Future's Thorns

Book III of The Quietus of Fate

By Brian C. Kershner

Acknowledgements

The Quietus of Fate Series is the textbook definition of a creation that consistently grew out of the control of its creator. At its core, it was never intended to be a series, at least not in the way that it exists today. It started as a single novel, and then a wild idea in the middle of the night while I was at college at Auburn University (War Eagle!) would forever change the destiny of this world that I had crafted. Three characters, conceived in rapid succession would be the foundation of the newly defined saga; Korrd, Aerith, and Emries. By now they have all made their initial appearances in the series, and those indelible markers will act as sign-posts for things to come. It was Korrd's creation that practically overnight doubled the initial novel.

And that reality has continued to be the norm as the Quietus of Fate has stretched from one book, to two, to four, to six, to fourteen, and perhaps will span a whole other saga of novels to follow. New characters have wanted to have their stories told, and at times older characters have found that their stories had not been fully told yet. Regardless of the impetus, the series has continued to grow and evolve and change.

Obviously, this kind of creative madness demands a lot of time and breeds a lot of sleepless nights. Fortunately I have had a great support system around me for the majority of my journey that has enabled me to continue to dream and be able to share that dream with my audience.

B.K.

Table of Contents

Appendicies

Heroes shall be born in the Kingdom of the Ancients,
The Walls of Safety shall crumble to an Enemy Within,
The puppet shall cut the Master's Strings,
And Gods shall sit in Harsh and Fatal Judgement.

A Daughter shall seek the forgiveness of her father,
The Broken Dragon shall be remade,
Ancient Flame shall give birth to Black and White,
When the Raven's Beak pierces its own Heart.

In Darkness there is no Light or Shadow,
And Truth shall be pricked by the Future's Thorns.

The future is not yet written,
The past never truly dead,
The present favors the driven,
Time is how legends are bred.

-   Aralias Imstra
Prophecies of the Coromor

Prologue

Game of the Gods

"I'm sorry Elwyne," Logan said holding her in his arms as her tears soaked through his shirt. These were not tears of sorrow, but rather of joy. Elwyne had told Logan her fears, and he had answered for the wrong that had been done to her. There were many things that were not said, and much of it revolved around the predictions of the mysterious man who had introduced himself as Emries. Whether he was the Creator as he claimed, or merely one of His agents, it did not matter. Logan trusted Emries and his declarations as surely as if the words had come from Logan's own father's mouth. There was so much that Logan still wanted to say to Elwyne still, but he could not find the words. How could he tell her that their son would rule the world in the years to come? How would she accept the fact that she would survive the quest, even if Logan didn't? Elwyne regained her composure quickly and smiled. Logan kissed her softly and then they watched the sun come up together.

"I thought I'd find you out here," Pike said as he walked out to the edge of the forest. "When I woke up and saw that both you and Elwyne were gone from the camp, I thought that the two of you had patched things up. I'm glad that I was right for a change."

"You're right more often than you think, Pike," Logan replied standing. "I just wish that I would remember that more often."

He smiled and clutched his old friend on the shoulder. When the trio returned to the camp, the rest of the party were up and around. To Logan's surprise, there were smiles all around, and no one seemed to be too shaken about the events of the day before. Despite Caris' attempts to sew deception and division, they were all friends, and now they had proven that nothing could break that friendship.

Talon was the first to speak.

"So, what do we do now?"

"I don't know Talon. For the first time since this quest started, we're on our own," Logan answered. "If there is going to be a decision made about our future, I think that we should make it together."

"Well said, Logan," Talos replied quickly. "What are the possible destinations that you would like to discuss."

"Kandor is still a possibility," Pike commented. "If it's true that the *Chosen One* is there, wouldn't it be the best thing to try to convince him to join us."

"I knew that the *Chosen One* would come up again eventually. That has bothered me ever since Gwydeon brought it up, and now it bothers me even more."

That was the complete truth, but Logan didn't know why it bothered him as much as it did. Something tugged at Logan's heart, and he had to find out what and why.

"Logan," Gideon said in his normally accented voice, "we've been meanin' ta talk ta ye 'bout dis fer some time. When Talon, Gwydeon, Pike and me were in Grawn's palace, he and Bryn made some comments 'bout da *Chosen One*, and we didn't know how ta tell ye."

"Tell me straight. If there is something that I need to know, then by all means, tell me what it is."

"Sit down Logan," Gwydeon said softly.

Gwydeon was never one for melodramatics, and with the tone in his voice, the gravity and somberness of the topic could not be denied. And in truth, it was a not a tone that Logan enjoyed hearing. Whatever it was that Gwydeon and the others had to say, Logan knew it wasn't going to be pleasant.

"The *Chosen One* is in league with the phase called Saurn, that much we already knew," Pike began, "but now we know the true identity of the *Chosen One*, and it worries us as to how you'll react."

"It's Korrd, Logan," Gwydeon said resting his hand on Logan's shoulder. "Your brother Korrd is the *Chosen One*."

For a long moment Logan wasn't sure whether or not he was still breathing. But, for every bit of shock that was streaming through his body, there was a kind of peaceful resignation to the news. For every part of him that didn't want to believe it, there was another part that knew it was true. Even before the strange dream in Taren, he had known that Korrd was still alive. For years, Logan had been told that his brother had died. His father would never speak about Korrd, much in the same way he rarely talked about Logan's mother, but Logan always sensed bitterness when it came to Korrd. Logan never really knew Korrd, but he had fragment memories of a voice and the fact that they were together at one time. Once, the only time that Logan's saw his father drunk, Arin had told Logan that Korrd had always blamed Logan for his mother's death. It had turned the boy bitter, hateful, and resentful of everything. Korrd placed the blame as much on Arin as he did Logan. Their last conversation was one of blame and recrimination, dissolution of every familial bond, and a shattering of what was left of Arin's heart.

* * * * * * * * * * * *

Arin was seated at the table in the center of the main room of the little farmhouse, dirt and sweat caked on his brow, and his nails still showing signs of his day spent with his hands in the dirt. Arin had just gotten Logan to sleep a few minutes earlier, the six year old so full of energy that Arin thought he would never fall asleep. He didn't realize that his older child was standing in the doorway until he looked up and caught sight of him out of the corner of his eye. Korrd's face betrayed the anger that must have been boiling inside of him.

"Why couldn't you have been content to have one child?" Korrd demanded. "Because of you and that baby, my mother died. If you wouldn't have..."

Arin was on his feet a second later, pushing Korrd out the door into the darkening night in an effort to keep Logan from hearing what was about to happen.

"Wouldn't have what?" Arin countered. "She was my wife, and we loved each other. What, do you think that I forced your mother into it, is that what you think? Do you not think that perhaps she wanted to have another child? Why do you take this out on your younger brother? All of us are now at a disadvantage, him most of all. He will never know his mother..."

"That's right, father," Korrd raged, "he won't know his mother, but I did. I will remember her for the rest of my life, and my loss is paramount. I will suffer more because I know what I have lost. Logan won't feel the same way. To him, a mother will be an empty word, but to me it means everything."

Arin balled his fist in an effort to keep the anger from rising out of control. There was a tug of war taking place in Arin's heart. No matter which won, the pain or the anger, Arin knew he would lose, but he thundered on just the same.

"And what about my pain, Korrd? Don't you think that I will miss your mother most of all? She and I have loved each other for the better part of twenty years. We were young when we fell in love, but that didn't stop us. Not even the war could stop us. Not even monsters, death, and the horrors of battle could kill our love, and in truth it only made our desire for each other that much stronger. During the war, we pledged our undying love and devotion for each other, and that I will never forget. When we came back to Aradon after the war, all we wanted was peace and to have a family. Then we did the one thing that we had always dreamed of, we had you. But your mother had come from a lonely family, as I had. We didn't want you to be lonely growing up, so we decided to give you a sibling. Little did we know that the second delivery would prove to be our undoing. No matter what you believe, all we wanted was to make you and each other happy, but for that we have all suffered a great loss."

"A needless one, father," Korrd replied coldly. "I will never forgive you or Logan for what you have cost me. When he is grown enough to not need my constant attention I will leave this place forever."

* * * * * * * * * * * *

"This complicates things," Logan said calmly. "We know who the *Chosen One* is, but I would think it foolish to believe that he doesn't know about me. In fact, I'm sure he's known from the beginning. Because of our past, I may not be able to convince Korrd to join us, even if he were to split from the phasia."

"But don't you think that you should confront him?" Midarin asked impatiently.

"I don't know."

The typical uneasy silence returned. There were a lot of unanswered questions that plagued all of their minds, and now that the completion of the quest seemed so much farther away without the guidance of the Lion or Aryx, desolation was something that was creeping around every corner and hung over every bad decision. It was amazing how they found themselves totally alone in the center of the raging storm. From the beginning they had been led around by the nose, but now, nothing. Logan remembered how much they had hated the constant invasive intervention. They wanted nothing more than to have their own free will, to have a voice in the narrative of their lives. Yet now that they had it, all Logan could think of was how much he yearned for the sage voice of experience. Elwyne seemed to be on the same page.

"Shouldn't we take this news to Lord Cedric? He said that he was going to Pramine to find out whether Aryx was really dead. I'm sure that he would be able to help us figure out what to do next."

"I agree," Logan answered. "There have been some things that I've been meaning to discuss with him anyway. I wanted to talk to him about Basille and Gideon's connection with him. Perhaps he will know what we should do about him."

"No me lord," Gideon countered. "I beg of ye not ta speak ta Lord Cedric 'bout Lord Basille. Cedric has dealt wit' Basille before, but he doesn't know dat Basille is a phase. Ye have ta let Basille reveal dat in his own time. Dere are too many things dat ye don't know, and I can't tell ye all of dem."

Logan pulled Gideon aside and spoke to him quietly.

"Does this have anything to do with a man by the name of Emries?"

He looked very shocked when that name came up. He looked around and then his eyes met Logan's again.

"Have ye seen Emries me lord?"

"Yes, he spoke to me late last night when I went walking. He mentioned both you and Lord Basille by name, and he also spoke of Basille's ward. Emries described her as a very beautiful girl."

Gideon's face changed from shock to one of marked caution. Mention of the girl seemed to place him on the defensive more than Emries' name had. There was something that was holding him back, but Logan was sure it wasn't to protect the group.

"I cannot speak of dis, me lord. It's not fer me ta reveal. I can speak 'bout Emries though, but only a little bit."

"Don't worry Gideon," Logan said leading him back to the others, "I won't press you to break oaths that you made before you met me. We'll talk about this later."

The others seemed concerned. They had watched the conversation, but were out of ear shot. Logan knew that Talon hadn't used his powers to hear the conversation, and that barrier of trust still stood, a fact that Logan had doubted given his recent behavior, but was glad still stood.

"Well, everyone, we have two possible destinations that have been suggested. Would anyone like to stick his or her neck out and make the decision?"

"For once," Midarin said quickly, "I agree with Elwyne. We should travel to Pramine and talk to Lord Cedric. He should know this new information about Korrd, and maybe he could help you figure out how to deal with him."

"Well," Logan said looking at Elwyne's sly grin, "are there any objections to Midarin's suggestion?"

Logan had expected Talon and Pike to chime in quickly. They had always been the most resistant to Lord Cedric's orders. But, the objection never came, and before too long everyone was prepared to travel. As the group walked back to Barer to retrieve our horses, Logan caught a stitch of conversation between Elwyne and Midarin.

"I really appreciate your support on this matter, Midarin," Elwyne said smiling, "I hope that you and I can convince the others."

"It's something that needs to be done soon. Though I don't like the idea, I find that it's necessary. I won't dispute that which makes perfect sense, no matter my personal feelings."

"I'm glad," Elwyne replied, sounding relieved, "I'd hate to have to fight you about this."

"Why?"

"I've seen you throw a punch, remember."

The two women laughed and parted company. Logan wanted to ask Elwyne about it, but he thought the better of it. She was the Lady Dragon, a fact that had become clear in the way that she had handled this situation in Barer. If nothing else, she had the best interests of no only Logan, but the quest in her mind. Logan knew he had to trust her decisions, and perhaps, somewhere deep insider, he knew that her judgment was the most sound of the group.

* * * * * * * * * * *

Brea. The city's beauty and gallantry had been heralded everywhere in the civilized world. The town was known well for its justice and military might. No invading army had ever been able to scale the walls of Brea, and only the blood of enemies had ever stained the white stone. There was a power and prestige that emanated from the city, but no one could ever realize the turmoil that ripped through the royal palace. Earlier in the year, the King and Queen of Brea had been deposed because of their age. Since they had no female heir to take their place on the throne, the captain of the royal guard assumed the throne. The new king had created an elite group of soldiers called the Light Keepers. They were commissioned to seek out the followers of Shau-ling and bring them back to the ways of the Light. No one outside of the palace suspected that these men tortured the so-called followers of evil until they admitted to whatever they had been charged with. Sometimes the accused would not be seen for weeks. During this time, they would be beaten, starved, burned, cut, and have various other horrible tortures done to them. The worst of what they endured was to be coupled with the fact that they were not allowed food or water during their torture. These sessions of brutality would not end until all of the man's conspirators had been revealed, and sometimes the accused would have to implicate his own family in order to escape punishment.

Arin Domae thought that he was being given a great honor when he was assigned to the Light Keepers. There was nothing he wanted more than to serve his city and his king. He had dreamed for many years of fighting against the scourge of Shau-ling like the legendary Lord Cedric Binosear, but that dream gave way to the reality of his station. He was the son of a warrior, and not that of a lord. Only the highest princes in the land were destined to become a member of the Lion's Mane, and so Arin feared that his dreams would never be realized. When the appointment to the Light Keepers came, he thought that it was a blessing. If he could somehow prove himself, than perhaps he would be noticed. Never in his wildest dreams did he realize the hell of what he would be forced to become.

The first time he saw a man tortured, he nearly threw up. It was the vilest, disgusting display that he had ever witnessed. While being whipped, the poor man cried and screamed, repenting every little crime that he had ever committed. He admitted to having an affair with a young maiden, and that she was pregnant with his child. The Head Inquisitor turned to Arin and ordered him to lead a team and dispose of the girl in order to cleanse the man's soul. Arin did not believe what he was hearing. He almost flatly refused, but that would have implicated him and left him open for torture. Like a good soldier, Arin did as he was commanded, and as he watched the poor girl, who couldn't have been more than fourteen, die he swore to himself that he would never again serve a king who would allow such travesties to occur.

When Arin faced the king with the deeds of the Head Inquisitor, all the king did was laugh. He was actually pleased with the actions of his appointees. Arin left the palace more worried and disillusioned than ever. From that point on, Arin had done everything in his power to stop the tortures without being discovered, and for almost a year his efforts had been fruitful. Then everything changed.

One day a man dressed in thick black robes walked proudly into the palace and entered the king's presence without being summoned. The guards moved on the man, but stopped short. They both dropped their swords and shields, and they fell to the ground clutching their throats, trying hard to breathe. The king stood and looked at his uninvited guest coldly.

"What do you mean by entering my presence and attacking my guards? If you mean to kill me, I assure you that my followers will strike you down before you could even . . ."

"Silence," the hooded figure boomed.

His voice was powerful yet aged. It must have been an old man under those robes. When the man pulled back the hood of his cloak, his wrinkled face was cast clearly into view.

"I have come to bring you tidings of the world King Vorin. I have been spreading the word of the *Coromor* all over the world, and now I bring the news to the place that holds the Light in the highest esteem. The Dragon will come here soon; of this you can be assured. There is no way that you can prepare for his coming, and any deception that you might plan in order to entrap his spirit will surely be thwarted. He is powerful, and you would be wise to follow all of his directives to the letter from the moment he arrives. I will stay here in your kingdom until I am sure that he has safely arrived, and then he will take the throne and rule your kingdom as he wills. You are in no position to stop these changes King Vorin, and if you try, you will be destroyed."

After the old man had spoken his words, he turned and left the throne room. For several weeks, the actions of the Light Keepers were halted. King Vorin did not trust the Proclaimer, but he was not willing to risk the retribution of the Dragon until he was sure that he had lulled the old man into a false sense of security. It seemed that the old man had a way of wrangling the wills of the people around him, and they flocked to him to hear the words of the *Coromor*, and to tell of the injustices visited upon them. In the light of day, King Vorin supported the Proclaimer, but in the shadows he plotted the continuation of his vile work. It took only a week for King Vorin to feel emboldened, and so the Light Keepers began their work again in earnest. The Light Keepers gave no heed to the words and warnings that were constantly spouted by the Proclaimer, instead fearing the wrath of their king more than the wrath of a legend. Arin Domae continued to do what he could to help the poor unfortunate souls who were being tortured, but he could only do so much. One night he had just retired to his bed when there came a knock at the door. When he answered the knock, he saw a young man and woman standing at the door.

"May I help you?" Arin asked softly.

"Are you Arin Domae?" the young man asked clearly.

"I am," the older man replied, "what can I do for you?"

"Lord Basille told me..."

Arin clasped his hand over the young man's mouth and looked around quickly. Seeing that no one was in ear shot, he pulled the young man and woman into his house and closed the door.

"What is the meaning of this?" the young man demanded.

"In this town," Arin answered, "you would be better off not to speak the name of a member of the phasia here in Brea. Your life could depend upon it."

The young man looked dumbfounded. He staggered backwards and fell into one of Arin's chairs.

"My father is not a member of the phasia," the young man said finally, "and I would have words with any man who would say otherwise."

"Your father? Is not the name of this man Lord Basille Mystic? And does this man not rule in the kingdom of Scalla?"

"Yes, his name is Basille Mystic, and he does rule in Scalla. What of it?"

"My dear boy..."

"Jerrard and this is my wife Erika," the young man replied.

"Jerrard, I hate to be the one to break this to you, but your father is a phase. I don't know how he has managed to keep this from you so long, but apparently you have been led astray."

Erika stepped forward quickly and knelt beside Jerrard.

"My father is a kind and gentle man, Arin, and I hope that you can believe that. Whether or not he is a member of the phasia is beside the point. He has changed his ways surely because he has sent Jerrard and myself to help the *Coromor* when he arrives."

This time it was Arin who took a step back and sat down.

"And Basille sent you to me?"

"Yes," Jerrard responded, "he said to stay close to you and we would all be safe."

"I wouldn't be so sure of that," Arin responded. "Things are quickly spiraling out of control here in Brea, and until the Dragon does arrive, you two had better stay indoors as much as possible. I will have to go to the palace tomorrow and I will be there all day. You may have free run of my house, and help yourself to whatever I have. We can talk more of this tomorrow night. As that I have only the one bed, the two of you will have to make do with the floor, at least until I can come up with something else. I shall bring you some covers and pillows. Please remember not to speak about this to anyone, and never to each other in public. All of the walls have ears, and I would not like to see you end up like so many other people have here in Brea."

With that Arin turned and went to gather the things that he had promised, leaving the two lovers to ponder the depth of their situation.

* * * * * * * * * * * *

Three days of uneventful travel later, Logan and the others found themselves in the small town of Pramine. To call Pramine a town at all was generous, as it seemed to be little more than a nomadic campsite that could be pulled up and moved at any moment. There was once central building, a lodge made up largely of logs from felled trees. It was very rustic, even by the standards that were common in Aradon. Cedric and the others were still in the lodge, though only Cedric was still there when Logan entered. It was just after mid-day, and Cedric was sitting alone at a table near the far wall of the common room, and he looked as though he wished he was somewhere else.

"I'm didn't expect to see you here in Pramine, Logan," Cedric said in a quiet contemplative voice. "According to the seers here in Pramine, Aryx is not yet dead, but his soul is in turmoil. They believe that Shau-ling is holding him captive."

"Alive is still able to fight. Diana must be somewhat relieved."

"If anything," Cedric said looking up, "it has just increased her resolve and dedication to finding her husband."

By this time, Elwyne, Gwydeon, and Midarin had joined them at the table.

"I understand how she feels," Elwyne said softly.

She squeezed Logan's hand tightly.

"We also have some news Cedric," Gwydeon commented, "but I don't know if you will be so happy to hear it."

His expression did not change at all.

"We know the identity of the *Chosen One*, as well as his current whereabouts," Logan said.

His eyes widened slightly, but the expression on his face did not change.

"Then why are you here?" he asked, looking up at Logan. "If you can wrestle him away from the phasia, then we have won."

"That's not the entire story Cedric," Logan continued. "You see, the *Chosen One* is Korrd Ranthall, my brother. We haven't spoken in over fifteen years, and I don't know if he still hates me or not. It could complicate the situation, and that's why we wanted to come here first."

He sat there thinking for a long time before he spoke again. Something was very wrong. The seers in Pramine must have said something more than the whereabouts of Aryx.

"This is not good news Logan, and it bothers me almost as much as the news coming out of Brea."

Midarin looked concerned for a moment but when she started to speak, Cedric cut her off.

"I'm sorry Midarin, your parents were killed in a coup, and there was nothing that anyone could do to save them."

She fled from the table in the next second. Gwydeon and Elwyne followed her away from the table to console her, and Cedric continued talking. He seemed unfazed by her reaction. It was as though the soul of the man no longer existed.

"The throne of Brea has renounced all ties to Marcwell and my rule. Instead a man called the Proclaimer has taken command. He says that Brea will only bow to the Dragon, and when he comes, the Proclaimer will step aside and give the *Coromor* what is his. As for the *Chosen One*, I don't know what I can say. If your brother will not join our cause, then you will have to make a very hard decision. You cannot let the *Chosen One* serve Shau-ling no matter what relationship you share with him. If he stands against you, than you must kill him."

The finality and dispassionate tone unnerved Logan, and anger began to boil. But no matter how he felt, there was still a decision that needed to be made.

"So what should I do, Cedric? Do I go to Kandor and confront my brother, or do I go to Brea and found out what this Proclaimer's scheme is?"

Cedric sighed, and it was obvious that his next words caused him severe discomfort.

"Neither I'm afraid. I received an interesting message from a courier a day and a half ago. The gods of Mount Tantis have summoned you. You are to leave for the mountain as soon as you are able, no questions asked. You cannot refuse this invitation, and I cannot go with you."

"What do they want?" Logan asked.

"I don't know. The gods of Mount Tantis do what they wish, when they wish. They have absolute power over everything in this world, but cannot flex that power without the permission of the Creator. If they had his leave to do what they willed, they would have just brought you there. In this case, it appears that their hands have been tied."

"Where will you go?"

"I will return to Marcwell with the others and start to rebuild. There is a lot that must be done, and it would appear that my role in this whole affair is changing. The gods will give you what help you require, that is after they have made sure you are worthy of their assistance."

It would take several days to reach the foot of the steep crag of rock called Mount Tantis, but apparently the ride was necessary. Once they reached the foot of the mountain, Logan knew he would be face to face with the ramifications of Emries' prophetic words.

PROLOGUE

Chapter XVII

The Path of Justice

The moment the group reached the foot of Mount Tantis, a white light flared, enveloping them all. When the light receded, the horses were gone and they stood blinking and slightly disoriented in a vast courtyard surrounded by pristine white columns and fountains that made no sound even as water splashed everywhere. They were standing in the City of the Gods on the highest peak of Mount Tantis. A moment later, a man appeared, walking slowly with his hands clasped behind his back. He was dressed in pure white, and his eyes beamed a brilliant blue. Around his head was a golden glow, a kind of noble haze that radiated around him. When he was standing before them, the tall man took a long moment to look over every member of the party before speaking.

"Welcome to Mount Tantis, Logan Ranthall. I am the god Azure. I have invited thee here for several purposes, none of which directly concern thy quest against Shau-ling."

"Then why am I here?" Logan asked quickly.

"I do not like thy tone, Logan," he replied angrily. "Be careful that thou dost not lose thy tongue the next time it wishes to wag so. Thou were created by our father, the Great One. Before he passed on to the next realm, he set down three tests that thou and thine companions must pass before thou art allowed an attempt to fight against the greatest evil. Cedric

Binosear was spared these tests, and his path nearly ended in catastrophe for those that love the Light. Chance could not be allowed to reign again, so Emries decreed that thee and thy allies must be tested and found worthy to face the living nightmare. "

"Ye mean Shau-ling," Gideon added.

"No matter what you believe, even the *Coromor* and the *Erieal* would not be able to destroy a creation of the Great One. Though at this time thee does not understand the full implications of what thou art or what thee art faced with. If thou and thine companions survive the three tests of the *Coromor*, thee will be told all which is needed to be known."

Logan took a moment to look across the faces of his companions, and he saw the doubt and uneasiness there. It was obvious that Azure knew much more than he was saying, and what's more, the edge to his voice spoke of resentment and hatred.

"What are the tests?" Gwydeon asked after a moment.

Azure smiled widely, like the proverbial cat that had just caught the canary and then responded.

"The first of the tests is called the Path of Justice. I can tell thee nothing more. In this journey, thou will be subjected to many tests, but the theme of the tests will remain the same."

"And what, pray tell, is the theme of the tests?" Pike asked shortly.

"That is for thee to discover on thine own. Logan, since thou art the leader of this band which thou so frivolously call the People of the Dragon, thee may select three to undertake this test. I must warn thee, if all fail in this test, thou dost also fail. If that occurs, thee will never leave this mountain. One other caveat has been set down by the Great One, thee who participate in this first task may not have a part in the other two."

"May I ask a question before I choose?" Logan said softly.

"Thou may indeed ask anything thee wishes, though thee may find the answer less helpful than thou might wish."

"Is this the hardest of the three tests."

"No," came the god's quick response.

"Will our powers work here?" Talon added quickly.

The god seemed to ignore Talon's existence entirely. Logan could feel the anger rolling not only from Talon, but from Pike as well, and the *Debuisa* on Talon's left hand began to become clearer as the moments passed.

"Will the powers of the *Erieal* and the *Coromor* function here as they do below?" Logan asked, rephrasing Talon's question.

"Yes."

"Very well," Logan said after a moment of thought. "I have chosen Gideon, Midarin, and Talos to undergo the first of the tests."

The combination of powers was a sound one, at least in Logan's mind. Gideon's speed and powers, Midarin's extended reach, and Talos' magic seemed as though they would complement each other well. Gideon shook Logan's hand, and Midarin kissed Gwydeon on the cheek before beckoning Azure to lead the way. Inwardly, Logan wished them luck and prayed that they would succeed. However, Logan wondered whether his prayers would be heard, even in the City of the Gods, and what's more he could not shake the feeling that something sinister lurked behind the pristine backdrop.

* * * * * * * * * * *

Gideon, Midarin, and Talos followed the god Azure down a long corridor away from the rest of the party. They entered an open door and found themselves in a pure white room. The walls and ceiling were smooth, and the floor was divided into five rows with three large tiles in each row. The four of them stood just outside the first row of tiles, and Azure turned to them and spoke.

"This is the Path of Justice. The object of this test is to cross the room and enter the door on the other side. Thee may move from tile to tile, and in any direction thee wishes, except for backwards. However, at some points thee may find the most direct path blocked. If thee wishes to survive, do not tread on the black tiles. Good luck."

After the last words from Azure, he left the room and closed the door behind him. After the door was completely closed, it disappeared. Gideon turned back toward the tiles on the floor in from of them and sighed.

"So, which will it be? Left, right, or center?" he asked his companions.

"Do you really think it makes that much of a difference, Gideon?" Midarin answered impatiently. "This whole thing about tests is a farce. Didn't you hear how Azure talked to Logan? He hates us. How do we know this isn't some plot by Shau-ling to kill us all? I say we walk right down the center of the room and open the door."

"Could it be that simple, Midarin?" Talos countered, trying to interject some wisdom into the conversation. "Could Shau-ling really create something such as this? And if they are not Shau-ling's puppets, but are indeed the servants of the Creator, how could they hate one who was supposed to save this world. I agree it is all very strange, but I hardly believe there is a sinister motive driving these tests. Perhaps they are exactly what they appear to be, a way to ensure that Logan is ready for the ultimate trial. Lord Cedric nearly fell in his battle against Shau-ling, and that had been attributed to his not knowing the full extent of his abilities. If the gods intend to ensure Logan's victory, these tests should acquaint him well with all of the tools at his disposal."

Midarin put both hands on her hips and frowned.

"If thee fails, thee will never leave this mountain," Midarin said, doing her best impression of Azure's superior tone. "Does that sound to you like something someone would say if their ultimate goal was to help?"

Talos was about to answer when Gideon cleared his throat and brought everyone's attention back to the task at hand.

"What say we test yer theory, lass. On three we step on the center tile."

Gideon had always been more for the direct approach then thinking every little detail through. That approach had kept him along thus far, and he was sure it would sustain him in this test.

"No, not the center one, the one to the left. While I may not agree with Talos' faith in these so-called gods, I think he's right that these are tests designed to ensure Logan can defeat Shau-ling with what he has at hand. If we were just supposed to walk down the center of the room, it wouldn't be much of a test. There has got to be more to this than meets the eye," she responded.

Gideon nodded, and Talos added his agreement after a moment. Gideon took yet another deep breath and began the short countdown.

"One . . ."

Midarin began to feel nervous, and then began to doubt her idea. *I feel like there are eyes all around us, measuring us. Why is it that I feel like they want us to fail? Maybe there is something more they want out of Logan. What if they think that we are standing in his way, and these tests are to weed out those who aren't going to be able to carry their weight? And why did Azure seem to hate Logan?*

"Two . . ."

Talos raised the hood of his cloak over his head and clutched his staff tightly. *This is not wise. Though at the present moment I do not see another option open. This can't be as easy as Midarin says it is, but then again, maybe the test is how we react and not what we do. Why is this place called the Path of Justice? I can see that there might be a specific path through the room, but what does that have to do with justice?*

"Three . . ."

As soon as the final number leapt from Gideon's lips, the three stepped onto the tile to their left. As soon as their feet touched the tile, the room around them began to fade away. Within a matter of moments, they were standing in the center of a town square. They noticed several people walking around them, but nothing in the town seemed familiar. There were no large buildings, just normal farm houses for a small community. Gideon stepped away from the group and grabbed one of the people by the arm.

"Oh please sir, don't hurt me," the shocked man said in a shaking voice, "I'll give you whatever you want . . ."

"I'm not going to hurt ye," Gideon responded. "Just tell me the name of this town, and I'll let ye go."

"Parn. This town is called Parn," the man said quickly. He then jerked free of Gideon's grasp and ran away in terror.

"I've never heard of a town by that name," Midarin commented after a moment of thought.

"Nor have I," Talos added.

"Parn is obviously a creation of the gods then," Gideon replied. "I wonder what it is dat we're supposed ta do here?"

The other two members of the party shrugged and began to walk quickly down the street. As they walked, a man passing by them tripped and fell. In his haste to continue on his way, he dropped a large bag on the ground. As soon as he was sure the man was gone, Gideon picked up the bag and opened it.

"By the gods," he said quickly, "there must be a thousand gold pieces here."

Gideon quickly stashed the bag in his pocket. Talos tugged on Gideon's sleeve the next moment.

"Wouldn't that be stealing?"

Gideon shrugged and smiled

"Once a thief, always a thief, you know?" Gideon said laughing.

Suddenly, Gideon felt a tap on his shoulder, and he spun around instantly with daggers drawn. The face he saw was that of the man who had dropped the bag of gold. The expression of shock faded quickly, only to be replaced by one of worry.

"Excuse me sir, I didn't mean to startle you," the man started, "but would you have by chance seen a small purse of gold lying in the street?"

Gideon thought for a quick moment in an attempt to lead the man into believing he was actually trying to remember if he had seen something. However, Gideon already knew what his answer to the question would be. He kept his body positioned so that the man could not see the obvious bulge in his pocket. Midarin marveled at how comfortable Gideon was lying, and how well he did it.

"Why no sir, are ye sure that ye dropped it around here?"

"Yes sir, very sure. Are you sure that you haven't seen it?"

"Very sure. I would have remembered seeing a bag of gold lying in the street."

The man nodded and turned away from Gideon.

"Thank you sir, I'm sorry for bothering you and your friends."

As the man walked away, everything faded, and the tiled room began to reappear. Gideon felt cold, and then began to lose consciousness. Midarin looked around quickly and found that she and Talos were standing where they were before the interlude in the town. However, Gideon floated over the now black tile to the left, and it appeared as if he could not move, and wasn't even breathing.

"I've figured it out!" Talos exclaimed. "Whatever we do during this test must follow common law, and must be just in all ways. We can't steal or lie, and if we do, we will end up like him."

Midarin shivered at the thought of ending up like Gideon, but she shook it off quickly and turned toward Talos again.

"So, which tile do we step on now?"

"I say we try the center one," he answered.

"I agree."

Quickly they both stepped on the center tile. Again the room around them began to disappear and they soon found themselves standing on a glade in the middle of nowhere. As they looked around, from over one of the hills a woman came running toward them. She was in very rich gowns, and the ornamentation of that type was usually reserved for royalty. The woman ran to Talos and tugged strongly on his arm.

"Please, help my father. His army is being crushed by another, and if you don't help him, he will be killed."

"Who is attacking your father?" Midarin asked calmly, the fact that this was a test and not reality easing her emotions.

"There's no time! Come on!"

At that she pulled Talos and began to run back the way she came. Without any discussion with Midarin, Talos followed quickly after the girl. As he ran, he pulled the hood of his cloak over his head and prepared for battle. Midarin cursed under her breath at the impulsiveness of her companion, drew an arrow from the quiver on her back, and nocked it on her bowstring. After she finished mumbling something about 'damned foolishness,' she ran after Talos.

Soon enough Talos and Midarin ran together after the princess. After a few moments, a small town was in sight. It was very much like the town of Parn in which they had failed the previous test. All of the houses and even the layout of the town was the same, except that this time there was a large palace in the center of town. Ahead of them, they could see the princess run through a guard post and down a street which must have led to the palace. Talos tried to run through the guard post as well, but the guard stopped him.

"What is your business here," he barked.

"The princess found me and asked me for help, now let me pass," Talos responded.

The guard drew his sword, and raised his voice.

"You have no business here old man. If you do not leave..."

An arrow flew past Talos' ear in the next second, striking the soldier in his helmet with such force that he fell backwards. The blow from the arrow, as well as the blow from hitting the ground knocked the guard unconscious. Talos did not have to look back to know that Midarin was behind him, and was impressed that Midarin had chosen a non-lethal way of dealing with the situation. Perhaps she felt that to kill the guard who was only attempting to fulfill his duty would have violated the conditions of the test. Without any acknowledgment to Midarin's actions, Talos ran after the princess. Midarin smiled a self-congratulatory smile and nocked another arrow on her bowstring before following Talos. As the two of them made their way through the town, they could see men locked in battle everywhere around them. No one appeared to pay them any notice, and continued with their own personal war. Before too long they had arrived at the palace.

As Midarin and Talos entered the palace, they caught a glimpse of the princess running up a flight of stairs to their left. They followed, and as they entered a set of doors at the top of the stairs they found themselves standing in front of the throne. The princess stood just to the left of them, both hands covering her mouth and tears beginning to stream from her eyes. On the throne in front of them sat an old man wearing an old golden crown on his head. A dagger had been thrust through his chest, and he sat there dying, blood dripping from the corner of his mouth. A young man dressed in black stood by the throne. He reached over and took the crown off the old man's head and set it on his own. He looked down at the old man and then to the new arrivals. Before the man could say anything, Midarin raised her bow and shot the man through the leg. The man in black fell to the ground and began screaming in agony. Midarin walked over to the man slowly, drew her sword and put it to his throat.

"Who are you?" she demanded.

"I'm the king's son," he groaned in pain.

"Did you kill the king?" Midarin demanded.

The prince faltered for a moment and then answered.

"No."

Midarin smiled.

"I know you're lying, you murderous bastard. You're coming with me."

She reached down quickly and grabbed the young man by the hair and proceeded to drag him across the room. Talos turned to leave when he heard the sound of breaking glass coming from behind him. Both Talos and Midarin turned sharply and were face to face with two new arrivals.

One of the men was holding a bow, the arrow aimed at the heart of the young prince being held by Midarin. The other man had a long red cloak that flapped behind him. The man with the cloak took a short step forward and spoke.

"Halt there! Turn that boy over to me and leave this kingdom."

Midarin looked the man over quickly and then responded strongly.

"And who are you to be making demands of us?"

"The king's son."

Midarin's head spun. The situation had gone from absurd to ridiculous. Before either Midarin or Talos could do anything, the princess crossed the room quickly toward the new arrivals. She grabbed the man who called himself a prince by the arm and slapped him across the face. As she turned to walk away, the man with the bow shot her through the back. Her mouth fell open and she looked down at the arrow head that protruded from her stomach just as the blood began to flow from the open wound. She began coughing and heaving, blood leaking from the sides of her mouth, and then she fell to the floor face down. The man with the bow drew back another arrow and pointed it at the prince lying on the floor.

"By capturing my younger brother, you have saved my kingdom from a war that could have raged on for centuries," the man with the cloak said clearly. "Now, if you will turn my brother over to me, he will surely be punished for his crimes."

"What would your brother have to gain by killing your father? He would surely have known that you would have inherited the throne," Talos asked.

The prince walked slowly over to the throne and picked his father's crown up off the floor and placed it on his head.

"Father sent me out of town on a mission of peace to our closest rival. I was supposed to be out of town for another week, but I got wind of a coup that had been planned by my brother and sister. Though it seems that at the last moment, my sister either thought better of the plan, or felt that she had more right than my brother to inherit. Perhaps she felt that she could dupe you into killing our brother and giving her the throne outright. Either way, I would have been banished from the kingdom before I could get back and inherit it as per the law. You have done the right thing..."

As the prince spoke those final words, the throne room faded out. Before they knew it, they were standing in the tiled room again. However, the tile they were standing on had tuned sky blue. Midarin looked over at the tile where Gideon was suspended in thin air. Before her eyes, she saw him descend from and start to move toward them.

"Well, I suppose I better keep me hands in me pockets from now on," he said quickly.

Midarin laughed and then looked to Talos. He understood and shook his head.

"So, where do we go now?" Midarin asked.

"Forward."

After it was agreed they all stepped on the white tile just in front of them. As their feet touched the tile, the room began to disappear yet again. This time when their new location materialized, they were standing on a black island of rock in the middle of a lake of fire. They could all feel the heat of the flames that leapt up around them. Gideon seemed to be the one who remained the calmest. He closed his eyes and held out his *Debuisa* which started to turn green. A rumbling sound came from all around them, and shelves of dirt and soil fell from the opposite shore of the lake and began to smother the lake of fire. Talos breathed a sigh of relief and then noticed something ahead of them.

"Look!" he said pointing.

Midarin and Gideon both turned and saw a dazzling spectacle. Two men dressed in long cloaks much like Talos' were engaged in a magical battle. Fierce tides of elemental forces leapt from each other's hands and lanced across the void with clear lethal intent. Most of the colorful and deadly projectiles met in the middle of the void between them and canceled each other out in bursts of breathtaking color. Talos began to move toward the combating robed men and was struck by a wave of the nullified energy and was thrown several feet backwards. The man in black looked to the trio and laughed maniacally. The man dressed in a white robe seemed to pay them no notice. Suddenly a huge ball of fire erupted from the man in black's hands and engulfed his opponent, and he fell to the ground screaming in agony. The victor walked slowly over to his now helpless adversary, savoring his victory and then kicked him into a pit of fire that had opened behind the fallen man. The man in the black robe motioned for the new arrivals to come to him. Midarin first moved to Talos' side and helped the older man back to his feet. He seemed to be simply dazed from the blow, and within a moment had his wits back about him. After Talos was ready, the trio walked over to the victor.

"You have witnessed my battle with an ancestral enemy, and for that the sacrilege is great. You must die, or perform a task for me."

"I assure you, we meant no offense, and surely if a task is required to cleanse the shame, we shall abide." Talos said in a humble tone.

If the man in black was impressed with Talos' words, it did not show in his face.

"Somewhere in the maze of buildings that lie through that door is a courier's shop. This courier has a flask that I require. When you find the courier's shop, ask the courier for the flask. He will know what you need. Then, when the flask is in your possession, you will bring it back to me, and my honor will be upheld."

"How will we know this courier's shop?" Midarin asked softly.

"Over the door of the shop is a sign. The sign is a large box and nothing more. Now, go. I shall be watching you the entire way."

The party turned toward the open door ahead of them and walked through, not knowing what to expect to see on the other side. As they entered the maze of buildings, they faced two doors and a passageway that lead further into the maze.

"I say we split up," Midarin suggested, "we'll be able to find the courier's shop a lot quicker that way."

"Aye," Gideon replied. "You two take the rooms, and I'll continue down the path."

Talos nodded and the group split. Talos walked into one of the two rooms. As he opened the door, he was faced with total darkness. He decided to close the door behind him in case there was some magical enchantment that he was unaware of. Upon shutting the door, the room was filled with a soft white light. Talos turned away from the door and was face to face with the man in the black robe.

"You have committed a great offense against me puny one. For that there will be no forgiveness."

Talos had no chance. Before he could even raise a hand to try and defend himself, a burst of flame leapt from the wizard's hand and engulfed him. Talos fell to the ground a smoldering lump of flesh and bone. The man laughed to himself and left the room in search of his next victim.

* * * * * * * * * * *

Midarin walked slowly to the door. She took a long deep breath and slowly twisted to golden doorknob. As she opened the door, a wisp of cold air surrounded her and sent a chill up and down her spine. She pulled the door open fully and entered with sword drawn. Something tugged at the back of her mind, and the familiarity of the face of the man in the black robe seemed just outside her understanding.

The room itself was black except for the light of one small torch at the back of the room. She stepped fully into the room, and the wind gusted again, this time slamming the door behind her. Now alone in the dark room, she made her way slowly forward. Eventually, she stood beside the torch. She removed it from the bracket on the wall, and suddenly the interior of the room exploded with blinding flashes of light. Midarin dropped the torch and fell to her knees covering her eyes. She began to feel sharp pains run through her arms and legs. When she forced her eyes open, she saw the cause of the pain. Apparently she had stumbled into the lair of large voracious rats. They clawed at her flesh, and tore large chunks of it from her body with their teeth. She screamed in agony and terror, but no one would respond to her pleas for help. For the first time she realized that another person was in the room. She looked up, and to her aversion she saw the black wizard standing over her laughing.

"This is the punishment for seeing what you should not see little girl. You should have stayed in your kingdom where it was safe instead of listening to the same lusty passions that put you in this situation. Now die, and feed my servants."

＊ ＊ ＊ ＊ ＊ ＊ ＊ ＊ ＊ ＊ ＊

Gideon walked down the hall, a dagger clutched in each hand.

I have a bad feeling about this. If this is as much of an offense as the old man says it is, then there is no way he would let anyone who saw what happened out of here alive.

Up ahead, Gideon saw a shop with a large wooden sign over it. The shop was clearly the one he was looking for, and Gideon felt an ambush waiting for him on the other side of the door.

"Hello my good man," the man behind the counter said cheerfully, "is there anything that I can get for you today?"

"I have come for the flask," Gideon replied shortly.

"One moment please sir."

The young man ducked into the back room, and then reemerged holding a small glass flask that was half full of a sparkling blue liquid. He handed it to Gideon and then went back into the back room. Gideon looked closely at the flask, and then slipped it into the pouch that hung on his side. He then walked back down the path he had taken, and ran into the man in black.

"Tis alright, one called Gideon," the wizard said quickly, "I see that you have completed the task that I have sent you on. Now, if you will give me the flask, you may leave whenever you please."

Gideon reached into his pouch and pulled out the small flask. He handed it to the wizard, and the world around him began to fade in and out. Before he knew it, he, Midarin, and Talos were standing in the white room, only this time, the tile they were standing on had turned from white to red.

"What was that?" Midarin growled, anger thick in her voice.

"A test," Talos answered matter-of-factly.

"A pointless test. What did that have to do with our sense of justice?"

Gideon shook his head.

"No time fer dis."

Midarin shot him a look of anger and displeasure and then answered.

"Forward then."

"Agreed," Talos added calmly.

The three adventurers tried to make their way to the tile that lay in front of them, but found their way blocked by an invisible barrier.

"So," Gideon said calmly, "which way do we try now?"

"I say we go to the right," Midarin answered.

"I hate to disagree with ye lass, but I say we go to the left," Gideon countered.

"Fine," Midarin shot back, "you go to the left, and Talos and I will go right. Right Talos?"

"Yes," he answered slowly, "I will go with Midarin."

Midarin and Talos walked from the tile in the center of the room over to the one on the right. Once they stepped on the tile they found that nothing happened. They were still in the white room, and Gideon was still standing on the tile to their left. Talos moved his hand along the barrier that separated them from the center tile of the next row, and found that it did not restrict their movement to the tile that was now in front of them. Without a word to the other, they took a step forward and the room around them vanished. This time though, nothing replaced the white room. The two of them found themselves floating in a void.

* * * * * * * * * * * *

Gideon watched his two friends as they stepped into the next row of tiles. Suddenly they vanished and the tile they had stepped on blackened quickly. Quickly Gideon realized that he was again alone. He looked at the black tile for a moment, and then stepped onto the tile to his left, half wanting to close his eyes as his foot touched it. However, he found that he remained in the white room, and the tile under him remained white. Gideon took a deep breath and then stepped onto the tile that lay in front of him. Just as with the last step, the room remained the same, and the color of the tile did not change. Gideon just then began to realize that he was one tile away from completing the test of the gods. Not wasting any time, Gideon stepped to the center tile of the next row. This time though the room faded away,

Gideon found himself floating in a clear blue sky. He looked around quickly and could not see a cloud anywhere. As he floated there, a small bird landed on his shoulder. Gideon jerked in shock, and reflexively knocked the bird off his shoulder. Suddenly, the sky blackened and then began to disappear. The white room reappeared, and Gideon found that he was standing on the tile by the left wall in the last row. The tile in front of him was the only one that led to the door that was recessed in the back wall of the room. The tile in front of him was black, marking his failure in the sky. He reached his arm toward the door, but found that as it penetrated the boundary between the two tiles, his arm began to disappear. He jerked his limb back quickly and found that it was still in one piece. He reached in again, and groped for the door handle. He found nothing and started to pull his arm back but found that he could not move. He was trapped by the black tile.

* * * * * * * * * * * *

Midarin and Talos floated in the nothingness listlessly. Suddenly a bright light streamed from a small crack in the void. Both of them swam through the void trying to reach the crack. However, Midarin seemed to move quicker than the older Talos and reached the crack first. Midarin moved through the crack and found herself back in the white room standing on the last tile in the right row. She looked across the row and saw a black tile ahead of her, and Gideon frozen on the far left tile. However, it appeared to her that one of Gideon's arms was missing. She reached her arm toward the door and found that as it breached the boundary between the tiles, her arm disappeared. She didn't pull her arm back but continued to grope around for the door handle. Her hand grasped onto something that seemed like the handle of a door, and she turned it quickly. The door to the chamber slid open, and the white room disappeared.

On the other side of the door, the trio was reunited. Midarin fumed.

"Pointless. How was that supposed to ensure that we're ready to face Shau-ling."

Talos' shoulders slumped.

"Should we question the motivations of the gods? They are aware of more than we can comprehend, and thus we as Logan must trust their judgment in these matters."

Midarin scoffed and was about to speak when a man in a white robe entered the room.

"You have done well," Azure said softly. "Here you will wait until the remaining tests are complete."

The cold blue eyes swept over the trio for a moment before the god turned to leave the white room. Once Azure had disappeared through an unseen door, a wave of realization hit Midarin. Azure had been the man in the black robe. Suddenly these tests seemed much less benign.

Kandor

Battle was becoming a predictable facet of Korrd's life. Saurn was using him well, and the remaining phasia were probably trembling at the thought of what the *Chosen One* was capable of. All of the phasia that is except for Basille.

He had been the only one that had not made the offer to rule beside me instead of over. He seemed to actually be concerned for my welfare. There was something more to his tale though. Logan is somehow involved in all of this, and it has nothing to do with the fact that he is the Dragon. Perhaps I have truly stumbled on my destiny. Could I have been so wrong?

"That is a distinct possibility."

There wasn't supposed to be anyone around. It was just before midnight, and all of the activity in Kandor had stopped an hour earlier. Korrd had set up camp about a mile from the city's gates, and he was well off the main road. If there was anyone reckless enough to travel this late into the evening, they should have stuck to the main road and never been aware of his presence. He had not bothered to make a fire as it was rather warm that night, but a fire would have also helped to alert others as to his location. And yet someone had stumbled upon him anyway. Korrd looked around but could see no one. The only thing that he could see was a thick evening mist rolling in.

Perhaps it was only my imagination. Ever since Basille and Asperon Thorne spoke to me, I have doubted what I have been doing. In the beginning all of Saurn's directives had seemed so right. But now, I can only think of what my brother is doing. Ever since the Guardian took me to see him, I can't get him out of my mind. Maybe that's why I'm hearing things.

"Or there could be someone else around, and that's why you're hearing voices, Korrd."

Just then a form emerged from the thick mist. He had long thick brown hair and a very unremarkable face and body. He reminded Korrd very much of Captain Antrobus, especially in the way that he held himself. There was no arrogance in the way he presented himself, or in his actions. He walked forward very slowly and sat across from Korrd. His features were only slightly cast in the pale moonlight, but there was something powerful about him. While he was not a man of powerful stature, power permeated his entire bring. With a snap of his fingers the stranger built a small fire, and he was finally cast in bright light. Just as with the moonlight, the man's features were very plain, except for his eyes. His cold blue eyes flickered like the fire that stood between them. Those eyes seemed to burn with all of the power of a thousand kings. Korrd looked deeply into the stranger's eyes for a moment and then was forced to look away, intimidated by the other man's vast power.

"Who are you stranger, and how do you know of me?"

"Worry not Korrd, I am not here to badger you or offer you riddles like the members of the phasia, nor am I here to offer you battle. Rather, I am here to offer you my assistance."

"Your assistance?" Korrd scoffed. "What could a man such as you know about my troubles? You may know me, but how could you see the pains that circulate in my heart and the troubles and uncertainties that cloud my mind. If you would not answer to this friend, you would be better served to disappear back into the mists and allow me to plan for my day tomorrow. I have much that I must attend to."

Korrd was shocked not only at his own candor, but also at the formality in his own words. Despite his power, the stranger's demeanor was disarming and oddly comforting.

"You discount me too easily Korrd," the stranger answered quickly. "What if I were to tell you of all of the troubles and turmoil that clouds your heart and mind? Would that convince you that I am here to help you? Very well."

The stranger paused for a moment and locked his gaze on Korrd. After a moment, a small smile came to the stranger's lips and he began speaking once more.

"In your heart you know that what you are doing on this world is wrong. However misguided, the deeds that you have accomplished are good deeds. It is a fine and noble thing to quest to destroy the members of the Brotherhood of Phasia, but the reason as to why you undertake such a quest taints all of your successes. Evil has always sought to destroy other evil in order to make the former stronger than that which remains. Without the help of good souls manipulated by the darkness, one evil would never be able to truly triumph over any other evil. That is why Saurn is using you. He knows that it would be futile to try and destroy the other phasia on his own. True he would gain power, but it would never be enough to accomplish his ultimate ends. He would waste as much as he gains. Do you know what Saurn's ends are Korrd?"

Korrd shook his head after a moment.

"I thought not. And that is what Saurn is counting on. He does not need a weapon who thinks about his actions. He wants a blunt obedient instrument."

There was clear contempt in the stranger's words, and there was no veiling the insult.

"I shall tell you Saurn's true motivations. He has more ambition than any of the other phasia that much is for certain. Not even Jeroch has had the courage to dream of the scheme that Saurn has already put into action. Saurn hopes to turn your talents and abilities against Shau-ling, and then take over the throne of power for himself. Without the other phasia to stand against him, there would be no prophecies or men alive who would have the power to stand against his schemes. By that time you would be so far under his power that you would be unable to break away from him. And yet there are layers deeper to Saurn's schemes, deeper even than my sight can delve. However, that is not what complicates this issue. You have a partial theory as to why you are able to fight the power of Saurn. Tell me."

Korrd thought hard for a moment, wondering how much his new acquaintance really knew about the whole situation.

"When Basille and I talked during my dream, he said a few things that really puzzled me. I have thought about them for a long time, and I know that I've been able to decipher a lot of the riddles, and I'm worried that I'm right. What if the reason that I'm able to resist the pull of evil is because I am the *Coromor*. The *Coromor* is supposed to be inherently good and not able to be swayed by any kind of evil. If I were the *Chosen One* as I have believed all along, I would never have questioned my role in evil. But because I feel the pull of good in my soul, I have no choice but to doubt what I have been led to believe all along. That would explain why Aerith Seth did not recognize me in the dream."

Korrd regarded the stranger for a moment and saw the grave look on his face. The stranger nodded his assent slowly and then spoke with a guarded voice.

"You have indeed stumbled onto your destiny Korrd Ranthall, and for that I am both happy and sad. Your brother has not yet fathomed why his heart is being ripped apart, and he seeks you as much as you hide from him. He plods along chasing the Light, hoping that the darkness inside of him will not grow any larger. But each day he is further from himself than he was the day before. Anger and doubt weaken him, and it is only a matter of time that he falls to the machinations of evil that swirl around him, or he crumbles under his own unreachable expectations. And the tragedy that will befall those around him will be horrific on a scale that cannot be imagined."

Korrd unconsciously swallowed hard, his mind immediately going to the young men and women that he too had grown up with, what seemed a lifetime ago.

"One day the two of you will meet, but not of your own free will. You will be baited to one another, and he will strike. A battle must be fought, and he will hate you more than you could possibly realize. When he finally learns the truth, he will fall victim to the very jealousy that once held your heart and mind. He will want you dead, but he must never succeed in the battle. You must turn his mind back to the Light, even if it means holding his friends and his own beliefs against him. Hostility will follow you everywhere until you finally admit the truth in the face of your brother. When that happens, I will appear to you again. He will believe me, as I have already earned his trust. The battle lies in your hands, as it always has, but it will not change what you have done. Soon enough you will be made to atone for your sins, and you will be truly punished by the Creator in the end."

"So there is no hope for my soul when this is all over?"

"I am afraid not, Korrd. You will fight the ultimate battle and save the souls of the world, but yet you can do nothing to save yourself. Though you have acted for evil in ignorance of what you are, you have still acted in the interests of evil. The Creator frowns on that truly, and you will be made to atone for your crimes. What form that atonement will take, I cannot say."

Korrd felt the knife twist deeper into the pit of his stomach.

"What are you, friend? You speak with a forked tongue indeed. All that you have told me, I know in my heart to be true, but I have never had the power to face it. It is like you are the conscience that I have never had. You tell me all of the things that I have needed to know all along, and for that I am grateful. Please honor me with your name and tell me what I can do to repay you for the great service you have paid me."

The stranger looked down, and for a moment Korrd thought he could see the faintest trace of a smile lifting the corners of the man's lips.

CHAPTER 17

"I am an agent of the true Creator my friend, and I am not of this world. In a way you could say that I am the conscience of all men, and I know what every man feels in his heart all over the world. My name, for all intents and purposes, is Emries. As for repaying me, there is no need. My reward is to see that good is done and in the end, the Creator's plans are carried out fully. That you serve your true purpose in this war is my only desire. Do you have anything else that you wish to know of me Korrd?"

"Thank you for your kind words Emries, and I do wish to ask you one more question before the night pushes me to sleep. What shall I do now that all of this has come to light?"

Emries made no attempt to hide his smile.

"You must continue on as you have to this point, Korrd. There is no need to change now. Nothing you can do will change the fate of your soul. However, you must not seek out your brother. Remember that you will not meet intentionally, and I cannot tell you where the two of you will finally meet for it is not for you to know. Saurn still holds the key to your future, and it is uncertain where that will lead you. You are here for a reason, and our meeting at this point in time has been ordained. It is to let you know the true path you must walk and to embolden you with the knowledge that you will triumph for certain. The adversary that you seek will not meet you, but once you battle your way to the throne room, Saurn will greet you as he has in the past. Then you will be given the hardest mission of your young life, and all of the world will depend upon your actions during that fateful mission. Now, I will take my leave and let your future guide you as it has in the past. Above all else, you must remember my words and heed my warnings. If you do not, the future is nothing but darkness. Now, sleep."

Emries walked back away from Korrd and disappeared into the mist again, leaving Korrd alone to his thoughts and the totality of night.

The next morning dawned long before Korrd had expected it. The previous night was like a haze on his mind, but Emries' words still rung out true. There were no doubts any longer, and the only thing that remained was the worry for Logan. But Logan would have to wait for another time, as the more immediate danger lay before him. Korrd gathered himself and approached the city gates ready to meet his future head on. It was apparent as he approached the city that the King of Kandor no longer ruled with an iron fist. The Vulture no longer flew over the palace, and soldiers filled the streets, battling each other for supremacy. The streets were also filled with the rotting bodies of the weaker knights and warriors who had fallen during the worst of the fighting. Korrd entered the city with no fear and no reservations; it was as though Emries' words had brought new confidence and conviction to his actions. His sword was out before the first of the fallen knights was upon him. Korrd lashed out without mercy. The soldier was able to parry the first slash, and countered with the dagger he held in his off hand. Korrd was not prepared for the attack, and the dagger struck true, digger deep in Korrd's side. However, Korrd ignored the pain and lashed out again. The knight just back out of the way, but Korrd pushed forward, closing the distance and catching the soldier on the top of the head with the hilt of his sword. A huge gash opened in the soldier's forehead, and he stumbled backward, the blood running into his eyes. Korrd however was not going to give the knight time to mount a counterattack. With a single hard kick to the soldier's knee, Korrd forced the man down and then slashed the knight across the side of his nock. Blood spurted in all directions and the solider went down. Korrd pulled the soldier's dagger out of his side and dropped it, the steel of the sword clanging against the ground. The wound in Korrd's side ached, and the warm flow of blood soaked his shirt. He concentrated on his powers and merged the threads of Water and Wind onto his wound. As the seconds past, the flesh sealed itself, and he was whole again.

Korrd walked through the main street of Kandor slashing at soldiers left and right, more to keep them at bay than to cause serious harm. He had only one purpose, and the whole-sale slaughter of these soldiers would not truly advance that goal. He could have been a god on the battlefield if he chose, but the more time he wasted on needless battles would give his prey more time to escape. Brave men died everywhere on both sides of the battle, and Korrd soon found himself inside the palace faced off against the royal guard. They held positions in front of the throne room, striking down every knight that would dare to approach their spears. The captain of the guard stepped forward and pointed his spear toward Korrd.

"Who are you infidel? I do not see the device of the Vulture on your cloak, nor do you wear the colors of the rebellion. However, I must warn you, if you wish to do our lord harm, we will strike you down as surely as if you were a rebel."

"Your lord does not deserve your loyalty. He is nothing more than a coward," Korrd responded proudly. "The Vulture has long since fled, and has probably already met his end. Farax is nothing but a pretender, and that is all he will ever be in every lifetime."

"Back up your accusations with your sword infidel," the captain of the guard taunted. "We'll see who is left standing afterwards."

One of the spearmen charged Korrd without warning. Korrd lifted his sword and spun to the side and avoided the spear. When he turned back, the blade of his sword shattered the wooden length of the spear and caught the guard in his unprotected thigh. The guard stumbled and fell, blood gushing from the open wound as another rushed Korrd. This time Korrd kicked the spear from the guard's hands and ran his blood soaked blade through the soldier's exposed chest. The handle of a spear cracked across Korrd's back as he tried to withdraw his blade from the dying soldier. The shaft pounded him again and again as Korrd was gradually forced to his knees. The punishment was incredible. Another of the spearmen kicked at the hilt of Korrd's sword, wrenching from Korrd's grasp. Another blow cracked Korrd over the head with the spear. Sensing the impending end of the conflict, Korrd rolled away from the swift attacks and staggered back to his feet. For the first time he reached for the strings of power that were at his disposal. Combining the flows of Earth and Water, Korrd created a sword of ice, whose crystal structure was strong enough to rival diamond. A guard charged him, but Korrd was engulfed by the adrenaline of battle. The *Coromor* that dwelled inside of him made him more than a normal man in battle, and he knew that he could do things that no mortal man was capable of. He caught the thrusting spear by its blade as it thrust toward him. The skin of his hand was split, but Korrd felt nothing. Crystal diamond met with soft flesh as the soldier went down screaming in agony. Korrd dropped the crystal sword, and it disappeared from existence. The other soldier who had assaulted him ran forward, intent on ending the battle once and for all. Korrd reached for the strand of Fire and burned the shaft of the spear in the man's hands. The soldier cried out as the fires seared his palm. Tendrils of Wind leapt from Korrd's fingertips and twined themselves around their victim. With a yank of his fist, Korrd crushed the soldier's throat and watched as he died. There were only two guards left to stand with their captain. One charged blindly, screaming his battle cry. Korrd sidestepped the attack and struck the soldier's ribs with his power-infused elbow that was stronger than stone. The spear clamored to the ground, and despite the resounding pain that came with every breath, the soldier drew his sword intent on continuing the fight. Korrd could feel his whole body tingling with barely restrained power, and with a mere thought made his fingernails extend. The soldier was dumbfounded as he watched the lethal instruments grow to a foot in length. Korrd slashed with his new weapon and ripped through the flesh in his adversary's neck. Blood poured everywhere as the soldier's throat was ripped free. The nails fell to the ground moments later, their purpose served. Korrd was quickly tiring of the game, and so he launched a lethal attack on the remaining guard. The stream of white flame enveloped the body, and when the burning was done, only the poor man's armor and helmet remained to tell the tale.

"So," Korrd said retrieving his blade, "what do you think your chances are now, captain?"

The captain looked at Korrd and smiled.

"Are you as dangerous without your powers, infidel? I am no match for you in that aspect I must say, but I believe that I could best you with steel. I was taught the sword by Arathorn Geoffry, and you are not man enough to defeat me."

"Arathorn Geoffry, eh? Well he may be captain of the Lion's Mane, and the second to Lord Cedric Binosear of Marcwell, but I have met and learned from his better. Gwydeon Sandar of Aradon could best Arathorn with his eyes closed, and Arathorn has admitted that. I am one of Gwydeon's students, and in duels, we have always fought to a stalemate. I would like to see you try to defeat me."

The captain thrust his blade without warning. There was almost no time for Korrd to defend himself, but he did manage to spin out of the way of the blade. When his elbow landed to the side of the captain's head, the captain began to circle him more cautiously. Each time the captain slashed, Korrd met his steel and return the stroke. Before long, the captain was covered with his own blood and panting feverishly. Korrd went in for the kill. With two swift strikes to the knee, the captain was left with no way to defend himself.

"I have been beaten," the captain said softly, groaning in pain. "You are a better swordsman even than my teacher, and for that you are a better man than me. Please kill me quickly so that I might die without too much pain."

Korrd stepped toward the man and measured his heart for the final stroke. The blade struck true and cleaved his chest. After wiping his blade properly, Korrd entered the royal throne room and found it empty as he expected. When he sat on the throne, the personage of Lord Saurn appeared before him with the normal haughty grin of approval written on his face.

"You have done well my pupil. I am most impressed with your progress and I have great plans for you."

"How goes the war, my lord?" Korrd asked with a coy smile on his face.

He now knew that Saurn had no power over him, but he was going to play the situation for all it was worth. Korrd might even be able to make Saurn slip and give him the one piece of information that he sought.

"The war fares well for our side young one. Zarsi and Farax fell to my treachery in the fields of Vesi Grath. They were fools to believe that I would actually agree to an alliance with the likes of them. How they ever survived this long is beyond my ability to understand. They should have been the first to die, but they were not nearly as impetuous as Aldridge and Erdric."

Korrd relaxed back on the throne, trying to look pleased.

"Why did you send me on an errand to kill Farax if you were going to dispose of him in the fields of Vesi Grath? Surely my talents could have been better utilized against one of the other phasia. Perhaps I could have gone against Warron or Basille."

Saurn frowned, his eyes narrowing.

"My, aren't we impetuous? I am beginning to find your questioning tedious, and so your next mission shall be my last for you. If you succeed in this, there will not be a need for me to order you around any longer, as my plan will be apparent soon enough. As for Farax, he has an interesting way of escaping the scene of battle without being noticed. Even though he was mortally wounded in the fields of Vesi Grath at the hands of his brother Zarsi, he might have been able to make it back to his palace to try and recuperate for a battle on another day. That of course meant he wouldn't have been much of a challenge for you, but still it would have ridded the world of another of my brothers. You are given due credit for your achievements I do dare say."

Korrd tried to unwind Saurn's words, but it was no use. With so many riddles and half-truths spun together, Korrd knew Saurn would always be a step ahead.

"What of Warron and Basille?"

Saurn shook his head.

"What of them? Basille is a fool to think that he can play both sides of the fence. Pretending to be Cedric's friend all of these years and still clinging to the dark secrets that go far beyond his service to Shau-ling. He believes that he can bribe the *Coromor* into serving his own ends and for that he will suffer. As a manipulator, he is an amateur at best. I have no need to hunt him down as of yet."

He doesn't know, Korrd thought to himself trying to hide his inner elation. *Saurn is more of a fool than I initially took him for. He may be mad, but he is still smart enough to figure out what is going on if I were to let it slip. I must remember what Emries told me.*

"As for Warron," Saurn continued, "he has already been destroyed by his own arrogance. Shau-ling decreed that he should be destroyed, and the winged assassin carried out those orders."

"The winged assassin?"

"Shau-ling in his infinite wisdom has decided to redesign the Shadowwalkers. Using the metal from a *Debuisa*, he designed a prototype. I don't know fully what he is capable of, but he has already demonstrated the ability to defeat a phase in single combat, and that cannot be overlooked. The assassin is none of your concern however. You have much more pressing matters to attend to. I assure you that this next mission is one that you have been anticipating for a long time . . ."

The Hall of Valor

For a long few moments, silence held between the five remaining members of the group. Logan was filled with an immense nervous energy, and Gwydeon paced back and forth. The god Azure had been blunt when it came to the precarious position Logan and the others were in. For so long the group had been fighting against creatures that had incredible power at their disposal, but now they were faced with a completely different situation. These were gods, but Logan took solace that the Creator himself had given Logan the best vote of confidence he could have ever received. If these gods were not satisfied with the will and wishes of the Creator, then why should Logan be concerned with their judgments? Then in thinking about the fact that he had been threatened with confinement to the mountain or death, the gravity of the situation truly hit. Regardless of what Emries had said, If the gods proved to be displeased with the actions of Logan and his companions, they could ensure that Logan never left Mount Tantis, at least until he was properly prepared and surrounded with those that would successfully complete the task to defeat Shau-ling. The last war had taken its toll on the world below, and the Gods of Mount Tantis were dedicated to making sure that the world was saved additional devastation, and they believed that an unprepared force could cause more harm than good. If Logan wasn't prepared for the road ahead, he could fail, and if he failed, everything would be shrouded in darkness for eternity. More than that, Logan could not help but feel continuous hostility coming from

Azure. There was something more to him, as though he had a personal stake in the war against Shau-ling.

They waited in an open foyer full of pillars and benches surrounding a still clear pond. Pike leaned against one of the pillars fidgeting nervously, watching Gwydeon pace around the area. Elwyne sat on a bench with Logan holding his hand and trying her best to keep him calm while Talon sat on the ground by the small pool lazily running his fingers through the still water. They had become so accustomed to action over the past few weeks that sitting around doing nothing was beginning to fray their nerves even more. Looking around quietly, Logan tried to take in the serene yet unnerving scenery. The entire mountain and city of the gods was white. The foyer itself was in the center of the city, and was surrounded by a garden. The fact that all of the plants in the garden were white gave the place an eerie solemnity, like that of a massive city of the dead. As the group sat there, Pike, Talon, and Gwydeon made several comments to each other about the palace of Sador. Eventually they started to tell the story of their capture by the forces of Zarsi and the battle in the castle. The more Logan heard of their story, the more he became leery of their surroundings and the lack of color that it afforded. A few minutes after Talos, Midarin, and Gideon left, the god Azure reappeared.

"Logan Ranthall, the Dragon of the Prophecies, and the *Coromor* as marked by the Creator. Thy friends hath succeeded in the test that they hath been presented with. They have performed well and all have survived."

They all breathed a sigh of relief when they heard those words. In the back of their minds, they had all worried about the outcome of the test and how that would affect the rest of the group.

"Thee shall see thine friends surely but not quite yet. Seeing the level of ability that we can expect, we have changed the nature of the tests. We are now ready to test the rest of thine companions."

"You're changing the conditions of the test?" Logan asked in disbelief. "The Creator set up those conditions in order to determine if I was ready to face Shau-ling or not. What gives you the right to change the words of the Creator?"

"That is enough!" Azure thundered. "Thee are not a god! What right dost thou have to question the actions and determinations of the gods? The Creator has moved onto the other realms to converse with the other Creators, and he left us with only a vague set of laws. We must be able to interpret those directives or we will never have any power over the people of this world."

"And yet you would be willing to risk the lives of those very people by changing the conditions of the tests and perhaps lowering Logan's chances of succeeding?" Gwydeon asked firmly. "The Creator underestimated the followers of the Dragon, and for that I'm sure he is pleased. Why do you have to turn a good situation into a punishment? Because we are superior, we should be rewarded."

"Thee are Gwydeon Sandar," Azure said softly, "I know of thee. Thine place in the realm of angels has already been confirmed, and yet thee still struggle to make thyself better in the estimation of others. Thee fight in this quest for reasons other than thou should, and it seems as if thee are fighting against the past instead of against Shau-ling. Thee hath been a puzzle to the other gods as well. We would offer thee piece of mind if thee would convince thy companions to follow with the path that we have chosen. We can give thee the one thing that thine heart has desired. We can give thee some solace to the pain that thou carry around inside of thine heart. With our help, thee can heal all of the scars that mire thine heart in a sea of blackness and despair. Will thou follow our directives, or must this end here and now?"

Logan started to say something as he stepped toward Azure, but Gwydeon brought his hand up in front of Logan, stopping him in his tracks. Gwydeon looked back at the rest of the group and visibly sighed. When he turned back to face Azure, his body went rigid and he drew his sword.

"What I do and don't want is not important, Azure. The reasons that we have for doing this are all different in some respect. Pike works now for revenge. Talon, out of love for his friends. Elwyne, fights for more reasons than any of us. Her pain runs deep on many levels, and she fights to resolve that pain and see that the man she loves walks away to keep his promises. Logan fights because he has no choice . . ."

"Ah if that were only true," a familiar voice said from behind them.

When the group turned to face the new arrival, Logan half expected to see the plain face looking back at him that he had met in the forest. Emries was the Creator, and Logan felt that he would have been a fool to think that Emries would have let him go through this test alone. Now that the gods were taking it upon themselves to test Logan for their own purposes, it would have only been logical for Emries to appear and set things right. However, Logan never thought that Emries would have picked such a way to enter the conversation.

"What are you saying?" Gwydeon said confronting what was probably just another petty god to him. "Do you expect us all to believe that we could have avoided this whole sordid quest if Logan would have just refused to fight?"

"No," Emries said quickly, "I'm not saying that at all, Gwydeon."

Emries walked toward him and laid his hand on Gwydeon's shoulder. Azure looked at the plain man quickly and then fell to one knee.

"Master, I did not know that Thee had returned to this world. What is it that Thee wish me to do? Give an order, and I will obey it as certainly as Thee command me."

Everyone else regarded Emries differently after that. Logan's posture never changed, and for some reason, no one else seemed alarmed. Pike stepped forward and took a closer look at the man.

"I remember you," he said reaching for his ax, "you were the bastard that sold us out in Rama. If it wasn't for you . . ."

"We never would have made it this far," Elwyne said as she held his hand back.

Logan had never made that connection. It was probably because of the poor light that he had not recognized Emries earlier, but Pike was right. The man that they had encountered in Illimar that later sold their identities to Lord Elouix in Rama was the same man that stood before them. Emries had been pushing Logan and the others along the whole way.

"My lord?" Azure questioned looking up at Emries.

"Assemble the rest of my followers in the Great Hall. There will be much to discuss in the next days. Our time on this world is finished, and we must make some preparations to move onto the next world."

"But my lord Emries . . ."

"No Azure, the beings on this world no longer need us to watch over them. They will soon learn that it is not the magic of the gods that have sustained them for this long, but rather the magic and power of mortals. They will be made to choose their own path, no matter where it leads them. For while the mortals may not always see the true cost of their actions, they are always willing to pay it, even with their own blood."

Emries considered his words for a long moment, the expression on his face never changing. His eyes shifted to Logan for a long moment before returning to Azure.

"Go! Prepare the Hall of Valor for the arrival of the people of the Dragon."

Azure bowed and left. Emries turned back to face Gwydeon and sighed deeply.

"Azure's words were not completely unfounded, Gwydeon Sandar. You have been promised to something far beyond this world, and when this battle is over, your time will come to join the gods."

"Does it matter?" Gwydeon said shortly.

He pulled away from Emries and sat on one of the low walls that surrounded the courtyard. After a moment, his eyes still cast to the ground, Gwydeon began speaking again.

"Throughout this whole quest we've been subjected to things that none of us would have ever expected. We live and die at someone else's command without ever thinking about why. Shau-ling is the greatest threat to the world, but if the Creator cared so much about the people of this world, why did he ever let Shau-ling live?"

Emries folded his hands behind his back and paced slowly from side to side, his eyes moving from Gwydeon to Logan and then across the face of each of the humans before speaking again.

"I cannot explain all of this to you, Gwydeon," Emries said finally. "I did not bring you here to answer the questions of existence, but I will answer the questions of your heart. You have all most likely surmised that I have been quietly guiding your path from the start. You needed some direction in your lives, and so I gave it to you. As for Logan, he would not have been able to stay away even if he would have wanted to. The will of men is much stronger than that of even the gods, and Shau-ling knows that fact well. If Logan would not have acted as he did, many more innocent lives would have been lost, and we would not be having this conversation."

"I only have one question," Pike said slowly easing his ax back into the loop of his belt, "why did we have to go through Rama? There was nothing that we did there that has made any difference in this quest."

"Your answer will come soon enough my friend," Emries answered sorrowfully. "There is much more than meets the eye when it comes to the tasks and will of the Creator. Your world is more complex than you are able to grasp, and mortal perceptions of time do not allow for a view of the same world that I see. There are many near collisions of fate, and many near misses of reality. If I were not there to steer you in the right direction at that particular point in time, one of you would have paid for it with your life."

"One of us?" Talon scoffed. "You come here without giving us so much as your name and you're making predictions about what might have been. And tell me whoever you are, which one of us would have suffered that loss?"

Pike took hold of his friend and started to pull him away from Emries.

"Talon, this isn't the time."

"Isn't the time? He seems to know everything else about us, let him answer."

"Talon . . ."

"NO!" Talon pulled away from Pike and stood straight before Emries with his hand on the hilt of his sword. "I said let him answer the damn question."

"I don't know, Talon," Emries said shaking his head. "The human heart is difficult to read when it comes to such things. But as with all other things in this frame of reality, it would have come down to Logan. He is the key to everything and without him, it is impossible to make predictions about the future or the past."

It was then that Logan felt every eye on him and for the first time he felt true doubt in his heart. Deep down, Logan knew that much of the quest relied solely on him, but for the first time there had been a price tag of lives attached to it. It seemed as if Emries was saying that the lives of all of Logan's friends had and would continue to hinge solely on his choices, and that was more troubling than any other possible threat. The actions of the servants of Shau-ling were out of his control, but now Emries made it seem as though it was Logan's choices that lead to the disaster at Taren. The massive weight that sat upon his shoulders only seemed to grow heavier.

"And yet you have come to give me the answers and rest to all of the questions in my heart," Gwydeon said shaking his head. "Am I so simplistic that you can read me easier than anyone else on the planet, or am I just lucky?"

Emries frowned.

"Sarcasm does not suit you, Gwydeon. But I forgive you your frustration. You have more pain in your heart than I originally thought young Sandar."

Emries turned fully to face Gwydeon.

"I cannot allow you to risk the lives of the rest of the people of the Dragon by continuing with the rest of the tests. You and I will journey elsewhere and finish some matters that you must face alone. Once that has been completed, and these demons of yours subdued, only then will you be allowed to rejoin the effort. Do not question my judgment, or you will not like what will occur."

Gwydeon just stood there for a moment and then nodded. No one knew what Emries was talking about, but it was apparent that Gwydeon did. Gwydeon's personal life, or lack thereof according to Pike, had always been a mystery even to his closest friends, but there had always been something deep inside of him that made him more passionate and loyal than the rest. Now this passion and pain was pulling him away. Logan only hoped that Emries would let him come back before too long. Gwydeon had become more than just another soldier. In many ways he had become the true leader of the People of the Dragon. While it was true that Pike and Logan could be strong at times, the only member of the party that had never been swayed by emotions, or even the ties of love, was Gwydeon. He showed strength of character and in battle, holding morale together with a soft-spoken word, or the lightning quick slash of his blade. If they encountered a battle while Gwydeon was away from them, the chances of surviving would be greatly decreased.

"Now," Emries said turning back toward the rest of the group, "Pike, Talon and Elwyne will undergo the next test. However, the Lord Dragon may make a choice as to whether or not he will risk the life of his consort."

Logan thought hard. Emries had told him not a day earlier that no matter what happened on this quest, Elwyne would survive. However, Emries also said that all of the lives of his friends hinged on what he decided to do. If Logan were to make the wrong choice, he could easily alter the future that Emries had predicted.

"What do you think Pike?" Logan asked cautiously.

"I don't know Logan, but I'm not really sure that I should be the one that you ask. You and I both know that no matter what you or I say, Elwyne is going to make her own decision and will fight tooth and nail until she gets her way."

Pike's attempt at levity did not go unnoticed, but Logan's grim state of mind did not let it have the effect that was intended. Elwyne looked Logan square in the face and then shook her head.

"Relax Logan," she said thoughtfully. "If you don't want me to go, I won't go. I'm sure that Pike and Talon are perfectly capable of handling whatever this test throws at them. Besides, aren't they members of the *Erieal*?"

The three of them laughed, but the only ease of heart that Logan felt was caused by Elwyne's acquiescence. She stepped to his side and wrapped her arms around him. For some reason she had always known Logan's moods better than he had, and she wanted to do her best to keep Logan in a good mood, especially in times like these where his patience and good humor were stressed to the breaking point. Without her, Logan don't think that he would have been able to make it as far as he had. Just knowing that she would live was not enough sometimes, but Logan tried to convince himself that it would have to do.

"What can we expect from this little test, Emries?" Talon asked.

"I can't tell you much, Talon. Even though the gods have changed the conditions of the tests, my hands are still tied. As the Creator, I am honor bound to let the gods test the Dragon and his companions. If I were to tilt the scales and give you any kind of advantage, the gods may not even allow you to continue upon your path."

"Well," Pike commented, "isn't that just great. What can you tell us?"

"There isn't really that much to tell even if I were allowed to speak freely. The test you are about to undertake is called the Hall of Valor. Once sealed in the hall, you will be tested for bravery and valor in battle. It is for this reason more than any other that I have allowed the Lady Dragon to stay outside of the battle. The danger is real my friends. You must fight your hardest and not give in to the pressures that will be put upon you."

"Us, give up? You've got to be kidding!" Talon commented brimming with his normal bravado.

"Do not be arrogant in your abilities Talon," Emries chided. "This will be the hardest test that you have ever had to face during the entire quest. Your lives and the lives of the rest of your companions and friends back home will be at stake. If you lose, they will suffer. You have already been warned that if any one of the companions of the Dragon were to fail in this quest, then he will not be allowed to leave this mountain until such time as the Creator were to spin out new companions, ones that were worthy of the task. Arrogance is wonderful in youth, but in battle it is pure suicide."

"You talk well Emries," Elwyne chimed in, "but you seem to know less than you say you do. Pike and Talon are the bravest and strongest people that I have ever met, save only Gwydeon. I doubt that you could find two finer companions in the whole of the world. If your sight as the Creator tells you otherwise, than perhaps Shau-ling is right to think that he can rule this world better than you!"

Even Logan winced at the severity of Elwyne's reprimand. Apparently she struck a nerve because Emries turned away from her and motioned for Gwydeon to follow.

"The gods await you in the Hall of Valor. Azure will take you there."

His voice was full of anger and rage. Logan knew that Emries was doing all that he could to keep it in check. Suffice it to say that Logan was most surprised when he turned back and glared at Elwyne.

"For your sake Ms. Tamerlane, you had better pray that my sight in the matters of this world is not wrong."

Logan knew what the response meant, and it struck him much harder than it did Elwyne. The only thing that puzzled Logan was why he had referred to her as Ms. Tamerlane. Before he had much time to dwell on it, Azure stepped forward and spoke.

"Pike Rhuiden and Talon Aielin. Thee hath been chosen by the Creator to face the trials of the Hall of Valor. Travel down the corridor behind me and enter the hall. Once inside, thy test will begin. Logan Ranthall, thee shall wait here until thee are summoned for thy test. As for thee, Elwyne Tamerlane, thee will accompany me, there are other purposes that await thee."

"What other purposes?" Logan asked.

"I am not at liberty to discuss that. The request does come from the Creator himself and cannot be disobeyed. However, I can say that it is concerning thy friend Gwydeon Sandar."

"I want Elwyne with me when . . ."

Elwyne took hold of Logan's arm and looked up at him.

"It's alright Logan. If Gwydeon needs my help, I want to be there for him. Besides, if Emries thinks it's important enough to swallow his pride and ask for me, than I can't pass up the opportunity to rub it in a little now can I?"

"But what about the test?"

"If Emries doesn't think you need me, than you don't need me. You'll do fine without me. Maybe I can teach him some humility like I did with Antrobus."

With that she turned and followed Azure out of the foyer. Pike and Talon stayed a moment longer, but soon left Logan alone with his thoughts. In his heart Logan could do nothing but wait and worry.

＊ ＊ ＊ ＊ ＊ ＊ ＊ ＊ ＊ ＊ ＊ ＊

Pike and Talon walked down the large white corridor, mentally preparing themselves for whatever test lay at its end. As the two friends emerged from the corridor, they were greeted by several gods standing in front of a large set of doors.

"Pike Rhuiden and Talon Aielin," one of the gods said proudly, "I am the god Nirrad. You have been chosen to undergo the tests of the Hall of Valor. Once you pass through these doors and enter the great hall the test will begin. Always remember that the future rests upon your actions and that no matter what occurs on the inside, you must act according to the will of your heart. Do what you would do were this not a test, and believe that your lives are very much in danger if you make the wrong choices. When you are ready, you may enter."

Pike and Talon looked at each other for a moment, and then Pike looked back at Nirrad.

"We're ready."

Nirrad nodded and then motioned to the other gods. They slowly opened the doors, and a bright white light flooded in from the newly opened chamber. After a second of hesitation, the companions stepped into the light and heard the door close behind them. When the light faded, Pike and Talon found themselves far from where they expected.

In front of them was the watchtower for a very large town. They could see buildings and people scattered over the countryside before them, and from the looks of the people, there was very little poverty or lack of finery among the townspeople. The guard in the watchtower motioned for them to enter, and without much thought, they entered the town.

"Where do you think we are, Pike?"

"I don't know, Talon, but I would doubt very much that this place exists in our reality. Hold on."

Pike stopped at one of the many merchant's shops that lined the main street of the town and began talking with the merchant who minded the store.

"Excuse me sir, could you tell me what town this is?"

"Heh heh, don't tell me that you folks don't even know where ya are and you've traveled all this way. Why, you're in the capitol of the vastest empire in the civilized world me fine boys. Welcome to the city of Brea."

"Brea?" Pike repeated. "This is where Princess Rice was born then?"

"Yes," the old merchant said sorely, "this was where the conniving tramp was sired. Because of her, we're now under the iron boot of that madman King Vorin and his pervert force of brutes, the Light Keepers. If she hadn't forced that poor innocent boy to her bed, she would be queen now, and the Light Keepers wouldn't be torturing people who are supposedly in league with Shau-ling and the *Coromor*."

"They're punishing followers of the Dragon? That's crazy!" Talon interjected.

"Watch your tongue boy. For even speaking the word 'Dragon' you could be sent away for life. When the Proclaimer took over, he decreed that no one may speak of the *Coromor* until he has arrived to take over the town. Any words spoken until then will be taken as heresy that is punishable by torture and death."

"What about members of the *Eriea?* Does the Proclaimer make any concessions for them?"

Pike pulled Talon aside and looked at him with a worried expression.

"What are you doing?"

"Look Pike," Talon said quickly, "if we can secure Brea and save these people from these Light Keepers at the same time, then maybe we could pass this test. If what we do here holds true in our reality, then we've done Logan and the world a great service."

"So you're saying that we should turn ourselves over to this man the Proclaimer and hope for the best?"

"Exactly."

"How did I know you were going to say that?" Pike sighed. "Alright Talon, we'll go with your plan, but I've got a bad feeling about this."

Talon smiled.

"Hey, trust me."

Before Pike could respond, Talon turned his attention back to the old merchant.

"Well, what does the Proclaimer say about the *Eriea?*"

"I don't know my boy," the old man said slowly yet with a sincere quality to his voice. "I don't remember the Proclaimer saying much about them."

"Thank you very much for your time my good sir, you have been very helpful," Talon replied.

Leaving the shop, the two wrapped themselves in conversation about how they were going to get in touch with the man who called himself the Proclaimer.

"I say that we just walk up to the palace and tell them who we are," Talon said finally.

"Do you really think that they'll believe us? Two crazy boys from who knows where walk up to the palace calling for the Proclaimer and yelling how they're the Erieal of legend? For all we know, they could say that we were member of the phasia and string us up on the spot."

"But what about the scars?" Talon asked.

"The scars probably won't mean that much to them. Remember Zarsi, he had that huge scar on his face. These people might think that the scars were either a marking of the phasia or some kind of tag for their servants. Either way, they'll probably think that we serve Shau-ling instead of the Dragon."

Suddenly they heard a shrill female voice ring out over the din of the crowd.

"Blasphemers! Blasphemers!"

By the time Pike and Talon spun around to face the one shouting, the whole crowd had stopped and were staring at them. The woman was short and pretty with long flowing red hair. Her face was red from the shouting, and she pointed directly at Talon. She kept screaming at the top of her voice for a few more seconds before ten men dressed in white armor ran up and formed a circle around the two confused *Erieal.*

"What goes on here," one of the armored men asked the red haired woman.

"Thank the light you came when you did Keepers. I was walking down the street here when I overheard pieces of the two strangers' conversation. I heard them speak of the *Coromor* using his animal name, and they also spoke openly of Shau-ling and the phasia. I even heard them give the name of a phase."

At this account, many of the surrounding onlookers gasped. The armored man turned away from the woman and approached Pike and Talon slowly. Pike had his hands on his hips and was shaking his head, while Talon had crossed his arms over his chest and was trying his best not to smile. After giving them a quick once over, he began his questions.

"Who are you strangers, and where do you come from?"

"I'm Pike Rhuiden, and my companion is Talon Aielin. We both come from Aradon."

"How did you come to be here in Brea? You are most assuredly far from home, especially for Aradon folk."

"We're adventurers," Talon answered flatly. "When we heard about the Proclaimer, we decided that we should bring some information to him that might help both him and the people of Brea."

"What would be this information?"

"We'd rather wait until we see the Proclaimer," Talon responded.

"Then you shall wait no longer," another voice entered strongly.

When Pike looked up, he saw a man dressed in thick black robes. The voice that spoke was very powerful, but the strained quality of the voice led Pike to believe that it was an old man under the robes. The man pulled back the hood of his cloak as he approached and his wrinkled face came clearly into view. All of the onlookers dropped to one knee and bowed their heads as the man approached, most trembling with either fear or adoration, Pike couldn't decide which.

"What is this information that you would like to present to me my young friends. Or is this just a ploy to by you some time before the Light Keepers and the Head Inquisitor have their talk with you?"

"Sir," Pike said strongly, "I am Pike Rhuiden. Because of the sensitivity of the situation in this world, I thought it best that we tell you who and what we are."

"Well?"

"Talon and I have been marked by the Creator with these scars," Pike continued indication the scar on his arm.

The Proclaimer smiled and then examined the scar quickly.

"They appear real enough. Now, tell me what these scars signify in the eyes of the Creator."

It sounded to Pike like they were being humored, but he continued undaunted.

"They signify that Talon and I are members of the *Erieal*."

Everyone was taken aback except for the Proclaimer who looked as though he had expected that very conclusion.

"And do you both have powers?"

"Yes," Talon answered.

"And you have knowledge of the *Coromor*, Shau-ling, and the brotherhood of the phasia?"

"Yes," Talon answered again.

"I don't like where this is going," Pike mumbled in Talon's direction.

"And you have indeed named one of the phasia within earshot of this entire town? Well, there can only be one conclusion. You yourselves are members of the phasia, marked just as Zarsi himself was marked by Shau-ling lifetimes ago."

Pike gave Talon a sidelong look.

"I hate to say I told you so."

Talon frowned.

"Shut up Pike."

The old man seemed unfazed by the interplay between the two young men.

"Either you will surrender," the Proclaimer continued, "or you will be killed here and now. You have one minute to decide."

"Well Talon," Pike said turning to face his friend, "what do you think?"

"Must you ask?" Talon said smiling and gripping the hilt of his sword.

"That's exactly what I was thinking."

Pike turned away from Talon and faced the Proclaimer once more. The haughty smile was gone from the Proclaimer's face, and a look of quiet determination replaced it.

"So, what have you decided?"

"I hope your men are ready for a fight," Talon said bluntly.

"Very well," the Proclaimer retorted. "Light Keepers, attack!"

The townspeople scattered as the men in white armor pulled their swords free from the scabbards at their sides. Not one managed to land a single blow to the awesome pair, and each one in turn went down to either ax or sword strikes. It was over almost as soon as it had begun, and at Pike and Talon's feet lay ten dead bodies. Pike and Talon had become so hardened battling Jeresei and Shadowwalkers that the resistance of common men had become almost a formality. They hadn't even had to call upon any of the powers at their disposal. Talon was smiling when he turned back to face the Proclaimer, but all Pike felt was pain. He was covered in blood and yet something inside him thirsted for even more. But that hunger was rivaled by something else, something darker, and something that resonated from the old man in front of them. It was something familiar, and yet at the same time horrible.

"Oh," Talon said thoughtfully, "is the battle over already? I was just beginning to get warmed up. Don't you have any more toy soldiers that we can play with?"

The Proclaimer smiled and began to laugh.

"You impudent fools. You really have no idea what you're up against do you? By meddling with the Light Keepers, you are disobeying the will of the *Coromor*. He has already arrived here ahead of you, and has decreed that his *Erieal* had met with some resistance during the journey and were killed. This more than anything has made your claim null and void. Isn't that right my liege?"

When a second man stepped forward, both Pike and Talon knew that they were in trouble. His face was very familiar to them, but it did not have the soft quality that they had come to expect in both the eyes and smile. The stark difference was the start of a beard and the sly mischievous grin.

"Pike, Talon," the hard voice said happily, "it's been a long time."

"It's nice to see you too, Korrd," Pike answered. "How long has it been?"

"Not long enough," Talon retorted.

"Oh Talon," Korrd said quickly, "you wound me. I trust that my brother is doing well."

"He is," Pike replied shortly. "What are you doing here Korrd, and why are you masquerading as the *Coromor*?"

"All in due time my friend," Korrd said quickly. "First though, I'm afraid that the Proclaimer and I must finish some business first."

They never even saw the streams of fire emerge from the Proclaimer's fingers. Before the veil of darkness fell over Pike's pained consciousness, he could see and hear the Proclaimer laughing over their writhing bodies, his violet eyes filled with malice and hatred. The look on Korrd's face was different; it looked almost like sorrow.

* * * * * * * * * * * *

Pike and Talon awoke in a white room. When Pike opened his eyes and sat up, he realized that they were alive and surrounded by gods. Midarin, Talos, and Gideon were also in the room.

"Pike, Talon," Gideon said walking over to them, "how are ye?"

"Much better now," Talon said rubbing the back of his head. "Where are we?"

"You are in a waiting area," one of the gods said softly. "You will stay here until the Dragon has completed his test."

"Then I take it that we succeeded?" Pike asked.

"You have done well Pike Rhuiden. The Dragon has chosen good companions for his quest against Shau-ling. Now you must wait until he has completed his test. If he succeeds, you will be set about your way with new direction. If he fails, the consequences could be disastrous."

Pike took in the words but his mind was still on the test. They had fought, they had died, but that couldn't have been the test. They had seen and done far more on the road that led them to Mount Tantis, greater proofs of their bravery and courage. No, this test was about something else. Was Emries preparing them for what might happen when they were face to face with Korrd, or was he preparing them for something else entirely?

Caged Animal

For many years before the War of the Lion, the Island of Mist was an obscure and peaceful place inhabited by small and friendly creatures that never knew the stamp of humanity, graced with a name lost to the ravages of time. For hundreds of years, the island lay untouched and a safe haven for the creatures of the world that could not survive mankind's tyranny. But then the wars of men and monster changed all of that forever. In a last ditch effort to hold the remains of Shau-ling's empire together, Zarsi and Warron led their army of Shadowwalkers and Jeresei back to the Island of Mist. For a strategist, it was a brilliant move, but the size of the army pursuing them was just too much for even a brilliant strategic move to even up. Eventually the forces of Shau-ling fell to the superior number of men under the command of Arathorn Geoffry. All of the wildlife had nearly been exterminated in the battle, and only a precious few lived to see the changes that would eventually turn their formerly beautiful home into a den of evil. Even as the men buried their dead, a mist began to roll in around the island. Many of the people on the mainland said that the mist was full of spirits of fallen heroes and agents of evil that could not find rest until the war between light and darkness was at an end. Others said that it was nature taking revenge for the damage done to the safe haven for the animals. Still others said that it was merely a natural occurrence and nothing more. Regardless of which belief people bought into, the fact that the opaque mist was there could not be ignored. Because of the mysterious nature of the mist, no one dared to try and approach the island, let alone colonize it. However, the mist was not the only change that affected the island.

From the beginning, the island had been flat and covered with gently rolling plains and small stands of forest that surrounded the lake in the center of the island. After the war, there was an upheaval in the island's foundation that caused crags of rock to leap into the sky. Flat plains erupted into mountains over a matter of days, and the forests that were scattered all over the island centralized themselves around the still lake. The lake too had changed. Nature had reacted badly to the taste of the blood of humans and monster, changing the face of the tiny island, but where it had ingested the most blood, it became a monument to the war. Because of the bleeding bodies that ended up floating in the lake, nature turned the water of the lake red, and from that point on, the color had remained. Only the soldiers that survived the battle ever spoke of Blood Lake, but it had become a symbol of terror and remorse for those who believed in the ghostly legend of the Island of Mist.

The island had not stayed devoid of life for long. Those little creatures that had survived the war were also changed by the upheaval of nature. Instead of the sweet, innocent, harmless creatures that were once protected only by the haven that the island provided, the newly evolved creatures were cunning, dangerous, and deadly. Nature had seen what the influence of humans had done to its sanctuary, and she in turn adapted to it with vicious, terrifying intensity. This more than anything led Shau-ling's hoards down upon the Island of Mist. The island was a place where monstrosities of every shape and size could call home, and where the den of evil could plot and scheme to take revenge upon their makers, the human race. Just as Shau-ling had been formed out of the nightmares of men, so too had his followers and the very place which he called home.

As it was rare for any being save the servants of Shau-ling to venture onto the island, the boat that came to rest on its shores was immediately brought to the attention of the sentries that sat high in the mountains. The newly redesigned Shadowwalkers with their shielded and powerful eyes were perfect choices to guard the beaches of the island, but even with the arrival of the stranger, they had yet to leap into action and thwart an attack by foolish trespassers. The stranger stepped out of the boat and looked around quickly. The person pulled at the robe and made sure that the hood concealed all features properly. Without a second of hesitation, the person walked up the beach toward the impressive wall of rock that kept out anything that did not know the secret path to Shau-ling's inner sanctum. This person was not a blind fool who had merely ventured onto the island for the sake of doing it. In fact there was a very dire purpose to an otherwise rash and risky action. Squeezing between the two opposing walls of rock, the person edged closer and closer to the entrance to the undersea palace of the master of all evils.

Within minutes, the stranger stood in one of the large receiving areas in the palace. After jetting down a few tunnels, the Pen came sprawling into view. Where there should have been hundreds of servants waiting upon Shau-ling's summons, there was nothing but stark and disturbing emptiness.

This is very odd. This place is supposed to be filled with Jeresei and Stone. If what I was told about the Shadowwalkers and the Kalbraks is true, there should be at least some of them here. I wonder what's going on. Maybe they knew I was coming and have prepared a little ambush for me in the Hall. Well, I don't intend to be caught off-guard.

The strange visitor breathed deeply and then traveled down the path that led to the Hall of Terrors. The darkness became more staggering the farther the person traveled into the bowels of the palace. Yet for every added shadow, there was a greater chance for something deadly to leap out. Only loyal and sworn servants had ever gotten this far, and deep in heart, the person hoped that luck would remain just a little while longer. But there was no way that anyone journeying into the pits of evil could do so unmolested.

Upon reaching the door that led to the Hall of Terrors, two guards stepped forward to meet the intruder. The Jeresei were armed only with their long, bladed fingernails, as well as their biting personalities. Their skin was its natural deep red, and they snarled ferociously as the stranger approached. With a raised hand from the intruder, the Jeresei fell to the floor, clutching their throats and writhing in pain. The stranger didn't hesitate long before entering the place most feared by all of Shau-ling's servants, the Hall of Terrors.

A single pathway of stone, suspended above the pit of fire by columns of stone, the Hall was a structure that should not have been possible. However, the nature of the stone was shrouded in mystery, and there had been some legends that said that this stone, berionite, was indestructible. So, even with the legend in mind, the Hall became an improbable structure at best, considering the rarity of berionite. The only light in the chamber came from the swirling pools of fire that lay over a hundred feet below the suspended platform of stone. There were also the occasional balls of flame that leapt up to the level of the walkway, but the increased light they gave off was only momentary. Looking from side to side during the slow walk down the length of the Hall, the visitor noticed the grotesquely huge cages that were placed in the rock face on either side of the walkway. Each of the cages was dark and empty where they should have been full of equally grotesque creatures shouting obscenities in foreign tongues. But the Hall was shockingly quiet, and that made it more frightening.

When the visitor reached the end of the Hall, flames leapt up from the pit below and separated the person from the door that led to Shau-ling's inner sanctum. As the flames receded, the Flame stood rigid in front of the door, vigilant of his eternal charge.

"I should have expected to see you before too long," the Flame said quickly. "The Master was not expecting you as of yet. He will be truly surprised by your presence."

"The more the better," the visitor answered. "You will allow me to enter his presence."

"Do not try to influence my mind, pretender. You should know well that your powers are useless against me. You should save what fight you have inside of you for Shau-ling. Shall I announce you?"

"No, just open the door, brother."

"Very well."

The Flame disappeared and the door to Shau-ling's throne room opened slowly. There was a faint pulsating of green light that emanated from inside the throne room. Taking a long deep breath, the visitor strode into the throne room waiting to face to embodiment of evil himself.

"So, you have finally come," Shau-ling's voice said from the far end of the chamber as the visitor walked slowly to the center of the black dragon etched in the floor, "I have been expecting you for some time, but never did I expect to see you alone."

The visitor did not answer.

"Why do you hide your face from me? Surely you did not come all this way to hide."

Shau-ling laughed at his own mocking words. The stranger reached up and pulled back the hood of the cloak. Green light reflected off long white-blond hair as the woman's face finally came into view. Her face was cold and pale. Her white skin was devoid of any pallor except for a little pink in her cheeks. She quickly locked her gleaming blue eyes on the human-like form of Shau-ling and waited for him to speak, half expecting an attack to precede any words.

"Welcome home my dear departed daughter. I thought that once the battle was taken to your comrades, you would come crawling back to your master."

"I don't know what you are talking about father. I came here to inform you of some plots, as well as some information that I thought you would find valuable."

"I'm not sure that there is much that you know that I have not already taken care of my dear. But I will humor you."

Ellis took a step back and then reset herself. The information that she had learned through Grawn, Bryn, and Saurn was very important, and if Shau-ling had already learned what she was going to tell him, then the war would already be over.

"Father," she said slowly, "I have learned through several sources that there is a group of phasia that are plotting to use the *Chosen One* and the *Coromor* to gain control of your throne. The names of these phasia include Saurn, Basille, Grawn, Bryn, Zarsi, Caris, and Warron. There is a danger because of the number my lord. If they were to link with either the *Coromor* or the *Chosen One,* they could complete the prophecies and one of them could take your throne."

"I know of this plot, my dear, but I never thought that my own children would be so vicious and blood-thirsty in their ambitions. I am almost pleased that they are so malicious," Shau-ling replied lightly.

"Are you not taking this seriously, my lord? I would think that even you would be a bit concerned considering that the prophecies are involved."

"I have no need to take this seriously Ellis, because the danger was as exaggerated as the belief that I could be so easily deceived. Zarsi was killed by Saurn, Caris lost her life to the *Chosen One* on Saurn's orders, and Grawn, Bryn, and Warron were taken care of by my own agents. Basille and Saurn are not dangerous enough on their own to worry me. With Jeroch and my secret weapon behind me, I need not worry about anything anymore."

"And the *Coromor*?" Ellis asked proudly.

"I have been given his identity by the Lion himself, and my old nemesis has already sealed the fate of the world he fought so hard to protect. It is fitting that it should all come full circle while he still lives. I should like to see the look on his face when I end his life again."

"I don't think that you truly realize the gravity of the situation my lord Shau-ling. It is possible that you and the rest of your phasia are mistaken in their beliefs and that they hunt the wrong man."

"Mistaken!" Shau-ling thundered. "You have grown impudent over the last few centuries daughter. You would do well to remember that you are still one of my children, one of my phasia. To think that you know something that I do not is bordering on madness. You were brave enough to come here unannounced, and even more so here to call your master a fool."

"You ceased being my master when Grawn, Bryn, and I were banished from the Council. If you are too much of a fool to listen to me now, then you deserve to die at the hands of those who would conspire against you."

Ellis turned to leave, but she found that she could not move. When she looked back there was a sly grin on Shau-ling's reptilian face.

"Do you mean to challenge me my dearest daughter?"

Suddenly the fear hit Ellis. Only once had any member of the phasia dared to challenge Shau-ling in one on one combat, and Zarsi had never been the same after that fateful fight. Ellis suddenly began to realize the mistake that she had made, and she inwardly wished that she had never left the confines of her little kingdom.

"No my lord," she answered quickly, "to challenge you would surely mean my death. My only intention was to make you realize the danger of your position and the obvious plots that are around you. I only had your safety in mind when I came here."

"And yet you insult me and wish me dead. Were you originally part of Saurn's twisted plan my dear Ellis, or were you merely playing along in order to find out as much as you could before returning to the very place where all phasia are forbidden to come?"

"Yet you do not forbid Jeroch," Ellis countered realizing that she would not escape the situation alive. "I have known for many centuries that he has been your favorite. You could not stand to see the first-born fail at anything, and that is why he is never sent out on any errand that could get him killed. After your experiences with the Flame, you had to make the rest of the phasia weak. After you made Jeroch, you found that you had made your children too weak, and so you coddled him until you thought he was strong enough to be your errand boy. Then you made your second mistake when Bryn, Grawn and I were born. You made us too powerful and too questioning. Jeroch has those seeds deep inside of him, and if any seeds of rebellion were to ever be planted in his heart, he could conceivably use his powers against you and win. He does not have the restrictions placed upon him that the rest of us do. You did not find that necessary until Grawn and Bryn challenged you because of Aerith Seth. How would you have handled both of them together had it not been for my intervention?"

Shau-ling sat still, but the sly grin was gone.

"That is right my lord," Ellis continued sharply, "you would do well to remember that I alone saved your life all of those centuries ago. Now I stand here before you trying to do the same thing, and you question my loyalty. What a mistake you would make to not listen to me now."

"There is no threat now, Ellis," Shau-ling replied after a moment. "All of the traitorous phasia have been dealt with appropriately, and soon enough Logan Ranthall will fall to the wayside with them. After that, the world will be mine, and not even the Creator will be able to save it."

Bells went off in Ellis' head when she heard the name. *So, he doesn't know after all.*

"And now that you have shown your true colors my dear," Shau-ling continued, "I have a small present for you."

Shau-ling raised his right hand, and a pair of red eyes appeared from the darkness beside the throne. As the metallic beast stepped forward, Ellis began to fear her own death. She that since she had been separated from the Council, her life was not renewable with ever generation. Once she was killed, her life was over, just like every other mortal's.

"Ellis," Shau-ling said smartly, "I would like you to meet Nightwing. He is the very man that destroyed your traitorous brethren Grawn and Warron. Soon enough he will rid the world of Saurn and Basille as well. Now my dear, he will end your life as well."

Nightwing stepped forward and pointed at Ellis.

"DO YOU WISH TO BATTLE FOR YOUR LIFE, OR WILL YOU KNEEL AND ACCEPT YOUR DEATH WILLINGLY. KNOW BEFORE YOU SPEAK THAT ALL PHASIA THAT HAD STOOD AGAINST ME HAVE FALLEN. NO ONE HAS EVEN MANAGED TO LAND A SINGLE BLOW."

"I have no doubt of that monster," Ellis remarked. "I will yield. Strike true and master will never have to fear my words ever again."

Nightwing's blade came down across the back of her neck a moment later. The secrets that she held about the Ranthall family would never be uttered, and the intentions that she had when coming to the palace would never be filled. If Shau-ling didn't find out about Emries and Korrd Ranthall before it was too late, there was hope for the world. If somehow one of the other phasia learned of the secret, then the world would be truly lost. However, there still was a chance for the one named Logan. If Bryn had gotten to him in time before she met her end and told him of his true nature, then perhaps he would seek out his brother and the two of them would learn the true meaning of power. Both of those were dying dreams. With Emries involved, there was no chance that the world would be whole again. The truth would come out, but not the way that it was intended. If one of the brothers knew the truth, and the other didn't, the war for power would cause the *Coromor* and the *Chosen One* to be forever at war, and their powers would not link properly when the time for the final battle came. That could be very dangerous in the end, and she hoped in her heart as the last strands of consciousness left her that Basille would find some way to make right what was going wrong, even if it meant doing the one thing that he had refused to do.

As Ellis' blood poured from the open wound where her head had been, Shau-ling laughed to himself.

"Well done Nightwing. I thought that my daughter would have posed more of a threat to you than that."

"SHE DIED WITH A PURPOSE MY LORD SHAU-LING. SHE SAID HERSELF THAT SHE HAD SOME INFORMATION ABOUT THE *COROMOR* AND THE *CHOSEN ONE*. PERHAPS HER INTENTIONS WERE TO TAKE THIS INFORMATION TO THE GRAVE IN AN ATTEMPT TO SEAL YOUR FATE."

"My sister was never that clever, Aryx," Jeroch said as he entered the throne room. "If anything, Ellis wanted to create that appearance in order to confuse the issue and buy time for the other traitors. Ellis has always been one to work with subterfuge, and she thought that it could save her life in this frame of time, but it appears that she was gravely mistaken."

"I agree with your assessment Shadow," Shau-ling commented. "Grawn and Bryn always represented the intelligence of the trio. Caris was always more cunning and forceful than her older sister."

"Yes my lord Shau-ling. Ellis' strength always did fall in the areas of diplomacy and reason."

"Totally useless qualities for a phase," Shau-ling added.

Jeroch felt something akin to disappointment in Shau-ling's voice. But it wasn't disappointment at Ellis, nor her actions. Was perhaps there more to this situation than Jeroch was allowing himself to see?

"My lord," Jeroch asked uneasily, "what should be done now? We have heard no reports about the activities of the *Coromor*, the *Chosen One*, or brother Saurn for some time now. I am beginning to wonder whether or not the final battle is coming quicker than we expected."

"The *Coromor* is out of my hands now, Shadow. The pitiful gods upon Mount Tantis have taken him for a test of his powers. Emries' concerns after Cedric's questionable victory has caused him to make hasty choices. Should Logan succeed, I have already devised a plan that will take care of him once and for all. I allowed the gods of Mount Tantis to intercept a message for your brother Taron. This message was of course false, but it sets the trap up wonderfully. I have sent Taron to a small town called Seren. There he and a Tarnae will make sure that our friend Logan Ranthall and his companions will die."

"And if Ranthall does not succeed in passing the tests laid out by the Tantis gods?"

"Then we can set our sights on the *Chosen One* and foil the prophecies of Aralias Imstra once and for all. Do not worry my dearest son. The prophecies can no longer hurt us. Aralias Imstra was a fool to think that I would bow so easily to his words. If there is any one being on this world that would control my destiny, it is I and I alone."

"Yes my lord Shau-ling," Jeroch responded. "What mission do you have for me to accomplish?"

"Ah," Shau-ling said gently, "I see that Ellis' words have rung out in your heart. Do not take her words for any value Shadow, her dementia caused by absence from the Council makes her words valueless. However, I do have a mission of vital importance that you must undertake. Saurn will not come to battle me openly, at least, not yet. There is one other member of the phasia that he must destroy before he would dare face me."

"I am a threat to him," Jeroch commented dryly.

"That is true, though not in the way that you are thinking. Because Saurn has lived in the Blight, my birthplace, all of these years, his power has grown to proportions above and beyond that of any of the phasia. His power might even be able to rival that of the Flame. He is not threatened by you personally, but more by your existence more than anything. Should I fall, because you are first-born, you would rule the forces of the Shau. That is why he fears you. You have the one thing that he does not, my favor. It is a gift that I do not bestow lightly. Cherish it."

"I do my lord."

"Good. Now, you would do well to seek out Saurn and challenge him to a duel. He will most assuredly want to battle you inside the confines of the Blight. That would favor you more than him because it would magnify your powers more than his. He does not realize that the powers of the Council are doubly strong for the first-born, and because of his absence from us for so long, his powers of merely a fraction of what they once were. Should you fail to defeat him, I will intervene. I need you alive, but this duel cannot go unfought."

"I understand my lord."

With that, Jeroch turned and left the throne room. The words from Ellis circled in his mind and what he called a heart. There were many old questions that popped up, and many more new ones. Perhaps the time had come to do the unthinkable. Perhaps it was time to realize the power of his status as first-born.

"WHAT OF ME, MY LORD SHAU-LING?"

"Nightwing, my loyal servant. I believe that it is time for you to seek out my youngest son Basille. He has been led astray, and I think that you should go and put him back on the right path again."

"AND IF HE WILL NOT LISTEN?"

"Then exterminate him."

"AS YOU WISH, MY MASTER."

Castle of Terror

Emries was never the kind of man you would expect to have great power within him, at least, that was the way Gwydeon had perceived him from the start. Because of his plain appearance and his calm demeanor, Emries could have been taken for just another man in a sea of humanity. There was nothing special or remarkable about him. Everyone Gwydeon had ever known had some distinguishing characteristic that set them apart from everyone else that he knew. That held true for all but Emries. How Pike had linked him with the man from Illimar and Rama Gwydeon would never know. Perhaps it was his plainness that set him apart. If one scanned over a crowd, Emries would have been the last person picked, and that was what made him special. Throughout the quest, everything special had been found in such common places. The *Coromor* and the *Chosen One* were brothers who had come out of a little farm village, and the same could have been said for two members of the *Erieal*. The third *Erieal* had been found in a forest, and he was nothing more than a thieving son of a commoner. The Jeweled Dragon's Flame had been found in the wine cellar of a little out of the way inn. Fate had played a hand in all of it, Gwydeon was sure, and not all could be attributed to the plain man named Emries.

"I shall give you the key to unlock the deepest desires of your heart, Gwydeon," Emries said as they left Gwydeon's companions standing in the foyer. "After this is over, you will be free to live the life that I had intended for you to live."

"The life that you intended for me to live?" Gwydeon repeated. "Is there truly freedom in that? Where is my freedom if everything has already been planned out for me?"

Emries look was one of amusement.

"You anger very easily these days Gwydeon, why is that? Are you afraid to face the demons that haunt your very soul? Are you afraid to look the Great Dark One in the eye only to turn back and fly to the realm of angels? These are the tasks that you must complete before you can be the man that you once were, and that you are meant to be. How is it that you have been able to make it this far in the quest without succumbing to the madness growing inside of you? What has held that bond tight this long so that it could be undone? Further still, what caused that bond to be torn asunder?"

"Love, Emries," Gwydeon answered without any hesitation. "Love is the answer to all of your questions."

Emries stopped walking and turned to face Gwydeon. The look on his face could have masked hundreds of different emotions, but confusion and pity would have been more accurate than any others.

"That is a valiant expression my son, but I am not sure that you fully know what you are saying. Love has been called both a thief and a tyrant by the woman you supposedly love now, and yet you would betray the trust of that solemn word to waste time on that one? She has no love in her heart for anyone but herself, and that is why she is on the road that she travels now. Perhaps your path would be filled with less pain were you to let her go and walk alone."

"No Emries," Gwydeon retorted, "you are the reason that she is on this path. You said yourself that you have chosen the paths of every mortal on this world, more so when it comes to the companions of the Dragon. She did not make the choices in this life that let her to this point, and neither did I."

"A profound statement Gwydeon, but one that you yourself do not believe. You would not be alive were it not for me, and if I were to let all humans make their own decisions, the world would become easy for Shau-ling to control. The human will is a very fragile thing, and if all humans were allowed to influence all others that they come in contact with, what would the world become? Take your Midarin as an example. Had she been left to make her own choices and not be tempted by my machinations she would not be at your side. She would not have been there in Sador, or Sarmeel. She would not have defended your lives in Illimar or Taren. What would have become of you all in Frontier? Choice is convenient when it works in your favor, but all humans must bow to the uncomfortable truth that you would all gladly trade that choice for certainty of result."

Gwydeon frowned, but would not allow his will to be shaken by words alone, regardless of who they came from.

"The human will is strong. We fight for freedom from the oppression of Shau-ling but in the end it may come down to fighting the Creator and the gods of Mount Tantis. You should not control us when we have fought so hard to destroy a foe that you cannot even touch. Without us, this world would die. It seems as if your circular argument had taken another turn Emries, I would like to hear you turn it back."

There was a faint smile that pulled at the corner of Emries' lips for a moment.

"Bravo Gwydeon," Emries said clapping his hands. "You have taken your first step toward the greatness that awaits you. Your strength will rise above the ranks of the mere mortals that fight blindly, and you will take your place at my side when your battle has ended, of that I am sure. It is not a path without pain and suffering, and your greatest tests lie ahead of you. First there are things that we must do to insure that you will be ready for this greatness. Are you prepared to face the very thing that you have run from all of this time?"

"I'm ready."

A subtle lie, but a lie nonetheless. His mind might have been prepared to face whatever lay ahead, but in his heart, the doubt raged like watch-fires in a never-ending night. Emries turned away from Gwydeon again and continued the slow walk down the long hallway. The time was the worst part for Gwydeon. Every second that passed was another second that he could dwell on the inevitable. Every second was another second that he could imagine what awaited him. The waiting was its own form of torture, and when Emries stopped and turned back to him again Gwydeon was thankful that the most trying part of the ordeal was finally over. Nothing that awaited him could have been as bad as some of the things he had imagined.

"Once you pass through these doors," Emries said indicating the plain set of white doors behind him, "the desire of your heart will be granted to you. What you do after you are granted this wish will determine much about your future and the future of your friends. For this reason, I have decided to give you some assistance to make sure that you do not allow your passions and your irrational emotions to cloud your judgment. Elwyne Tamerlane awaits you in the Dream Chamber. I will not interfere, and even with the assistance of Ms. Tamerlane, you must be the one to make the choice. In time you will see the benevolence of this act, and though for a time you will hate me for giving you this burden, you will one day see the mercy of it."

"I understand."

Yet another small lie. Emries opened the door before him and stepped to the side. Gwydeon regarded him for a moment and then walked into the room that Emries had called the Dream Chamber. The room was pitch black, but when Emries closed the door behind Gwydeon, a warm white light grew in the room, and seemed to float about like clouds around his feet. In fact, the longer he stood looking around, the clouds seemed to grow more solid and float throughout the room as if one was looking down on the sky.

"Elwyne," Gwydeon called.

There was no response.

"Alright," Gwydeon said aloud, "I'm ready. Grant me the one wish that Emries has seen in my heart."

The light in the room flickered for a moment, and then the clouds a few feet in front of Gwydeon began to shift more abruptly than the others in the chamber. It was as if they were parting the way for someone to walk through. Then a shadowed figure began to come into view. When at last Gwydeon recognized the person before him, his heart nearly stopped.

The woman who approached was a woman of such beauty that not even the greatest poet that had ever lived could do her justice. She had the face of an angel. Her skin was soft and white, but not fragile or pale. The eyes were the one feature that Gwydeon remembered above all others. They were like two beacons shining out from the heavens. While they were a stark shimmering blue, those eyes had a warmth to them that could never be described in words. Eyes like whirling pools of azure with a single blazing star in the center of each. Each look so deep and full of meaning that it would take lifetimes to understand all of the subtle levels. Gwydeon could remember a time when he was captivated by every glance and every beat of an eyelash. Her auburn hair was light and soft, just as it was in all of Gwydeon's memories. He could remember the nights when they would lie together and all he could do was run his fingers through her hair as he watched her sleep. There had never been anything subtle about her, and yet there was always the mysterious shroud that hung about her, almost like a sensual veil that enticed one to examine the person below.

"Gabrielle?"

Her name was fitting for her beauty. It was a name that dripped from the tongue like honey and made all sweet things in the world pale by even the slightest comparison. None could match her beauty or grace in Gwydeon's eyes, and he truly began to believe the old saying that his father had taught him all that time ago. 'Beauty is in the eye of the beholder son,' his father had said all those years ago, 'but love has a funny way of reshaping the lens.' His father never thought that he listened, but it was times like these when he realized how much his father really knew.

"Gwydeon, my love, it's been a long time."

The voice. It was as if all of the music in the world could not compare to the tone that came from her throat.

"Yes it has, Gabrielle, how are you?"

Stupid question, Gwydeon thought to himself, *she's dead, how is she supposed to feel?*

"I'm fine Gwydeon. The gods here on Mount Tantis treat me very well, and the man they call Emries checks in on me now and then to make sure that I have everything that I want. At least I know that one of my wishes has been granted."

"You wanted to see me?" Gwydeon said in disbelief. "I didn't expect such a warm welcome after . . . well . . . I mean . . ."

"The accident?" Gabrielle finished. "I hope that was the word you intended to use. What, did you think that I would hold that sword breaking against you all this time? I know that you didn't intend to hurt me, and I could never blame you for what clearly wasn't your fault."

"But . . ."

"No Gwydeon. It wasn't your fault no matter what you believe. I know you too well, and I know you've been beating yourself up over this for a long time now. You can't blame yourself for what you couldn't control. Besides, it doesn't matter now. You and I can be together again, and things will be like they were."

"What do you mean?" Gwydeon asked blindly.

"You came here for a reason. You wanted me back, and so the gods here on Mount Tantis have given me back to you."

A year earlier, in a cruel twist of fate, Gwydeon's first love had been taken from him by a horrible accident. From that time on he had always believed that there was something that could have been done to prevent that terrible tragedy from ever occurring. It had haunted his dreams every night since then, and he didn't see that there was any rest in sight. But then love had come again into his life. Leane Torne was a woman who reminded him so much of his lost love that he could not help but let his emotions take him to the place he never thought he could find again. But that had ended too soon for the emotions to be realized, and just when he thought she had forsaken all they had forged in that short time, he realized that her life had been stolen from her, just as Gabrielle's was. But once awakened, those emotions were not ready to fall back into the deep sleep that had claimed them for that year. A woman had indeed claimed his heart again, but this time, she had not been stolen away from him quickly, nor did she appear to intend to leave him. Midarin truly loved him, and Gwydeon knew in his heart that he loved her back. But now the one thing that he had secretly wished in his dreams and prayers had come true. Gabrielle was alive again, and she wanted him back. She wanted to go back to the way things were, and she wanted him to love her again. The truth was, he never stopped loving her.

"There is so much that we must catch up on Gwydeon. You must tell me all of the things that you have done in the last year, but before that, I have a surprise for you."

She turned away from Gwydeon and walked back toward the clouds. When she returned a few seconds later, she was holding a bundle in her arms. Before Gwydeon looked at the small child in her arms, he knew what the surprise was. The boy she held in her arms couldn't have been more than three or four months old.

"I'd like you to meet your son, Gwydeon," Gabrielle said with an unfamiliar look in her eye, "this is Gwillim. Gwillim," she said in a soft pleasing voice as she looked down at the baby, "this is your father, Gwydeon."

For the first time the baby stirred, but it was obvious that he was aroused more by the tone than the actual words. The child had no idea what had occurred, and Gwydeon felt the pangs of regret harder than they had ever struck him before. Without much thought he took the child from his mother and held him close. Gwillim had his mother's eyes, and the face of his father. There was no doubt in Gwydeon's mind that the child would someday grow up to be greater than he had ever been or ever would be, but that was only if the child would be allowed to grow up at all. Only in his wildest fantasies did Gwydeon ever dream of being a father. After Gabrielle died, it seemed like he could never love another woman with the kind of devotion that he had given her. When the quest came along, it sealed the thoughts in his mind and a child bearing the name Sandar would never again grace the earth. But now was his chance to change all of that, however, the cost was almost as much as what he would gain. But there was something more, something that gnawed at the back of Gwydeon's mind. Emries' words crawled through the shadows of Gwydeon's mind like a like a rat through a pristine palace. Words of the loss of choice in the face of necessity. Gabrielle's words of forgiveness for an action that Gwydeon had felt responsible for. Had Emries only been trying to help Gwydeon absolve himself of what he considered to be his greatest mistake? Or was there more, something deeper that lingered beneath what most would have considered a way out of the darkness? Gwydeon turned away from Gabrielle for a moment and prayed under his breath.

"Elwyne, if there was ever a time that I needed your help, this is it."

"I'm right here Gwydeon," Elwyne's voice responded from the shadows. "Emries told me that I can't come into the room, but I can stand here at the edge of the clouds and help you as much as I can."

Gwydeon nodded absently and gave Gwillim back to his mother.

"I need to think this over for a second Gabrielle, I won't be too long though."

She nodded her assent and watched as Gwydeon walked to the edge of the clouds. Elwyne waited there as he expected, and the look on her face told him quickly that she knew almost everything.

"I'm sorry Gwydeon," she said tenderly, "I know how hard this must be for you."

"That's just it Elwyne," Gwydeon responded, "it's not hard at all to make the decision, it's just the consequences that I'm afraid to deal with. How can I tell her that I can't be with her ever again? Won't she think me callous and cruel to cast her away like this?"

"I see," Elwyne responded sadly, "I guess I should have expected as much. I suppose were I put in the same situation as you are now I would make the same choice. Don't worry Gwydeon, Midarin is an understanding woman and I'm sure..."

"No Elwyne," Gwydeon said shaking his head, "I was talking about Gabrielle. I can't jeopardize the quest and the rest of my life by holding on to the past. I have come to terms with the fact that Gabrielle is dead. The fact that she had my child may make the pill a little harder to swallow, but what kind of world would Gwillim have to grow up in if I don't follow Logan into the den of evil."

"Can't you have it both ways?" Elwyne asked. "Why can't you take Gabrielle out of here and send her back to Aradon to wait for our return?"

"Because I wouldn't return," Gwydeon responded with a marked finality in his voice. "I've known from the beginning that I won't survive this quest, Elwyne, and I don't want Gwillim to grow up without a father."

Elwyne opened her mouth to speak once more, but suddenly she disappeared from sight, her words lost to the swirling clouds of the Dream Chamber. Gwydeon knew what she would have said, and it was clear that Emries had only wanted Elwyne there to reaffirm the decision that he had already wanted Gwydeon to make.

"So you have decided then?" Emries' voice said from somewhere in the shadows.

"I have," Gwydeon responded. "I have long dreamed of seeing Gabrielle again, but my desire was never so bold as to wish that she was alive so that I could have her again. I guess I could never be that selfish. The most that I ever wanted was to know that she had forgiven me for what I did and that she dwelled with the angels."

"Your words confirm the majesty that has been foreseen for you my dear boy. You have faced your greatest fear head on, and for that you will be rewarded two fold. The forces of the Dragon need your valor and greatness. You are hereby allowed to return to them as soon as you are ready."

"And the other reward?" Gwydeon asked.

"Because of her undying faithfulness and your love that burns inside of your heart, the gods of Mount Tantis have decided to return Gabrielle and her son Gwillim to the world below. They will not remember anything of their former lives nor will they need to worry about anything for the remainder of their lives. The gods will see to it that they will be taken care of, and it has been foreseen that this child will know greatness that will rival that of his father."

Gwydeon smiled for the first time since entering the Dream Chamber, and he knew that all of his dreams were coming true. He would probably never know the man that was his son, but he would know that somewhere in the world was a man who fought with the protection of gods and was kin to the angels.

"Do not worry, Gwydeon," Emries said as they left the chamber together, "the world below will always need those who fight for those who cannot fight for themselves. Some call them heroes; I prefer to think of them as the greatest of my children."

* * * * * * * * * * * *

It wasn't long before Azure came back to collect Logan for his test. For the first time since their arrival on Mount Tantis, Logan thought that Azure actually looked pleased. Perhaps it was because each one of the tests had been passed thus far and he was pleased that he had underestimated the so-called People of the Dragon, or perhaps it was because one of them had failed and he was happy with himself for being so clever in redesigning the tests. Logan hoped it was the former and not the latter.

"Thy companions are very impressive, Lord Dragon. Thee hath done well in thy choices, and we applaud thee. However, the time of celebration is not yet upon us for there is still one test that must be completed before the journey to confront Shau-ling can be allowed to continue. If thee complete the test, thee and thy friends will be given everything that thou needst to continue and thee will do so with the honored blessings of the gods of Mount Tantis."

"Thank you for your kind words Azure, I will be sure to pass your praise onto them when I see them. Now, are you allowed to tell me anything useful about this test or do I have to stumble through it as the others were made to?"

"There is little that I can tell thee without undermining the purpose of the test, however, I can tell thee this. The test is known as the Castle of Terror. Thee will be placed on the ground floor of a castle. From then on thee must go on with the test alone. There is but one way out of the castle, but thee cannot leave until thee hath completed the task laid out for thee. Thee will know if thou dost fail."

"I hope it doesn't come to that, Azure," Logan responded. "I'm ready whenever you are."

Azure nodded and pointed to a stone arch that had begun to rise out of the ground. It was made of the same stone as that of the rest of the foyer, but there was something different about it. When the arch had finally stopped moving, Logan approached it and gave it a cursory examination. There was nothing special about its appearance, but Logan couldn't shake the feeling that this was not an ordinary arch. Then it hit him. When he looked through the open space beneath the arch, the image was cloudy and seemed to shift back and forth. It would have made him seasick were he to look at it for a long period of time, but the second Logan realized that it was something like the portals that the phasia used, he stepped through the arch.

A second later Logan was standing in the middle of a dark room. It looked a lot like the huge receiving hall of the palace of Marcwell, but there were no banners that lined the walls. The only banner that hung in the hall was a lit torch in front of a field of gold. The banner hung over a large passageway in the far wall of the chamber, so Logan made his way toward it. It seemed like the most logical place to start. A few feet from the entrance of the passage was a flight of stairs. As he started to climb the stairs, he heard a man's yell, and suddenly ten guards were upon him. Logan freed his sword from the scabbard at his side and sliced through the first two that rushed in. It became apparent that he was greatly outnumbered, so Logan closed his eyes and clutched the string Fire. When he opened his eyes again, Logan saw what remained of the men strewn all over the stairs. Most of their chests had exploded and cast charred innards all over the walls, but one man was mostly intact. He was dead enough, but it appeared as if Logan somehow missed connecting with his heart, but rather his head exploded. It was obvious that the result had been just as devastating, but inwardly Logan wondered how he could have missed the soldier when he had stuck true to every other member of the attacking party. The emblem on the chest of the man whose head exploded matched that of the banner on the lower floor, but added to the torch was a ring that encircled the base of the torch. Making a mental note of the different symbols, Logan continued up the stairs and was shocked to find an arch at the top of the stairs. The arch was the same color and shape as the one in the foyer of Mount Tantis, and it was apparent that this was to be the way out when time came. As Logan moved cautiously past the arch, he set his sights on an open door at the end of the long carpeted hall. There seemed to be no other opposition waiting as Logan continued down the hallway. When he entered what turned out to be a grand and opulent throne room, it too turned out to be absent of threats.

Two golden thrones sat on the other side of the room atop a small raised dais, and stood empty. Other than the door that Logan had come in, there were no other obvious entrances or exits to the throne room. However, Logan's initial evaluation proved to be wrong when a hidden door in the far corner of the room opened and a single man stepped proudly into the room. Logan couldn't get a clear look at him for a few moments, but when his face finally came into view, it was like looking in a mirror. The other man caught a look at Logan at about the same time.

"Korrd?"

"Logan?"

Korrd approached and the two estranged brothers met in the center of the room. Face to face and eye to eye, there was very little difference between the two men, save for a few scars and wrinkles on the face of the older of the pair. They stood roughly the same height, and their physical features were almost identical. It was hard to believe that there were minutes let alone years between their births.

"What are you doing here, Logan?" Korrd asked. "Where is everyone else?"

"That's not important, Korrd. What is important is that we settle a few things while I have the time. I know what you are, and I know that you're working for the phasia. As the *Chosen One*, you're the link we need to destroy Shau-ling once and for all. Tell me where you are, and I'll come and get you. Together we can end this once and for all."

"It's not that simple Logan," he replied. "The time is not right for us to meet yet. You're not ready. Your friend Emries has already assured me of that. But you don't know that you are being lied to."

"Lied to?" Logan said staring at him, "how? And how do you know about Emries?"

"He has come to see me, Logan, and he has told me the truth about us. The gods are lying to you Logan, you aren't the *Coromor*. I am."

Logan laughed in his brother's face.

"You're crazy, Korrd. You're the one being lied to. The phasia have twisted your mind and the power is going to your head."

"How would I know about the words of the Elder if Emries didn't tell me? Think about the prophecy of the Black String, Logan. You broke it and robbed Cedric of his powers, yet you retained yours. If you were truly the *Coromor*, you would not have been able to find the string, let alone break it. You are the *Chosen One*, and those words come from Emries' lips, not mine."

Anger swelled up inside of Logan. He had known this would happen. The phasia had twisted Korrd's mind, and he was having delusions of grandeur. The power had gone to his head.

"So you won't join us, brother?"

"It's not the time yet Logan. Emries . . ."

"Then die!"

He never even saw the strings that sealed his fate. The fire was set in his heart before he could move a fraction of an inch of even think about drawing on his own powers. His chest exploded and belched forth roaring flames that spread his melted flesh all over the room. Logan did the only thing that he could have in the situation. There was no way that he could allow Korrd, mad or not, to stay in the possession of the phasia. If Korrd truly knew about Emries, then it was safe that the phasia did too, and the forces of the Light were all in more danger than Logan had initially expected. With those thoughts in mind, Logan sprinted back down the hall and leapt through the arch, half expecting to end up back in the foyer. Instead, Logan found himself in a black space.

"Logan," Emries said walking slowly toward Logan, "the gods are very disappointed with you, and so am I. In your heart you did what you thought was right, but you have failed the test."

"I failed?" Logan echoed disbelieving Emries' words. "How is that possible?"

"You did not complete the test, and therefore you have failed. I can tell you no more than this. Destiny is rewriting itself, and you must now atone for the wrong you have done. Because of the mitigating circumstances that you did what you thought was right, you will only be required to sacrifice one of your own to appease the gods. This must be done, or you will all be confined to the mountain for the rest of eternity."

"What do you mean 'sacrifice'?"

"One of your companions will die for your failure, and you must choose which it will be."

CHAPTER 17

Chapter XVIII

The Circle Closes

Kandor. Saurn's words rang in Korrd's mind, but it felt much different this time. The truth was clear and bright in the back of his mind, but he could never let Saurn know that he had been in control of the *Coromor* all this time. Such information could be deadly. Saurn had done everything in his power to thwart the will of Shau-ling. By using the *Chosen One* to do his dirty work for him, Saurn could look almost innocent in all actions. If he were to challenge Shau-ling directly, that foolish action would be sure to seal his fate. Then there was the question of the other phasia. Looking into his mind where the strings of the primal forces hid, Korrd pushed past the obvious and felt for the Blaze. He knew it was there, but as of late he had a harder time finding it. Perhaps the more he admitted his true nature, the less likely he was to be able to touch the side of him that Saurn had implored him to embrace. Finally that part of his consciousness came to the forefront in his mind again. The strong green inferno that was Shau-ling's life and power burned in Korrd's mind, radiating power and a sickening seductive call. Any who embraced the power of Shau-ling for even a moment would be at his mercy for the rest of eternity. That soul would never find rest, and could not be ripped from Shau-ling's grasp by the Great Dark One, or even the Creator himself.

Inside the burning maelstrom of power were thirteen different lines of power that fed on the Blaze. Only four burned as bright as before, but now there was a strange addition to the lines that served as the power for the phasia. Three of the lines of power had melded themselves together and pulsated as one. Saurn had spoken about the redesign of the Shadowwalkers and their new leader, the one Saurn had called the winged assassin. If Shau-ling had combined the powers of three of the phasia in this new creation, he was more of a threat than any of the phasia. Not only that, if their skin was truly made from a *Debuisa* that made them more dangerous.

Korrd looked back at the palace of Kandor as he rode to the north. Saurn had indeed waited a long time before giving him the mission that he had always known would come. Logan was out there somewhere, and Saurn had ordered the bait to be set. Brea would serve as a perfect location for the trap. Saurn wouldn't say what, but there was something there that was important to the quest, and if Logan didn't go there, he would be doomed to fail. So, Saurn had already prepared the people of Brea for the coming of the Dragon. In Saurn's twisted plan though, Korrd would be playing the part of the Dragon in order to keep the people of Brea on the side of evil for just a little longer. Saurn had played the part of a Proclaimer, and now he had summoned Korrd. But the night had passed slowly before the trip, and his mind was clouded with dreams.

The first had been no more than fragments in time. Saurn with an old and wrinkled face, but the power and voice still belonged to the maniacal phase. Pike and Talon ripping a force of Light Keeper's to shreds mere seconds before Saurn burned them to a crisp. But it was more than a dream. He could smell the charred flesh and hear their screams of terror as they lay dying. He even heard Pike's cry for mercy as Saurn looked back at Korrd with those evil and hate filled eyes. Korrd wanted so much to help those men who should have been his allies, but in the dream he could not disobey the will of his former master. Maybe in that subconscious state, Saurn still held some power.

But then the dreams turned even stranger. Korrd was pulled from Brea and was set down in the throne room of a dark and mysterious castle. There was a cold in the room that Korrd had never before felt. It was as if all the life in the palace had been sucked out and replaced with a fog of loathing and dread. The palace exuded hate, and as the seconds passed, the rage in the castle grew and covered him like a blanket. Outside of the throne room he heard cries of battle and of death, and so he mentally prepared himself for a fight. But when the doors at the far end of the throne room finally burst open, the face that greeted him was the last one that he expected to see. For the third time in as many days, Logan had entered his dreams. This time, the circumstances were much different. The conversation between the two brothers was short and anything but sweet. Logan didn't take the news about his true nature well. The burst of fire came quickly, and just before Korrd's chest ruptured and spewed forth flame, he woke up drenched in sweat. He could only hope that the real meeting would go better.

Korrd tried his best to push those thoughts aside. If there truly was still a place in his mind that believed the words of Saurn, then it was possible that his own thoughts could betray him. Time was growing shorter, and Korrd knew that he had to be strong. The order had finally come from the mad phase's lips, and Korrd was supposed to kill his younger brother and doom the world to darkness. Even though the latter would not have been totally accurate, it was a safe bet that the three *Erieal* and Gwydeon Sandar would be able to kill both Korrd and Saurn once Logan fell. Saurn was crafty, but in his current state of mind there was no way to tell if he considered that contingency. Korrd hoped that it wouldn't come to that, but as he rode toward Brea, that's all that was on his mind.

Four days passed before Brea was in sight. Korrd had made good time but was puzzled by the lack of travelers on the main roads. It was only when he saw Brea that he realized why the people weren't traveling there. Hordes of men in the grab of the Light Keepers were stopping all travelers and searching their belongings. Three or four horses in front of Korrd, one of the Light Keepers found several daggers hidden in a man's pack. When they pulled off his cloak, the scabbard and sword strapped to the man's back was revealed. The man was striped and forced to his knees by the soldiers around him.

"Speak Shadow-man," the apparent leader of the troops demanded. "You come to the City of the Dragon hiding your weapons. Unless you tell me why, I will be forced to believe that you intend to assassinate the Dragon when he arrives as your hated master Shau-ling has ordered of you."

The man looked down at the ground for a moment and shook his head. He was humiliated beyond the point of speech, but that was not how it seemed to the soldiers or the by-standers.

"He does not have the tongue to speak of his treachery my liege," one of the other soldiers said to his commander.

"Worry not traitor, you shall be absolved of your sins in the Light. See to him my warriors, and let the others see that we here in the City of the Dragon do not tolerate the scourge of Shau-ling within our walls."

The soldiers moved quickly and swarmed around the naked man. Within seconds they had wrapped him in blankets and tied the blankets tight around him. There were shackles on one of the outer walls, and as they chained him both at the wrists and the ankles, one of the men brought forth a torch.

"The fires shall cleanse you of your sins. Pray with all of your might that the Creator will receive you into the glory of the Light."

The man's screams of agony were drown out by the cheers of the on-lookers. As they set him to blaze, many of the people in line to enter Brea turned and fled. One of the soldiers took hold of the reigns of Korrd's horse and led him forward to the commander of the Light Keepers.

"Welcome to Brea, the City of the Dragon as named by the Proclaimer. We tolerate no deceivers inside our walls as you have seen, and we will listen to whatever transgressions you have in your soul if you so desire. Now, state your business here in Brea."

Korrd looked coldly at the commander of the Light Keepers for a moment and then looked back at the man who was strapped to the wall burning. Korrd reached into the blackness of his mind and found the strands of Fire that surround the man and ripped them away. The fires went out, and Korrd dismounted and approached the prisoner. A few of the soldiers started to go after Korrd, but a simple motion from his hand froze them in their tracks. Using the strands of Earth, Korrd willed the pins in the wall to tear free, and then he helped the man to the ground. The on-lookers watched in silence as he freed the prisoner from the remains of the charred blankets and laid him flat on the ground. Without so much as a word, Korrd laid his hand on the forehead of the prisoner and drew on the threads of Wind and Water to heal the rather extensive wounds. As the wounds healed on his body, many would not stay healed. They reopened, bringing new cries of pain from the man. Korrd closed his eyes and pictured the man's body in his mind, looking for the reason for the rejected healing. Threads of Fire were laced in with the wound, and they were the reason that the Wind and Water had not been effective. Korrd emptied his mind and reached for the string of Fire. Just as he was about the grasp it, it flashed bright red light all around. Korrd stopped dead and watched in his mind as the thread of Fire pulsed quickly. He watched the flashing for a moment and the grasped the thread anyway. After another few moments all of the prisoner's wounds were healed, and he was trying to struggle to his feet.

"Relax my friend," Korrd said in a soothing voice. "Your wounds are all healed, but you will be weak for a while."

"Thank you," the man managed to croak out. "I am . . ."

"You can tell me later young one. I believe that you and I will have a long way to go together. Come, let me help you. We must find you something for you to wear."

Korrd helped the weak man to his feet and walked him over to Korrd's horse. He supported the man with one arm as he reached into the saddlebag and retrieved a small parcel. This simple white package was supposed to be used for something else, but this way, it would serve two purposes. Korrd quickly unwrapped the ropes on the parcel and covered the naked man with the cloth of the parcel. As the man turned 'round, all of the on-lookers dropped to one knee. The man was stunned, but Korrd seemed rather happy with what had occurred. The man wrapped in cloth spun around and looked at the masses of commoners and soldiers who had fallen to one knee. In that instant he realized that they were all looking at his savior. He looked around again and then looked at the cloth that covered him. There was the shape of a huge red dragon spread down his back, and only then did he realize that he was clothed in the banner of the Dragon. The man started to drop to one knee, but Korrd held him up.

"There are enough people on their knees already my friend. You are my ally. Now, how do you feel?"

"Much better my lord," the man answered.

"No," Korrd said smiling and shaking his head. "My name is Korrd, and I insist that you call me that, or I just might let the Light Keepers have at you again."

"As you wish Korrd," the man replied quickly. "My name is Gwillim. I pledge that wherever you go, my sword will be at your side."

"I accept your sword willingly, Gwillim," Korrd said. He then turned to the people on their knees and spoke. "Friends, please rise. I have heard of your vigil and I have come to seek out this man called the Proclaimer. I am the one of which the ancient prophecies have spoken. I am the second coming of the *Coromor*. I am the Dragon."

A huge cheer rose from the crowd, and they rose to their feet to welcome the man on which all of their hopes and dreams relied. The Light Keepers were quick to surround Korrd and keep the massing people from harming him.

"You know Gwillim," Korrd said in a voice that only Gwillim could hear through the din, "you remind me of someone. You wouldn't by any chance have relatives in Aradon would you?"

"I don't know, Korrd," Gwillim responded. "I was born in Palacia, a little town across the sea. My mother and I lived there for a long time, but when we got news of the *Coromor* I felt draw here. I don't know what it was, but something in my heart told me that I could do more than just sit around and hear about the war."

"Well," Korrd replied walking toward the gates of Brea, "you're in the thick of the war now my young friend."

* * * * * * * * * * * *

Jerrard paced impatiently in the front room of Arin Domae's house. Erika sat in the chair watching him.

"Do you think you could sit down for a while, Jerrard?" Erika said lovingly, "you're starting to make me nervous."

Jerrard looked at his wife and sighed.

"I'm sorry, Erika, this situation seems to be going from bad to worse all of a sudden."

Jerrard stopped pacing and sat on the chair beside Erika.

"Still upset about your father?"

"I don't see why," came Jerrard's short reply, "I mean I haven't seen or heard from the man in all these years, I shouldn't really care who or what he is. I mean, what does it matter if he is a phase?"

"It matters to you my love," Erika replied taking her husband's hand and caressing it. "You're worried about how it's going to affect you. You're worried that you're going to turn out like that boy Hawk."

"To tell you the truth, I didn't even think about him. I suppose that I should have. He and his narcissistic father made our lives miserable for a few years before this war started, and I was actually glad to see that they had set their sights on another town. I guess deep down I was worried what that kind of power would do to me, I suppose I'm about to find out."

"I disagree," Erika replied pulling closer to Jerrard. "You have always been a wonderful man, and I don't think the power will change you one bit. I told you before that it didn't matter to me what you are, and that is still the true because I know in my heart that our love is stronger than any power in this world. Remember when you told me that Hawk had been a lying deceitful bastard all of his life, well I willing to bet he was raised that way, and it wasn't just because of his power."

"You're probably right."

"I am right," Erika corrected. "Now, let's see if we can't find a better outlet for all that pent up energy."

As she leaned in to kiss him, the door opened and Arin rushed inside. Erika stopped short of her mark and dropped her head with a sigh. Jerrard looked up at the new arrival and laughed.

"You definitely are the king of timing, Arin, what's happened?"

"Sorry," Arin said quickly, "but the Dragon has arrived. He just rode up a few minutes ago."

"How do you know it was him?" Jerrard said springing from his seat.

"The Light Keepers were torturing this poor man, and then they set him on fire. This man, Korrd, he got off his horse and saved him. Then he healed all of the man's wounds and wrapped him in the Dragon Banner. Then he proclaimed himself as the Dragon."

"Impossible," Jerrard said looking for his sword, "my father told me that the Dragon's name was Logan, not Korrd. It is highly possible that this man is a phase, and he is using this ploy to trap the real *Coromor*. Is there any way that you can get me close enough to this man so I can find out the truth?"

"The palace is locked up tighter than I've ever seen it, but I think there's a way. There are some secret tunnels that the old king used to use to sneak his mistresses in and out at night. Because of the Light Keepers' activities, I've been using the tunnels to save some of the prisoners in the dungeons. Recently though, I've been afraid to use them because of the Proclaimer. However, the word is that he's left to spread the word of the Dragon's coming to some of the other towns in the area."

"So you can sneak us in?" Jerrard asked.

"Yes, but I don't know how much good it will do us. How are you going to be able to tell if he is the real Dragon or not?"

"You leave that to me Arin. Remember, I'm the son of a phase, and I should be able to tell if he's one or not. All I need is for you to get me in and get me close enough to him to make sure he is the Dragon. If he's not, I might be able to try and use a few of my powers against him. If I catch him by surprise I may be able to kill him. If not, well, I don't think my parlor tricks will be much good against a phase who has had lifetimes to practice using his powers."

* * * * * * * * * * * *

Korrd sat on one of the two thrones in the huge throne room and looked around. This was the most restless he had ever been in his life. Saurn had only been in Brea but for a few moments after he arrived, and then went on with his charade as the Proclaimer and went to tell the world of Korrd's arrival in Brea. Now, he was alone in a massive kingdom with no one. Gwillim was only with him for a few moments before heading off for a bath and a change of clothes. Korrd had been taken to the throne room and installed as the ruler by King Vorin, and that was the last time he had seen anyone. Inwardly he wondered if that was what it was like to be a king. If so, he never wanted the job.

The door opened a few minutes into his reflection on the boredom of kingship and a beautiful young servant girl entered the room.

Perhaps there are some perks to the job after all.

"My lord Dragon," the girl said eloquently, "Sir Gwillim has been cleaned and dressed. Would my lord like to see him now, or would my lord rather I attend to his bathing instead?"

"As tempting as that offer is my dear, I would like to see Sir Gwillim. Don't worry little one, I may have need for you soon enough."

The servant girl smiled and giggled as she left the room. It was a moment of two later when Gwillim walked into the room wearing red armor with a white dragon on the breast plate. His sword and scabbard were on his left hip, and he held his helmet under his right arm.

"Well look at you, Gwillim," Korrd said rising from the throne. "I must say, it's a far cry from that banner you were wearing."

Gwillim laughed and then responded. "The Light Keepers and the wise ones thought that since you chose to clothe me in your banner that I was special or something, so they knighted me and gave me this armor and the sword. I am now the commander of the Army of the Dragon, as well as the leader of your personal security force."

"My personal security force? How many people are in this force?"

"Counting me?"

"Yes."

"One."

"How did I know that was coming?" Korrd responded laughing.

"Well," Gwillim answered lightly, "you have to find people that you and I can both trust. I don't think the personal security force will get much larger before that happens."

"Agreed. So, what do we do now?"

"That's what I was going to ask you. Brea is nice and all, but I get the impression that we are being watched all the time."

"I know the feeling," Korrd responded, "and the Proclaimer being gone doesn't help that feeling any. Take my word for it, Gwillim, just because he's not here doesn't mean that he's not watching us. Understand?"

"Yeah," Gwillim answered, "I think I know what you mean."

"Well, I suppose there are some people out there waiting to be blessed or healed or something."

"Yes. Would you like to start with the people of Brea, or maybe Illimar, or Kandor, or . . .'"

"I get the picture," Korrd replied sitting back down.

"Oh, Arin Domae, a member of the Light Keepers has asked to see you. It's something about the security of the palace I think."

"Well, that's as good a place to start as any I guess. Send him in."

Gwillim bowed and left the throne room. Moments later he returned escorting the man who Korrd assumed to be Arin Domae. This Domae was a man of average height, but he had a large chest and broad shoulders. His blond hair was cut rather short, military style, and his gray eyes mysteriously calm. Every person that Korrd had come in contact with since entering Brea, save Gwillim, had been nervous and a little scared of him. But this man Domae seemed to be feeling something different. As Arin approached, there was a flash of red light behind Korrd's eyes, and Korrd fell back into the golden throne clutching his head in pain. Both Gwillim and Arin stopped, and when Korrd recovered and looked at his visitors, Arin was cast in a red outline of fire.

"You," Korrd said pointing at Arin, "come here."

Arin looked around for a moment and then obeyed. Arin walked up to the twin thrones and stopped about a foot short of Korrd.

"Arin," Korrd said softly, "I only want you to answer one small question for me before we talk about whatever it is you wanted to talk about. Do you understand?"

"Yes my lord Dragon."

"Arin, do you happen to have a scar on your left leg that runs from your ankle to the back of your knee?"

Arin looked Korrd dead in the face and nodded.

"Yes my lord, I've had it since I was born, and no one knows why. How did you know that?"

"Arin, I have some good news for you. That scar means that you are the fourth member of the *Erieal*. To tell you the truth, I didn't expect to run into you here, and I thought that perhaps the phasia had gotten to you before I did."

Arin just stood there trying to fathom what he had just been told. No wonder Basille had told Jerrard to stick close to him.

"Are you alright?"

"Yes my lord Dragon," Arin answered, "though I must say that I am a bit surprised and taken by the news. All my life I thought I was nothing but a commoner, and now I find out that I am one of the *Erieal*. That is wonderful my lord. I am here to serve my liege."

"I am glad to hear it Arin. You can start by calling me Korrd. I'm afraid that with all of these people fawning over me that I'll start to get a swelled head."

"Yes sir."

"Now," Korrd said relaxing back into his seat, "what is it you wanted to talk to me about."

"Well Korrd," Arin started, "the security here in the palace is . . ."

As Arin began to speak about the situation in the castle, a veil of darkness fell over Korrd's vision. He got up from his throne and looked around. Arin stopped his briefing mid-sentence and asked a question.

"What's wrong Korrd?"

"Gwillim, has the Proclaimer returned?"

"No Korrd," Gwillim answered, "you know he would have come right back here if he had. Remember what you told me?"

"Yes, but if he's not here, we're in trouble. I feel the surge from one of the phasia. It's like a veil of blackness. Well Arin, it looks like we're going to have to test your powers out sooner than expected."

"That won't be necessary," a strange voice called from the shadows.

Korrd turned and watched as a young man emerged from a displaced panel in the wall. The man was tall and thin with short black hair and the start of a beard.

"Who are you young sir?" Gwillim asked drawing his sword.

"I am Jerrard Mystic, son of Basille Mystic, lord of Scalla, member of the Sacred Brotherhood of Phasia, and youngest born son of Shau-ling. I am here to offer my sword and my powers to help the true *Coromor* of the prophecies."

Korrd stood fast. He remembered Basille's words to him from the dream, and he started to believe that Basille was really out to help him. But just when his fears started to abate, Jerrard continued speaking.

"However, the Dragon's name is Logan Ranthall. I have heard this name come from both my father and from the palace of Marcwell from the mouth of the Lion. Now I have been listening to you for some time, and I can tell that you are not a phase, nor are you the son of a phase. So, that leads me to ask you, who are you?"

"My name is Korrd Ranthall. The man you speak of, Logan, is my brother. Listen carefully. The Proclaimer may be listening to every word that we speak, so I cannot say fully all that you must hear. All I can say right now is that I am who I say I am, and you're just going to have to trust me for a while. Jerrard, Basille has been an ally to me for a little while, though I have never seen him outside my dreams. I ask you for your hand, and for your sword. There are rough times ahead, and I need all the help I can get."

Korrd extended his hand to the boy and waited. Jerrard hesitated and then approached slowly. He extended his hand and laid it on top of Korrd's. Arin and Gwillim then added their hands to the circle.

"The circle is closing my friends, and soon enough the People of the Dragon will strike their blow at the heart of Shau-ling."

Somewhere Emries smiled.

Trapped

Never make a decision that is totally influenced by emotions. That was the phrase that Logan's father had instilled in him from the first day that he could remember. Logan's father Arin had always been the kind of man that wanted every thought and every decision to be rational and clean. He often said that in battle there are two kinds of warriors. A warrior that acted on instinct and hacked at whatever crossed his path would soon die from the stroke of a blade he never saw. The other kind of warrior was one that laid out his strategy and knew exactly where everyone was at any given time. This kind of warrior was the one that attacked the leader of the force counting on the rest to break ranks after the leader was dead. Arin had always said that there was nothing rational thinking couldn't solve, and only when the heart was in conflict with the mind does something go wrong. The only thing that Logan never understood was how to settle those disputes between the heart and the mind without losing.

Emries stood before Logan with that eerie blank look on his face. He was waiting for the younger man to sentence one of his friends to death, and Logan couldn't make up my mind as to which one he should sacrifice. After all, how could he, after all that they had been through, simply chose and name, knowing that moment that the person would simply cease to exist? Was that the weight that came with the title of the Lord Dragon? Was knowing that some had to be sacrificed so that the majority could be saved enough to make the sacrifice less terrible? Pike, Talon, and Gideon were members of the *Erieal*, and so the success of the quest would be greatly reduced if one of them were to be sacrificed. Elwyne was the woman that Logan loved, and he couldn't very well let her die on Mount Tantis. There was something about Gwydeon that had always made Logan very dependent upon his strength and skill. He exuded this kind of power that made everyone stop and take notice. Logan had seen this man take cuts and blows that any other man would have fallen from. But he would not just curl up and die, he fought back with every ounce of his being. Sometimes it was like he was fighting against death. Logan remembered asking Gwydeon once why he fought so hard, and all he said was that it was all he knew how to do, and losing was never an option. Simple as it was, Logan could accept that explanation. The only two options left were Midarin and Talos. Logan went over the situation twenty or thirty different times in his mind, and every single time, he came up with the same answer. Midarin had to live, there was no question in Logan's heart or mind. Gwydeon loved her with all of his heart, and Logan wasn't about to tear her away from him and put him through the same pain he felt with Gabrielle and Leane. Talos was the only option. Though sacrificing Talos meant the loss of the council of a wise sage, one who had the weight of the entire Moridon tribe on his shoulders, and the wisdom of ages. Once again, love and wisdom found themselves on opposite sides of the ledger, and yet again, love would win out.

"Have you made your decision, Logan?" Emries asked impatience thick in his voice.

"Unfortunately, I have. Let me just say before I make my choice that I don't understand this at all. I can understand testing the People of the Dragon for the task ahead, and I can even understand testing the *Erieal*. But I'm the *Coromor*. Whether you believe I'm worthy of the task ahead of me or not, the path is clear. I'm the one who is going to face Shau-ling. I'm the one who has the fates of six generations on my shoulders. No matter what happens here on Mount Tantis, nothing can change that."

Emries crossed his arms, his eyes narrowed.

"Valiant words Logan, but no amount of speaking will change what has occurred. Because of your failure in the Castle of Terror, you are made to sacrifice one of the People of the Dragon so that you may leave this mountain in peace. Past that, I have no need to explain the motives of the gods of Mount Tantis, or for that matter my own. This may be a difficult decision for you to make, but it must be made if you are to continue on in an attempt to save this world and the future. Do not compound the difficulty of this situation by forcing me to choose the one to be sacrificed. I don't think that you would like the outcome."

The threat was clear, and Logan exhaled a long breath.

"Now," Emries said finally, "will you choose, or shall I?"

"I see no other choice than to name Talos of the Moridon as the sacrifice."

Emries nodded.

"The choice has been made, and Talos has gone to meet his brethren on the Other Side. You made a wise choice, and Talos has served his purpose in this quest. Do you remember the question I was asked about why you were made to go through Rana and Rama?"

"Yes."

"Now you know a portion of the answer."

Logan flashed back through his memory and with a start of shock and horror realized what Emries was talking about. On the battlefield between Rana and Rama they had met the old man who had called himself Talos of the Moridon. It was there that he offered to join with the People of the Dragon. Had they not gone through Rama, Logan would have had to sacrifice one of the other members of the group. Emries had known all along that Logan would fail the test of the Castle of Terror, and so he steered Logan in a direction that would ensure that no decision would have to be made that would have affected the result of the quest. In effect, Talos had been sacrificed twice.

"Come Logan, the time has come to reunite you with your companions," Emries said in a soft voice. "I have much to tell you all before you return to the world of mortals."

Off in the distance, a door of light opened into the darkness. Emries walked quickly through the door, leaving Logan alone for a moment in the darkness. In his mind he wondered how he was going to tell the others about Talos. Logan had never been good at accepting failure, nor was he good at admitting it. His father had always told his about the times when Arin himself had been faced with a no-win scenario. Up until that moment, Logan never believed in a situation with no right answers. Arin had always said that in situations where there was no way to win, you must try to get through it losing the least amount possible. It was what he had called acceptable losses. Sometimes loss was inevitable, but if you survive with as many people as possible, perhaps with as little as one more than you thought you could, you have won the day. A moral victory he called it. In that moment, Logan's conscience could not abide such a rationalization. It was a fallacy to make one feel better about failure, nothing more. As Logan walked through the door of light, he emerged a moment later in a totally white room. As he looked around, the other members of the People of the Dragon stood from benches and surrounded Logan with looks of confusion and worry.

"What's going on Logan?" Pike asked quickly. "Emries came through and took Talos with him saying something about a failure and a sacrifice. What happened?"

"I failed my test, Pike," Logan answered plainly. "I didn't do what I was sent to do, and so I was made to sacrifice one of you in order for us to continue on our quest. Believe me when I say that I tried every way possible to get out of the sacrifice, but in the end, that was the only option that I had."

"And Talos?" Talon asked.

"He was the only choice. He said that he would do anything to serve the *Coromor* and that he would gladly give his life as his brethren had. I couldn't think of parting with any of you, and so Talos was the one who was sacrificed to the gods. Don't worry, he is on the Other Side, and he is serving our cause there."

It was yet another rationalization, and though Logan could have also added Emries' revelations about Talos' purpose and their path through, it seemed like nothing more than rubbing salt into a fresh wound. There was a very uneasy silence for a few moments, and then Pike broke it with the obvious question.

"So, what are we going to do now?"

"I suppose that I should answer that question, Pike," Emries said returning to the room.

Emries was no longer in his plain clothes, but had changed into a long flowing white robe. It was almost like the robe was giving off pure white light. His face was different too. The plain appearance was gone, and his face was bright and radiant.

"You are going to be returned to the world of the living. However, you must decide to which town you will travel."

"Can't ye just send us ta Shau-ling's palace?" Gideon asked.

Emries smiled, seemingly briefly caught off-guard by the straight-forward question. For being the Creator, Logan found that Emries had been very inconsistent in judging the actions and intentions of those he had chosen to save the world.

"No. The gods do not have the power to send you into Shau-ling's presence or into the lands that he controls."

"During our test," Pike commented, "we were in Brea. As we were walking through the town trying to figure out what we were supposed to do in the quest, one of the townspeople overheard our conversation about Logan and called out the army. Supposedly, the town is under the protection of a man called the Proclaimer. So, we ask to see this Proclaimer, and he just shows up and orders the Light Keepers or whatever they were to attack."

"They weren't competition," Talon interrupted proudly. "So, we challenge the Proclaimer guy. Then he starts babbling on about how the *Coromor* was already in Brea and how the *Erieal* were dead and that we were impostors and members of the phasia. So we politely ask to see the *Coromor*."

"Politely?" Elwyne interjected. "Talon, I didn't even know that word was in your vocabulary."

"See," Talon responded, his attempts to lighten the mood working slightly, "you are rubbing off on me."

Laughing, Pike continued.

"I think demanded was more the word he was looking for."

"Hey," Talon remarked, "I was nice."

"Nice huh? I think your exact words were, 'don't you have any more toy soldiers that we can play with?'"

Everyone laughed but Talon.

"The Proclaimer thought it was funny," Talon added under his breath.

"Anyway, then Korrd walks up, acting like he's the bloody *Coromor* and the Proclaimer fries us on the spot. I thought we had failed until we showed up here. Apparently, the Proclaimer is really one of the phasia, and he's got Korrd on a pretty short leash."

"Well," Gwydeon added, "we had heard those rumors about the *Chosen One* being under the control of one of the phasia. So, Pike's conclusion is probably sound. And if what we've been told about the powers of the *Chosen One* is true, it would be easy for common people to accept Korrd as the *Coromor*."

"What about these Light Keepers?" Logan asked. "What do you know about them Midarin?"

"They were my father's personal guard. They used to look for Shau-ling's servants in town to make sure that no one was trying to assassinate the king in Shau-ling's name. Over the years they took more power until they became the majority of the army of Brea. Less they were guards of the royal family, and more they were the enforcers of some abstract purity. If you ask me, they took what Cedric stood for a perverted it in a way that got the leadership of the Keepers whatever they wanted. Before long you could see their banners flying over every town in the kingdom."

"Let me guess," Logan said, "a golden torch with a ring around the base."

"Yes," Midarin answered giving him a puzzled look, "how did you know that?"

"In my test, I think I was in the royal palace of Brea. The banners of these Light Keepers were all over the walls of the palace. I think I killed a few of them before I got to the throne room."

"Was Korrd there?" Gideon asked.

"Yes. He tried to tell me that he was the *Coromor* and that I had been mistaken all this time. When he wouldn't turn to our side and leave the phase's control, I killed him."

"Is that why he failed?" Elwyne asked turning to face Emries.

"Logan didn't not complete his quest in the way that would have been considered satisfactory. That is why he failed."

Pike rounded on Emries, and his hand instantly went to the axe that hung from his belt.

"Why won't you give us a straight answer, Emries?" Pike questioned angrily. "You've been pulling our strings this whole time, and you won't even tell us why."

Gwydeon interjected himself between Pike and Emries, his hands up.

"I've been through this with him, Pike," Gwydeon commented. "It won't do any good to try and get any information out of him. He isn't going to tell us anything."

"But why?" Pike badgered.

"Because you are not ready to hear the truth."

For the first time, Emries furrowed brow showed annoyance and the start of anger. Every other time he had spoken, his voice had been calm and even, but now his voice was hard and cold.

"You have fought all this time without knowing even half of what truly is occurring in this world, and yet you expect to become suddenly knowledgeable and see all that I can see. Do you want me to simply hand this knowledge to you and hope for that a blunt instrument like you can understand?"

Emries moved past Gwydeon and stared hard into Pike's eyes.

"Do you want to know the true nature of power? Can you hope to understand what you are truly capable of? Or what your enemies are capable of? Can that rage inside your heart hold you together against the awesome burden that lies ahead? Do you truly believe you are either prepared or worthy? Do you?"

"I think you made him mad Pike." Talon muttered in his friend's direction.

Emries held his ground, now towering over Pike, the glow in his robes seeming to intensify.

"I am tired of your constant questioning and your ingratitude for all that I have done for you."

If Emries was trying to intimidate Pike, it didn't work.

"All that you've done?" Pike shot back. "Let's talk about what you've done. You gave us these powers that we didn't want and put us out there for all of the evil in the world to take a shot at. Those people you didn't deem important, like my wife, you let die."

Pike jabbed a finger into Emries chest and thundered away,

"You don't give a damn about anyone or anything but your own plans and schemes. You can't take out Shau-ling yourself, and so that's why you need us. You don't care about us, you're just trying to save your own ass."

Pike turned his back on Emries, but looked over his shoulder and continued his assault.

"So, you want me to be grateful. Okay, thank you for letting my wife die. Thank you for making my life a living hell."

Emries' face was bright red. Pike had pushed him to the farthest limits of his restraint. Just when Logan thought it was over, Pike turned back to Emries and fired away again.

"Oh, and if that isn't enough gratitude, come find me in hell when this is all over. I'm sure the Great Dark One would love to watch me kiss your ass for the rest of eternity."

A brilliant white haze rose up around Emries, and his restraint broke.

"Enough! I had expected some impertinence, but I never thought that this would be your reaction. You have forced my hand, Rhuiden, and for that you will all suffer. You will be sent back to Pramine, and no more aid will be extended to you by myself or the gods."

Emries turned back toward the door and started to leave. Logan was about to say something to Pike when Emries turned back and spoke again.

"And one more thing. You may not think this a loss now, but if I were you, I'd watch my back a little more closely than I have been in the past, Miss Tamerlane."

With that he turned and left.

"And what did he mean by that exactly?" Elwyne asked.

"He's just trying to scare us," Midarin commented.

And he was doing a good job. No one else knew what Emries meant, but Logan did. He had promised that Elwyne and her unborn son would survive the quest no matter what happened. Now, because of Pike and Emries' own stubborn nature, that protection had been revoked. Logan tried his best not to look hurt by Emries' warning, and as he scanned the faces of his companions he found that his deception was holding. Pike still looked mad, and everyone else was puzzled by Emries' last words. However, when he got to Gwydeon's face, there was a look of pain and sorrow there that Logan had not seen in a long time, not since Gabrielle. Elwyne noticed Gwydeon's look too, and it seemed like she knew what was going through his mind. Just as Elwyne was about to say something to Gwydeon, Azure entered the room.

"Thee have done well in the tests of the gods, but because of Lord Emries' orders, thee will be set down in the town of Pramine, much as thee were before thee came to this mountain. There is one other thing that thee must be told before you are free to leave Mount Tantis. While thee were undergoing our tests, one of our agents intercepted a message from Shau-ling to his son Taron. Apparently he is in Seren awaiting further orders. If thee were to go there, thee might be able to learn the location of Shau-ling's palace from him. Thee may leave whenever thee are ready."

Azure turned to leave, but Gwydeon cut him off.

"I need to see Emries."

"That is impossible Gwydeon. Lord Emries has forsaken thee to the wills of fate, and no one will see him again until the time has come for the *Coromor* to end the life of Shau-ling and plunge his perverted soul into the depths of hell."

"I don't care about that Azure," Gwydeon replied strongly. "I need to see Emries one more time before I leave this mountain, and I will not leave until he will see me."

"Leave it alone Gwydeon," Pike commented. "If Emries doesn't want to see you, he won't see you. Remember, he is the almighty Creator."

"Shut up Pike. Try to remember that it was your mouth that got us into this whole mess in the first place."

Gwydeon's tone was not one that anyone was familiar with. Even when angry, Gwydeon never raised his voice or put venom in his words. Even in jest, Gwydeon's words never stung. That all changed.

"So, Azure, will you take me to see Emries?"

"Worry not Gwydeon," Azure answered. "There is no reason for you to see him. I will answer thy questions. Thee need not worry about the promises that were made thee. All will be and have been kept. Fate smiles upon thee."

Gwydeon smiled and nodded.

"Thank you Azure."

"So," Logan asked as Gwydeon rejoined the rest of the group, "are we all ready?"

Everyone answered in the affirmative.

"Good. Alright Azure, we're ready."

Azure nodded and raised his hands. A brilliant white light flashed and Logan had to shield his eyes against the brilliance.

* * * * * * * * * * * *

The next thing Logan knew, they were back on their horses riding away from Mount Tantis in the direction of the little town of Pramine. He pulled up on the reins and the seemingly startled horse skidded to a stop. Everyone else followed Logan's lead and the now seven members of the People of the Dragon tried to decide their next move.

"So," Gwydeon said looking around, "what now?"

"I say we go after Taron," Pike chimed in quickly, "I still owe that overgrown ox a piece of my axe."

"I agree with Pike," Talon seconded. "If we take out Taron, that's one more phase out of the way when we get to Shau-ling's palace. We already know that six of them are dead. That leaves four who are still alive. If we take out Taron that puts them down to three."

"Two," Gideon countered, "remember dat Lord Basille is on our side. He's no threat ta us."

"That still remains to be seen," Logan cautioned. "I can't bring myself to trust any member of the phasia, and I've seen how they can twist people's minds. What do you think, Gwydeon?"

"I say we fight. The danger cannot be ignored. If we let this opportunity to strike slip away from us, we may well regret it later."

Gwydeon still seemed distracted, but his tone had at least gone back to normal. Midarin was beside him, and Logan thought for a moment that he saw concern in her eyes.

"Elwyne?"

"I don't like this Logan," she replied. "This just feels all wrong. I say we just go on to Brea like we initially intended. We'll have enough to worry about with Korrd."

"I agree with Elwyne," Midarin added. "However, I don't see the two of us out voting the rest of you. Especially when Pike and Talon have their blood-lust up. I understand wanting to get revenge for Eldar, but we have to be smart about this. Seren is about a half a day's ride from Brea. If we get trapped there, this Proclaimer and Korrd could swoop down on us before we could even handle Taron."

"So you think it's a trap?" Logan asked.

"Yes, Logan, I do. This is just too convenient. Taron is responsible for the death of Eldar and Lane, and he knows that it could cause us to do something rash and foolish. I think he's baiting us. Not to mention that Emries gets done ripping Pike's head off for being rash and ungrateful and then dangles this in front of us? No offense Pike, but I don't think that you're ready to face him."

Logan expected Pike to fire back, but a calm and even voice is all that followed.

"Look everyone," Pike replied, "I may not be in the most rational frame of mind right now, but I do know one thing, we can't just talk about this and hope it will work itself out. The only thing these bastards understand is power and steel. Right now, we have the advantage. We know where the *Chosen One* is, and we have a connection to him that they don't. We also know that Taron is just sitting there, waiting for someone to tell him what to do. Logan beat him once, and I know that he can do it again. First we kill him, and then we get Korrd. The rest will take care of itself."

"But what if it is a trap?" Talon asked.

Pike smiled.

"Don't turn tail on me now Talon. You want that bastard as much as I do. I don't think it's a trap, but if it is, we can remedy that right now. You guys don't want to take on Taron nearly as much as I do, and that I understand. So, you go to Brea and find Korrd. I'll go to Seren and take care of Taron. When I'm finished, I'll bring his head to you."

"No Pike," Logan answered without hesitation. "If we're going to take on a phase, we're going to do it together. Besides, I want to see the look on his face after you beat him."

Pike's smile widened, and with that the decision had been made and the group turned their horses toward Seren. As they rode, Logan could feel Elwyne's eyes on him. She was not happy with his decision.

"I can't believe you did that."

Logan sighed.

"Did what? You know as well as I do that if I would have said no, he would have gone off by himself one night and attacked Taron alone. There was no way to get around it Elwyne, we were going to end up in Seren one way or another."

Elwyne's shaking head conceded the point.

"You're right," she said after a moment, "I'm sorry."

Logan knew that Elwyne was partially right, but in the end, it was safer to aim Pike at a target than let him control where his rage was loosed. It was nightfall before the group reached the forest on the edge of the town called Seren. Seren itself was nothing more than a little farm town on the edge of a huge kingdom's capitol. It reminded Logan a lot of Aradon in that respect. As they roped their horses to the trees, Pike and Talon started foraging around for loose twigs and leaves to build a small fire. For some reason, the nights had been colder than normal, but the days had been almost intolerably hot. Within an hour there was a roaring fire on the edge of the forest, and the group did their best to settle in for the night. There were still many frayed nerves and questions that could not be answered, and so silence was the order of the evening. Elwyne sat with her back against one of the trees, and she started to nod off. Suddenly a hand emerged from the darkness and grasped her around the neck. She was forced to her feet, and then Taron emerged from behind the tree and held her close to his body.

"Hello Logan, Pike, others," he said in the deep gloating voice. "It's good to see you again."

Pike pulled the ax from the loop in his belt and started toward Taron. He would do everything in his power to keep him from hurting Elwyne.

"I wouldn't come any closer if I were you, Pike. Don't you remember the last time I held one of your pretties in my grasp? She was so fragile, I barely had to squeeze before her little neck snapped. I doubt it would take much with this one."

"Stop, Pike," Logan ordered.

Pike growled and lowered his ax. The air around him started to show his breath, and the *Debuisa* on his hand was a deep blue.

"Don't bother with your powers either Pike," Taron chided. "Even if you could render me immobile, I'm sure I would still have enough time to kill her. You're not nearly as fast as you think you are."

The color faded in Pike's *Debuisa*, and he backed away from Taron.

"That's better. I didn't think you were stupid enough to come chasing rumors of my whereabouts, but I guess the sour taste I left in your mouth last time was enough to make you come back for more. And yet, this close you still aren't smart enough to keep your presence quiet. A roaring fire, horses, exuding power like a blazing lantern in a dark room. You were practically begging me to find you."

"What do you want Taron?" Logan demanded, cutting off the giant's boasting.

The phase laughed.

"Just your head Logan, nothing more. But, there are a few matters that I have to take care of before I kill you. Master wanted a trophy of our victory, so I think the *Coromor's* lover would be a good enough present, don't you?"

Suddenly a whirling blue portal opened beside Taron. As it opened, the familiar form of a man became visible. When the man stepped out, Logan clutched the hilt of his sword even harder. Logan's knuckles were white with rage, and he could see that all three *Debuisa* were instantly the colors of the primal forces. Just the mere sight of the first born of the phasia was enough to make any sane person angry.

"Jeroch," Logan said letting the thoughts of the *Coromor* take over his mind, "I didn't expect to see you out of Shau-ling's palace. Is he not holding your hand as tight anymore?"

"A pitiful maneuver my little Dragon," he replied, "you should know that taunts like that will have no effect coming from you. I have had to endure worse from my brothers for hundreds of years. But, my errand is not to banter with you, I have come here to collect your woman. I must say that your taste in women is improving. Don't worry Logan, we won't kill her...yet. But, that doesn't mean that she will not be good for a little sport. From what I hear, this one has fire."

With that he grabbed Elwyne by the arm and pulled her into the portal. Logan launched himself into the air after her, but the portal closed before he reached it, and he fell flat on my face at the foot of Taron. Pike wasted no time in leaping toward Taron, but before he got half way across the distance, a yellow object rolled out from behind a tree. Pike's motion became slower, and a fine yellow mist began to engulf the campsite. Even as the winds swirled around them, Taron's laughter echoing in all of their ears, all Logan could think about was getting Elwyne back.

Dreamscape Revisited

When the unnatural wind died down, Logan found himself lying face down in a crop bed. As he looked around from the prone position, he noticed that there was a faint trace of yellow smoke around each of the individual tall plant stalks. Fighting through the hauntingly familiar pain that wracked his body Logan stood up and looked around. As the son of a farmer, it was easy to recognize that they had been dropped into the middle of a huge corn field. Off in the distance was a two story white farmhouse. One by one each of the other members of the party made their way to their feet, and Midarin was the first to ask the question that Logan dreaded already knowing the answer to.

"Where the hell are we, Logan?" Midarin asked.

"Welcome to Dreamscape, Midarin," Gwydeon answered. "The yellow smoke all around gives the place away."

"I thought dat we had seen da last of dis place," Gideon said reaching for his sword and one of his daggers. "I can't say dat I'm happy 'bout bein' in here again."

"I'm with you there, Gideon," Pike growled, "but you can rest assured that we aren't alone in here. Taron's in here somewhere, and I'm willing to bet my life that the coward isn't alone. He's probably got hundreds of Jeresei crawling around in here looking for a chance to take us out."

"Just like the last time we tangled with him," Logan added.

He hadn't intended to bring up painful memories, but from the look in Pike's eyes, Logan knew that it wasn't he words that brought Pike's mind back to the tragedy in Taren. It was important though to know the tactics of the enemy. Despite his size and physical power, Taron preferred to let others take the fight to his opponents and then set up ambushes where his considerable power could be used swiftly and without chance to counter. He was arrogant and vain, and the last thing Taron wanted was a fair fight to bring his weaknesses to light.

"I think our best bet is to head for that farmhouse in the distance. Taron's probably hold up there with his army around him waiting for a chance to strike at us."

The rest agreed, and slowly the group started toward the farmhouse. The stalks of corn were placed very close together, but when pushed against, they felt as firm as tree trunks. It created a very unrelenting path toward the farm house, one that gave many opportunities for ambushes.

"Is it just me," Talon said after a few minutes of walking, "or is it getting darker."

He was right. Logan looked up into the sky and saw huge black rain clouds rolling in over the sun that hung high in the sky. Within a matter of moments, the sun was blocked out completely, and it was eerily reminiscent of the Shadowwalker attack that nearly leveled Aradon and killed dozens of people. The black storm clouds heaved and lightning arched out across the sky, thunder bellowing out in every direction, echoing back on itself as though they were standing in a bubble. Then the rain began to fall. The cold hard rain fell in short bursts at first, but then it poured down in sheets making it impossible to see more than a couple of feet in any direction.

"Keep an eye out," Gwydeon called out over the din of the storm. "This would be a perfect time for an attack."

As if on cue, a Jeresei popped out from the corn stalks and swung razor-sharp claws at Logan. He ducked the blow, more as a reflex than anything, and pulled the Dragon Sword free from the scabbard at his side. One set of claws came up from behind and ripped across the back of Logan's right hand, his sword hand. Though he tried his best to control the pain Logan's hand continued to spasm as blood flowed from the open wound. The twitching muscles became too much to control and the hilt of the Dragon Sword slipped from his grasp falling into the clutches of one of the Jeresei. The Jeresei immediately turned the blade back on its owner and slashed wildly at Logan's head. Logan was barely able to duck the blade, and when he reached for the thread of Fire, the heart of the Jeresei wouldn't ignite. It was like the Jeresei was concealed in a bubble of power that Logan couldn't reach into. The tip of the Dragon Sword thrust again, and this time caught Logan's flank. It was a clean cut, wide and deep, sending hot blood flowing down Logan's side. Just as Logan turned his entire focus to dodge the next assault from the sword-brandishing Jeresei, another leapt up from behind and ran its claws down the length of his back. The armor was somewhat able to protect Logan from the assault, taking the brunt of the punishment before it was sheared off completely. Without thinking, Logan turned and hit the Jeresei in the face with all of his might. The force of the blow shattered the bones in the right side of its face and caused its neck to jerk so violently that its spine snapped. Turning back quick enough to dodge another slash of the Dragon Sword, Logan caught the glow of green around his still-clenched fist. When the blade flashed by again, the green-wreathed hand caught it. As steel struck flesh, it sounded like the blade was hitting solid rock. The Jeresei shrieked with surprise as Logan ripped the hilt of the Dragon Sword out of its grasp and ran it through.

Looking for another opponent, Logan turned sharply to see Taron's figure ducking out from behind one of the wide bundles of corn stalks. Uncontrollable Rage built inside of Logan and he swung wildly in that direction. The Dragon Sword contacted with the stalks, but ricocheted off as if the stalks were made of stone. Apparently the others had made the same assumption about the stalks. Talon's *Debuisa* was clear, almost to the point of being translucent, and he was casting Jeresei into the huge stalks, breaking bones with each impact. Gideon's strategy was to bend the stalks of stone to his will, and he struck out with the extensions of earth like they were extensions of his sword. Stalks grew and flexed, smashing unsuspecting Jeresei in the skull and chest, killing them on impact. Pike concentrated his powers on a more direct form of devastation. Shards of ice shot from his fingertips and ripped through Jeresei after Jeresei. If they didn't fall to the projectiles, he followed up quickly with his ax.

Gwydeon and Midarin stood side by side near a dense group of stone corn stalks. As Jeresei leapt up near them, Gwydeon cut through them with his sword. Meanwhile, Midarin used her bow to take down any that were in her range which meant that many would-be attackers never came close to feeling the steel of any of the other members of the group. However, the odds were quickly becoming more than even the Coromor and the People of the Dragon, no matter their powers, could handle. For every Jeresei that fell, it would seem like three or four more took its place. As outnumbered as they were during the battle of Sarmeel, the odds in Dreamscape seemed much worse. At least in Sarmeel there were wide areas and more of them to combat the odds. In this pitched battle however, the landscape moved and twisted to constantly keep them at a disadvantage and to reduce sight-lines making any of their attacks that much less effective. More bladed fingers and teeth flew in from every direction, and Logan knew before long one would slip through. The *Coromor* inside of Logan clamored something almost unintelligible. It took every part of his control to keep it from seizing the reigns of his body. Logan pushed it out of his mind and hung tight to the threads of power. All four primal forces flowed through his body and made his reactions quicker and more deadly. Logan killed Jeresei before he ever saw them. All he saw was red all around. But even his unnatural reflexes and powers were not infallible. Finally he missed. One set of bladed claws ripped completely through Logan's right arm. The bone snapped loudly, and the arm fell away just below the shoulder. Logan screamed in pain as his blood poured everywhere from the vicious wound. Suddenly, the restraint on the *Coromor* snapped. It took Logan's body and snatched wildly and wrathfully at the strings of power. This was the first time that it had ever been given full control. The *Coromor* drew on all of the power of the *Erieal* that was available to it and stored that power inside of Logan's body. He had never dared to draw on that much power, or even half that much power, but the *Coromor* continue to draw more. It drew power from sources that Logan couldn't even see in the blackness of his mind where the primal strings dwelt, but there was power coming from a fifth source. Logan's whole body sang with pain, shaking from his toes all the way to his head. His skin felt as though it were on fire, and his awareness was so sharp that he could feel each and every hair on his body burning. His blood boiled, his brain filled with a fog that was a mixture of pain and rage. Just on the edges of the hate, Logan caught glimpses of memories; standing in the middle of a battlefield, the fallen enemies and friends all around, and himself being the cause of all the devastation and destruction. Then, just as Logan thought he would burst from all the power the *Coromor* had gorged itself on, it turned its attention skyward and released all of its fury and strength. The huge black clouds in the sky above them were suddenly filled with a different light; a red glow that could only be called an incarnation of hate. Lightning lanced between the clouds, and as the confused Jeresei looked skyward, the bolts of pure energy launched from the darkness and struck down the creations of evil. Needle thin ice-rain fell from the sky with such force that the thin drops passed completely through their victims leaving only a thin bloody trail. As more of the deadly rain fell, Jeresei began to scream in pain under the assault.

"Everyone to me!" Logan yelled as best he could over the cacophony of wrath and the din of dying. "Hurry before my concentration on you breaks."

Seconds later the other five members of the group had gathered around Logan, and Gideon created a ledge of rock over their heads to shelter them from the onslaught. Midarin was the last to reach the alcove, but when she saw the extent of Logan's injuries, she winced and turned away. It was that reaction that caused Logan to realize exactly how bad his injuries were. Midarin was certainly not the squeamish type.

"What can you do?" Logan asked Pike.

"We've healed some bad wounds before, Logan, but we've never seen anything like this."

Logan looked up at Talon, and he shook his head. Logan was barely aware of the cold feeling slipping through his whole body. The pain was gone, and so to was the influence of the *Coromor*.

"What about you, Logan?" Gwydeon asked. "Do you have anything left?"

"I don't think so. That release was the best that I had, and it drained me completely. It's up to Pike and Talon now."

The look on Pike's face was grave to say the least. In his eyes, Logan could see the doubt and the fear that he had only seen one other time. However, the gravity of this situation seemed to dwarf any other they had seen. There was no doubt in Logan's mind that he was dying. While the wound itself was grave, the release of power had stolen all strength and ability to fight from the young man's shockingly frail body. His heartbeat was slow, and the blackness was creeping into the edges of his vision, threatening to steal the last remnants of consciousness. Gwydeon had packed a shirt around the stump of the arm that remained, but blood still leaked through.

"I got it!" Pike exclaimed after a moment. His face had brightened, and the fear was gone from his eyes.

"What Pike?" Logan asked meekly.

"Talon and I probably can't heal your wound on our own, but we can with your help. Talon and I will start to reconnect your arm, but you'll have to hold the mended arm together with your powers."

"How can that be possible?" Midarin asked, concern thick in her voice. "He said that he doesn't have anything left."

"That's why Gideon's going to feed Logan with his powers."

"Right!" Gideon commented after it dawned on him.

"Whenever you're ready Gideon."

Gideon removed his *Debuisa* and concentrated on Logan. Cedric had said that the *Debuisa* took away some power, but increased control. For this little chore, it was obvious that raw power was the most valuable commodity. The moment Gideon's hands touched Logan's shoulder he could feel the power flood through his body, but it seemed almost insignificant to what Logan had experienced moments earlier. Logan longed for the sweet rush of power, and as Gideon poured more and more into Logan's body, he felt a portion of his strength return. However, as the cold numbness in his body was being pushed away, the pain began to slowly return. He could feel the stump of his arm throb and twitch with ache. Again Logan's body sang with pain, but this time the power of the *Coromor* was not there to hold him together.

"Hold on Logan," Pike said looking down on is longtime friend.

Pike's words sounded like a faint and distant echo against the choir of Logan's muscles and nerves. However, Logan did his best to help Pike and Talon with their work. Most of that however was confined to simply not allowing the fear and panic creep into his conscious thoughts.

"Gwydeon, I need you to hold Logan's arm in place."

Logan felt a tickle of skin and bone rub against the pieces of nerve that were left in his shoulder. It felt strange to have that piece of his body gone and then for it to move back to where it once was. It was as though his nerves had already adjusted to the absence of the arm. Tendrils of Wind and Water touched the arm in the next moment. Agony rocketed through Logan's body as the skin, bone, and muscle pulled themselves back together. All he could do was try to stay conscious and push all of Gideon's strength into the wounds. After what seemed like hours of suffering and horrible pain, the arm was again attached to Logan's body, but it would take some time before any strength would return to it, and it would do anything more than hang uselessly at his side.

Pike and Talon stood, but were visibly fatigued. Between the battle and stitching Logan back together, they looked like they needed to sleep for a week. As Logan made it slowly to his feet, with a lot of help from Gideon, he could not help but look toward the little farm house in the distance.

"I know you're tired," Logan said in the strongest voice he had left, "so am I. But remember one thing. Taron is in that house, and he's laughing at us right now. If we don't kill him now, we're not going to make it any farther in this quest. He and his Tarnae pet of his won't give us a minute's rest until we're dead."

Pike nodded and patted Talon on the shoulder.

"Now, where's my sword?"

Gwydeon looked his friend up and down for a moment, and then handed him the Dragon Sword. When Logan reached and took it from Gwydeon and pulled it free from his hand, Logan's arm went numb and the sword dropped to the ground.

"Are you alright, Logan?" Midarin asked.

"I'm not sure. I guess it's going to take some time for me to get my strength back."

"What about your powers," Talon added, "is your strength returning?"

"Slowly, but it is returning. I may have to draw on you three a little deeper than usual, but I'll be fine. For the meantime though, I don't think I'll be much good in a fight."

"That's alright Logan," Pike commented, "you never were."

Pike never took anything too seriously, but of course much of that changed after Eldar's death. It was comforting however that he was willing to joke, even if it were in the face of something so daunting.

"Alright," he continue, the momentary levity gone, "we need to protect Logan at all costs. Let's use the same plan from Barer, but we'll modify it a little. Remember, Logan isn't our target this time."

Logan looked at Pike and when he answered the puzzled look with a stare, Logan realized what he meant. Pike nodded with understanding and continued with his explanation of the plan.

"Gideon, you take the lead. You should be able to feel or see anything that gets in our way before we get to the farm house. Talon, Midarin, and I will stay close to Logan and make sure than nothing gets to him. We'll be his sword and armor while Midarin will act as his extended reach. Gwydeon, you stay behind Logan and watch our backs. You know how Taron has a way of just appearing behind people, and I know that he won't hesitate in snapping Logan's neck if he's in that position, and in Logan's current condition, I doubt he'll have too much resistance. Does everybody understand what you're to do?"

Nods all around.

"Good, let's go."

The clouds had since dispersed above, and the bright imitation sun beat down upon them. It was hard to remember sometimes that none of what they saw really existed. The Tarnae were masters of their domain, and it was easy to see how they could trick their victims. Distance was another disorienting facet of Dreamscape, and what seemed like a mile could be ten miles, or it could be three feet. The latter was true in the current case. As they started walking, it seemed like it would take forever to reach the house, but suddenly it was right in front of them, and then in another few steps they were standing on the front porch.

"Does anyone else have a problem with this?" Midarin asked looking around at the others.

Pike grimaced by did his best to keep everyone focused.

"No change in plan. Gideon, you're first in. Nothing fancy, just secure the entrance and make sure it's safe for us to come in. Once inside, we'll probably be trapped, but we'll worry about that later."

Pike's tone was a strong one. He wanted everyone to know that he was in control of the situation and that nothing would come as a surprise. However, there was a waver in his tone that was almost imperceptible, and it seemed as though he was really trying to convince himself. Gideon hesitated only a moment before busting through the door. Within a moment or two, he motioned for the rest to follow. The interior of the house was plain. It had high ceilings and brown walls. The entry foyer was small opening not to a larger room but a long corridor. Along the length of the hall were doors, and there was a door in the far wall. Once everyone had stepped inside house, the entry door slammed shut.

"As we expected," Pike said. "Alright. Midarin, you stay here with Logan while the rest of us check these doors. If we do find something and we have to run for our lives, you can cover us with your bow."

Midarin nodded. Pike, Talon, Gwydeon, and Gideon moved down the hall and took up positions in front of one of the four doors. Only the door in the far wall was ignored.

"Okay," Pike said, "on three."

The others nodded and looked forward at their doors.

"One . . . two . . . Three!"

Four doors cracked and splintered as they forced their way into the rooms. Seconds later reappeared.

"Nothing in mine," Talon said.

"Not one damn thing," Gideon added.

"Same here," Pike commented walking back toward me.

"Well," Gwydeon said emerging from his room, "all I found was this note from Taron."

Pike glared at him for a moment and then sighed.

"All huh?" he said. "That's a hell of a lot more than we found. What does the arrogant bastard have to say?"

"Not much. Here, I'll read it. He says, *'Welcome to my house, weaklings. I trust you made it through my little welcoming committee if you are reading this, and so congratulations, you made it farther than I ever expected. So, you're probably wondering why I've brought you here. Well, that's the fun part you see. I am on the second floor of the house, and all you have to do is find a way to get to me. One problem though. There are no stairs, and the floors and ceilings are so thick and warded from your powers that it would be impossible for you to break through them. This is my little game for you, Logan. I hope you enjoy games. Oh, by the way, your friend Elwyne says hello. She is a very interesting woman, Logan, and I assure you she loves to play games. See you soon, or perhaps not. Good Luck.'"*

"Bastard," Logan cursed.

"Well," Gwydeon said, wading the note up and casting it aside, "all we have to do is find a way up to the next floor."

"There's still one door we haven't tried," Midarin commented.

"What the hell," Talon said heading for the door, "he couldn't have that many Jeresei hidden behind here."

Talon pulled open the door and slammed it shut quickly.

"I was wrong. We have a bit of a problem."

"What kind of problem?" Pike asked.

"What's slim, red, has three thousand horns, three thousand arms, and fifteen thousand nails?"

"That kind of problem," Pike said nodding his head.

"What are you two talking about?" Midarin asked.

"Oh nothing," Pike said calmly, "Talon was just telling me about the fifteen hundred Jeresei that are standing behind that door waiting to make us all dead."

It was Logan and not Pike that came up with the next plan.

"Alright, we're not in the grave yet. Talon, how much room did they have to maneuver in there?"

"Not much, they were packed in tighter than cattle at the marketplace on Sunday. But this is Dreamscape, so you never know what that room really looks like."

"Good, then a steady stream of fire ought to take them out quick and easy. However, the only problem is that if there's anything valuable in there, it'll be burned up in the fire."

"No problem Logan," Talon replied. "There are three ways that we can get around it. I can create a wind wall around the walls of the room, or Pike can do a quick freeze, or . . ."

"Wait," Logan interjected. "Pike, do you think you can freeze and break that many?"

"I'm sure I could. I've taken that many before, but I had Lane's help. Because they're so close, I think I can get them."

"Good, do it."

Gwydeon stood by the door and waited. Pike readied himself and motioned for Gwydeon to open the door. As the door opened, water flowed from Pike's outstretched fingers and coated the mass of red bodies in water. Seconds later, the water began to crystallize, leaving the Jeresei trapped in ice. Talon finished off the army of evil with a huge gust of wind which left piles of red and clear ice strewn all over the floor of the chamber. As Pike let the ice melt, blood streaked over the floor and eventually conglomerated into drying pools.

"Well done gentlemen," Logan complimented, "a little messy, but very effective. But I don't think the Tarnae will let us get away with that again, so we better keep our eyes open. Now, let's see what we have."

The room itself was very much like the other rooms of the house. Flush with the back of the wall however was an enormous wardrobe. Other than the wardrobe, there was nothing in the room.

"Well, who wants to open that door?" Talon asked.

Gwydeon stepped forward without a word and opened the doors of the huge wardrobe. It was empty except for the picture of a sword that was etched in the back wall, and a note hung on the inside of one of the doors.

"Another note?" Logan asked.

"From Taron," Gwydeon replied, "and he is no less joyful about his position. He says, *'you've done well to make it this far, and I am very impressed. The Jeresei are failing more and more these days, and it's starting to become annoying. Well, when you can read this from inside the wardrobe, you've found the stairs.'*"

"What does dat mean?" Gideon asked.

"I think it means we're supposed to get in the wardrobe. Since the note was on the inside of the door, it probably means we're supposed to close the doors and then we'll be able to see the stairs."

Midarin frowned.

"And we're simply going to trust Taron's word?" she cautioned. "Need I remind everyone that this would be a pretty obvious trap?"

"Do we have a choice?" Gwydeon answered.

Midarin shrugged and finally shook her head. The wardrobe was certainly not designed for the comfort of its occupants. Gideon was the last one to push himself in, and when he shut the door, there was a faint sensation of movement. When the movement stopped Gideon opened the doors, and they found themselves in a different room. This room was much larger than the previous one, and the most redeeming feature was that it did not have blood smeared all over the walls. On the far wall of the room however was written the word *Zaltahz*.

"Blade," Gideon said.

"What?" Talon asked.

"Dat word *Zaltahz*, its Old Tongue fer Blade."

"Okay," Pike said. "Now all we have to do is figure out why the word blade is written on the back wall of this room."

"Look at this," Gwydeon said.

They returned to the wardrobe and found Gwydeon examining the sword on the back wall of the wardrobe.

"What does this look like to you, Logan?"

Gwydeon moved out of the way and Logan took a closer look at the scrawled picture. The sword was very familiar. It wasn't the way the blade curved, nor was it the general shape. The dead giveaway was the intertwined dragons that made up the hilt of the sword.

"Let me guess," Logan said to no one in particular, "I'm supposed to put the tip of my blade through the back wall of this wardrobe."

"The Tarnae and his stupid riddles," Pike growled.

Logan took the Dragon Sword in his left hand and thrust it through the picture of the sword. A seam appeared in the center of the wall, and it opened to reveal yet another large room. At the far end of the room stood Taron and the Tarnae. His smile was the same haughty one he had worn when Jeroch abducted Elwyne, and he held a huge sword closely at his side.

"Well Taron," Logan said as they cautiously approached, "we made it through your little tests, and now we've come to collect our reward."

Taron's smile widened.

"And what reward were you expecting, Logan?"

"You're head," Logan replied, "and the location of Shau-ling's palace."

He laughed loudly.

"Fool! Do you honestly believe that you can defeat me in your weakened condition? Your powers are diminished, your sword arm is lame, and not even three of the mythical *Erieal* can destroy a phase without the help of the *Coromor*."

Pike circled behind Logan and pushed a parcel into his hands that he held behind his back.

"Now," Taron continued, "how would you like to die?"

"I think you're going to be the one dying this day Taron," Logan shot back.

With that Logan revealed the Jeweled Dragon's Flame and pointed it at Taron. The smile melted immediately from his face, and his next act was to drop his sword and attempt to open a portal. Seeing his instinct to flee, Logan reached into the depths of the powers left at his disposal and tried to activate the Flame. There was a brilliant flash of light as Logan poured the energies of the *Coromor* into the Flame, and a searing heat ran through his arms. Unable to hold onto the Flame, it dropped out of Logan's grasp, hit the ground, and shattered into millions of pieces.

"By the Light!" Logan cursed.

Taron turned his attention back to Logan, released the swiftly forming portal, and brought his red aura back up around his body. The beam of force leapt from his hand a second later and slammed into Logan's chest, knocking him across the room. Pike jumped into the fray and sunk his ax into Taron's back before he had a chance to dodge. Taron howled in pain and threw Pike across the room. When he turned back toward Logan, Talon was in his face. Tendrils of wind wrapped around the phase's body and lifted him off the ground. Taron tried again to open a portal, but Talon's air prison shifted and propelled him into the far wall of the room. By that time Logan was back on his feet, and was using his remaining powers to strengthen the net of wind around Taron. Midarin had her bow poised and was about to strike Taron in the heart when Gwydeon put his hand on hers and lowered her bow.

"This is Pike's. Let him finish it."

Pike was on his feet by that time. He walked slowly over to Taron and touched him lightly on the foot. Taron howled in pain as soon as the contact was made. Pike broke the contact a second later.

"Oh, I'm sorry, does that hurt?"

Taron couldn't answer. Talon and Logan had cut off his ability to speak using the net of wind. Pike walked away from the helpless phase and grabbed hold of the Tarnae that was doing its best to escape attention. Logan could see Pike channel ice into the Tarnae, and when all motion in the ball of yellow had stopped, Pike formed it into a bucket. That chore done, he set the bucket down in front of Taron, well within his line of sight.

"Now you know what it feels like to be helpless."

Pike reestablished the painful contact, only this time water was pulled out of Taron's pores, rolled through Pike's arms and into the Tarnae bucket.

"Think of every soul you've ever tortured. Think of every life you have stolen over the years, Taron. Now you know what each one of them felt at the moment of their death. Now you know why they looked the way they did, the fear in their eyes, the look of sorrow and loss, and the pain that all of their family felt."

The volume of water increased, and Taron cried out even over the restrictions that had been put on his voice. His cries had no substance but pain.

"I do this to avenge all of the families that you have destroyed, all of the mothers of fallen children, all the children who will never know parents because of you. I do this for my friends, and for myself. Most of all, I do this for the wife you stole from me!"

The last gush of water came out of Taron's chest with such force that his ribs and breast bone shattered as the torrent was pulled out by Pike's hatred. When it was over, Logan and Talon released the remains of the phase and watched as he slid to the ground. That concern had been violently ended, but a more important one remained.

"What happened to the Flame, Logan?" Pike asked.

"I don't know. It was like the power turned on me instead of Taron. I dropped it, and it shattered."

As they looked at the pieces of the Flame, it started to liquefy. The pieces pulled themselves together slowly and retook the solid black shape that they had become accustomed to. When Logan bent down to pick it, and stream of fire enveloped his hand and he was forced to retreat.

"What the hell?"

Logan tried again with the same result, but when Pike reached down, there was no burst of fire and he took it into his possession without incident.

"You keep it Pike," Logan said finally. "We'll have to deal with that later. Now, the real problem is that we are no closer to finding Shau-ling or Elwyne than we were before we went through this. Suggestions?"

"I say we keep going to Brea," Midarin answered quickly. "Korrd's there. Maybe he'll have the answers."

Midarin was right. Logan's brother was at the heart of everything, and if they were going to solve the increasingly costly puzzle, several of the pieces were in his hands. Everything had been pushing them to this point, and now the confrontation was frighteningly close. Dispatching the Tarnae shattered Dreamscape, returning the group to the outskirts of the town of Pramine. The sun was just beginning to dawn in the east, and though every member of the group was exhausted, a new purpose and urgency filled them. Sleep would have to wait until they reached Brea. Even then would there be an end to the nightmares that plagued the darkness?

Chapter XIX

Agendas

Basille sat in his palace in Scalla waiting for some sign of what he was to do next. Trouble was brewing all around him, and it wouldn't be long before his father, Shau-ling, would see it fit to have him exterminated. At least he had gotten his son out of it alive. Jerrard had always been precious to him, and his memory had kept Basille going for all those years when he thought his son dead. But now, Jerrard was alive, and the Mystic family would soon have a legitimate heir to carry on the line of blood that had been stagnating for so long in the evil fires of the Blaze. The phasia had always been proud, and had always plotted and looked for some way to make themselves out-live their maker and master. But those were pipe dreams that they had been chasing. Basille had found the research done by the 'forgotten phasia' Grawn, Bryn, and Ellis. Though their sources and steps in formulating their theories had never been clear, their conclusions rang out clearly. When Shau-ling was finally killed by the forces of the *Coromor*, no matter which generation it occurred in, all of the phasia would lose their immortality. The only problem with that, aside from the fact that the phasia could die, was that time from the last rebirth would hit. So, if the phase had been alive fifty years before Shau-ling was killed, that fifty years would hit the phase all at once. It was very possible that some of the phasia would die because of this aging. However, because the children of the phasia were not affected in the same way, they could hope to lead normal lives. However, the children of the phasia did have one problem and one advantage.

The problem was that they were pulled to use the powers of the Blaze. Some of the children of the phasia, and there had been dozens over the centuries, were taught to feel the powers of the Blaze and harness it. Because of this teaching, they became some of the most awesome and fearful agents of evil. Children of the phasia were not mandated to the service of Shau-ling, and they did not suffer the restrictions that their parents did. So, seven children of the phasia could band their powers together and overthrow Shau-ling, and there was nothing that could be done about it. That was why all of the phasia did everything they could to spawn their seed. Shau-ling knew of this threat well, and so he hunted down every last one of the children of the phasia until they were all but extinct. Many of his lapdogs were used for this purpose, and Jeroch had killed many himself. Basille had never, in his early days, thought of overthrowing Shau-ling. He was the youngest of the phasia, and so he did everything in his power to make sure that Shau-ling made note of his loyalty and his prowess in all things. Needless to say, he made enemies very quickly, most of which were the eldest of the phasia. So, for reasons of loyalty, Basille never thought to try and have a family. As the centuries and lifetimes rolled on however, he saw that his wishes and dreams of advancement in the ranks were merely false hopes. So, Basille secretly took a wife and had a child. When Shau-ling learned of this new threat, Jeroch was dispatched to deal with the child. Jeroch killed Basille's wife in the fire, but Jerrard managed to escape. Later, Basille learned that Jeroch had sired a child. When he reported this to Shau-ling, his master merely laughed and dismissed the child as another one of the many leniencies granted to the First of the Shadows. More and more hatred built between the two, and ultimately it would have become a matter of a duel.

But Shau-ling would never have let it come down to that. For centuries, Shau-ling had believed that only the strong were meant to survive, but he would be the one to determine which were strong and which were not. He fancied himself a god, not fettered by the ambitions of man or beast, and he truly believed down in his black heart that not even the Creator or the *Coromor* could touch him. In the end, it would come down to him against his phasia, and now he was exterminating the last vestiges of hope for humanity. It would only be a matter of time before the phasia would fall in a similar way. Warron had forecasted that. He said that agents of Shau-ling had already started pruning the tree of power. Basille's thoughts had led him in a circle again and again. And each time they went through those corridors, he found himself again in the same position, sitting in his palace, waiting for someone else to make a move. It proved to be a short wait in the end.

The large set of double doors at the far end of the throne room opened to admit a familiar man. Basille had never expected this man to come to him, and in truth he had never even expected to see him again.

"Hello, Aryx," Basille said standing from his throne and drawing his sleek black sword from the scabbard on the table, "or should I call you Nightwing?"

"I didn't think that I needed my armor to face the last-born of the phasia, Basille. To tell you the truth, I hope that this doesn't come down to a one on one confrontation. Master sent me here . . ."

"To kill me," Basille interrupted. "I know all about the famous 'winged assassin' and his many conquests. Shau-ling thinks that I've gone rogue, and so he ordered you to bring me back to his side, or die. Tell me I'm wrong."

"You are correct in your account of the situation, Basille, I am impressed. I take it by your tone that this is going to be a fight. A pity, I was hoping that I would have at least one ally."

"You have Jeroch," Basille countered.

"Jeroch is a weak and pitiful fool. He is blinded by ambition and power. Besides, once Saurn is finished with him, there won't be a Jeroch to be allied with."

"So," Basille said nodding, "Saurn has gone through with his master plan. He wanted to be the eldest, and he just might get his wish."

"But it will be a short lived one. If Jeroch does die, Shau-ling will finish him. And if he does not, I'll be glad to do it for him."

"Provided that you survive this battle," Basille added.

"Please," Aryx scoffed, "do you really think that you are a match for me? None of the other phasia were able to land a single blow, and not one escaped their fate."

"Until now."

Basille leapt into the air and seemingly flew over Aryx's head. He continued into a full flip with a twist, and landed behind him. Aryx spun to face the phase and brought his sword to bear. Aryx was first to lash out with his steel, but Basille blocked the slash easily and returned one of his own. As the seconds past, black and silver metal clashed and recovered over and over again. The black sword of the man called the Raven by the brothers of the inner circle glowed green and then a bolt of the Blaze fired across the gap between the two combatants and slammed full into Aryx's chest. The very human flesh peeled away as Aryx cried out in agony. Even though the fires of the Blaze melted easily through the flimsy human flesh, once it burned down to the metal stored inside the human shell, it quickly died out. Though it was smeared with blood, the black *Debuisa* metal that was Nightwing glowed with that same evil fire. The pain had stopped, and Aryx turned his cries of pain into laughter. Basille was not hindered or surprised by the turn of events, and in the turmoil of the next few seconds, he was able to land a critical blow. The black metal of Basille's blade sparked to life with green ferocity. Basille had used his birthright to charge his blade in such a way that had never before been tried in the memory of any of the phasia. He channeled the Blaze out from inside himself and put it into the blade of his sword. Almost always, the Blaze was used as a last resort to save the phase's life because of the destructive power and consequences. The Shadowwalkers had always been able to pull on the Blaze, but their power and control was limited. For the phasia, there was no such limitation. They could draw on it whenever they wished to whatever extreme they wished. The danger was that the Blaze was a seemingly bottomless source of energy. If a member of the phasia drew on it deeply enough, they would be absorbed by the fires that created them.

Basille knew the danger he was placing himself in, but he needed time to pull off his plan, and a pure sword of Blaze energy would serve as an impressive enough distraction. The fiery sword hissed and cracked with power as Basille brought it slashing across Aryx's chest with all of the power he could muster. The sword sliced through armor and bone, sending pasty blue blood splattering in every directing. The light and fury of the Blaze sword diminished as it sliced slowly through the tough metal. Nightwing had been forged and molded in the fires of the Blaze, and only through the overloading of ability to absorb that energy was damage able to be done. As the seconds past, the sword cut through the armor slower, until eventually, all of the sword's power was gone, and the blade of black metal shattered. Aryx howled, and Basille staggered back, not expecting the result he had witnessed. A huge jagged scar was etched across the front of Aryx's chest and Nightwing's armor. The blue blood had stopped flowing, and Basille could see glimpses of human skin from under the scar. That was the true Aryx under the armor, the skin on the surface was merely for show. While Aryx was distracted, Basille opened five portals all around him, and split his body, trying to keep his opponent off balance. Aryx recovered quickly enough to make an attempt to halt Basille's escape. He dove at one of the five Basilles, but found himself diving through an illusion. Before he could regain his footing, the five portals had closed, and Basille was gone. With a scream of rage, the skin that covered the black metal armor split and the wings of the huge beast sprung out. As the cry of anger ripped from his throat and chest threads of fire and Blaze mixed in with the hatred and spewed out into the spacious throne room. Crossbeams snapped and collapsed under the assault, and soon, Nightwing hovered over the ruins of Basille's palace. His rage wouldn't die so easily. The onslaught continued. Houses and stables burned as people ran from the black assassin. In a matter of minutes, the entire city that was Scalla was reduced to a smoldering pile of ash. After surveying his handiwork, Nightwing turned his flight back to his home and to whatever punishment Shau-ling saw fit to place upon him.

* * * * * * * * * * * *

For some reason, the Hall of Terrors seemed darker than it had been before Nightwing left. The flame spurts no longer leaped to the level of the walkway, and there was only a faint glow cast on the walls by the whirling torrent of flames below. As he reached the end of the Hall, the Flame appeared and laughed maniacally.

"Did you truly believe that the last-born of the phasia could be defeated that easily Nightwing? He may be the youngest of the breed, but he is by far the most intelligent and cunning in battle."

"I DID NOT EXPECT HIM TO BE ABLE TO USE THE BLAZE IN SUCH AN IMPRESSIVE WAY. HE TRULY SURPRISED ME BY HOW WELL HE COMMANDED HIS FEAR AND HIS POWERS. WHEN WE MEET AGAIN, THE RAVEN WILL NOT ESCAPE MY WRATH SO EASILY."

"If there is another opportunity for the two of you to meet," the Flame replied with a note of finality in his voice. "This is your first failure of the Master's orders Aryx, and I warn you now that he will not be lenient. I would be surprised if you survive."

"WE SHALL SEE."

The Flame nodded and disappeared. Just then, the giant stone doors that led to Shau-ling's inner sanctum opened, and a pale green light flooded out into the Hall. Nightwing hesitated only a moment before entering.

"Ah, Aryx," Shau-ling said as Nightwing stepped into the throne room, "I'm glad to see that you made it back, in one piece that is."

Immediately Nightwing fell to one knee and looked up at his master and creator.

"I APOLOGIZE FOR MY FAILURE MASTER, BASILLE PROVED TO BE A MORE CUNNING AND SKILLED OPPONENT THAN I EXPECTED. HIS MASTERY OF THE BLAZE RIVALS ANY THAT I HAVE SEEN IN ANY OF THE OTHER PHASIA, AND AS A RESULT, HE WAS ABLE TO WOUND ME MORE SERIOUSLY THAN EVEN THE FORGED *DEBUISA* ARMOR COULD ACCOMMODATE."

"I am well aware of the actions and skills of my children Nightwing," Shau-ling chided. "You of all people should know that my phasia have infinite ability to pull from my Blaze, and they only do so in attempts to save their pitiful lives. You posed a great threat to Basille's life, so he did what he thought was necessary, and you were out fought. Admit it Aryx, for the first time in your whole life, you were beaten by a lesser adversary."

All Nightwing could do was hang his head in shame.

"But I am not concerned with this failure," Shau-ling continued. "I am more concerned with the bumbling of the phasia that I once thought capable. How easily the strong have fallen to the depths of disgrace."

"OF WHOM DO YOU SPEAK MY LORD?"

"Need you ask, Aryx? Can't you surmise that Taron has botched his mission and sealed his own fate in the mire of the Other Side?"

"HOW WAS HE KILLED MY LORD?"

"The man named Pike Rhuiden used his control over the forces of Water to torture him. This man Pike drew all of the water out of his blood and caused his heart to swell and explode. I must say, Aryx, I am becoming more and more impressed with the new generation of *Erieal*. They have found much more lethal and painful ways of executing my phasia than you and your allies ever did."

"WE NEVER HAD REVENGE AS A MOTIVATING FACTOR, MY LORD SHAU-LING. TARON KILLED THE WOMAN THAT PIKE RHUIDEN LOVED, AND THAT WAS THE REASON FOR THE TORTURE OF YOUR SON. PIKE WAS ALWAYS VICIOUS IN BATTLE, BUT HIS FEROCITY WAS TEMPERED BY HIS UNCANNY HUMAN NEED FOR MERCY. WERE HE NOT SO INCLINED, I MIGHT VENTURE TO SAY THAT HE COULD CHALLENGE YOU."

"That is a very bold statement Nightwing, and I am now sorry that I had not gotten this information from you earlier. I have obviously overlooked a valuable source of information about my adversaries. I intend to correct that mistake. Now, tell me about the rest of the members of this party."

"ANOTHER OF THE *ERIEAL*, TALON AIELIN, HE IS OF LIKE MIND WITH PIKE. THEY FIGHT ALMOST AS ONE IN BATTLE, IT SEEMS AS THOUGH THEY HAVE SOME SORT OF RAPPORT

WITH ONE ANOTHER THAT ALLOWS THEM TO COMMUNICATE WITHOUT WORDS. THIS RAPPORT ALSO ALLOWS THEM TO USE THEIR POWERS IN COMBINATIONS THAT I HAD NOT SEEN IN THE PREVIOUS GENERATION. HOWEVER, I WOULD NOT CHARACTERIZE THIS DEPENDENCE AS A WEAKNESS THAT COULD BE EXPLOITED."

"Explain."

"I HAVE SEEN THEM FIGHT APART ON MANY OCCASIONS, AND EVEN APART THIS RAPPORT IS FUNCTIONING. I WOULD ASSUME HOWEVER THAT THE DEATH OF ONE WOULD ONLY MAKE THE OTHER FIGHT HARDER."

"Interesting. I had made the same conclusions from their actions in Dreamscape and the battle in Sarmeel. They are obviously the strongest of their generation, and it would be hard for me to resist them as targets if I could corner them somehow. What of the third *Erieal*?"

"THAT ONE IS CALLED GIDEON VIRUCI. MY KNOWLEDGE OF HIM IS LIMITED."

"Yet mine is not," Jeroch said emerging from a newly opened portal in the back of the room. "This man is merely a thorn in our side that has been placed there by the Raven. My own brother has been secretly tutoring this man Viruci in the shadows of his palace."

"Welcome home, Shadow," Shau-ling said sitting back in his throne. "I trust you have heard about your brother's defeat at the hands of the *Erieal* and the *Coromor*."

"I have indeed my lord," Jeroch replied, "but I think we may have come out of that battle with something more valuable than Taron's life. One moment."

Jeroch turned back to the still open portal and stepped through. When he returned, Nightwing stood in shock as Jeroch pulled Elwyne Tamerlane into Shau-ling's throne room.

"My lord Shau-ling," Jeroch said proudly, "may I introduce you to the Dragon's concubine, the Lady Dragon, Elwyne Tamerlane Ranthall."

At this Shau-ling stood and nearly ran down the dais in delight. Elwyne had been gagged and tied with bars of pure light, and while she struggled against Jeroch's firm grasp, she was totally powerless.

"Welcome to my home," Shau-ling hissed as he examined her face with his clawed hands, "I trust that Jeroch has not done anything to harm you . . . yet."

"She is in perfect health my lord," Jeroch replied. "I must say that when Taron captured her and summoned my to retrieve this prize, I never thought her to be so valuable. But then, after I saw how recklessly the Dragon fought in the next battle, I was indeed impressed with Taron's strategy. Tis a pity that he had too many battles to fight. He may have actually been successful."

"TARON WAS A FOOL TO THINK THAT HE COULD DEAL WITH THE *COROMOR* AND THE *ERIEAL* ON HIS OWN. ONLY A STRONG FORCE OF PHASIA WOULD BE ABLE TO DESTROY THEM AT ONCE, AND NOW THAT IS ALL BUT IMPOSSIBLE. BUT THERE IS A REAL DANGER NOW MY LORD. THE *CHOSEN ONE* IS STILL OUT THERE SOMEWHERE, AND HE MAY NOT STILL BE IN THE CONTROL OF SAURN. IF HE IS NOT, IT MAY NOT BE LONG BEFORE HE IS ROPED IN BY LOGAN AND HIS ALLIES. ALSO, BASILLE HAS BEEN BORDERING ON TREASON THROUGHOUT THIS ENTIRE LIFETIME, AND MY ATTACK ON HIS PALACE AND HIS PERSON WILL NOT STRENGTHEN HIS LOYALTY TO YOU. HE MAY CONSIDER SEEKING OUT THE *COROMOR* IN AN EFFORT TO STAY ALIVE. TO ADD TO ALL OF THAT MY LORD, THE FOURTH *ERIEAL* HAS STILL NOT BEEN FOUND BY EITHER SIDE. THE NUMBER IS DANGEROUS MY LORD, AND I WOULD FEAR FOR YOUR LIFE."

"Fear not Aryx, the time for my demise is not yet at hand."

Only Aryx caught Elwyne's disturbed reaction to his name.

"But my lord," Jeroch commented, "Nightwing speaks the truth. The number is very dangerous. If the *Coromor* were to unite six powers under his own, your life could end. If you will not take steps, I will."

"YOU WILL DO NOTHING THAT I DO NOT COMMAND SHADOW!"

The Voice ripped through the throne room and forced both Jeroch and Nightwing to their knees. Shau-ling's temper was becoming more and more erratic over the past days, and this was not the first time that he had used the Voice to inflict pain.

"You really shouldn't let your temper get to you like that, Halicon," a plain voice spoke out as a man entered the throne room.

Shau-ling stopped dead in his tracks. His intent had been to beat some sense into the eldest of the phasia, but that name had caught him in the pit of his black heart. No one had called him that name in centuries. No. No one had called him that since he had awakened into the world of men all those millennia ago.

"Who dares speak that name?"

"I dare," the plain-faced man said as he strode into the light. "Don't you recognize me Halicon? I know it's been a long time."

"Emries," Shau-ling hissed, "I should have known it was you. It's beyond presumptuous of you to come here. Perhaps I should just kill you now and be done with all of these games?"

"Now," Emries said trying to fake a hurt expression, "is that any way to treat your brother?"

"Brother?" Jeroch said scrambling to his feet. "What does he mean my lord?"

"Jeroch, my son," Shau-ling answered, "when I was born in the fires and torrents of the Blight, Emries was born with me, and we grew and learned as brothers. In those days, he and I were the only things in this world, and all of nature was our friend and companion."

"An interesting account of the facts," Emries mused.

"But then man started its dominance of this world," Shau-ling continued, ignoring Emries' words. "It looked at nature as an obstacle to be tamed and used as a servant. They cut down trees to build cities and burned off whole forests so they could have room for the animals that they had trapped. My anger with these beasts grew and I vowed to destroy every last one of them. So, I gave up the name Halicon and took the name of Shau-ling, which in the original man's tongue meant Dream Killer. Emries, my so-called brother thought it would be better to work with the men instead of trying to exterminate them. So, he went among them and tried to change their destructive ways."

"The humans of this world were mine to command," Emries interjected. "Halicon started his reign of terror for his own aims, not the altruistic goals he espouses now. I was forced to defend the people that I had so magnanimously promised my protection to. They gave me the name *Coromor*. Our personal war has lasted for thousands of years. Halicon spawned his phasia, and I created my *Erieal*. As the generations wore on, neither side had a true advantage in the war, and all we succeeded in doing was killing. But you know much of this Jeroch, you were there."

Jeroch grimaced, but Shau-ling continued.

"But my own creations got greedy, and so they conspired to usurp my powers and take over my throne. I learned of the plot quickly enough, and I banished Grawn, Bryn, and Ellis from the Council. When I replaced them, Emries created the *Chosen One*, Aerith Seth."

Emries smiled and waved his hand dismissively.

"Seth was a great man, Halicon, but his existence was not my doing. A higher power has always guided us, and He saw fit to bring another piece onto the chess board. Your phasia gave Aralias Imstra the information that my followers needed to even up the playing field. And just as in this generation, it was the actions of Jeroch, Basille, and the *Chosen One*, that sealed your fate. Your time is over brother," Emries chided, "and your cause is lost."

"You are not my brother, Emries, you gave up that privilege when you chose to spread your blasphemes across this world. You protect these humans as if you were one of them, but the truth is that you are just like me."

Emries self-satisfied smile turned to a frown.

"I have not come here to answer ancient recriminations, nor have I come here to rehash old ideological bitterness. My mantle rests on the *Coromor* of this generation, and he shall ensure that my aims are met. I have come here though to give you a warning. My word and my wishes still carry much weight on this world. I have laid my word of protection on Elwyne Tamerlane and the child that she carries. You will not harm her, Halicon, or your life will be forfeit to the Great Dark One. If you or one of your servants harms her in any way, the prophecies will not be able to protect you from the places that I will damn your soul to."

Shau-ling's expression was passive, but Jeroch could see the hate burning in his eyes.

"I recognize your warning Emries, my brother, and I will heed them. Now, you will hear me. Never again will you set foot in my palace or in my presence. If you do, all of the rights that you possess as a First One will be forfeit, and the battle will continue as it should have. Your prophecies will no longer exist, and your mantle will return to your weary shoulders."

"By your word, Halicon," Emries answered bowing, "farewell."

Just as mysteriously as he appeared, the plain man who had called himself Emries departed. Shau-ling watched as he left and then returned to his throne.

"Nightwing," Shau-ling said after a long moment, "you will deliver this letter. You know whom it is to be delivered to, and you know what it means. You need not worry, its conditions will not be challenged. Ensure that no one sees you other than the recipient of this missive."

"BY YOUR WORD."

"Jeroch?"

"Sire?"

"Take the woman to my private chambers and then find Saurn. I am sure that he awaits you in the Blight."

"Yes my lord."

"Now," Shau-ling said finally, the light in the room fading, "leave me. I have much to think about."

Fire and Ashes

On the Island of Mist, red rains fell onto the hillside as Shau-ling ripped through his palace loosing his fury on anything and everything in his path. Many of his minions could count themselves lucky that their master had cleared the palace days earlier. His rage caused storms and calamities on the surface. From the time that Shau-ling picked location for his palace, he created a bond with that place. Shau-ling had always been able to connect with nature, a talent that had both positive and negative repercussion. His peace and concentration had created the fog of mist that protected the Island of Mist, but now his anger and rage threatened to tear the surface of the island apart. Taron's failure did not sit well in the pit of his stomach, and while he was sent up against the *Coromor*, a power that no one but Shau-ling himself should be able to combat, the phase's power should still have been able to battle the cursed mortal to a standstill. But, with the influence of the *Erieal*, the *Coromor* was able to best a phase with only partial command of his powers. A phase of Taron's obvious physical power should have been able to at least kill one of the *Erieal* before he was taken down. But Taron had not managed to kill one member of the People of the Dragon. Not even the mortal Gwydeon Sandar or Midarin Rice was touched by Taron's legions. He had sacrificed thousands of Jeresei and a very valuable Tarnae on that failed scheme, and that proved to be too high a cost for such an unfavorable result. Now, Shau-ling found himself in a position that he never wanted to be in. Yet another of his phasia had fallen by the wayside, but this time, it was a phase that he could ensure would be loyal. In the beginning, there had only been five phasia that Shau-ling was sure he could trust. Now though, Basille proved that he could not be trusted. However, out of the ones he could trust, Erdric, Aldridge, Taron, and Jeroch, only Jeroch was still alive. His children were dropping left and right, and only Saurn, Basille, and Jeroch still survived. Shau-ling's rage subsided, and he found himself back in the Hall of Terrors. The Flame appeared as he approached the open doors to the throne room.

"How do you fare my lord?"

"Not well, child. You were always loyal to me without question, and I may have need of your services before too long."

"My service to you is out of love for my father, lord, and I would never dream of acting against you. Though you banished me to servitude and holding your door all those lifetimes ago, I have never wavered in my devotion, and I did not put my own needs or desires above those of the one that held the key to my life. You gave me a home in the fires of the Hall of Terrors, and you made me the master of all that I surveyed, and for that I will be forever grateful. I knew from the start of my life that I might be perceived as a threat to you my lord, and that my power dwarfed that of the phasia if I were allowed their freedoms. You could have easily destroyed me, but you saw fit to let me live, and for that I am grateful."

"You remind me so much of your brother Erdric. I never thought that he was as sincere as you are in his praise of me. You have always been a loyal and proud servant, and if I had it to do all over again, I would let you have been my standard bearer instead of the phasia. But, we must make do with the mistakes that we have made in the past. You and Jeroch are the only ones that I can be sure of now, Flame, and that disturbs me."

"What about the impetuous Aryx Terian?" the Flame asked shortly. "Did you not design him to be completely loyal to you and follow without question?"

"That I did, Flame, but I did the same with my phasia, and we have seen how effective that strategy has been. However, my own shortsightedness is not what worries me about Nightwing. Terian's soul is too far routed in the Light, and I do not believe that I could ever fully pull him from it. Perhaps it has always been so with him. But perhaps I won't need to rend him from the Light."

Shau-ling went silent for a long moment as a new set of thoughts cascaded through his mind. There was one possibility that he had yet to envision, but it was such a drastic act that it would take more power than he had ever thought to use at one time. The Flame could sense his master's hesitation, and when Shau-ling turned back to face the Flame, he realized that his master had a truly devious plan in mind.

"What is it you wish of me master?"

"My loyal servant, the time has come to break the bond that I have imposed on you all this time. I have a need of your power and of your life. I'm sorry that it must come down to this my eldest son, but the time has come for me to make my phasia live and breathe again."

"But my lord, what of the Other Side? If you pull the phasia from the Other Side and bring them back to life in the same generation from which they were stolen, they would no longer be immortal and they cannot be born again into the next generation were the Dragon to succeed."

"He will not succeed Flame," Shau-ling thundered. "Whether you realize it or not, the Dragon is not as much of a problem as I initially believed him to be. If my phasia can destroy the Dragon before he reaches my palace, then my power would be supreme and not even the Creator or the blasted members of the *Erieal* could do anything about it. Then, once the danger has been dealt with, I can finish off the phasia. No longer will their selfish schemes come between me and total domination."

"Yes my master."

"Now, Kamen, follow me to the throne room."

"By your word."

The bond broken, the former Flame entered the throne room for the first time in centuries in his natural form, the phase Kamen. The body that he had originally been given was very much like that of the humans but much taller. His size and strength dwarfed that of Taron. Later, Shau-ling had used his original form as the model for the Stone, yet they were not given the mind or the power of his original creation. Before the door to the Hall of Terrors closed, Shau-ling turned back to the dim Hall and closed his eyes. The flames in the room leaped higher than ever before, and Shau-ling pulled them all together into a copy of what had once been the Flame. Carefully he blended the powers of the Blaze with the natural fire, and his servant had once again returned from the ashes, but to a much dimmer Hall.

"You shall now hold my door like your predecessor did for all these centuries. You will hold it steadfast, and you will not allow anyone to pass who does not hold my favor. Use the memory of the Flame and of the Blaze as your own. Do you understand?"

"Yes my lord," the creature said in the same demonic voice of the Flame, "I understand completely."

"Good."

Abruptly the doors closed, and Shau-ling was left with his servant in the giant dark throne room. Shau-ling made his way toward the golden throne, only to realize that the Flame had not followed and was still standing in the center of the large black dragon that was etched in the floor.

"Master," Kamen said slowly, "I have never been one to doubt your orders or your beliefs, but I have some reservations about this newest plan of yours that I cannot help but dwell upon."

"By all means my most loyal of servants," Shau-ling said sitting down on his throne, "tell me of these fears so that I make quell them."

"By your word. You have said yourself that the phasia have proven themselves untrustworthy. Do you believe it is wise to bring these same phasia back into existence? Wouldn't it be wise to think that perhaps they would see this rebirth as a show of weakness on your part?"

"Ah, my son, you are very wise. Indeed my children would find weakness in my actions were I to remake them into this same generation.

However, that is not my intention. I said that I would make my phasia live and breathe again, but I never said that I would remake my existing phasia. They are weak and have served their purpose. The time has come for a new generation of phasia, ones that can be more easily bent to my will. It has taken me many lifetimes to find the faults in my phasia, and I think that I finally have the information that I need to make my warriors perfect."

"My lord," Kamen responded approaching, "is that possible? The only reason that you were able to create the phasia in the first place was because of Emries and his *Erieal*. Then, when the rift caused by Grawn, Bryn, and Ellis became apparent, and the new phasia were created, the *Chosen One* was born into the world. If you create new phasia, what creature will be born into the world this time to balance the power? In protecting yourself my lord, you may very well be signing your own death warrant."

Shau-ling nodded. His look was one of pride and happiness. That look scared the Flame deep in the core of his being. It was not because of the possible meanings behind the look, but it was because he had never seen that look on the face of his master. He could remember a similar look on the faces of the phasia, but it had an evil underlying it. As Kamen searched his memory, he remembered the name of that look. His master was smiling.

"I should never have changed my original design, Kamen. If I would have known then what I know now, you would have forever been my servant in the field instead of those bumbling idiots who think they hold my favor. I am sorry that I have to do what I must. To avoid that very contingency my dear child, I must make my new phasia from an existing creature. Unfortunately, the remaining phasia are flawed, and my other creatures do not have the power that it requires to form my phasia. You are the template and source from which I will draw my new creations. I am sorry that I have freed you from your bonds just to destroy you, but believe me when I say that your essence will serve me in every generation and will probably save my life. Now, follow me to the Council chamber where you can be reunited with the fires of the Blaze that gave birth to you."

"No."

Shau-ling stopped dead. When he looked back at Kamen, he stood resolute in the center of the black dragon. The look on his face was one of marked defiance, but there was no fear in his eyes.

"What do you mean no?"

"No, father. I will not sacrifice my life so that you can make more of your flawed servants. You have made it clear that I am the superior one of your creations. If you destroy me to make cheap replicas of your phasia, then you are a fool. Send me against Ranthall and his companions, and I will guarantee you that I will succeed where my pitiful siblings have failed. If not, then you will have to destroy me completely."

Shau-ling walked back down the stairs of the dais and approached Kamen slowly. The smile was gone from his face, but no expression replaced it. Shau-ling's face was now cold and emotionless, more like a snake than it had ever been. That look had broken the constitution of many men and phasia alike over the centuries, but Kamen stared back into his master's eyes, refusing to let himself be intimidated.

"You would dare to challenge me here in my own throne room? You were always my most loyal servant. How can you not follow my orders?"

"You gave me strength of will father," Kamen replied. "None of the other phasia possesses the kind of power or control that I do. Just as with the phasia, I can call upon the Blaze at any time, but I have a level of control that they could only dream possible. Grawn and Bryn once showed me the kinds of power that have been made possible by my simply being born, and if I were so inclined, I could be as powerful as the *Coromor* and the *Erieal* combined. Your biggest mistake in the end was giving me a free will that was unfettered by the laws of good and evil. At the beginning of your war, it was for the side of good, but you have forgotten that. I have not."

Shau-ling was becoming angrier with every word. He had destroyed people for less. First it was Grawn and Bryn, then Zarsi, then the Shadowwalkers, then that clan of Jeresei, then Saurn and Basille, now Kamen was becoming rebellious. The circle was closing all around him, but he could not allow the deeds of his servants to hinder his cause. The war had to be won, even if it meant killing all of his children.

"Do not trifle with Kamen. If you do not sacrifice yourself for the good of the shadows, then I will be forced to kill you. No matter what power you think you have, you cannot match me. If you try, you will perish."

"I will not yield," Kamen replied defiantly.

"Then prepare yourself for the end of your life. You have served this long on your knees; it will be pleasurable to see you die on them."

Shau-ling backed away from his servant, and waited. If this was truly going to be a battle, he did not want to show his hand too soon. Deep in the pit of what was supposed to be his heart, Shau-ling did not really want to kill Kamen, but if attacked, he would not hesitate. Before his very eyes, Kamen disappeared. Shau-ling looked around puzzled for a moment, and then a blast of green flame struck him full force in the back. He flailed around helplessly and fell to the ground. When he rose to his feet, Kamen was waiting, perched just in front of the throne of power. Shau-ling extended his hand toward the former Flame, and a large globe of darkness leapt out. A stream of the Blaze engulfed the globe, and it bounced back toward Shau-ling. Unprepared for the attack, the globe of Blaze energy surrounded Shau-ling and slowly began to contract on its victim. Even though the Blaze was the source of energy and life for Shau-ling, it could also harm him. The fires burned him more severely than he had ever imagined. Kamen approached slowly and cautiously, unsure of what his former master's next move would be.

"I do not want to hurt you father. Let me leave this place to hunt the *Coromor* and I will release you. Please father, do not make me kill you."

"KILL ME!"

Suddenly the globe around Shau-ling extended outward and slammed full force into Kamen's chest. It was like Shau-ling had thrown a Stone directly into the Flame. He was propelled backward into one of the walls, and as he slid to the floor, Shau-ling approached.

"You dare believe that your pitiful powers are a match for me? You dare believe that you are in a position to offer me mercy? If you had one iota of the intelligence that you think you do Kamen, than you should not have spoken of mercy and killed me when you had the chance. For that you will surely parish."

Tendrils of green fire leaped from Shau-ling's extended fingers and twisted themselves around the Kamen's neck. The tendrils should have been enough to kill him, but Shau-ling had not realized what he was really doing. Living in the fires of the Blaze and the pits of the Hall of Terrors for all of those centuries had made the former Flame dependent of the burning that fueled him. Now, instead of the Blaze causing damage to his body, it only made him stronger. Kamen stood up, even under the brunt of Shau-ling's assault and laughed. When the fires stopped spewing from Shau-ling's fingers, a shield of Blaze flames had formed around the Kamen's body. It was as if Kamen had formed armor out of the Blaze.

"You are a fool father. Your own powers are nothing against me. You had your chance to let me go free, but now, you must die."

Kamen clasped his hands in front of his chest and closed his eyes. All the lights in the room went dim, and thunder resounded throughout the palace. Slowly, Kamen pulled apart his hands, and a ball of green flame formed. In contrast to the light green of the fires of the Blaze, the green of the ball of flame was much darker, much more powerful and menacing. As Kamen's hands pulled farther apart, he began to tremble and shake from the power that he was exerting. For the first time, true fear touched Shau-ling, and he was transfixed by the power of his son. Suddenly, the former Flame opened his eyes, and the ball of energy sped toward Shau-ling. The ball moved faster than should have been possible, and when it slammed into Shau-ling's chest, he was propelled backwards. The force of the impact carried Shau-ling across the length of the throne room, and he collided with the doors to the Hall of Terrors, shattering them. He found himself balanced precariously on the edge of the Hall's walkway. As he pulled himself back to a sitting position, safely away from the edge, Kamen approached and laughed.

"I cannot believe that you are still alive. Cedric Binosear did not assault you with nearly that much power, and yet you cowered in fear and died in shame. Perhaps my type of power is just not as strong as his. No matter, before too long, I will be the Lord of the Shadows, and you will be a distant memory. Fitting don't you think that your servant takes your throne. That's what you wanted after all, isn't it? Only, you wanted Jeroch to take your place, not me. Well, I intend to make you pay for that oversight."

Shau-ling forced himself to his feet and nearly stumbled backwards into the pit of fire that lay below. The force of the blast had made him considerably weaker than he had imagined possible, and if it wasn't for the fact that he was so close to the source of the Blaze, the blast probably would have killed him.

"Don't be a fool, Kamen. I have never forgotten your loyalty or your courage against the terrors of the Hall. I put you hear to make you stronger, and it appears as if that goal has been accomplished."

"Fitting isn't it father," the former Flame said with a note of marked irony, "that you should die in the same hell that you consigned me to all those lifetime ago. I wish Jeroch were here to see this, I think he would enjoy that. Afterward he could grovel at my feet for a while before I send him to the Great Dark One to meet you."

"You shall be the only one dying this day traitor!"

Jeroch leapt from the ruined door of the throne room and buried his blade deep into the back of his much larger opponent. He then flipped over the head of the former Flame and landed in front of Shau-ling.

"Father, are you alright?"

"I shall recover, Shadow, do not concern yourself with me. Surprise may have served you well for the first strike of the battle, but do not believe for a second that it will be very much good against Kamen. His power is incredible."

Jeroch stood again and faced his brother. By the time, Kamen had recovered from the assault, and he pulled Jeroch's sword out of his back and threw it into the pit below.

"You are supposed to be with Saurn, Shadow," the former Flame said coldly. "It's not like you to disobey master's orders."

"I came when master summoned me. He knew that this might happen. You were always too proud for your own good Kamen."

"Proud?" the former Flame asked laughing. "You speak to me of pride? I have served, silent, waiting for the opportunity to prove myself. And yet you, brother, you and the rest of the dysfunctional group that comprises my family walk through the palace entitled and arrogant, and what have you to show for this misappropriated pride? You have failed at every opportunity. How many of the *Erieal* have you cut down since my banishment to the Hall of Terrors? How well did you fare against Emries and Cedric Binosear? You grovel and cower at master's feet, not willing to use the power that has been granted you. I have no such reservation, and after I dispatch you, I will finish off my former master."

Lightning lanced across the room and struck Kamen in the chest. The assault was quickly followed by blades of steel that looked a lot like feathers. Nightwing landed beside Jeroch and retracted his bladed wings and the black armor under his imitation human skin.

"Aryx," Jeroch said relieved. "I never thought I would be happy to see you."

"Don't be, Jeroch. If we survive this, then you can thank me. If not, I'll see you on the Other Side."

"Touching brothers," the former Flame retorted. "Now, die!"

A huge stream of flame leaped toward Jeroch. Before he could move, Nightwing stepped in front of the blast and was propelled backward into the darkness. Jeroch responded without hesitation and shards and daggers of ice ripped through the air and through the Kamen's skin. By this time, Shau-ling was back up to his feet, but this time with much more balance. Rocks that formed the roof of the Hall of Terrors collapsed and struck to the head of the Flame burying him in rubble. Seconds later, Aryx had recovered, and the pillar of stone that held up the walkway under Kamen collapsed, and the former Flame was cast into the pit of fire below the Hall.

"That will not hold him long my children. What's more, we cannot fight the Kamen here. Help me get to the throne room, and there I can call on the full force of the Blaze to finish him."

"By your word," the two servants replied in unison.

Jeroch helped his master to his feet and started to help him to the door to the throne room. The path in front of them had been shattered, but with a thought, Jeroch created a bridge of ice. Before they reached the bridge, flames erupted from the pit below and shattered the ice bridge. The shock wave of heat propelled Jeroch and Shau-ling backwards. Aryx stood his ground and watched as the former Flame, coated in an armor of the Blaze rose out of the fires and hovered in the air above the ruined pillar of stone. Before Aryx could move to attack, the path reformed under Kamen, and floated back down and crossed his arms in front of his chest.

"Now did you really believe that I would allow you to get to the source, Shau-ling? We can't have that, now can we? If you were wise Aryx, you would kill Jeroch and then help me finish Shau-ling off. You and are more alike than you know. If you only knew what I knew, remembered what I remembered. I know the answers to the questions that plague you. I know why you are drawn to serve. But I can free you of those bonds. I can free your mind and return you to what you were always meant to be. Stand beside me now, brother."

Aryx made no move in any way. He clutched his hands behind his back and waited. Slowly, the skin in his left palm split, and the arrow tipped tail emerged.

"I stand with my master, Kamen." Aryx responded strongly, "and if you do not yield, we will have to destroy you."

"I will not yield, and you will be the one to die."

Aryx's hand swung forward, and Nightwing's tail sprang from his palm. The attack that had ended Warron's life was averted when the former Flame caught the tail.

"Pitiful maneuver, Aryx," the Flame laughed. "Remember, you were forged in the Blaze, and I am a creature of the Blaze. What you know, I know. There is not a thought in your head that I do not know. So, if I were you, I would try not to be clever."

"It is me that you want Kamen," Jeroch said stepping away from his fallen master. "You have always been jealous of my position that I took from you. Your jealousy is far worse than Saurn's. If you destroy me now, master will have no choice but to give you back the seat on the Council that you have always deserved."

"You blind pathetic fool," Kamen chided. "Do you really believe that I want your seat on the Council when I can make the whole Council bow before me when I take the throne of power? Look and tremble at the sight of the true power of the Blaze!"

Suddenly the whole room erupted in flame. The fires of the Blaze leaped up from the pit below the walkway and created burning walls all around the walkway. Heat filled the room and stifled the air. Jeroch helped Shau-ling to his feet and they started toward the door that led to the Pen. The doors shut violently, and a wall of the Blaze leaped up to further seal the exit. As Jeroch turned, a ball of wind slammed into his chest and cast him into the wall of Blaze fire. In Shau-ling's weakened state, he was unable to hold onto his favorite son.

"Nightwing," Shau-ling wailed, "please save Jeroch."

Aryx hesitated only a moment before diving into the flames. When he returned from the wall of flame, he had Jeroch's limp, burnt body in his arms. He laid the body on the walkway and stood straight. The imitation human skin had been burned away, and only the armor remained. The scar from Basille's blade was still very evident, and would probably be with him for the rest of his life.

"ALRIGHT KAMEN," Nightwing said, all remnants of Aryx's personality gone, "IT'S TIME TO FINISH THIS."

"Whenever you're ready Aryx," the former Flame baited. "I've always wanted another shot at the infamous White Lightning."

Nightwing charged hard and slammed full force into Kamen. Unable to maintain his balance, the former Flame staggered backwards into the throne room. Nightwing recovered from his charge and drew one of his bladed feathers from his right wing and pushed all of the Blaze energy that still radiated from the wall of Blaze fire into the blade. It sang with power, and when Nightwing thrust it into the former Flame's armor, Kamen howled in pain. The blade pierced the armor, drawing on the armor's own power to make the blade itself stronger. The armor shattered, and Kamen again staggered back, and ending up falling at the foot of the dais. Shau-ling leapt at the opportunity to take his revenge for his fallen son. A gust of wind picked up the fallen adversary and hurled him into the swirling blue portal that has appeared behind him.

"Hurry Nightwing," Shau-ling commanded, his voice strong again, "we must hurl Kamen into the source of the Blaze before he recovers his strength. If we do not, I fear that I will not be powerful enough to stop him from killing us both."

Nightwing didn't waste time with a response and leapt into the portal. He found himself a second later in the chamber of the Source. The huge pillar of Blaze flame rose out of the floor, and the glass walls showed the ocean of flame around the chamber. Kamen leaned against one of the walls, trying to pull the bladed feather from his stomach. Calling on all the reserves he had, Nightwing grabbed onto the former Flame and lifted him over his head. Just as he was about to hurl Kamen into the Source, Kamen took hold of Nightwing's right wing and pulled hard. The wing ripped free from Nightwing's back, sending pasty blue blood splattering everywhere. Nightwing howled in agony and fell to the ground, releasing Kamen. Seconds later, Nightwing found himself encased in an invisible prison, unable to move. Kamen turned to the imprisoned warrior and laid his hand on the barrier that separated the two men.

"Remember, my brother," Kamen said somberly, "remember and be free."

By this time, Shau-ling had made his way into the chamber. Kamen turned his attention to his Master, and gritted his teeth.

"It comes down to you and I again, Shau-ling," Kamen said proudly. "The first one thrown into the Source dies."

"Agreed."

Light shimmered all around, and a portal appeared underneath the invisible prison that held Nightwing. Even before he was all the way through, a portal had appeared under Shau-ling. Kamen screamed something barely audible over the growing roar of flame. Seconds before Shau-ling fully disappeared, he motioned with his hands toward the glass walls that held back the tides of flame. Released, the true limitless power of the Blaze flooded into the room and began to slowly engulf the Flame.

Back in the throne room, Nightwing and Shau-ling emerged from their portals and breathed a sigh of relief.

"WHAT HAPPENED MASTER?"

"Kamen thought he knew all there was to know about the powers of the Blaze and what it took to control it. What he didn't realize was that because the Blaze was infinite in power, he could not hope to absorb and channel all of it. So near to the source, I could release the barriers that I had placed there for my own protection. To put it simply, his own powers ate him alive. Perhaps in his next incarnation he will not be so presumptuous."

Nightwing nodded and then remembered suddenly.

"JEROCH!"

"Do not worry about the First of the Shadows, Nightwing. He will recover in time, but he will be badly scarred for the rest of eternity. The Blaze is not forgiving in inflicting pain. Now, I have more things to worry about now that we had to destroy the Flame. His power has been added to that of the Blaze, and I have much that I must do. Nightwing, follow me to the Council."

"BY YOUR WORD."

A new portal opened on the dais, and Nightwing followed his master into the black Council chamber. Shau-ling walked toward the center circle and stopped just short of the boundary. With a wave of his hand, the floor opened, and a single column of Blaze extended into the chamber.

"Step inside the outer circle, Nightwing. I will need your assistance for this. Focus the three strings of power inside of you into the Blaze. Give yourself over to the power and make your powers one with the powers of the Blaze."

Nightwing obeyed, and three strands of power flowed from his scarred chest into the column of energy. One by one, the circles of power, which were the seats of the phasia, opened and a stream of colored energy entered and merged with the Blaze. As the seconds past, Shau-ling slowly added his own power to the mix, and a form began to take shape inside the flame. Instants later, the strands of power disappeared, and the Blaze flames receded, leaving a naked human body standing in the center of the Council chamber. As the lights came up, a black shirt and breeches appeared around the body, and he raised his head and opened his eyes. As the man stepped forward, he clutched his head in pain, and fell to the floor. Shau-ling gasped as the newly formed phase cried out in pain. The clothes ripped and fell away as the man's body expanded and then split into two. When the two newly formed people stood, there was now the original man and the newly formed woman. Clothes formed again, and the man was again dressed in black with the woman dressed in white.

"Incredible," Shau-ling said to himself, "there was enough power inside of Kamen to create two new phasia. That should not be. There is something wrong. Emries must have broken one of the covenants of the gods, and the Creator has spun out an equalizer. Wonderful."

The two new arrivals regarded each other for a moment and then looked to the man they knew to be their creator. They each had the memories of the Blaze and of the Council, and they both knew they purpose in life was to serve the man called Shau-ling. The man was stocky. He had broad, muscular shoulders that were just the top of his powerful frame. He had a full black goatee, and his gray eyes were cold and seemingly unfeeling. His black hair was medium length, and hung almost like and mane around his head. The woman was very similar in many ways. She also had a very powerful build and a narrow face. Her hair was red and long. The ends of her hair were curled in an intricate patchwork that seemed to somehow lend more power to her piercing green eyes.

"Ah, my children," Shau-ling said gleefully, "you will be the ones to lead me into the future. Do you know who I am?"

"Yes my lord," they answered together, "you are our master."

"Very good. Now, you," Shau-ling said indicating the man, "you are Rael, the Panther."

The young man smiled and bowed.

"And you my dear sweet daughter, are Trece, the Tigress."

She bowed and then they both stood firm. Shau-ling found himself impressed with the control the two had showed since their birth. Usually when born, the phasia would ask a multitude of mundane questions which would generally center around what they could do and what was expected of them. As the man opened his mouth, Shau-ling wondered if his hopes were about to be destroyed.

"When are we to meet and destroy the *Coromor* my lord and master?"

Shau-ling's laughter echoed through the palace, signaling to all his pleasure with his new arrivals.

"Ah my son and daughter, how I wish you would have been born many lifetimes ago. The time is now. Take whatever army you wish from the secret pens below the palace. Also, take with you one of my shape changing beasts. When you dispose of Logan Ranthall and his companions, the shape changer will be able to get close to the *Chosen One* and finish the job."

"As you wish my master," Trece replied.

"If you fail," Shau-ling continued, "you may return here without shame. I need you now. So, do not push a bad position if your army fails you. Return here and we will find another way to destroy the Light."

"By your word," the evil twins responded.

With that, two portals appeared behind the twins, and they disappeared into the torrents of swirling blue light.

"WHAT DOES MY LORD WISH OF ME?"

"Complete your mission, and then follow them. They are young and inexperienced, but must taste the conflict. Make sure that you kill one of Ranthall's companions. Bring me a head if you can, everyone needs to have trophies."

"BY YOUR WORD."

Nightwing hesitated for a moment, a torrent of new thoughts swirling through his head. They moved too quickly to understand, but there was a torrent that froze Aryx's heart. He wanted to give the new thoughts voice, the new memories, but as he looked into Shau-ling's eyes, he thought better of his actions. Seconds later, Nightwing had disappeared into a portal leaving Shau-ling alone in the Council chamber.

Prepare yourself Elwyne Tamerlane, Shau-ling thought to himself as the portal formed in front of him, *you have much to answer for. I'm going to get all of the information out of that pretty little head of yours, even if it kills you.*

Chapter XX

The Cave

The storm clouds had just begun to roll in when the familiar shades of reality returned. The transition from Dreamscape had gone just as Logan had expected, and as soon as he awoke back into reality, the pain and weakness from all of their ordeals had vanished. Everything about the situation in Dreamscape with Taron still filled Logan with a combination of confusion and frustration. He had no control over his powers nor of his actions once the *Coromor* decided to take control. What's more, Logan finally realized what it took to use his powers at their most efficient level. Unfortunately, the power that the *Coromor* had drawn upon was still largely unknown. The strangest thing was that Logan could feel all of the *Erieal* not just Pike, Talon, and Gideon. The fourth was close, close enough for those powers to be felt. But that wasn't all, there was another close source of power that Logan had drawn upon. He could only imagine that it was Korrd, but that didn't feel right. However, the mysteries of the battle did not stop there. The actions of the Jeweled Dragon's Flame concerned Logan more than the identity of the fourth *Erieal*. Perhaps the only creature the Flame was meant to be used against was Shau-ling. But why did it resist so strongly when Logan tried to touch it after the battle was over? Something was very wrong, and had been since their return from Mount Tantis. The path that had once been so clear was beginning to fill with undecipherable complications.

Logan's heart was rolling over and over inside his chest, and that wasn't helping him to comprehend the situation any better. That bastard Taron and his equally maniacal brother Jeroch had kidnapped the woman that he loved. Emries had said that she would survive the quest even if Logan didn't, but after Pike's little outburst in the city of the gods, that had probably been revoked. If Logan didn't know any better, he probably should have been mad as hell at Pike, but it wasn't really his fault. This quest had put the most strain on him, and Logan couldn't find it in his heart to fault him for what Logan would have done if he were placed in the same position. Pike was the one person that Logan could count on to not lose sight of the importance of what they had gotten themselves into. After the death of Eldar, he had turned his sights onto the battle and nothing else. This had become his own personal war, and just as much of a personal hell. Logan knew in his heart that Pike wouldn't stop fighting until every last one of them was dead. As far as they could all tell, they were well on their way to fulfilling that wish. Ten of the phasia were already dead. One, named Saurn was supposed to be crazy and fighting his own war against Shau-ling. Another, Basille, was supposed to be on their side. The only one that Logan knew of that might pose a problem was the one called Jeroch. He was the one that had rudely interrupted the feast in Marcwell. Lucky, Jeroch's thirst for revenge against Cedric won out over his impulse to kill Logan.

The rest of the members of the slowly dwindling People of the Dragon had begun to make camp. Gideon used his powers to erect a shelter for the night, and Gwydeon built the fire. By the time the shelter was finished and they had all sat down, Pike and Talon reemerged from the forest and brought with them some of the local animals to serve as dinner. Lightning lanced through the sky, the advance warning of a storm. If the lightning and thunder were any indications of the storm to come, Logan seriously doubted that Gideon's little shelter would be able to weather it. As Logan sat down to warm himself by the fire, Pike looked up with a questioning look on his face. Once before Logan had read his thoughts, and he could see the words in Pike's mind even before he opened his mouth.

"Pike," Logan said calmly, "I'm fine."

"How do you do that?" Pike replied without concern or irritation.

"I don't know. It's like I hear your thoughts and I can tell what you are thinking sometimes. The more I try to do it, the easier it is to do. However, it only works with you, Gideon, and Talon. I suppose that it would make us all able to react to each other quicker in battle if we knew what one another are thinking."

"Clearly it would me lord," Gideon responded, "but could ye try not ta do it without tellin' us first. I don't know 'bout de rest of ye, but it makes me a bit uncomfortable."

"I agree, Gideon," came Logan's curt response, "and I'm sorry if any of you are threatened. My intent was not to invade your privacy, but if there is an advantage to be gained from this type of communication, then by all means I say we exploit it."

"Agreed."

Pike was always quick to jump behind a good idea, and he was equally as quick to strike down a bad one.

"Logan, I have a feeling that there is something that you aren't telling us. I may not be able to read your thoughts, but I know you, and I know that look. If its concern for Elwyne, I understand, but I know that is not what is on your mind."

It was that moment that Logan was reminded how much he truly appreciated having his childhood friends around him to see him through the nightmare that had become their lives. Someone would be there to pick him up when he was down, be there for him when you stumbled, and when necessary to give him a swift kick in the right direction.

"You're right Pike, there is something wrong. I neglected to mention it because I'm not really sure myself what it means. There have been a lot of things in my head for a while now, and I've been trying to make sense of them by myself, but it hasn't helped. You see, I get echoes of thoughts and feelings from the past lifetimes. Up until now, I thought that those thoughts came from the *Coromor* of the past, but the more I think about it, the more that seems impossible."

"What do you mean impossible?" Midarin asked.

"Some of the memories are of the phasia and what they were like in the past. These memories were not of battle, but more of companionship and trust. The most powerful ones were awakened when I confronted Bryn. All of the love that I had in my heart for Elwyne was immediately seized by the memories and all of a sudden I was in love with Bryn. After Bryn died and I had regained control of my thoughts, that love was back where it belonged, but the echo was still there and still powerful. I also have memories of conversations between the phasia and Shau-ling that I was present for. I remember a meeting between myself, Jeroch, Basille, and Shau-ling. The end of that encounter is a little vague, but the memory is still there."

"Where are you going with this Logan?" Gwydeon asked concerned.

"Think about it. Emries never came out and said that I was the *Coromor*. He only called me the Dragon, and I got the impression that he was never comfortable with that label. Then, there were the hints dropped by the tests of the gods. Pike, you saw Korrd as you died, and you said he looked sad."

"Yeah. But come on Logan, that's pretty thin thinking. Korrd's always been unstable. You don't know all of the things that went on in Aradon after he supposedly left."

"What are you talking about?"

"Logan," Gwydeon said softly, "Korrd never really left Aradon."

Logan was shocked. Actually, shocked isn't a strong enough word to describe how he felt at that moment. Utter devastation comes close, but still wasn't quite strong enough. All those years, Logan was told by everyone that his brother had died the year after he left home, but now Logan was finding out that even his best friends knew that Korrd was alive.

"Why wasn't I told?"

"For your protection as well as his," Talon responded, "at least, that's what we were told."

"Told?" Midarin asked.

"Logan's father always knew that Korrd was alive, but he was so mad that he wanted him dead. So, he told Logan that Korrd was dead. Meanwhile, Korrd and the rest of us kept the secret, and made sure that Korrd and Logan were never near each other long enough for Logan to make the connection. In the years that followed, it got harder and harder to keep them apart. Logan was inquisitive about everything, and Korrd was not exactly the recluse type. In fact, Korrd was enrolled at the fighter's training school under an assumed name. It wasn't always easy," Gwydeon said uneasily, "but we managed to make sure that their training schedules never put them in the training grounds at the same time. However, all of our plans and schemes were really put to the test when Lord Cedric showed up after the war. After one long meeting, Logan's father and Lord Cedric came to my house and woke me up. After dragging Pike, Talon, Eldar, Elwyne, David, and Lane out of their beds, we all sat down and Lord Cedric told us the secret that we have all been holding until today."

Gwydeon was the master of dramatic pauses, but this was not one of them. Logan thought that he was really scared of Logan's reaction, and that suspicion was confirmed when he looked over to Pike, and Pike continued the rather intriguing story.

"Lord Cedric said that there was something special about both Logan and Korrd. At the time, he wasn't sure what it was, but he said that it was so important that if we failed to keep the two of them apart, all of our lives would be in grave danger. A threat like that coming from a living legend is a very powerful motivation for children. So, we obeyed. But, it wasn't as hard as we thought. Not long after Lord Cedric departed, Korrd disappeared. About a year after that, Logan stormed out after Mayor Tamerlane all but exiled him for proposing to Elwyne. We heard nothing from either of them until Logan returned."

Logan was dumbfounded. Lord Cedric had known all along. All of Logan's fears were beginning to be realized, and the entity that was crawling around inside of his was not what he thought it was. But, perhaps Logan's fears were not justified as Pike had said. Was it not Lord Cedric who sent Aryx to find Logan? Didn't Lord Cedric proclaim Logan as the Dragon from the top of his palace in Marcwell? Wasn't Korrd the one who had been waist deep in evil since day one? Maybe Logan was getting thoughts from the *Chosen One* because they were so closely bonded by blood. Perhaps the reason that he thought that he was the *Coromor* was because he was getting the same patchwork of memories that Logan was. Emries was the only foil in the whole thing. Logan knew that Emries was the Creator, but he was interfering in a way that was almost destructive. If he had told Korrd that he was the *Coromor*, maybe that meant that Emries was not the Creator at all. Maybe he was just another one of Shau-ling's agents who had fooled everyone. Yes, the pieces were slowly falling into place. Emries was the enemy, Korrd was the *Chosen One*, Lord Cedric was responsible for all of the misdirection and lying. Logan and his friends were merely pawns in a war that Lord Cedric still thought that he was fighting. It all seemed so clear.

"You did what you thought was right," Logan said after a moment, "and I won't fault you for that. Lord Cedric was right to say that we were important, but I think that if he would have let us be together, this war would already be over. For too long, other people have taken stakes in our lives and tried to make us bend to their will. First there was Aryx, then Anne, then Cedric, then Asperon Thorne and Basille, and now finally Caris, Bryn, and Emries. I'm tired of all of this, and I say that from now on we do what we think is right. There is no force in this world that can stand up to us now that the phasia are all but dead, and after we deal with my brother, we can finish this bloody war."

Pike and the others looked happy with my declaration, but Gwydeon seemed to be holding back. Logan knew now that he and Korrd had been very close, and that they were probably better friends than Gwydeon and Logan had ever been.

"Don't worry Gwydeon," Logan said in an attempt to quell Gwydeon's fears, "we won't kill him unless we have to. I didn't know I had a brother until recently, and I don't intend to lose him again so easily."

"Is that true, Logan?" Gwydeon replied harshly. "Don't you remember the Castle of Terror, and the confrontation that was set up for you by the gods?"

"That wasn't real, Gwydeon," Talon countered.

"It was realer than you think, Talon," Gwydeon commented. "But more to the point, it showed how we would react in a given situation. When confronted with the possibility that Korrd was the *Coromor*, Logan reacted like a jealous child and he struck his brother down in a split-second. That failure cost us one life, Logan. What if the same thing happens again, and Korrd swears to you on your father's grave that he is the real *Coromor* and that he will not follow you unless you admit the truth? You yourself have said that you have doubts about your identity, and no matter what we say to try and reassure you, you're the only one who knows the truth. So tell me Logan, how many lives do you think it will cost us if you lose your temper with Korrd again?"

Before Logan could defend himself, Pike jumped in.

"That's not fair Gwydeon. The test was just that, a test. When you know that what is going on is a test, the only thoughts that are on your mind are trying to pass the test and get out alive. You think differently when you are being tested. But then again, you didn't have to go through a test, now did you Gwydeon? Emries thought you were so special that you didn't have to take part in any of the tests. Besides, aren't you the one who is supposed to take his place with the angels after this is all over?"

Even Logan thought that Pike's reprimand was harsh, and Logan was the one who Pike was defending. There was one thing about Pike that served him both well and ill. He was passionate about his beliefs, almost to the point that he let his passions govern all of his actions. If he felt strongly enough about something, he would tell you how he felt, and Pike was not the kind of guy who pulled punches. If anything, when a person debated him, Pike became more vicious and opinionated. Some of the arguments between he and Eldar had drawn crowds larger than the ones at the yearly sword tournament. The only problem with the passion was that his emotions fed his passions, and anger was usually the fuel of choice. Pike would store up his anger for a long time, not wanting to face it, but when an unsuspecting person started an argument, Pike was quick to loose all of his stored-up venom. More than one of his biting comments had sent men and women alike running home crying their eyes out. Gwydeon was no stranger to Pike's rages, in fact, the only person in Aradon who had never lost an argument to Pike was Gwydeon.

"You think that I didn't have to go through a test, Pike?" Gwydeon challenged. "What I went through was more of a hell than you could ever imagine in your life. I know that you're still upset about Eldar, but just you remember that you're not the only one who's ever lost someone you loved. Remember Gabrielle?"

Pike's faced changed from rage to one of shock. Apparently he had forgotten, and to tell the truth, until Gwydeon brought it up, Logan had forgotten too. Back when the incident happened, it was hushed up quickly, and no one wanted to hear any mention of it made. Gabrielle's parents moved to Trelon, and Gwydeon spent more and more time in the training grounds away from everyone. By no means though was this a self-imposed exile. Even though he was cleared of all blame, no one in the town would train with him, except for Eldar, David, Talon, Pike, or Logan. They knew he was dangerous, and they could not forgive him for Gabrielle's death, even though her parents and his true friends had. There was even talk that if he entered the next sword tournament, he and Eldar would be the only ones. Luckily and unluckily, the quest started before the next tournament rolled around.

"Yeah, that's right Pike. I see that you had forgotten just like everyone else. Well, I didn't forget. How could I? Do you think that for one second I could close my eyes without running through every second of the accident in my mind? Do you think that I don't lay there every night praying that I don't dream of her? But the worst part was the Emries knew, and he put my feelings and my loyalty to the test. He offered me the one thing that I had always secretly wanted in my heart. He told me that if I chose to, Gabrielle could be mine again, and our child that she was pregnant with when she died could live. Do you think that I wasn't tempted? Of course I was tempted, but in the end, my sense of loyalty to my friends, my future wife, and the quest were more important to me than a dream. So, do you really believe that I wasn't tested?"

Pike had no answer to Gwydeon's accusations, and Logan didn't think that he could have answered either. To be faced with the dream of your heart and then say no because of your friends and your loyalty to a cause is one of the toughest things that any person could ever do. But Gwydeon had done it. Logan had no doubt that he would not have been that strong.

"I'm sorry Gwydeon," Pike said after a moment, "I didn't know."

"I know you didn't Pike," Gwydeon replied, "I just had to keep my string of victories."

Pike smiled and laughed. But there was the unsaid feeling of dread that still hung over the entire conversation. The storm clouds rolling in thicker and the increasing volume and rapidity of the thunder wasn't helping the situation any.

"Logan," Midarin said as she massaged Gwydeon's hand softly, "how's your arm feeling?"

"Fine, thank you. It's just like nothing ever happened. I must say that you all did a great job in there looking out for me, and when this is all over, I'll owe you."

"I doubt that," Talon retorted. "Just remember who saved us from all of those Jeresei after he got his arm cut off in the first place. Without that storm that you created, there's a good chance that we wouldn't be having this conversation right now."

"Point taken," Logan replied. "By the way, when our powers were linked, did any of you feel anything strange?"

"What do ye mean strange?"

"I don't know," Logan replied. "Power that wasn't familiar, things like that."

"Now that you mention it," Pike commented, "there was this feeling of strength and total power that I had never felt before in battle. For a while I thought it was just because we were in Dreamscape, but if that was the case, the feeling should have been negative, not positive."

"I had the same feeling," Talon added.

"Me too," Gideon said.

"Well," Logan responded, "that's what I was hoping you would all say. I didn't want to be the crazy one. So, does anyone have any good reason for this?"

"I don't know much about your powers Logan," Midarin answered, "but could the fact that we are so close to Brea make any difference? Could you be getting some of your power from Korrd?"

"That was my first thought," Logan replied. "We don't know much about how our powers link, or if there is any kind of limit to how far away we can be for the link to still be effective. Recently, every time I use my powers, there is an echo of the strings in my mind. Maybe if I pull enough power from the link, I can make the echo stronger and figure out where the power came from."

As Logan closed his eyes, the darkness that usually held the strings of power had changed. He stood on a stone floor in the center of a huge room. One look at the banners on the walls and Logan realized that he was in Brea again. The floor had a circle cut into it, and in the center of the large circle was a smaller circle. When he stood in the center of the smallest circle, six lines appeared in the stone floor. These lines ran from the outside of the circle into the center. As Logan turned, the lines began to gain color. One of the lines was red, another was blue. There was one that was green, one black, one was clear, almost invisible, and the sixth was bright white. Acting on a hunch, Logan walked back up the length of the blue line, and when his foot touched the outer circle, the image of Pike appeared before Logan. Satisfied that his instincts were correct, Logan returned to the center of the circle and tread down the clear and green paths. As he reached the outer circle, Logan was greeted by the images of Talon and Gideon. Then Logan was left only with the three mysteries. He took the most obvious first. Korrd had to be the owner of the black string of power. However, when the image appeared, it was that of a stranger. After standing there for a moment looking at the stranger, a voice said the name Jerrard Mystic into Logan's head. The next investigation took Logan down the white path, and at the end, he was greeted with the image of his long-lost brother. Logan was immediately astonished at how much they looked alike. Of course Logan had seen him since the quest began, but standing there in his mind was the first chance Logan had to really look at

Korrd. The last point of investigation led Logan down the red string. The image of a stranger again greeted him, but this man's name turned out to be Arin Domae. When Logan opened my eyes to the outside world again, the amount of time that past was little more than a blink.

"Well, I've got something."

"Already?" Pike asked.

"Well, it seems like I've been gone an hour, but if you think about it, our powers wouldn't be worth that much in a fight if we had to be gone into our minds an hour before we can do the simplest of parlor tricks."

"So, what did you find?"

"Well, in some of my memories from the *Coromor* I know that there is this council where all of the phasia meet. This Council is in the shape of a circle with a small circle in the center where Shau-ling stands. In my mind, there was a chamber a lot like that, but this was in the floor of one of the castle chambers in Brea."

"That's very possible," Midarin interjected, "there was always the rumor that the very first *Coromor* held his court in Brea. However, we've never been able to confirm that. The chamber itself was called the Heart of Turbulent Light."

"Do you know where this might be?" Pike asked.

"If it's anywhere, it's in the lower levels. No one's been allowed down there for years, and the entrance is guarded constantly by the elite members of the Light Keepers."

"That makes sense," I commented. "If Korrd's there, the Heart of Turbulent Light will feed off his powers and increase the link. The fourth member of the *Erieal* is there. His name is Arin Domae. Does that name ring any bells, Midarin?"

Her face was beet red. From that reaction, Logan gathered that the answer to his question was yes. Looking around, Logan noticed that Pike, Talon, and Gwydeon had also made a connection to that name.

"Arin's a member of the Light Keepers," Midarin said finally, the color slowly leaving her face. "He was the one who is directly responsible for my banishment."

"Oh," was the only reply that Logan could manage.

"Don't worry, Logan," she said trying to smile, "I won't kill him, at least not until the quest is over."

Logan nodded absently, trying to let the veiled threat pass.

"The other source of power was a man named Jerrard Mystic. The string of power that he used was black. That means that he must be a member of the phasia or one of their children. The only problem I have is why is a member of the phasia being included in the circle of power for the *Coromor*?"

"Jerrard Mystic is Basille's only child," Gideon answered. "Gotta be dat Lord Basille has finally made up his mind as ta which side of de line he's gonna tread. He sent his son ta Brea ta wait for us and give us de seventh player dat we need."

"But now Korrd's got him, and it may be a fight before we can bring him to the side he was initially supposed to serve," Pike added.

"I agree." Logan said finally. "Tomorrow morning, we make our way to Brea."

The conversation turned to topics of a happier quality. There was talk about plans of marriage for after the war, and they talked of the good times and innocence that had been left behind in the ashes of Aradon, Sarmeel, and all of the other towns along the way. Without warning, the storm broke. Hard driving poured down onto the ground, beating it so hard that in places the ground buckled and pitted. Gideon's shelter proved to be little protection against the storm's fury. Pike stood, covered his head and yelled out over the din.

"There's a cave not too far into the forest. We should be safe there until morning."

Running through the driving rain turned out to be an exhilarating, if not painful experience. The rain drops stung on impact, and Logan wondered as they all ducked into the shelter of the cave if there would be any welts left from the attack of the heavens. The cave itself was warm, and Logan heard the crackling of a fire. When he looked back into the large cavern, Logan saw two people, a man and a woman, sitting next to a fire.

"Come in," the man said kindly, "the fire's warm, and we would enjoy the company."

For some reason, as friendly as they appeared, Logan couldn't help but think that they had just sought shelter in the eye of the storm.

Stone

The man and woman at the fire were physically attractive in just about every sense of the word. He had large shoulders and a barrel chest atop a thin waist and muscular legs. His face was one that anyone could pick out of a crowd quickly. With somber gray eyes and the well maintained goatee, he was easily distinct, but the mane of black hair that hung down was thick and wild, making him more singular. However, the woman who held his company was easily his equal in beauty and uniqueness. She had a powerful frame for a woman, but not a frame that detracted from the positively feminine curves of her figure. Red ringlets of her hair hung down to her shoulders, and her piercing green eyes seemed to give off a light of their own. As much as they were alike in appearance, their dress was both contradictory and complimentary. He wore all black while she was draped in a wardrobe of all white. The duality was too much to ignore. On one hand you had the opposing factor, but in the same token you could not have light without dark, white without black, or good without evil. Not a comforting thought when you get right down to it, but it was a true one. From the very beginning, Aryx had tutored Logan about the delicate balance between good and evil. Aryx's theories and life practice was confirmed by the intervention and information provided by the Elder and Emries. From first impressions, Logan still hadn't made up his mind what to expect from the two strangers. But, he had to remind myself that they did intrude upon the pair, and they were probably doing their best to be hospitable considering the circumstances. To make matters worse, the intruders were all armed, and from what Logan could see, the couple were not. All the same, the two strangers seemed at ease with the new arrivals, and as they sat down around the fire, the couple began to speak plainly and happily. The two halves of Logan's brain were in conflict. One said that they should be wary and slow to trust, because these people could be in league with Shau-ling. The other said that to be suspicious of everyone while the safe approach gave a grim accounting of the world they were trying to save.

"Again," the man said, "let me extend my greetings. This is not a storm that I would want to be trapped in myself, and so I am glad to offer to share the shelter of this cave with you. Now tell me, where are you coming from and where are you traveling to? Perhaps after the storm is over our paths will lead us in the same direction."

"Perhaps," Midarin responded before any of the others. Her tone was different than her normal speaking tone, and it seemed to be the more diplomatic one that she had used during her courtly days in Brea. "We have recently come from the town of Barer on the edges of the frontier. Now we are on a pilgrimage to seek the wisdom of the Dragon in Brea."

"Ah, so you are also seekers of wisdom and truth?" the woman said quickly. "We have met many like you over our long journey. My husband and I learned of the works of the Dragon in our home of Jahandar, and decided to make the journey here. The word is that he sits on the throne of Brea and is waiting for the rest of his companions to arrive."

Midarin nodded, and her face was calm, not wanting to give anything away.

"That is the same story that we have heard on the road. I'm sorry that we are being so clumsy, but we have been on the road so long that courtesy is not one of the points that have demanded of us on a constant basis. My name is Midarin, and this is my fiancé Gwydeon. The rest of the men are our valets. Their names are not important."

Logan bristled a little at the thought of being reduced to a nameless valet, but Midarin's quick thinking may have proved to be a better disguise than the one that the persona of Lord Merrick had offered earlier in their travels. This at least had a piece of truth woven into it. In another life, Midarin had been a princess, and the simple farm boys that Logan and the others had been would not have allowed them to be elevated to any role much above that of a common valet to a member of the royal family.

"We forgive you for the breech of court etiquette, Midarin, for we ourselves are as much to blame as you are. My name is Rael and this is my wife Trece."

"A pleasure my lady," Gwydeon said calmly.

"Now, again if you will forgive us," Rael continued, "my wife and I were about to retire for the evening when you arrived. If you wish, you may enjoy the fire. There are some private alcoves that you and your husband may enjoy farther back into the cavern. I'm sure that your valets will be happy with the floor of the cave, it seems comfortable enough."

"Thank you," Gwydeon answered. "And you're probably right about the floor. After all, they're only valets."

The two strangers excused themselves from the fire and retreated back to the darkness of the cavern. Before long, they had completely disappeared into the shadows. After Logan was sure that they were out of earshot for whispered communication, the remaining members of the People of the Dragon sat near the entrance of the cave and held their conversation over the roar of the pouring rain.

"Does anybody else have a bad feeling about this whole situation?" Pike asked calmly.

A show of hands made the feeling unanimous.

"Well, unfortunately we have no other choice but to stay here until the rain lets up and we can part ways," Pike concluded. "I don't see any other choice but to get out of here before they wake up, rain or no rain."

"I agree," Talon added.

"I just have one question," Midarin said after a moment. "I know we all have a bad feeling about this, but isn't this chance for new allies a little too good to pass up? I know that our record with the last few prospects hasn't been very good, but there is a distinct possibility that these could be the two people who we have been waiting for. Besides, with the recent odds we have seen in our battles, we could use their obvious strength to help cut down the disadvantage a little."

"She's right Logan," Gwydeon said, "they both look like they could handle a good fight, and you've always said that the more blades you have behind you, the better chance you have in succeeding."

"Yeah," Gideon retorted, "but fer every sword behind ye, dere's dat much more chance dat one of dem will end up in yer back. I'm with Pike and Talon, I say we leave well enough alone and git ta Brea as is."

"Before I make any decision, I want to know why the three of you are so against us making an offer to Rael and Trece?" Logan asked turning to Pike.

"Remember that feeling that we all had about Leane when she started taking over in Barer?"

"Yes."

"There you go. That should be all the reason that you need to justify our apprehension about these new people. We've been tricked before. There was Jasmen, Hawk, Gideon, no offense . . ."

"None taken," Gideon replied smiling.

" . . . Aldridge, Erdric, Aryx, shall I go on?"

"I get the picture," came Logan's defeated reply. "But, there is a way that we can know for sure. The four of us have been around the phasia now, and we know what their strings of power look like. Maybe if we concentrate hard enough on Rael and Trece, we can feel to see if they have any kind of power."

"Wait," Gwydeon cautioned, "do you really think that's necessary? We know for a fact that ten of the phasia are out of commission, one is crazy and on a rampage, one is on our side, and the other one is out there somewhere doing Shau-ling's dirty work. That's thirteen phasia present and accounted for, and that's the exact number that there should be."

"But for a long time we thought there were only ten of the heartless bastards. Then we got the surprise that there were thirteen. Who's to say that we weren't wrong about that figure?" Talon interjected.

"Along the same lines," Pike added, "we've already seen that the children of the phasia have their powers. I know you remember Hawk, Gwydeon. So, even if these aren't full-fledged phasia, there is a possibility that they could be the spawn of those demons."

"Since you put it that way," Gwydeon conceded, "I suppose that you should find out if they are a threat or not."

That having been said, Logan closed his eyes and pictured the cavern in his mind. Pushing back into the darkness of the dark gray stone cave, Logan found the slumbering forms of Rael and Trece. As he drew on the powers of the *Erieal* to make his vision and feelings more acute, a huge flash of blackness covered his vision. Logan fought against the darkness to release his, and when he finally shook it away, Logan opened his eyes.

"Get ready, we're in trouble. Rael and Trece..."

"Are servants of the master of evil," Rael said entering the light cast by the fire, "Shau-ling himself."

Logan and the others sprang up in an instant and all of their weapons were brought to bear. Whether those two were phasia or children of the phasia was irrelevant, the only other time that they had ever dared to take on two phasia at once was back in Barer. They had been lucky that Farax came in when the battle was just about over. Still though, Alexander had been lost in that fight, and Logan was bound and determined not to lose anyone else.

"So," Logan said slowly as he pulled the Dragon Sword free from the scabbard on his hip, "I'll bet you have an army of Jeresei farther back in the cave that is causing this storm, and you were waiting on us to go to sleep so that you could kill us quietly. Only, you hadn't planned on our suspicious nature and knew your cover was blown when you felt my powers being used. Am I missing anything?"

"No," Rael replied dully. "Had we expected your pedestrian attempts at subterfuge, we would have simply annihilated you before you set foot inside this cave."

"We may be the last born of the phasia, Logan Ranthall," Trece added, "but we are more than strong enough to kill you."

The firelight of the chamber blew out, and a dim blue glow cascaded through the room and hung on the walls of the cavern like paint. The new lighting allowed Logan to see the massive chamber behind the two phasia, and the massive host of Jeresei and Shadowwalkers approaching quickly. Logan almost didn't recognize the Shadowwalkers. Their body was slimmer in some ways, but the skin looked more like steel than flesh. Also, instead of leathery wings, the feathers of the wings were like sword blades. The force of twenty or so Shadowwalkers soared past the phasia and closed in on their targets quickly. One of the huge monstrosities opened its mouth and a stream of white fire erupted towards Logan. The attack came too fast to move, and Logan hoped that in some way his powers or the *Coromor* would take over and shield him from the assault. Instead, Logan held up the blade of the Dragon Sword and the fiery onslaught struck the blade. To Logan's surprise, the flames dissipated leaving the Dragon Sword glowing with the power that it had absorbed from the attack. More of the Shadowwalkers continued the fire tactic, sending the rest of the People of the Dragon sprawling in different directions trying not to get caught by the blasts. Pike created an ice shield and everyone dove behind it to escape the fire. Talon and Logan were the only ones to remain outside the shield. Logan continued to use the Dragon Sword to avert and absorb many of the attacks while Talon used his powers over the wind to keep the airborne opponents off balance. Between incoming shots of flame, Logan looked back at the army of Jeresei and noticed that they were no longer advancing and just waited, cautious to not be caught in the cross-fire. Suddenly there was a scream from behind Logan.

"By the Light!"

Two of the stone-like creatures that they had encountered in Marcwell had entered the cave while all attention was focused on the Shadowwalkers. That was why the Jeresei were hanging back. It wasn't because they were afraid, but they saw that they weren't needed yet. They had their prey trapped literally between a rock and a hard place. Gideon leaped out from the protection of the ice shield and started an assault on the Stones. His *Debuisa* was deep green, and a single punch shattered one of the Stones into little pieces. One of the Shadowwalkers took exception to the death of one of its compatriots and a stream of fire sped toward Gideon. As if it was what he wanted to happen, Gideon leapt out of the path of the flame and let it burn straight into the other Stone. After a howl of pain, the Stone recovered its senses, or at least some of them, and lumbered through the human force on a direct path toward the Shadowwalker that had assaulted him. The rocky hand came up as soon as the bat-like creature was in range, and seized the Shadowwalker by the throat. Very quickly and brutally, the Stone ripped the wings and head off of the Shadowwalker. Pasty blue blood splattered everywhere, and when the Stone dropped its victim and turned back toward the humans, its entire front was drenched in dripping blue remnants of the Shadowwalker. The other Shadowwalkers were quick to act on behalf of their fallen brother and started spewing flames at the Stone. Many of the shots were poorly aimed, and Logan still had to use his sword to absorb the energy and prevent injury. Amazingly, no matter how many times the Stone got hit by the full force of one of the streams of flame, the huge beast plodded on as if nothing had happened. The sound of the Stone ripping through each and every one of the Shadowwalkers was stomach turning at best, and after it was over, all that was left was carnage and gory scenery. The Stone quickly refocused its attention on Logan. Gideon stepped up behind Logan and prepared to strike. However, instead of immediately attacking, the Stone just stood there and looked at Logan. No, it wasn't looking at Logan, it was looking at the Dragon Sword.

For the first time since the battle started, Logan looked down at the Dragon Sword. Nothing about it had really changed except the blade. Now, instead of the normal mirror-like steel, the blade was almost completely comprised of pure energy. The longer Logan looked at it, he could see the energy in the blade was not just the energy from the fire, but it also wasn't the energy from one of the primal strings of power. After closing my eyes, Logan searched the blade with my mind. Suddenly there was a huge flash of green light that arched across his field of vision, and when Logan opened his eyes, he could see the peaks of green flame jutting off the blade of the Dragon Sword. Now he knew why the Stone was so interested in the sword. It had been taught to follow not its commanders, but to follow the power of Shau-ling. The Shadowwalkers apparently had the ability to channel that power to a limited degree, and now that the Dragon Sword had absorbed that energy, Logan was the holder of the power, and of its loyalty. Slowly, Logan raised the Dragon Sword and approached the Stone. Pike grabbed Logan's shoulder and tried to hold him back.

"What the hell do you think you're doing? Didn't you see that thing just take out twenty Shadowwalkers without even blinking?"

"I don't think they can blink Pike," Logan replied.

"You know what I mean, Logan," Pike cautioned again.

"Look, just trust me okay?"

"Trust you. Why is it that everyone I know says 'trust me' before doing something incredibly stupid?"

Logan shrugged off the connotation of the question and continued to approach the Stone. It backed away for a moment, and then when Logan stopped, so did it. Logan chanced a look back at the army of Jeresei, but they stood in the same position behind Rael and Trece as they had before the Stone started ripping apart Shadowwalkers. On a hunch, Logan tried to communicate with the Stone.

"Can you understand me?"

The Stone nodded.

"Good. Can you speak?"

"Y...E...S..."

Its voice sounded like a raging river crashing over a break of rocks into a waterfall. The din of background noise was incredible, but Logan could make out every syllable and word.

"Great. Do you know who I am?"

It shook its head.

"Do you know what the *Coromor* is?"

"B...A...D../..M...U...S...T../..K...I...L...L..."

Not exactly the response that Logan was looking for. The voice of the Stone was difficult to understand as each word and syllable flowed into the next as though the entire sentence was one long word.

"What if I told you that I was the *Coromor*? Would you try to kill me?"

"N...O../..C...A...N../..N...O...T../..K...I...L...L..."

"Why?"

"Y...O...U../..H...O...L...D../..B...L...A...Z...E../..Y...O...U../..L...E...A...D ..."

That was the answer that Logan was looking for. The energy that the Shadowwalkers used evidently was the power of Shau-ling and the phasia, and was called the Blaze. Logan's theory about the strongest power must have been true. The Stone would follow Logan as long as he displayed the greatest control over the Blaze.

"Turn around."

The Stone stood straight for a moment and just stared at Logan. Its eyes didn't exactly have much expression to them, but compared them to those of a human, Logan would have said that the Stone looked confused.

"W...H...A...T../..I...S../..A...R...O...U...N...D..."

"Look behind you."

"B...E...H...I...N...D..."

Again, the same puzzled look. No wonder that the Stone had never been used by themselves against them. They had no sense of direction.

"Do you know where the Jeresei are?"

"Y...E...S..."

"Can you kill them if I ask you to?"

"Y...E...S..."

"Well, have at it."

Logan should have known that he would get a blank look to that statement. Not only were the Stone bad with human language and the concept of direction, they also weren't very well versed in expressions or euphemisms.

"Kill the Jeresei."

"Y...E...S../..K...I...L...L..."

The Stone turned and lumbered in the direction of the Jeresei. Even before it was half-way across the chamber, the Jeresei swarmed the massive and started tearing at its hard exterior with their long claws. The battle turned ugly at that very moment. The Stone did not hesitate before attacking any of the Jeresei, and when it did the assaults were vicious and deadly. One of the Jeresei leapt toward it face, but the Stone punched its massive fist toward the attacker's chest. Instead of repelling the attacker, the fist slammed through the body of the Jeresei and the dead body slid up the Stone's arm like some twisted evil bracelet. As one of the Jeresei hacked at the Stone's knee, it brought down its fist on the Jeresei's head strong enough to create a large red smear on the cavern floor. More and more of the Jeresei fell to similarly powerful assaults, while still others went down screaming after having their arms, legs, or other pieces of their anatomy ripped off. Still others were crushed by the Stone's massive feet or in its strong hands. The battle was over almost as soon as it was started, and after all of the Jeresei had stopped kicking, the Stone turned and walked back toward Logan. Unfortunately, there was now a collection of red splotches mixing in with the blue from the Shadowwalkers.

"The first thing we're going to have to do is teach this guy some personal hygiene," Pike commented.

"Sure," Talon replied, "how do you tell a fifteen foot stone giant that he has to wash of his body after he gets done killing an entire legion of Jeresei?"

"Point taken," Pike laughed.

The Stone stopped short, observing the same distance to Logan as it had in their previous conversation.

"R...E...D.../..O...N...E.../..S...D...E...A...D..."

"Good. Wait here for me, I'll be back in a minute."

"W...A...I...T..."

Logan again received a glazed look for the misunderstood word.

"Don't move until I tell you to. Do you understand?"

"Y...E...S.../..W...I...L...L.../..W...A...I...T..."

With a motion, Pike and the rest of the People of the Dragon fell in behind Logan, and they approached the two rather alarmingly undisturbed phasia. Even after the defection of the Stone as well as the loss of their entire army, neither Rael nor Trece appeared the least bit concerned for their own welfare.

"You are more impressive than we were led to believe, Logan," Rael said smugly, "we will not make that mistake again."

"You know," Pike said smartly, "you phasia should compare notes more often. It seems like every time we meet one of you, you always say that you have underestimated us and that it won't happen again. Granted than none of the phasia has had more than one shot at us, except for Taron, but I would think that by now you guys would have figured it out. I'm glad you haven't but I guess that I've just overestimated you, being the scourge of the world and all."

"Strong words from a man who is about to die," Trece said.

With that the two phasia disappeared from view. Logan felt a tug at his shirt and was pulled into the center of a defensive circle. Gwydeon, Pike, Talon, and Gideon served as the perimeter of the circle while Midarin stood beside Logan with her bow ready for action. There was a flash of light out of the corner of Logan's eye and a yelp of pain from Talon. He turned back toward Logan, and there was a huge bloody slash across his chest. Midarin pulled him into the circle and started to treat his wounds.

"Damn!" Pike said in frustration. "How the hell are we supposed to fight and kill something that we can't see? Wait a minute."

Pike's *Debuisa* was already brilliant blue, and he closed his eyes and concentrated. Logan felt cold all of a sudden, and every second that went by, the temperature in the cave dropped. Then Logan realized the plan. When the temperature dropped low enough, Logan began to see the breath of their adversaries as they circled. Instinctively, Logan closed his eyes. The energy in the Dragon Sword pulsed angrily, and when Logan's eyes opened again, the energy released itself from the sword and slammed fully into the bodies of the two phasia. They sprawled to the ground, visible again. Talon and Gwydeon were quick to act, encasing the two evil children in prisons of wind and rock. However, any chance at celebration was cut short by lightning lancing across the top of the cavern. Two seconds after the battle should have been over, lightning slammed into the two prisons, and sent the two phasia sprawling across the floor again. When Logan turned, he was shocked to see what was hovering near the entrance of the cavern.

It was very much like a Shadowwalker but it seemed larger. The beast had the same black metal skin and blade wings, but it also had a large set of horns and a whisper thin tail that floated around in the air behind it, almost like the ones that they had seen attached to the demonic little balls of fur called the Snags. More than all of those other factors, the beast was set apart by the huge jagged scar in the armor plate of its chest. With a voice like rolling thunder, the beast called to the fallen phasia.

"LEAVE HERE NOW. THE BATTLE IS LOST, BUT THERE WILL BE ANOTHER TIME."

The phasia were up and through portals before any attempt could be made to stop them. The other beast just hung there in the air as it watched the phasia flee.

"Stone!" Logan yelled. "Kill the Shadowwalker!"

"Y...E...S..." it replied.

But the monster proved too quick for the Stone's assault. The Stone flailed out with both arms in an attempt to grab the Shadowwalker, but the beast darted through the air and then through the portal that appeared a second later. The Stone looked puzzled for a moment and then lumbered toward Logan.

"F...A...I...L...E...D../..W...I...L...L../..P...U...N...I...S...H..."

Logan shook his head.

"No, I'm not like your former master. I know that you did your best to follow my orders, and I forgive you."

The Stone looked down at Logan for a moment like it was confused as to the meaning of the words, but just as Logan was about to explain himself, the stone held up its hand and for a moment Logan thought that it smiled.

"U...N...D...E...R...S...T...A...N...D../..W...I...L...L../..F...O...L...L...O...W../..T...I...L...L../..D...I...E..."

"Well my friends, I think we have ourselves a new ally."

Destiny

As the group explored the cave, Logan began to realize that the cavern was much more extensive than he initially believed. Fortunately, the height of the cave easily accommodated the Stone's significant size. As they moved further back into the cave, Logan began to wonder exactly where they were and how far back the cavern could actually run. Part of him entertained the thought that the cave ran through the entirety of the mountain chain and had some secret exit under the city of Brea. The mysterious light in the cave was still an eerie subdued blue, but it was enough to see by. There were many shadows that could conceal enemies, but with the Stone standing with them, they could easily discourage any kind of assault. Logan never thought that any creature alive would have been able to handle an entire legion of Jeresei and several Shadowwalkers and still come away with all of its pieces and no visible marks except the blood of the enemy. In the enclosed space of the cave, even Logan and three of the Erieal would have had problems dealing with just the Jeresei alone, and that would have been with serious losses. The longer that Logan walked through the cavern with their new companion, he wondered more and more about it. Before long, exhaustion won out over curiosity, and the group settled down at the edge of a pond that had been filled by rain water through a series of cracks in the cave ceiling. Logan figured that it was as good a time as any to question their new compatriot.

"Stone?"

"Y...E...S../..F...R...I...E...N...D../..L...O...G...A...N..."

"Do you have a name?"

"W...H...A...T../..I...S../..N...A...M...E..."

"A name," Pike answered, "is what we call someone else. Logan is his name, and Pike is mine. Do you understand?"

"U...N...D...E...R...S...T...A...N...D../..F...R...I...E...N...D../..P...I...K...E.. /..N...A...M...E../..I...S../..S...T...O...N...E..."

"No," Talon said, "I don't think you do understand. You are a Stone, but your name is not Stone. What do others call you when they want to get your attention?"

"S...T...O...N...E..."

"What is Logan?" Logan asked.

"L...O...G...A...N../..I...S../..F...R...I...E...N...D..."

"No, you are a Stone, what am I?" Pike said, exasperation thick in his voice.

"D...O./.N...O...T./.U...N...D...E...R...S...T...A...N...D..."

"You are a Stone," Talon added. "There are Jeresei, Phasia, Shadowwalkers, and others. Understand?"

"Y...E...S..."

"Then, what is Logan?"

"L...O...G...A...N../..I...S../..L...O...G...A...N..."

"No, I am a human," Logan replied, starting to see true comedy in the conversation. "Do you know what a human is?"

"W...E...A...K../..F...L...E...S...H../..C...R...E...A...T...U...R...E...S../..T...H ...A...T./.T...H...E./..P...H...A...S...I...A../..L...O...O...K../..L...I...K...E..."

"In a manner of speaking, yes," Gwydeon commented. "Now, I am a human, Logan is a human, we are all humans."

"U...N...D...E...R...S...T...A...N...D../..Y...O...U../..A...R...E../..H...U...M.. .A...N../..W...H...A...T../..I...S../..A../..G...W...Y...D...E...O...N..."

Gwydeon was a shocked by the question as the rest of the members of the party were. However, as puzzling as the entire conversation was, Logan was beginning to understand what the Stone was saying.

"It's no use," Logan said finally, "Stone doesn't understand the concept of names and it probably won't understand what it is to be an individual. It is a Stone. Shau-ling probably doesn't differentiate between them, and so with their obvious limits in intelligence, they have accepted the fact that they are all alike and therefore inseparable. My bet is that they do not realize what they are, more than saying that they are Stone."

"So," Gwydeon said making the connection, "if one goes, all go."

"Yes," Midarin continued. "If some are left behind, it is because they were not told to remain with the group. That is why Stone went so crazy when the other Stone was killed. It didn't know what it was like to be alone and simply reacted to the situation. It killed because it was threatened."

"Stone," Pike said turning to it, "you see that we are all very different."

"D...I...F...F...E...R...E...N...T../..B...U...T../..S...A...M...E../..E...X...C...E. ..P...T../..F...O...R../..F...R...I...E...N...D../..M...I...D...A...R...I...N../..M...U... C...H../..D...I...F...F...E...R...E...N...T../..F...R...O...M../..F...R...I...E...N...D.. /..P...I...K...E..."

"Thank the Light," Midarin mumbled under her breath.

"Yes, Midarin is different from us. You are different from us too."

"Y...E...S../..S...T...O...N...E../..D...I...F...F...E...R...E...N...T../..B...U...T.. /..S...A...M...E..."

"How are you the same?" Logan asked.

"F...I...G...H...T.../.A...G...A...I...N...S...T../.S...H...A...U...L...I...N...G../.
.N...O...W../.W...I...T...H../.F...R...I...E...N...D../.L...O...G...A...N../.W...
E../.N...O...W../.S...A...M...E..."

"Yes," Logan replied after a moment, "we are the same now."

"B...U...T.../.F...R...I...E...N...D../.M...I...D...A...R...I...N../.N...O...T../.
S...A...M...E..."

"Why aren't I the same Stone?" Midarin asked, genuine curiosity thick in her voice as to how the creature actually saw her.

"S...O...F...T...E...R../.S...H...A...P...E...D../.D...I...F...F...E...R...E...N...
T..."

Midarin blushed a little at the description, but finally nodded in ascent.

"Yes," she said, "I am a woman. I am a female human."

"H...U...M...A...N./.F...E...M...A...L...E../.H...U...M...A...N../.M...A...L.
..E../.A...N...D../.S...T...O...N...E..."

"Does that mean..."

"Don't ask Midarin," Gwydeon said putting his hand on her shoulder, "we probably don't want to know."

"You're probably right," she replied, the color still evident in her cheeks.

"Well," Logan said seeing that the conversation had died down, "there is another chamber that we haven't searched farther back in the cavern. Anyone want to volunteer?"

"S...T...O...N...E../.W...I...L...L../.G...O../.F...R...I...E...N...D../.L...O...
G...A...N..."

"Alright Stone," Logan replied, "I'll go with you."

"N...O../.F...R...I...E...N...D../.L...O...G...A...N../.W...O...U...L...D../..
L...I...K...E../.F...R...I...E...N...D../.M...I...D...A...R...I...N../.G...O..."

Midarin was puzzled by the large creature's request, but after a moment she nodded and the two went off into the cavern together.

"Don't look now Gwydeon," Talon said laughing, "but I think you have some competition for your bride-to-be."

* * * * * * * * * * *

Midarin and the Stone continued into the cavern silently. After a moment, the Stone broke the silence. Its voice was different this time. The background noise was greatly decreased, but the hard quality was still very apparent.

"F..R..I..E..N..D./.M..I..D..A..R..I..N./.S..T..O..N..E./.S..P..E..A..K./.T.. O./.Y..O..U./.A..W..A..Y./.F..R..O..M./.O..T..H..E..R..S./.D..O./.U..N..D.. E..R..S..T..A..N..D.."

"Yes," Midarin said. "What do you want to talk about Stone?"

"B..O..T..H./.D..I..F..F..E..R..E..N..T./.F..R..O..M./.O..T..H..E..R..S./. B..U..T./.Y..O..U./.M..O..R..E./.D..I..F..F..E..R..E..N..T./.Y..O..U./.F..E.. M..A..L..E.."

"Yes," she responded, "I am a woman."

"W..H..A..T./.M..E..A..N..S./.T..O./.B..E./.A./.W..O..M..A..N.."

"Well," Midarin said after a moment of thought, "being a woman is different than being a man. Men are supposed to go out and fight while the women stay at home and have children."

"W..H..A..T./.A..R..E./.C..H..I..L..D..R..E..N.."

"I was afraid you would ask that," she said shaking her head. "When humans come into the world, they are born small and defenseless. Those young humans are called children. How do the Stone come into the world?"

"S..H..A..U..L..I..N..G./.T..A..K..E..S./.O..L..D./.S..T..O..N..E./.A..N.. D./.C..R..A..C..K..S./.I..T./.I..N..T..O./.H..U..N..D..R..E..D..S./.O..F./.P..I ..E..C..E..S./.A..N..D./.E..A..C..H./.O..N..E./.I..S./.S..T..O..N..E.."

"Interesting."

"H..O..W./.H..U..M..A..N..S./.M..A..K..E./.C..H..I..L..D..R..E..N.."

"Yet another interesting and awkward question my large friend. Two humans, a man and a woman get together and a few months later a child is born."

"I..T./.T..A..K..E..S./.M..A..N./.T..O./.M..A..K..E./.C..H..I..L..D.."

"Unfortunately, it does. It seems that there are not too many things in this world that women can do without men."

"S..O..U..N..D./.M..A..D./.D..O..E..S./.N..O..T./.F..R..I..E..N..D./.M..I..D..A..R..I..N./.L..I..K..E./.M..A..N.."

"Yes," she replied defensively, "I do like men, it's just that it frustrates me sometimes that men don't think about how we feel and are too worried about themselves and their honor. You know, if it weren't for a man who was so worried about his honor that he didn't care what happened to me, I wouldn't be here right now."

"F..R..I..E..N..D./.M..I..D..A..R..I..N./.W..O..U..L..D./.N..O..T./.H..A..V..E./.M..E..T./.F..R..I..E..N..D./.S..T..O..N..E.."

Midarin politely laughed at the comment.

"F..R..I..E..N..D./.M..I..D..A..R..I..N./.W..O..U..L..D./.N..O..T./.H..A..V..E./.M..E..T./.F..R..I..E..N..D./.G..W..Y..D..E..O..N.."

Midarin marveled that the simple giant grasped the situation so completely. Perhaps they had been fooled by the barrier of language, but Stone certainly was not as simple as his linguistic skills.

"F..R..I..E..N..D./.M..I..D..A..R..I..N./.W..O..U..L..D./.N..O..T./.B..E./.W..I..T..H./.C..H..I..L..D.."

She was dumbfounded. The Stone said no more and stopped dead in its tracks waiting for Midarin's response.

"How do you know that I'm pregnant with Gwydeon's child?"

"S..T..O..N..E../.S..E..E../.D..I..F..F..E..R..E..N..T./.T..H..A..N./.H..U..
M..A..N..S./.D..O./.H..A..V..E../.B..E..T..T..E..R./.E..Y..E..S./.H..A..V..E./
.K..N..O..W..N./.S..I..N..C..E./.F..I..R..S..T./.S..A..W./.F..R..I..E..N..D./.M
..I..D..A..R..I..N./.B..U..T./.D..I..D./.N..O..T./.U..N..D..E..R..S..T..A..N..D
./.W..H..A..T./.S..T..O..N..E./.W..A..S./.S..E..E..I..N..G./.I..S./.F..R..I..E..
N..D./.M..I..D..A..R..I..N./.H..A..P..P..Y./.N..O..W.."

"Yes my good friend Stone," she replied in a mixture of awe and joy, "friend Midarin is very happy now."

"G..O..O..D./.W..O..U..L..D./.N..O..T./.L..I..K..E../.S..E..E../.F..R..I..E.
.N..D./.M..I..D..A..R..I..N./.A..N..G..R..Y./.B..U..T./.N..O..W./.S..T..O..N.
.E./.W..O..R..R..I..E..D.."

"Why?"

"P..O..R..T..A..L.."

Midarin spun quickly on her heels to see a familiar whirling blue portal opening behind her. She reached for the short sword that Gwydeon had given her and took up a position behind the Stone.

"Guys!" she yelled back toward the dark passage. "Get back here! We've got company!"

* * * * * * * * * * * *

At Midarin's rather harried summons, Logan and the others picked up their weapons and sprinted toward the cavern that she and Stone had gone to investigate. Inwardly Logan was cursing himself for letting just the two of them go, but then again, he couldn't tell them that they couldn't go. Logan had to start trusting his companions more and stop worrying so much. Logan had learned that they could take care of themselves, but he still wasn't comfortable with them taking risks on his behalf. As irrational as it may have seemed, Logan liked taking the risks on his own terms. Granted, it probably would get him killed sooner or later, but that would be his preference anyway.

When they reached the chamber of the cavern, they saw the portal as well as Midarin and Stone. Stone stood facing the portal, and it looked ready to smash whatever came walking through. Midarin was safely perched behind one of Stone's massive legs, looking back every now and then to see if and when the others had arrived. When they did, she ran back to the others and took position at Gwydeon's side, her bow ready to strike.

"Nothing's come out yet, Logan," she said after a quick moment. "Stone felt the portal before it actually appeared, and he's ready to act if something hostile makes its appearance."

"Stone."

"Y...E...S./.F...R...I...E...N...D./.L...O...G...A...N..."

"Step away from the portal. I don't want to make this uglier than it has to be."

"Y...E...S..."

"Do you think that's wise, Logan?" Gwydeon asked. "Rael and Trece could be coming back with more help."

"I don't think so, Gwydeon," Logan replied, "besides, if Rael and Trece bring back more Stone, we could turn their own army against them. Stone?"

"Y...E...S./.F...R...I...E...N...D./.L...O...G...A...N..."

"Could you talk to other Stone and tell them to follow me?"

"D...O./.N...O...T./.K...N...O...W./.I...F./.O...T...H...E...R./.S...T...O... N...E./.W...I...L...L./.F...O...L...L...O...W./.F...R...I...E...N...D./.L...O...G...A ...N./.W...I...T...H...O...U...T./.B...L...A...Z...E./.I...N./.H...A...N...D./.B...U ...T./.W...I...L...L./.T...R...Y..."

"Good enough Stone. Well everyone," Logan said trying to keep the tension at bay, "let's be ready in case this thing turns ugly."

Suddenly a body fell through the opening of the portal. It look almost as if he had been thrown through the portal instead of walking through. When he landed on the hard floor of the cavern, Logan knew something was not right. The man was stark naked and lay there on the floor shivering. This was apparently not an everyday occurrence for him. Logan removed his cloak and approached the fallen man slowly. With a little help, he sat up and looked Logan square in the face.

It was almost like looking into the mirror. Except for the fact that he had blond hair, the stranger could have easily passed for Logan's twin. But the more Logan looked at him, the more subtle differences he could identify. He had the same narrow face and sharp features as all of the men in Logan's family, but his eyes were different. They weren't set as deep into his face as Logan's or Korrd's, but they were more like someone else's. If Logan didn't know any better, he would have said that the stranger had Elwyne's eyes. There was an immediate connection between the two men, and before either of them could say a word, Logan wrapped the stranger in his cloak and helped the young man to his feet. As the pair approached the others, many looked startled and more than a bit surprised when they got a good look at the stranger. Logan waved off all inquiries until they had returned to the fire and the man had pulled on a set of clothes from Logan's saddlebag. After dressing, the man looked up and around at the assemblage for the first time. When his eyes crossed the massive bulk of Stone, he shrank back as if something had bit him.

"It's all right my friend," Logan said quickly, "Stone won't hurt you; he's on our side."

"I'm sorry," the man said clearly in a voice that sounded much like Logan's, "where I come from, the Stone are enforcers that are used to strike fear into the hearts of all men and women who dare to oppose the will of the Shadow."

"Well," Pike commented, "that leads to the most important question that I can think of right now stranger. Where are you from, and who are you?"

The stranger looked up at Pike for a moment and took a deep breath. Then, he smiled.

"Pike Rhuiden," the stranger said, "your name is legendary where I come from. All of your names are recorded in history. Especially Gwydeon

Sandar, the man who risked and sacrificed all to save the life of the *Coromor*."

That comment froze everyone. The only person that had ever talked of the future in the past tense was Emries. Logan didn't like it when Emries did it, and he surely didn't like to hear it coming from the mouth of the stranger.

"Oh," he said after only a moment of reflection, "I'm sorry. My sense of history is what you will term to be your future. My name is Fion Quinn. This is going to sound really strange, but I come from about thirty years into your future."

None of them had been prepared for Fion's revelation. Logan thought that the only one who wasn't effected by the comment was Stone. For a few moments, all they could do was look around at each other as if they were all still trying to make sense of the strange words.

"So," Gwydeon remarked finally, "you are from thirty years into our future, and the world is still under the boot of Shau-ling."

The young man sighed, his thoughts clearly troubled.

"Yes," Fion answered. "I don't have all the particulars, my study of history is not what it should be, but then there is little time for study of such things when you spend every moment training to fight for your life. Eventually, all of you will make it to the throne room of Shau-ling. There is no record of the battle, but it is certain that the side of the Light triumphed. Unfortunately, only three people walked away from the battle alive. Those three were Logan Ranthall, Elwyne Ranthall, and Midarin Rice."

Gwydeon and Midarin looked at each other for a long moment, and though it was clear that the news impacted Midarin, there was almost a quiet expectation in her eyes. Pike was probably the calmest about the news. He had a long stick in his hand, and he kept turning over the ashes in the fire. His face was cold and unreadable, much like the night that Eldar died. Talon had his eyes focused on the young man, and Gideon was taking in the reactions from all of the others. As for Stone, it just sat there looking at Fion. Logan heard a low rumble from somewhere behind him. It was barely audible, but when Logan glanced, he noticed that Stone had balled its fist and appeared ready to add Fion to the smears that already covered the walls of the cavern.

"After the war," Fion continued, "Logan and Elwyne returned to the kingdom of Marcwell where they ruled for the next twenty years. Unfortunately, there is no record as to what happened to Midarin Rice. However, the problem started after Logan Ranthall's death twenty years after the battle. By that time, the generation fold had already occurred, and Shau-ling raised himself from the ashes of his palace and pulled the phasia back from the Other Side. The reign of terror began again in earnest, but Shau-ling was very quick to move and did not hide the actions of his minions. The first town to fall was Marcwell. The royal guard put up a valiant fight, but the walls crumbled and Jeroch took his place on the throne and claimed Elwyne Ranthall as his bride."

Logan winced at the thought of Jeroch coming within five feet of Elwyne, let alone bedding her. The thought made his skin crawl and his stomach turn.

"Fortunately, the remaining members of the royal guard were able to sneak back into the palace and kidnap the queen before she was to be wed to that devil. She fled to the kingdom of Brea were she sat on the twin thrones with my father Élan Quinn. From there, my mother Elwyne was able to plan the assaults on Shau-ling and try to keep as many kingdoms on the side of the Light as possible until the *Coromor* was found. Unfortunately, the *Coromor* never did surface. With Logan and the other *Erieal* long since dead, there was no one with the power to seek him out. Many towns and kingdoms fell in the next few years, but they were never able to take down the walls of Brea. The last remaining tribe of the Moridon came down from the mountains and helped to defend the city. But, the time eventually came when the struggle looked futile, and Brea fell. All of the survivors of the battle were put into camps by the phasia. Every blood member of the former royal court was executed, and so were all of the remaining members of the Moridon. Elwyne was the first to die. She took up a sword in her own defense of her nine week old son and was cut down by the blade of the phase you call Taron. The child was then burned to show the dangers of impudence."

"By the Light," Midarin said shocked, "how did you survive?"

"You saved me, Midarin," Fion said curtly. "I said that there was no record of Midarin Rice. However, there is a record of a Midarin Sandar, but I am the only one who will remember you. You pulled me out of the ruins of the palace of Brea and nursed me back to health. Then, you led me to the sight of an underground resistance that you had formed. One of the members of the resistance was a man called Basille Mystic. He taught us all how to fight and how to kill the things in the army of the Shadow. But even his skill and power were not enough against that much force. The day came when they found us. As they were breaking through our fortifications, Basille pulled me back into the farthest chamber of this very cavern and told me that he had a great mission for me to accomplish. He said that something in the previous generation, this generation, had gone terribly wrong. Somehow, the *Coromor* did not pass on his legacy into the next generation, and the line of saviors was cut. This one mistake was enough to doom the world to eternal darkness. So, Basille summoned all of his strength, using forbidden abilities given to him by a secret ally named Emries to create a portal back to the past so that I could right whatever wrong had been done. As I stepped through the portal, Jeroch and his force broke into the chamber and tried to get me before the portal closed. The last thing I saw of my home was Basille being cut down."

Fion went silent for a long moment. The rest were silent as well. There was nothing really to say. But something wasn't right. Logan was the *Coromor* and Elwyne was carrying his child. If she survived the quest, she would have given birth to Logan's heir, and that heir was supposed to inherit the powers of the *Coromor* to save the next generation, at least that was what Logan had inferred from all of Emries double talk. The prophecies said that 'from the ashes of the Dragon, the third *Coromor* shall rise.' The first part could have meant anything, but the connotation was clear.

"Fion," Logan said finally, "answer me this. Right now, Elwyne is pregnant with my child. What happened to that baby? Why didn't that child have the powers of the *Coromor*?"

Fion stared Logan straight in the face. It looked as if he either didn't understand the question or that he couldn't believe that the question had been asked.

"Logan," he said in a shaky voice, "the baby survived and was born in Marcwell seven months after the final battle. He was raised as a member of the royal court, but he had no powers. No one knew why, but your son does not have the powers of the *Coromor*."

"What happened to my son?"

"You're staring at him."

Logan was shocked. That was why Fion looked so much like Logan. Fion was his son.

"But your name?"

"Father, after you died, and mother remarried, I had to take the name of my new king both as a show of loyalty and for protection. Even though I did not have your powers, I was still a liability to the forces of the Shadow. But maybe I can serve a purpose after all."

"I'm sure we'll find the problem, Fion," Logan said after a moment, "but let's wait till morning. The storm has cleared off, but we all need our rest for the tough tasks we'll probably have to endure tomorrow. Let's turn in for the night, and leave the mysteries for the dawn."

* * * * * * * * * * * *

Midarin pulled Gwydeon into the same alcove that she and Stone had found Fion in and smiled.

"What's this all about Midarin? There I was about to get a decent night's sleep for once and you wake me up and say that you have something important to tell me. Now, are you going to tell me, or are you just going to stand there grinning all night?"

"Okay," she said, "I'll tell you."

She just stood there for another moment, waiting to see what kind of reaction she would get out of her fiancé. He just kept staring at her, and when she started laughing, he smiled.

"This must be good news, because you never tease me this bad when we're not in bed."

"Well," she commented, "you're on the right track."

"Oh? This has something to do with being in bed together?"

He walked up to her and took her into his arms. After a long deep kiss she looked up at him and smiled.

"I'm pregnant."

Gwydeon's expression didn't change for a moment and then he laughed.

"That's wonderful. I can't believe this Midarin, you're wonderful."

He kissed her passionately again and then held her tight in his arms. About that time, they both heard soft but familiar rumbling footsteps coming toward them. When Stone entered the chamber, he stood silent for a moment and then spoke softly.

"F..R..I..E..N..D./.G..W..Y..D..E..O..N./.I..S./.H..A..P..P..Y./.A..T./.N.. E..W..S./.O..F./.F..R..I..E..N..D./.M..I..D..A..R..I..N.."

"Yes, Stone, I'm ecstatic. How did you know what she was going to tell me?"

"Stone there was the one who told me. He says that he can see things that we can't and now that he understands what it means to be pregnant, he could tell me that I was."

"Amazing. So, what are you doing up at this hour Stone?"

"S..T..O..N..E./.D..O..E..S./.N..O..T./.S..L..E..E..P./.B..U..T./.S..T..O.. N..E./.H..E..A..R..D./.F..R..I..E..N..D./.M..I..D..A..R..I..N./.A..N..D./.S..T ..O..N..E./.H..A..D./.S..O..M..E..T..H..I..N..G./.S..T..O..N..E./.N..E..E..D. .E..D./.T..O./.S..A..Y.."

"Okay, Stone," Midarin said puzzled, "what is it?"

"D..O./.R..E..M..E..M..B..E..R./.W..H..E..N./.S..A..I..D./.F..R..I..E..N.. D./.M..I..D..A..R..I..N./.D..I..F..F..E..R..E..N..T.."

"Yes."

"F..I..O..N./.D..I..F..F..E..R..E..N..T./.T..O..O.."

"Yes," Gwydeon said, "but Fion is from another time."

"That wouldn't make a difference to a Stone, Gwydeon. Remember, they don't have any concept of what time is."

She then turned to Stone and continued.

"How is he different, Stone?"

"D..O./.N..O..T./.K..N..O..W./.F..R..I..E..N..D./.M..I..D..A..R..I..N./.
D..O./.N..O..T./.U..N..D..E..R..S..T..A..N..D./.W..H..A..T./.S..T..O..N..E.
/.I..S./.S..E..E..I..N..G./.L..I..K..E./.F..R..I..E..N..D./.M..I..D..A..R..I..N./.
A..N..D./.C..H..I..L..D./.B..U..T./.D..I..F..F..E..R..E..N..T.."

"What's he talking about, Midarin?"

"The Stone can see things that we can't but most of the time they don't have the context to interpret what they see. Stone knew I was pregnant, but he didn't know what pregnant was or what he was seeing until I described to him what it meant to be pregnant and how humans reproduced. Until he figures out what it is that he is seeing, it doesn't mean much more to him than the fact that Fion is different from the other humans in the cave."

"F..R..I..E..N..D./.M..I..D..A..R..I..N./.U..N..D..E..R..S..T..A..N..D.."

"Yes, Stone," she said smiling, "I do understand. And don't worry, we'll keep a close eye on him. For now though, let's keep this between the three of us, because I don't want Fion to find out."

"U..N..D..E..R..S..T..A..N..D.."

"And since you don't sleep, you might want to keep an eye on him."

"Y..E..S.."

"And if he does anything that threatens one of us," Gwydeon said strongly, "I don't care what he says he is, I give you permission to do to him what you did to those Jeresei."

"T..H..A..N..K./.Y..O..U./.F..R..I..E..N..D./.G..W..Y..D..E..O..N./.L..O ..O..K./.F..O..R..W..A..R..D./.T..O./.S..M..A..S..H./.F..I..O..N.."

As the Stone turn and walked back to the camp, Midarin pushed herself back into Gwydeon's arms and snuggled close to him.

"You know," Gwydeon said after a moment, "I'm starting to like Stone."

"Yeah, he does grow on you."

Captured

Korrd sat uneasily on one of the twin thrones of Brea, waiting for some word from Gwillim. There had been some trouble in one of the lower chambers when Korrd ordered an inventory taken of all the assets of the kingdom. Jerrard and Arin, probably the only people besides Gwillim in the entire kingdom of Brea that Korrd could trust, had gone down into the unused sections of the palace to try and find out what was going on. Arin and Jerrard had returned nearly an hour later stating that they had encountered some interference from members of the Light Keepers. Korrd wanted to go himself, but Gwillim insisted that he could handle. After all, Gwillim was considered the anointed champion of the Dragon, and so if the Light Keepers were going to take anyone seriously, it was going to be Gwillim. But now, all Korrd could do was wait, and Korrd hated waiting. Moreover, Korrd hadn't had to depend on anyone but himself for a long time, and it would take some getting used to again. Moments later, rescuing Korrd from his growing restlessness, the door to the throne room opened and Gwillim walked in.

"Well, Gwillim," Korrd said standing, "what happened?"

"It's strange Korrd. I got down there, and the guards again refused to let us pass. They said something about the Proclaimer ordering them not to let anyone pass, not even the *Coromor*. As you yourself have said, it's not our prerogative to follow the orders of the Proclaimer, so Arin, Jerrard and I altered those orders."

Korrd smiled.

"Any losses?"

"Four members of the Light Keepers. After they fell, the others scattered."

"How many were down there?"

"Ten."

"Well," Korrd said rubbing the back of his neck slowly, "I wonder what's down there that is so important. The Proclaimer wouldn't lock me out of that place without good reason. There's something down there that he doesn't want me to find, and he's not afraid to let me know it."

Gwillim put his hands on his hips in a posture that looked very familiar to Korrd.

"Then shall we thwart the Proclaimer's plans or should we just sit here like good little boys?"

"Let's go," Korrd replied smiling.

The passageways of the palace narrowed greatly the further down they went. Before too long, Korrd and Gwillim had made their way down to the bottom level of the palace. The passages on the lowest level Korrd and his companion had to walk through single file, but after twenty or thirty feet, the passageway opened into a huge chamber. Arin and Jerrard waited in the chamber near a small door in the far wall of the chamber. The four dead Light Keepers were still on the floor of the chamber, and bother Arin and Jerrard had their weapons drawn to ensure that there were no further obstacles.

"Well gentlemen," Korrd said as he approached his two newest allies, "let's see what's behind door number one."

"We would love to Korrd," Jerrard said quickly, "but we've got a bit of a problem. You better come over here and take a look at this door."

Korrd shrugged and then crossed the chamber. As he approached the door, he saw what Jerrard was talking about. Around the edges of the door, symbols from the Old Tongue were carved into the wood of the door, and in the center of the door was a plate of metal that had the outline of a hand drawn onto it.

"Well, does anyone here speak the Old Tongue?" Korrd asked.

"I speak a little," Jerrard said, "it comes from instruction by my father early on in life, though I must say that I'm a bit rusty. These first symbols at that bottom left of the door mean power. These, mean hand. The rest read like gibberish."

"That's because you didn't remember that Old Tongue reads right to left, not left to right," a female voice said from behind them.

Korrd spun on his heels reaching for his sword. The voice was a very familiar one, and he tensed when he saw the woman's face. The memories that flooded into his mind were not his own, and they were all jumbled. For a moment he saw two faces, then they merged into one, and for a long moment the eyes held a power that made Korrd shiver down to his soul.

"Caris," Korrd said to himself.

"Erika," Jerrard said aloud as he approached the woman, "what are you doing down here?"

The name shook Korrd even further.

"I heard that the four of you were poking around down here, and I thought it would be a fine time to meet this Korrd and Gwillim that I have been hearing so much about."

Jerrard smiled and led the woman back toward the door.

"Korrd, Gwillim, I'd like you to meet my wife, Erika Mystic."

Gwillim was the first to greet her. He took her hand and kissed the back of her hand softly.

"Tis a pleasure to meet you my lady."

"And to meet you Gwillim," Erika replied, "and you are every bit as charming as Jerrard said you were."

"You are too kind."

Korrd stood there staring at Erika, trying to figure out the strange familiarity that he felt in his heart. There was something tugging at him inside, but he couldn't put the pieces together. Again the memories flooded, but they collided with one another in a way that made Korrd almost feel like someone or something was preventing him from seeing the whole picture.

"Korrd?"

He shook himself back into the real world and took Erika's hand lightly. At the touch of her flesh to his, the *Coromor* screamed bloody murder in his head, and Korrd pulled away as if he had been bitten. Arin was there to catch him as he lost balance, and the other three just stood transfixed.

"What's wrong Korrd?"

"I don't know Arin, but something isn't right. No offense intended my lady, but I keep feeling something inside my head and my heart. Every time I look I you I feel like I should know you already, but I don't know why. And just now as I touched your hand, I felt as though some dark and cold force was squeezing my heart. I can't make much sense of the rest of it right now, so, you will forgive me if I seem less than hospitable."

"I understand Korrd," Erika replied gracefully, "and I forgive you."

She held his gaze for a moment, and Korrd felt the moment stretch on for what seemed like forever, setting his soul on fire. When she finally turned back to the door, the burning stopped, but the ache didn't.

"Now, shall we see what this door really says?"

Gwillim waved a hand in the direction of the door.

"By all means."

Erika walked over to the door and began to read the symbols as they should have been read, right to left.

"It says, 'This is the Heart of Turbulent Light. Only the worthy may enter. Power makes the door appear. Only the *Coromor* holds the key.' Anyone have any clue what that means. I mean, the Old Tongue is usually cryptic, but this is a little more vague than usual."

"I think I understand," Arin said quickly. "The chamber is the Heart of Turbulent Light. It's like the grand throne room of the *Coromor*, at least, that's what I would guess. Since the chamber is locked, only the *Coromor* can unlock it, but being in the presence of those with the Power will make the door appear. No wonder the guards looked so frightened and puzzled when Jerrard and I got down here. When we came close enough to the door for it to recognize our powers, the door appeared and spooked the guards. Well, Korrd, do you feel up to unlocking a door for us?"

"I'll give it a shot."

Korrd walked slowly over to the door, still shaken by the unfamiliar and unwanted feelings that had rushed through him. He looked at the metal plate for a moment and then at his hand. Nervously, he placed his hand on the plate and waited. Nothing.

"Are you using your powers Korrd?"

"No, Arin, I'm not. I suppose that I should, shouldn't I?"

Before an answer could be given, Korrd focused his powers on the plate in the door. Under his fingers, lights began to appear. First the plate glowed red, then blue, green, and then clear. Then the plate turned black and then bright white. The white light began to get stronger and then suddenly flashed and enveloped everyone in the chamber in brightness. The next thing they knew, they were standing in the center of a new chamber. On the floor of the stone chamber was a circle that had been carved into the rock itself. From the outside of the circle, six long channels were carved that led to a small circle that was in the center of the larger circle. When Korrd took a step into the circle, a large flash of light blinded everyone. After a moment, the five of them regained their sight and noticed that they had been joined by a new arrival. He was a stranger to everyone but Korrd.

"Emries," Korrd said quickly, "what are you doing here?"

"You found the Heart of Turbulent Light my dear boy, and I came here to congratulate you. More than that, I wanted to congratulate you on gathering the remainder of the force that will be needed to topple Shau-ling's empire of Shadow once and for all."

Korrd took the compliment in stride, but there was something about the man who called himself Emries that Korrd did not trust. Perhaps it was because every part of him was telling him that Emries was good and true and that he should have been followed and trusted unconditionally.

"Thank you Emries. But, I don't understand why you are here and not the image of the first *Coromor*. This place has been sealed so long, but it is still filled with his power. I feel as though I'm swimming in it."

"The first *Coromor* is here Korrd," Emries said smiling, "you're looking right at him."

"You?" Korrd replied in disbelief. "But you are the Creator, how can you be the first *Coromor*?"

Emries folded his hands behind his back and moved in close to Korrd, his voice low so that only Korrd would be able to hear.

"There is too much to explain my dear boy, and not nearly enough time to begin. The journey is quickly coming to a close, and before too long, you shall be on your way to fighting the most difficult and most important battle of your young life. Now, listen to me carefully Korrd. Shau-ling's palace is known to the man called Basille. I have learned that his son is with you, and so I am sure that Basille will fight on your side. You will be able to learn the location of the palace from him. But, there is still danger. As we speak, Saurn is on his way back here to Brea, and he will be here sooner than he should be. After I leave here, you must return to the throne room and post a guard here so that he believes nothing has been disturbed. Do you understand?"

Korrd did understand. If Saurn learned the truth before Korrd was ready, everything could spin wildly out of control. As long as Saurn thought that he was in command, he could be managed.

"Yes, Emries."

"Now," he said raising his voice so that all could hear, "I know that you have all had some doubts as to who the real *Coromor* is, but this is proof that Korrd is the one that has been chosen to fight the battles of the gods in this generation of the prophecies. There is danger ahead, more than you could realize. In my attempts to save lives and keep promises, I myself broke a covenant of the gods. In doing so, the Creator has pushed a new player into the game. There are two new phasia afoot, a man and a woman. Logan and his party have already met these two with a measure of success. However they were unable to kill these new phasia. The twin phasia, Rael and Trece, were saved by the winged assassin known as Nightwing. Before you ask, I cannot describe this Nightwing to you, nor can I tell you anything more about his origin or I will break another covenant and expose you all to even greater danger. What I can tell you is that the circle is closing, and you are all on the right path. Logan and the others will be arriving tomorrow, so be ready. The Proclaimer has his own plans for Logan, and I'm sure that it will come down to a fight. Be strong and be proud. Long live the Light! Long live the People of the Dragon!"

With those last words, Emries disappeared. Korrd stood there staring at the place where Emries stood for a mere moment and then turned back to his companions. Despite it all, Korrd still felt empty and confused.

"Alright, you heard Emries. Saurn, the Proclaimer, is on his way back here, and is probably already in Brea. In case you haven't figured it out yet, the Proclaimer is a phase, and he will stop at nothing to kill the person that he thinks is the *Coromor*. That man is my brother, Logan. Now, we have to do everything to keep him safe, but we can't risk an open confrontation with Saurn until Logan gets here. It's not that I doubt your abilities, but the facts are clear. Arin, you didn't even know you had powers until yesterday, and Jerrard, as you said, your parlor tricks wouldn't be much good against a phase with many lifetimes of experience. I'm not even sure that I could handle Saurn by myself."

"Then we won't try," Gwillim interrupted. "I have gathered a personal guard from the officers that both Arin and I trust. I'll put them down here to guard the door to the Heart of the Turbulent Light. Korrd and I will get up to the throne room and wait for Saurn. Jerrard, you and Erika better go back to Arin's house and wait until we call you. I don't know how close a phase has to be to detect the powers of another, but just to be safe, we better get you to the palace. Arin, you mix in with the rest of the members of the Light Keepers and do what you can."

"Got it boss," he said smiling.

"Alright," Korrd said. "Let's go."

Korrd closed his eyes and channeled his powers into the chamber. A second later, the room filled with bright light and the five of them found themselves back in the chamber under the palace. The five then split off from one another, and Korrd and Gwillim sprinted up the flights of stairs back up to the throne room. Seconds after Korrd rested himself back on one of the thrones, the door to the throne room opened again admitting Saurn. He was no longer in the guise of the Proclaimer, but was back in his violet robes and full regalia.

"Ah, child," he said walking through the throne room, "you have done well to pull the entire kingdom under your reign."

"You have done much to that effect Lord Saurn," Korrd said trying his best to sound subservient. "What has happened to bring you back so soon my lord?"

"The *Coromor* is on his way here. Several of Shau-ling's attempts to kill him along the way have failed, and so it has come down to you and I. I have dispatched the Light Keepers to detain the one called Gideon so that we may interrogate him and make the entire group less powerful. If the Light Keeper's fail, you and I will have to finish them by ourselves. If they succeed, I will question this Gideon personally and then devise a plan to bring the rest of the *Coromor's* pitiful band to heel. Do not worry Korrd, we will have your brother in irons in our dungeon before too long."

That's what you think, Korrd thought to himself, *after this is all over, you'll be the one finding himself face down in a shallow grave.*

* * * * * * * * * * *

Logan and the rest of his group awoke early the next morning and were on the road just after dawn. Logan spent most of his time talking to Fion, trying to get as much information about the young man as possible. In the future that Fion described, he would not get the chance to know his son, and Logan wanted to take every opportunity he could to keep that from happening. To make themselves less conspicuous, Gideon used his powers to make Stone invisible to humans. Logan didn't know how Gideon did it, but it was very effective. There were times when Logan even forgot that Stone was behind them. By noon, they had covered a great amount of the distance were in the glade outside of Brea, well within sight of the town.

"What can we expect when we get there Midarin?" Logan asked.

"I don't know, Logan. It's been a long time since I've been in Brea, and with Korrd and the Proclaimer there, things have most likely changed a great deal. Lord Vorin was the man who was supposed to take over the throne from my parents. He is a vicious man who has nothing but conquest on his mind. My bet though is that he had yielded his place on the throne to Korrd, either through thoughts of advancement for himself, or because his vanity required his violent removal. Regardless of who is on the throne, the best way into town is by the front gate. There should be no guard in the tower, so unless we make our appearance know to everyone, we should have no problem."

"What," Gwydeon asked, "don't your people react to strangers in their town?"

"Brea is such a big place that strangers and visitors are an everyday occurrence. Don't worry Gwydeon, I doubt we'll see any interference until we get to the center of town."

"Why do you say that?" Pike asked.

"The palace of Brea stands in the exact center of town. Around the perimeter is a fortification that is always watched by members of the Light

Keepers. I doubt we'll have to deal with any of them until then. But, as much as I would like to have Stone with us for this, I think that he would hurt our chances of going through town unnoticed. Even though his is invisible, people can still run into him, and many of the paths in Brea are narrow."

"Okay." Logan said, considering Midarin's words. "Stone?"

"Y...E...S.."

"You will wait by the gate until I call for you."

"H...O...W../..W...I..L..L.../..F...R...I...E...N...D../..L...O...G...A...N../..C..A..L..L../..F...O...R../..S...T...O...N...E../..I..F../..H...E../..I..N../..B..I..G../..T...O...W...N..."

"I can talk to you with my thoughts. Do you understand what that means?"

"Y...E...S../..O...L...D../..M...A...S...T...E...R../..T...A...L..K...E...D../..T...O../..S...T...O...N...E../..L..I..K...E../..T...H...A...T..."

"Good," Logan responded. "So you will stay by the gate, away from the road until I call for you?"

"Y...E...S..."

That having been settled, the group crossed the plain and made our way up the long road to Brea, trying their best to look like they belonged exactly where they were. Midarin and Gwydeon rode at the fore of the group alongside Gwydeon while the rest lagged behind, keeping up the appearance of valets in the lord and lady's service. About three fourths of the way to the gate, they began to meet travelers along the road who were telling tales of the deeds of the *Coromor* in Brea.

"I heard that he has a woman by his side who is supposed to be a phase," one would say.

"I heard that the Proclaimer is a phase," responded another.

Many of the stories contained similar facts. While some of them might have been true, none of the people had proof for any of the stories. One of the stories they heard that Logan found almost impossible to believe was that Korrd had saved a young boy from the torture of the Light Keepers and covered him in the Dragon banner. That was said to be the way that Korrd proclaimed himself. The story seemed completely out of character for the Korrd that Logan had come to know over the past days. He was too hard and bitter; too interested in his own goals to risk his own life to save someone else. Logan wasn't even sure that he would have done what the stories had said Korrd did. Would he have risked the completion of the quest for one life? When they finally arrived at the gate, several members of the Light Keepers approached and started to question them.

"What business do you have here in Brea?"

Midarin drew herself up in the saddle and spoke proudly and evenly, though there was an edge to her voice that made it clear that answering the man's questions were a waste of her time.

"My name is Midarin Rice and these are my companions. I have come to seek an audience with the *Coromor* in an effort to have the name and title that were stolen from me by the jealousy of lesser men and women returned. I would respectfully ask for you to allow my companions and I to pass and to ask for an audience with the Dragon at his earliest possible convenience."

The guard looked Midarin over for a moment and then looked back toward the gate. Another man stepped forward. He was taller, and his face was crueler.

"Lord Vorin," Midarin said as the man approached. "I did not expect to see you out here today. I must say that I am surprised to see this many of the Light Keepers guarding the gate."

"The *Coromor* must be protected at all costs, Midarin. You know that we treat all dignitaries with equal reverence. The Dragon is no exception. As for your request, I have no choice but to let you pass. Were your parents still sitting on the throne, you would be killed for even attempting to set foot back into the town of Brea, but with the *Coromor* having seized control, the decision will be left up to him. I will inform him that you are here, and I would expect that you will stay at the *Royal Lodge* while you stay here in Brea."

"Yes," she answered, "I will."

"Good. Now, are any of your companions armed?"

"Yes," she answered curtly, "all of the members of my entourage are armed. I would ask that you allow them to keep their weapons while we are in town. Many of the townspeople may still hold me ill will, and my protectors would not be much good to me unless they were armed."

"I will agree to that, Midarin," Lord Vorin said after a moment, "but once you reach the inner ramparts, all of your weapons must be left at the gate before you will be allowed to enter the palace."

Midarin nodded her assent and started to walk past Lord Vorin. They all made it through the gate, but as Gideon attempted to pass, one of the Light Keepers took hold of him by the shoulder and pulled him aside.

"Where do you think you're going, you Alimidarian thief? Your arrest has been ordered by five of the towns in the kingdom of Brea, and you must be taken to the dungeon."

Vorin's face turned to a dour frown, and he rounded on Midarin quickly.

"Has this man been traveling with you Midarin?" Lord Vorin asked.

Midarin gave her best look of shock and revulsion.

"Yes, but he said that he was from Scalla. I had no idea that he was Alimidarian, nor that he was a thief. I apologize for trying to bring such a rogue into your town my lord."

Vorin's frown soften slightly, and he nodded in agreement, a gesture Logan found all too convenient.

"It is not your fault, Midarin. Rogues like this will do anything to pervert the will of the righteous, or those seeking redemption. We will deal with this criminal and make him pay for ever deceiving you."

Midarin put her hand on her heart nodded her head gratefully.

"Thank you again, my lord."

He nodded curtly and Midarin led the group further into the city of Brea. As soon as they were far enough away from the main gate, Midarin led them into a side alley where they could speak more openly without being overheard. Logan was quick to round on Midarin.

"Why did you let them take, Gideon?"

Midarin sighed.

"Logan, if I would have fought them for him, none of us would have gotten into town without a fight. Look at it this way, once you convince Korrd to join us, he can free Gideon from the dungeon and we can be on our merry way. Besides, I'm sure this isn't the first time that Gideon has ever been in a dungeon."

Logan nodded and they continued on in the direction of the *Royal Lodge*. This was definitely not turning out the way that Logan thought it would. Sinking back into the peace of his mind, Logan reached out and tried to touch Stone's mind.

Stone? Are you in position?

I…AM../..H..E..R..E../..F..R..I..E..N..D../..L..O..G..A..N../..S..A..W../.. W..H..A..T../..H..A..P..P..E..N..E..D../..W..I..T..H../..F..R..I..E..N..D../..G.. I..D..E..O..N../..W..A..N..T../..S..T..O..N..E../..H..E..L..P...

No, Stone. You stay where you are and I'll let you know if I need you. Do you understand?

Y..E..S..

Good. Wish us luck.

W..H..A..T../..I..S../..L..U..C..K...

Logan smiled to himself and shrugged of the comment. Stone was turning out to be a good addition to the force. If getting out of Brea turned out to require much more force than it took to get in, Stone would be invaluable. Inwardly Logan hoped that it wouldn't come to that.

* * * * * * * * * * * *

Gideon never had liked the scent of any dungeon that he had ever been in, but the one in Brea was the worst by far. The black stone walls were covered in this green slime that seemed to seep from the ceiling and ooze down the wall just fast enough to let you know it was moving. The whole place smelled of stagnate water and rotten eggs. It was the smell of rotting flesh that had been left in a closed chamber for a long time. Once long ago Gideon had been put into a cell with the remains of a thief. Gideon found himself watching the man decay, day after day, and finally he was able to use one of the dead man's bones to escape. Though it was not always the most pleasant experience, Gideon usually found one way or another to survive.

One of the guards shoved him hard in the back, and Gideon walked slowly down the steep stairs that led to the lower dungeon. Apparently, the guard didn't think that Gideon was moving fast enough, so he shoved Gideon again, sending him tumbling down the stairs. Gideon tried hard to focus his powers on the floor below in an effort to soften the impact, but for some reason, his powers didn't work, and he landed hard on the cold stone floor. As he pushed himself up to his knees, he noticed that another person was waiting for him in the dungeon.

"Welcome to my new lair, Gideon," Saurn said looking down at the fallen *Erieal* with a wide smile on his face. "It's been a long time since you were a little boy in Basille's kingdom."

"I wasn't scared of ye den Saurn, and I don't intend ta let ye scare me now."

"Oh," Saurn said stepping back toward the dungeon, "I don't intend to scare you Gideon, I intend to kill you." Saurn then turned to the guards and pointed at Gideon. "Bring him."

CHAPTER 20

Chapter XXI

Insurgence

"Your silence is maddening, little one," Shau-ling growled as he settled back onto the ivory throne which stood in the middle of his private torture chamber located deep inside the palace on the Island of Mist.

Elwyne glared into his serpentine eyes with all of the strength that she had left in her body, but that strength was slipping away as the seconds crept by. His torture had been excruciating, but the fact that he had relented just in those few seconds before she was about to break played in her mind. Part of her wanted to believe that she had beaten him, but she knew in her heart that he had only stopped in some attempt to prolong the perverse pleasure that he was deriving from watching her suffer. But still the voice in her mind swore and spat at the evil demon.

No one breaks a Tamerlane you soulless bastard. You may kill us or the ones we love, but you can never break our spirits.

However, she could not help but to admit that her iron will had almost slipped. Logan had taught her so much about harnessing anger without meaning to, and it was taking every little bit of that knowledge to keep from crying out in pain and frustration. She had seen the man she loved before all others in the world take all of his pain and anger and shove it deep inside to make himself stronger, and she could never remember that stone-cold face of his cracking one iota when it mattered most. But Elwyne had never imagined that she could accumulate the amount of hate inside of herself to stand up to the kind of torture that Shau-ling had inflicted upon her. Even remembering Emries' words and the warning about the wrath Shau-ling were to incur were she to die did not help her. Those words, and that was all they really were, could not shield her as the blade of Shau-ling's dagger ever so gently yet terrifyingly crept down the side of her cheek as his yellow eyes glared at her, searching for some chink in her armor that he could exploit. The steel of his knife lifted and was placed back on her cheek time after time, and the whole while Shau-ling stared at her with those eyes, just waiting for the fear to engulf her. But he began to get frustrated. He tried to goad her farther down the road of reckless abandon by bringing the blade of the dagger across her neck. Elwyne fully expected that Shau-ling would chance the wrath of the gods and the Creator, and she waited for that stinging pain to crawl through her flesh and free her from the world of shadows that held her. But that fatal sting never came. What he had done to her though was almost worse than death would have been. Death would be a release, but this hell never relented. The long lazy strokes of his blade caught and sliced the fabric of her clothes easily and before long, she had been stripped down to the thin white shift that had kept her warm so many nights before she found warmth and comfort in Logan's arms.

"So," Shau-ling said relaxing back on his throne, admiring his handiwork, "this is the warm caressing body that has been snuggling against my mortal enemy? This is the body that will give birth to his foul heir and the next generation's answer to my evil? You are nothing more than a child yourself, and with Logan you would aspire to be the queen of the world? Emries always did have poor taste in women, and I see that his successors have that same loathsome taste."

He was up from the throne again, and he approached slowly. His clawed hand scratched his cheek as his eyes examined every inch of her trembling flesh.

"Why he chose you I will never be able to guess my dear little one. I offered him two of my three daughters, but he would not take them. Your Logan is not a fool like those who proceeded him. Cedric was blinded by rage and morbidity and he easily fell into the bed of Caris, my then youngest daughter. And then there is Bryn and her many conquests over the years. Tis a pity that she was killed before she was able to add Logan to that list. She always did have a way with the rebellious types. Yet you tamed him, or is it that he tamed you? Yes, the woman Jasmen was ready to take your place, but I'm sure that he would have been much happier with a girl that he could control and make to do his bidding. And he would have had his way until her dagger was plunged into his chest. But you bested her before that blow could be struck. Still, girls such as you are so hard to come by, and it is a pity that you will be the one who would kill a king, and that you would do so through pride and ignorance."

His hands slapped her face back and forth as his insults stung down to her very soul. Yet he had been content with seeing her embarrassed. When his hand ripped the shift away from her body that hung to the wall supported by unseen shackles, his only aim was for utter humiliation. His fascination did not stop there. His talon-laden, scaly finger traced every inch of her naked flesh as she shivered under his gaze.

"Perhaps I am wrong in my estimation of your worth little one. Maybe you are too good for Logan," Shau-ling said on further reflection of the point. "Perhaps you and your unborn child should be given to Jeroch as a present. Under the careful watch of my eldest, your child could become a powerful agent for the Shadows, and you would be the lover of the second most powerful being on the face of the world."

Shau-ling hesitated for but a moment, though his serpentine eyes never left hers.

"He could try to take me," Elwyne said defiantly in as cold and heartless a voice as she could muster, "but you'd be without your eldest son by the dawn of the next morning. He may be a phase and your first-born, but a knife through the heart will still dispatch him as quickly as it would any other man."

Much to Elwyne's surprise, Shau-ling laughed. As soon as his laughter ceased, he lightly stroked her cheek while his other hand rested on her hip.

"Perhaps I should keep you for myself. I would most certainly be a better teacher for your son than Jeroch, and I would be sure that I could trust him to be loyal. Would you try to kill me as well, even knowing that such an attempt would be futile?"

"Logan will take care of you for me."

Again Shau-ling only laughed.

"Which? The killing or the futility? It seems that he is better at the latter than he is the former."

He looked her dead in the eyes again and saw that her will was as solid as ever. How this woman, this mere piece of frail flesh was able to confound his wits so was incomprehensible. Yet she held some sort of power over him. No matter what he tried, she would not relent, and he began to wonder inwardly who was really in control.

"Stubborn to the last. Have it your way," he said shaking his head. "Let us test this will of iron once again shall we? This is the last time that I will ask this question, and before the night is over, I expect to have the answer I want. Tell me everything you know about the man Gwydeon Sandar and the prophecies that my brother Emries made concerning him. Leave something out, and I will know. Lie, and I will know. Now, are we going to be sensible?"

She spat in his face.

"I thought not."

Shau-ling sighed and raised his hand back up to her face . . .

* * * * * * * * * * * *

...and the back of the hand connected so hard to Gideon's face that he thought he could have spit all of his teeth onto the floor at Saurn's feet. Blood poured from both corners of Gideon's mouth as he returned his stare to the cold violet eyes of his captor.

"I've waited a long time for this Alimidarian. You've been a thorn in the side of the phasia for a very long time, and now that you have joined with the Ranthall boy, that thorn has turned into a dagger. Make this easy on us all and tell me what you know about Basille's involvement with the Dragon."

Gideon hung his head and laughed softly to himself.

"Roast in hell ye flintin' fairy."

This time, the volley of violent, gut-wrenching slaps came not from the hands of the phase, but from the power of the Wind. Gideon had tried many times to reach for the green string of Earth since the moment he saw Saurn in the palace of Brea's dungeon. However, Saurn knew enough even in his madness to rob Gideon of his powers before he could react.

"Tell me what I want to know, Gideon," Saurn growled with the power of the Voice, "or I swear by the Blaze that I will tear you limb from limb."

"Ye will have ta get yer answers from somebody else den, Saurn. Ye could 'ave killed me anytime, but ye waited. Dis is more den Basille dat ye want isn't it? Ye want Shau-ling, and ye know dat controllin' Korrd ain't enough to pull it off. Tell me I'm wrong."

Saurn hesitated a moment and then laughed. It was an uneasy laugh however much as he tried to hide it.

"So, you know about my little toy? I thought that it would be fitting to use one Ranthall brother to dispatch the other, but I must admit that I had never dreamed that it would come down to such a grandiose showdown. Korrd's power is growing every day, and I believe that soon enough he will have enough control to destroy my father without so much as a stray thought. After the Dragon is dead, there will be nothing to stand between me and toppling the walls of Shau-ling's kingdom and taking the Throne of Power for myself."

This time Gideon laughed and looked into Saurn's face, smiling.

"And ye really believe dat, don't ye Saurn? Dat is a very interesting plan dat ye have dere, but ye seem ta be forgettin' three very important points."

"For an Alimidarian, you seem to be either very brave or very stupid. Let's see which."

Saurn released the bonds of Wind that held Gideon to the wall and used Wind to carry him over to the little chair on the other side of the room. As he sat, Gideon pawed at the cuts on his face and wiped the sweat off of his brow.

"Now Gideon," Saurn started as he sank into his high-backed, cushioned chair, "what are these glaring omissions that I have so clumsily overlooked?"

"First off," Gideon said trying hard to ignore the pain surging through his body, "what are ye going ta do about Pike and Talon? Together with Logan, dey should be enough to take out Korrd."

Saurn clicked his tongue and laughed.

"You overestimate their abilities my dear old friend. Pike Rhuiden and Talon Aielin could not stand against the *Chosen One* by themselves, and Logan has not yet proven to me that he knows all of the abilities he possesses when linked to members of the *Erieal*. Besides, Korrd can draw on their strengths as well as Logan can, and believe me, he is very well aware of what he is capable of."

"And da Jeweled Dragon's Flame?" Gideon fired as soon as Saurn finished speaking.

"I doubt that Logan knows how to use it. Besides, it takes all of the *Erieal* to activate the weapon."

Gideon rubbed his neck and smiled.

"Ye seem ta have all of dose points well accounted for Saurn."

"Your three points were pitiful, Alimidarian."

"I might agree wit' ye had I named me third point. And if ye have already counted on dis one, I'll gladly kiss a Jeresei and eat me own foot ta boot."

"I'm sure I can find you a Jeresei around here somewhere Gideon," Saurn teased, "and if you like, I'll even get you some salt for your foot."

Gideon just smiled and crossed his fingers. This was what he had been waiting for, and now it was time for the biggest gamble of his life.

"Saurn," Gideon began relaxing as much as he could in the chair, "let me tell ye a little story about da Ranthall family, and a little bit about why Basille has taken such an interest in me..."

* * * * * * * * * * * *

As the rain beat softly against the pane of glass on the far end of the royal bedroom, Korrd tossed and turned, trying to find a position that would let him sleep. He had not felt comfortable since he had gotten to Brea, but now thing were different. Something was wrong, but he could not place his finger on what. Then, right on cue, the door to his bedroom opened and Gwillim strode in.

"Korrd?"

"Don't worry, Gwillim," Korrd said shifting around and then sitting up, "I wasn't asleep anyway. What's wrong?"

Gwillim turned back to the doors and shut them quickly. Sensing the state of urgency, Korrd created a shield of Wind so that no one could hear their conversation even with the use of powers.

"Jerrard reported to me that your brother and his force are here in Brea. They are posing as valets in the service of Princess Rice and her husband. Jerrard said that he had a very familiar face but could not determine where he had seen it before."

"That would be Gwydeon Sandar," Korrd commented as he searched around the floor for his breeches. "Where are they?"

"They left a request for an audience with the guards at the front palace gate and then took rooms at the *Glass Tiger*. But there is a problem."

Korrd sighed as he pulled on his shirt and buckled the sword belt around his waist.

"There is always one problem or another, Gwillim. What's happened?"

"Under Saurn's orders, the guards at the outer gate took Gideon Viruci prisoner and then took him to the palace dungeon. According to Arin, Saurn is questioning him personally. Also, Saurn has left orders with the commander of the Light Keepers to seize your brother and the rest of his force."

Korrd shot up off the bed and was out the door with Gwillim right behind.

"When was this attack supposed to take place?"

"At dawn. Korrd, relax."

Korrd spun on his heels and stared Gwillim right in the face.

"Gwillim," Korrd said trying to make his voice sound as even and calm as humanly possible, "is there some reason that I should relax when you just told me that my brother and his friends are about to be ambushed by a group of trained killers?"

"I've already mobilized your security force, and there are enough of them to keep the Light Keepers busy while Arin sneaks in and wakes up your brother. None of us can be seen in the battle though, and I know you want to be there. Just remember what you told me about the walls having ears."

Korrd sighed again and then walked to the throne.

"You're right, Gwillim, but I want you there anyway. If I know my brother half as well as I think I do, he'll finish off the Light Keepers and then storm the palace looking for me. You have to convince him that I'm trying to help."

"Korrd," Gwillim said fingering the hilt of his sword nervously, "I don't really think that Logan will listen to me, especially if the Light Keepers press him as hard as they press everyone else."

"Then take Jerrard with you for insurance. He may not know much about his powers yet, but maybe it will make Logan sit up and take notice of the situation. He may think twice when faced with the Fire Brother and Basille's son."

"By your word, Lord Dragon," Gwillim said as he bowed and then left the room.

Korrd watched him go and then looked back at the bed. He knew he wouldn't be able to get to sleep, and there was no real reason to try. It took only a moment to pull on a shirt and strap his sword around his hip. There was a secret passage that lead from the royal bedroom back to the throne room, and so he slipped quietly into the throne room and Korrd relaxed back onto the throne taking some solace in the peace and darkness. As he scratched his newly shaved chin, the doors to the throne room opened and a woman walked quietly into the room.

"Not tonight dear," Korrd said as he rubbed his temples madly trying to make his head stop pounding, "I have too much on my mind."

"I know you do, Korrd," the woman said softly as she continued to stroll down the center of the room toward the throne, "and that's why I'm here. We have a little unfinished business you and I."

Korrd leapt to his feet and clutched the strand of Fire quickly. With a thought, all of the torches in the room lit instantly and the shadows that hid the woman's face disappeared. The being in the back of Korrd's mind screamed, and the traces of red in the woman's hair ignited Korrd's memories in circles of fire.

"I know you," Korrd said as he tried to work through the jumbled images in his head. "No, the *Coromor* knows you."

The woman laughed and approached slowly, the tight red dress clinging seductively to every curve of her body as she moved.

"I should hope so Korrd," she said finally, "after all, you and that voice in your head are one and the same."

The woman did not slow her approach one iota and seconds later stood with her hands on Korrd's chest as she looked him square in the eyes.

"All of the memories I have of you are not my own," Korrd said as he tried to remain calm. "And I can't even remember your name."

"Then perhaps we should try to jog that memory of yours."

Korrd began to speak, but was cut off as the woman's lips met his.

* * * * * * * * * * * *

Nighttime was quickly becoming one of Logan's least favorite times now that Elwyne was gone. A few times when he had slept, he could not help but reach out in the night to hold her and find that she wasn't there. There were even times when Logan would swear that he could feel her snuggling up against him in the night when the cold wind would blow. The touch of her warm body against his was something he could never forget or make his skin neglect. As Logan lay in the bed in the inn called the *Glass Tiger*, his mind could not be pulled away from his missing love. Playing the mute valet and learning all of the things that servants could hear in a day got him through the bustling daylight hours, but when the sun went down and they were told to retire to their rooms, the new loneliness crept back into Logan's heart. Midarin and Gwydeon had managed to get the other members of the group their own rooms on the same floor as the couple stayed without causing too much suspicion. She said something to the mistress of the house about needing 'constant attention' as was her right under Breaen law. The mistress laughed and allowed them to have the two rooms adjacent to Gwydeon and Midarin's.

"What is this right of constant attention under Breaen law?" Gwydeon had asked.

"As a member of the royal house and namely the Princess and future ruler of the kingdom, arranged marriages are expected," Midarin explained. "Sometimes the matches were not favorable, as in my case. But, according to law, after the consummation of the marriage, the bride may have any amount of lovers at any time, and there is not a thing that her husband can do about it legally."

Gwydeon had balked severely at that comment, and seeing him stumble, Pike chimed in.

"Well Gwydeon, after you two are officially married under Breaen law, you're going to have to put some heavy locks on the door, or be more of a man than you have been."

Talon and Logan both roared at the comment, but before Gwydeon could get a good grip on his hilt, Midarin eased his hand back and laughed.

"Don't worry Gwydeon," she had said. "When you and I are King and Queen, there are a lot of Breaen customs that I would like to see go. From all that I have seen and heard from you Aradonians, I might think of adapting some of their customs to fit our people."

Gwydeon smiled a little and then let himself enjoy the humor a little. When Talon opened his mouth to comment, Logan knew it wouldn't be good.

"What if the Queen is an undesirable match? Doesn't the King get to take lovers too?"

Midarin growled and said something very unladylike under her breath. Logan had honestly thought she was kidding about the custom until he saw the mistress of the house unchain the connecting doors between their rooms.

It was still rather early when Logan decided to turn in, and by early, it was before sunrise. When Logan went up to his room for the night, the common room was still packed, and Pike and Talon were doing their best to act like gentlemen. Logan had just laid his head down onto the thin pillow when the room began to feel wrong. When he opened my eyes and sat up, the walls of the room glowed red, and there were two men standing in his doorway. At first Logan thought it was Pike and Talon, but the mistake was revealed when he saw the symbol of the Dragon on each of their shoulders. Logan threw himself out of bed and instantly reached for the red string of Fire. The stream of flame leapt from Logan's outstretched fingers a moment later, and the two strangers flew for cover. In the flickering light of the flame though, Logan had seen their faces, and it triggered something in his memory. He had seen those faces before, but he didn't know where.

"Logan," one of the men shouted, "please. We're here to help you."

"Help me die I bet," Logan countered pulling the Dragon Sword from the scabbard under the bed. "If you truly do know me, then you know that there is no way that the two of you can defeat me by yourselves. Surrender now and tell me what you want or I'll be forced to kill you."

One of the men stood from where he dove to avoid the flame attack and spoke.

"I'm Jerrard Mystic, Basille's son, and my companion is the fourth member of the *Erieal,* Arin Domae."

The names sparked Logan's memory even further. He had seen their faces when he had stumbled on the Heart of the Turbulent Light. Basille's son was not what Logan expected at all. His eyes were his father's but the rest of his body was stocky, and he wore his hair very short. Arin Domae looked exactly like a soldier should. The broad chest and large arms made him an impressive sight, and in full armor, he would have been very intimidating.

"What are you to doing here? And why would you try to sneak up on me when you damn well knew what I would do when I felt your presence?"

"There's no time for subtlety, Logan," Arin said looking out into the hall. "Any minute now, a force of Light Keepers is going to attack under the orders of the phase Saurn. They were sent here to capture or kill you and your companions. Your brother sent us here to make sure that you were warned and to help you fight if it came down to that."

"Oh it will come down to a fight alright," Logan said ignoring the fact that his brother was trying to help slaughter the soldiers that Saurn had no doubt ordered Korrd to send. "But if you are truly here at my brother's behest, you can tell me why he's trying to help."

"Now's not the time, Logan," Jerrard countered. "Korrd will tell you when we get you into the royal palace."

"Alright," Logan conceded. "How are you two with your powers?"

"The only help we'll be in that department is for you to draw on our strength. I only know parlor tricks, and Arin just found out two days ago that he was an *Erieal*."

"Wonderful. Well at least you have swords."

"The other man Korrd sent is named Gwillim," Arin interject as he led Jerrard and Logan through the door. "If you see a man in red armor hacking at the enemy that will be him."

Logan made mental note of the fact and plunged into the crowded common room with sword drawn and the two strangers following behind. As the rest of the remaining People of the Dragon gathered their wits and Jerrard explained the situation, Logan began to wonder if he could trust the strange pair. Fion was the first to chime in and denounce the new arrivals.

"I can't believe that you are listening to this rabble, father," he said in disgust. "Korrd is your enemy, you've said it yourself a hundred times. And now you're going to blindly follow his assassins into battle so that when your back is turned they can plunge their daggers into you. Kill them now, and then we can storm the palace and take care of your brother."

"I don't know who you are boy," Jerrard said reaching for his sword, "but you've just made a mistake by accusing me of being a murderer. However, I gladly make you out to be telling the truth if you'll just open that mouth of yours again."

Without a thought Logan stepped in front of Jerrard.

"You should watch your tongue Jerrard," Logan said growling. "If you so much as look at Fion the wrong way again, I swear that I will gut you and hang you from a pole in front of Basille's palace. The same goes for the lot of you. I know you don't trust him, and I've heard all of you talk. Now is not the time for us to be divided."

Jerrard drew his sword and stuck it in the floor.

"You want to kill me Logan?" he said defiantly. "Go ahead. But think about this. If you kill me, you'll have to kill Arin, and Gwillim, and Korrd, and Basille, and all of the others who would gladly support you. Now I don't care what this boy means to you, but I know what Shau-ling's permanent demise means to me. Now let us help you, or kill me now."

He dropped to one knee and bowed his head. Part of Logan wanted to kill him for the insults and for the possibility that he was lying, but the other told him that he was being paranoid. Paranoia had gotten Logan far, but he had also seen what it did to him in Barer at the hands of Caris. Logan looked over his shoulder and saw Fion's angry face staring down at Jerrard. Logan could feel the hatred radiating off the young man, and if the places had been reversed, Fion would have already stuck Jerrard down. For a man who was dedicated to correcting the mistakes of the past, it seemed that he was alienating everyone that could have helped Logan succeed in the task ahead. Was that where everything had gone wrong? Had Logan been betrayed by one of his own? Or was it an alliance with Korrd that had brought the world crumbling down? All that remained were questions, and Logan hoped that soon they would have answers.

"Get up and take your sword, Jerrard," Logan said turning toward the door. "We have an ambush to walk into and I need every sword that I can muster at my side."

The Hunter Becomes the Hunted

The Light Keepers apparently thought that they were quire clever when they planned out their assault. The *Glass Tiger* was on the far end of one of the more secluded streets near the royal palace. Thieves had a habit of hanging around the dimly lit corners, and according to Midarin, that was why there were very few guests that patronized the *Glass Tiger*. The fact that the Light Keepers had this battle planned out well was not what bothered Logan. All of this time they had been most effective when fighting as a cohesive unit, but now several wildcards were thrown into the mix. First there was Logan's son, Fion. From his own words, he had proclaimed himself a better than average swordsman, and if he learned his skills from Basille and Midarin, Logan was sure that his boast was well justified. Then there was Jerrard Mystic. He had admitted both to being the son of a phase, even though that phase happened to be Basille, as well as being one of Korrd's agents within Brea. Both of those facts made Logan slow to trust him, but the fact that he had offered his sword so willingly made Logan feel the need to respect him. The last new player was Arin Domae. Again, he was an admitted member of Korrd's army. But the one fact that forced Logan to trust him was the fact that he was the fourth member of the *Erieal*. Gideon may have hid secrets about his past and his connections to the phasia, but he had never gone against Logan's wishes or proven himself to be a traitor. Dissension was back in the ranks, but this time it seemed to have a lethal edge.

If this were a normal battle situation, Logan would have sent Gideon out to verify the information that Jerrard and Arin had provided and also to provide accurate intelligence about the movements of the enemy. Unfortunately, he didn't have that luxury. Fortunately Logan still could feel Gideon's power, and as he opened his awareness to Arin, Logan could feel the power inside him grow until he thought he was going to explode. The *Coromor* inside of Logan was singing with elation at the feeling of being whole again, and it was all he could do to keep it from pulling another stunt like it had back in Dreamscape after his arm had been severed. The only problem was that Logan could not resist the temptation to see how far he could push the envelope of control. As he began to open up his awareness to the powers of the four *Erieal* and Jerrard, Logan began to feel the presence of everyone and everything around him. The more he pulled upon the power, the clearer the picture became in his mind. Within a matter of seconds, Logan was able to lay out an entire plan of attack. It was as though suddenly all of the tactical knowledge he could ever want was there at his fingertips. He thought he had it all figured out when Arin brought forth an idea that Logan had overlooked in his assessment of the situation.

"Logan," he said pulling Logan back into the common room, "Gideon is still down in the dungeon. Don't you think that some attempt should be made to rescue him?"

"I don't know, Arin," Pike replied, "it seems awful risking splitting up the party. Every time that we've tried it in the past, we very nearly wound up dead, and most often only escaped by the skin of our teeth, if by that much. Odds are that our luck is bound to run out sometime. Besides, our numbers aren't what they were."

"Sorry Pike," Logan said after a moment, "I have to disagree with you on this one. If Saurn is as powerful and as insane as Jerrard and Arin led me to believe, then we are going to need Gideon when we get to the throne room and Saurn reveals himself for what he is. Gideon has had training that none of us has, and for all we know, he may have dealt with Saurn in the past, and we will be able to draw on him for information. Every little bit helps when it comes down to fighting a phase."

"But Logan," Gwydeon interjected, "Arin also said that Saurn was personally questioning Gideon. Wouldn't it be safe to assume that whoever goes after him would tip our hand?"

"Gwydeon's right," Talon commented. "Saurn would have the rescue party for breakfast, and then you would have no chance in defeating him. Better to be down just one man instead of five or six."

"Saurn is not just going to wait around down in the dungeon," Jerrard said shaking his head. "Korrd said that he would see to it that he was in the throne room when we arrived with you and your friends. He is going to send word that the ambush failed and that you were on your way to settle the score personally. Arin knows all the secret passages and he can take a team in and get them out before Saurn even knows what happened. Then they can meet us outside the throne room."

Pike lowered his eyes and picked at the golden dragon etched into the blade of his ax.

"All of this planning is well and good, but what if Gideon's dead by the time we get there. I don't like to think about it anymore than the rest of you do, but what are the chances that Saurn is going to leave Gideon alive after he's done questioning him?"

"I'd say the chances were pretty damn good," Gwydeon remarked in frustration.

Logan had seen Gwydeon mad before, but this was something else. Gwydeon was tired of all of the fighting and bickering that was going on, and Logan knew he had thought all of this out and was just waiting for an opportunity to point out the problems with the plans. He had a gift for keeping a level head when the rest of the group were just running on pure emotion and working within the heat of the moment. That's why Gwydeon had the best chance of surviving the growing madness. Or at least he should have in theory, but according to Emries, theories weren't much good when it came to the fate of the *Coromor* and his followers.

"Think about it everyone. The reason Saurn latched himself to Korrd was because Saurn wants to take over control of the army of the Shadow. It isn't about the *Coromor* anymore, not with him. He is making the king of all takeover attempts. With the *Chosen One* at his side, Saurn has a chance to kill Shau-ling. But, with a member of the *Erieal* at his side, that chance greatly increases."

"That's crazy," Talon said without thinking, "why would Gideon ever follow a pha...oh. Never mind."

"Yeah, Talon," Gwydeon answered grudgingly shaking his head, "that's exactly what I was thinking. But see, it wouldn't even need to be treachery. As long as a member of the *Erieal* is alive and in the general vicinity, his powers can be drawn on. Thus, Korrd and Saurn would have more power at their disposal the more *Erieal* they can draw on."

"Therein lies an advantage," Midarin added.

Apparently, she and Gwydeon had been on the same line of thought. That had been happening more and more lately, and for some reason Logan found it both distracting and almost annoying.

"Saurn will want Logan dead, but if can leave the battle with Pike and Talon alive, he will have more of an advantage. He won't try to kill them unless he absolutely has to."

"The same goes for Arin and Jerrard," Gwydeon said finishing the thought.

"He doesn't know about us yet," Jerrard said.

"But he will when we get to the throne room," Logan replied. "I was able to tell that the two of you had power the instant that you were in my line of sight. I'm willing to bet that you both found the same to be true when you first met Korrd. With a member of the phasia, I'm sure this ability is much more advanced and with lifetimes of practice..."

"We get the point Logan," Pike interrupted. "No sense in beating it into the ground. Well, it seems as if our strategy is well laid out, but I still don't trust Jerrard."

"I have to agree with Pike, father," Fion offered for the first time. "He may be Basille's son, and he may not. There is no way to tell what line he is touching, or what his motives might be. If a rescue attempt is going to be made for Gideon, let Jerrard and Arin go after him, and the rest of us will attend to the more important task of finding Korrd and getting out of here alive."

"Look," Jerrard said stepping toward Fion, "you don't like me, and I can't say that I'm too crazy about you either. You could die in the first battle for all I care, but I have a job to do. I promised Korrd that I would keep an eye on Logan and watch his back until we get to the throne room. I intend to keep that promise. Now, Arin should lead the party that goes after Gideon, because he is the only one who knows the tunnels and passages. Those members of the party who are stealthy and who don't have any powers will be the best ones to go with him. Gwydeon and Midarin are obvious choices because of Gwydeon's ability to fight against great odds, and Midarin's ability as a sniper. The rest of us should help Logan get to the palace. Trust me when I say that Talon, Pike, Logan, and Gwillim will be enough to take care of the Light Keepers, even without the help of Korrd's security force."

"And you actually believe that your choices for these groups will be honored?" Fion asked with his lips curled into a frown. "My father may have been wise enough to spare your life for the time being, but if you think that he will accept your strategy now, you have another thing coming. At this point you are making it obvious that you are leading us into a trap, and your words are acting as a noose. Once our force is split, the Light Keepers and Saurn will most likely attack you, father, and then once we are out of the way, Gideon, Gwydeon, Arin, and Midarin will be easy pickings."

"Sorry to say it Logan," Pike said as he rotated his grip on the handle of his ax, "but I'm really starting to hate Fion and doubt his sanity. Jerrard's plan is sounder than any other one that I could come up with, and I'm sure that Gwydeon would agree with me."

"I would at that," Gwydeon chimed in. "Midarin and I will go with Arin. The rest of you should have no trouble. This problem with Fion can go on later."

Before Logan could say anything in response, Arin led Gwydeon and Midarin out the door of the inn and around toward one of the secret passage. From that point on, the common room was silent. Fion's scowl told the story of his feelings, but as for Jerrard, Logan could not get an accurate impression of what he felt. He was not left too much time to mull over the situation in his mind because Pike and Talon were the next people out the door, followed quickly by Jerrard, and Fion. Finally Logan followed, his heart and mind filled with a growing conflict.

* * * * * * * * * * * *

The problem with these paths is the fact that they are too damn small to maneuver through.

That was the tamest thought that came to Gwydeon's mind as Arin led he and Midarin through the winding streets of Brea. He knew that Midarin knew the paths as well as Arin, and that she could probably have been a better guide to Logan than anyone else in the party, but there were two factors that almost precluded the decision that she would go with him. The first was that in a secret operation like this one where stealth is the most important factor, her bow would probably be the one thing that helped the mission to succeed. The other was the fact that she was also a great threat to Fion. It would only take a single arrow through the throat to silence him forever, but the funny thing was that this thought came to mind as they were leaving Logan's company. There was something very wrong about the man who had called himself Fion Quinn, even without the warning that Midarin and Gwydeon had received from Stone. It fit all too well. Here was this son who came from the future to warn Logan of some mistake that he had made. If this Fion was a phase in disguise, it was obvious that he was trying to destroy Logan's confidence. Gwydeon had to admit to himself that who or whatever this Fion was, he was finishing the very plot that Caris had started when she took the guise of Leane. However, that time, Gwydeon was the target of the attack, as well as Elwyne, Pike, and Talon. This time, this Fion character had targeted Logan and Korrd directly, and it was almost as if the tension was building to the point that a duel between the Ranthall brothers was eminent. Gwydeon had had these concerns for a while, but it wasn't until Jerrard and Arin made their appearance that some of the pieces began to fall together. His words and attitude were too pointed. It was as if he knew the entire situation with Korrd, even though there was no way that anyone could know who or what

Korrd was. Korrd wasn't even supposed to be alive. Really, Fion had never said one thing about Korrd's role in this entire plot except the fact that Logan had to kill him. But who would want Korrd dead? He would be a great asset to the forces of the Light if he were to come over to Logan's side, and that would be a great blow to Shau-ling. Then again, Shau-ling never had control of Korrd; that control had always fallen with the phase named Saurn.

As Gwydeon thoughts trailed off about Fion and Korrd, Arin ducked around a corner and pulled up a grate in the ground. No words were spoken as the three adventurers ducked under the heavy metal plate and climbed down into the sewer system of the city of Brea.

The sewers were dank at best, and the smell that rose up from the water was nearly enough to make Midarin lose what little remained of the dinner she had eaten the previous night. Luckily there was a narrow ledge along the wall so that the three of them did not have to wade through the dirty water. So, the three of them edged slowly down the narrow path until they reached a large smooth recess in the wall. Arin hesitated for a moment and then pushed on a small rock in the upper right corner of the recess until the wall began to slide backward. Within seconds, a new passageway was in clear view, and this passage was dry and well-lit by torches. Arin didn't say a word and ducked into the passage. Midarin turned and shrugged at Gwydeon before she followed their newest companion into the passageway. Gwydeon could not help but finger the hilt of his sword for a moment or two before he entered the passage. As more time passed, Gwydeon was becoming more uneasy with the entire situation. It wasn't Arin that he was distrustful of, in fact, Gwydeon had this strange faith in the man who was supposed to be the fourth member of the *Erieal.* In the back of his mind where some of the more illogical thoughts seemed to roam, Gwydeon secretly thanked Arin for finding Midarin in bed with that guard all those years ago. Had Arin not done his job, Gwydeon would have never had her in his life. He made a mental note not to ever divulge that little piece of information, but he knew that he owed Arin one.

The passage diverged at one point and Arin hesitated and then stopped at the fork.

"The path to the left leads down to the dungeons. After we rescue Gideon, we'll come back here and take the path to the right. It leads to the throne room."

Gwydeon stopped and looked down the length of the right hand passage. Midarin glared at him after a moment when she realized that the knuckles on his right hand were white because he was gripping the hilt on his sword so hard.

"Don't even think about it Gwydeon," Midarin admonished, "Logan will deal with Korrd soon enough. There's no reason for you to rush up there and get yourself killed."

"You don't understand Midarin," Gwydeon said shaking his head. "Fion's got Logan so brainwashed that it will come down to Korrd killing Logan. Then, after Logan's dead, Pike and Talon will rip Korrd apart. Or, Korrd will destroy all of us. Logan is a good swordsman, but I trained with Korrd, and he challenged me on a consistent basis, that's much more than I can say for Logan."

"Logan has his powers," Midarin commented.

"I hate to jump into the conversation," Arin said shortly, "but Korrd has his powers too, and not only that, he has had a phase teach him everything he knows. Trust me when I say that his powers are very lethal."

Gwydeon frowned but nodded.

"Arin's right. Now, if I can stop this stupidity from happening then I want to try. You know me Midarin, if there is even a chance that I can . . ."

Midarin put up a hand and shook her head.

"Go, Gwydeon. The only way that I could stop you would be to kill you, and I don't think that would leave any of us in a good position. Besides, I know I couldn't live without you. Just remember, when the fire starts flying, get your cute butt down and let the people with the powers take care of their business. You remember what happened last time."

Gwydeon nodded, kissed her lightly on the lips and then raced off down the right hand passage. After a moment, Midarin turned back to Arin and sighed.

"Ok Arin, looks like it's just you and me now."

Arin nodded and started down the path toward the dungeon. Arin had had this same dream many nights not long after Midarin had been banished from the kingdom. In the dream, Midarin was to be thrown in the dungeon, and then to be killed the following morning in a public execution. Feeling remorse for his role in her punishment, Arin took to the secret passage and rescued Midarin. But, while they were making their escape up this very passageway, Arin felt a dagger stab him in the back. As he rolled over and felt his life slipping away, he looked up into the eyes of a woman who had taken her life back from the man who stole it. That was a dream that he had banished to the farthest reaches of his mind, thinking that he would never see Midarin again. But now, as they walked together, he could not help but revisit those old fears. At one moment, he thought he heard a sword being drawn, and he stopped abruptly, turned, and reached for his sword. Midarin's face wore the shock of the situation, and she took a step back.

"What's wrong Arin?" she asked slowly.

"I heard you draw your sword, and..."

"And you thought that it was going to be buried in your back. Don't be surprised, Arin, you have been stiff as a board since you first saw me."

"Then you don't..."

"Oh, I still hate you," Midarin replied lightly, "but I know that you are good for the quest, and besides, I've gained a lot since you had me expelled from my kingdom. Now, let's stop all this foolishness and get Gideon out of that hole in the earth."

Arin nodded and led the way to yet another series of small grates in the floor. At one of the grates, Arin pushed a finger to his lips as a signal for Midarin to stay silent. Midarin nodded and also looked through the grate. There below them they saw Gideon, stripped to the waist, covered with bloody cuts and scrapes, tied to a chair. Before him was a man dressed in all violet robes, holding a long staff in hand. Arin looked up at Midarin and mouthed the word 'Proclaimer'. Midarin nodded and looked back down at the situation.

Saurn stood in front of Gideon shaking his head. Gideon didn't seem to react to anything that Saurn did, and as Midarin looked closer, she could see that Gideon's eyes were closed. At that point, Saurn raised his staff and struck Gideon across the face with it. Gideon shook his head violently and spit blood onto the floor at Saurn's feet.

"Still the proud and resilient servant of the Dragon aren't you, Gideon? I'm surprised that you are as strong as you are. I had always been told that Alimidarians were cowards and weaklings, more interested in their graft than any form of self-preservation. But your strength has caused me to rethink that. Oh, and as to your little confession earlier, I have considered it, and I must say that I have not laughed so hard in all of my life. How did you expect me to believe that you were Bryn's son by way of Aerith Seth, and that Basille knew all along that Korrd and Logan were the *Coromor* and the *Chosen One*? Hopefully my plan will continue, and Logan and Korrd will kill one another trying to sort out the truth."

Gideon looked up with a look of horror written across his face.

"Oh," Saurn said laughing. "You think that I was a fool like Shau-ling? No, Gideon, I knew all along that I was in possession of the *Coromor*. And yes, I could have killed him at any time. But what purpose would that have served? This way, Logan will have to face his brother, and I will be rid of both Ranthall brothers in a single stroke. Besides, using Korrd for my purposes has made the War for Power too easy to win. Once I eradicate the Ranthall brothers, I'll kill Jeroch and then Shau-ling."

"But without the *Coromor* of the prophecies..."

"Shau-ling is vulnerable. His own creations have proven that they can turn on him. He will no longer be protected by the Creator's words, and anyone in this world could destroy him. But that's hardly common knowledge is it? Then, once I destroy Shau-ling and take the throne, no one will be able to touch me."

Saurn laughed maniacally and started out of the room. As he reached the door of the dungeon, he turned back toward Gideon and the guards that were apparently behind him.

"I now go to meet with my pupil for the last time, and to watch as his family's fate is sealed. I will spare you the pain of living in my world, Gideon, and so I now give to order for your death. Be thankful, Gideon, that you won't be alive to see everything that you have worked so hard for be destroyed in a matter of seconds."

At that Saurn laughed loudly again, and the guards moved up into Midarin's and Arin's line of vision. Two of the guards were armed with swords, while the other had his ax ready to lop Gideon's head off. Arin looked up at Midarin with a question written on his face. Midarin held up two fingers and pointed at her sword. Arin nodded and held up three fingers. Midarin nodded and loaded her bow. Arin silently counted to three and then stomped on the grate, sending it crashing to the floor. The man with the ax jumped back out of the way, and the first of Midarin's arrows claimed one of the sword-wielding men in the chest. Arin jumped through the now open grate and landed just in front of Gideon. The second swordsman ran toward Arin, but Midarin's second shot came fast enough that he dropped to the floor a matter of inches from his striking distance. As Arin reached for his sword, the man with the ax chopped downward. Arin was able to roll out of the way and then bury his sword in the larger man's gut. The man groaned as his life slipped away and then fell to the floor with a crash. A few seconds later, Midarin jumped down to the floor of the dungeon and help Arin cut the bonds that held Gideon.

"Thanks to ye, Midarin," Gideon said after a moment of pawing the cuts on the side of his mouth. "Who's yer friend?"

"This is Arin Domae, a friend. Korrd sent him to us to keep Logan from getting killed."

Gideon's face and body froze. Midarin looked closely at him for a moment and tried to read something in his eyes.

"Where's Logan now?" Gideon asked forcing his tired body to stand up.

Midarin reached in to him and braced him against her body. Gideon accepted her help for a moment, but once he found his balance, he pushed her arms away.

"He's up with the rest of the party trying to force their way into the palace," Midarin answered. "Saurn sent the Light Keepers to kill Logan, but thanks to Korrd we got wind of the ambush and have taken steps to make it work in our favor."

Gideon looked up at her and then started toward the door of the dungeon.

"We have ta get ta Logan before he can get into da palace. Saurn has dis whole damn place ready for a war between Logan and Korrd, and believe it dat if Logan and Korrd get in the same room together, dere's going ta be trouble."

"Then let's get back into the tunnel and follow Gwydeon."

"Gwydeon?" Gideon asked.

"Yes," Midarin continued. "He had a bad feeling about this whole situation, so he went to find Korrd on his own."

"Well," Gideon said as Arin help him up to the tunnel, "I hope he's still alive when we get ta da throne room."

* * * * * * * * * * * *

Gwydeon walked quickly down the passage that was supposed to lead him to the throne room and to the man he had known nearly all of his life. Korrd was the one constant in his life from the very beginning, but it was also one facet that he would like to have removed from his past. He was old enough to remember the day when Korrd left the Ranthall house after the fight with his father, but then the next year, Korrd returned to find that he was supposed to be dead. The first person Korrd sought out was Gwydeon. Gwydeon always thought it was strange that Korrd would have come to look for him, but since the beginning of this quest, Gwydeon began to believe that things happened for a reason. Emries had said that there was something special about Gwydeon, and maybe that was the reason that Korrd felt so drawn to him. However, Logan was growing in popularity in the town, and people were known to talk, so Korrd's visit had to be kept a secret. It all started innocently enough, Gwydeon and Korrd trained together in the ways of the sword. Logan's father had taught Gwydeon everything he knew, and so in a way, Gwydeon was fulfilling the circle of father to son learning. As the years went by, it became harder and harder to keep Korrd a secret. Subtlety was not one of the greatest characteristics of the Ranthall family, and Korrd was no exception to that rule. So, it became necessary to involve most of the circle of friends that would become the People of the Dragon in the fact that Korrd was alive. After a few arguments about what was best for Logan, the Korrd secret went quiet for good. At least, it was quiet until a little less than a year before the tournament that claimed Gabrielle's life.

Korrd and Gabrielle were close friends from the beginning, and Gwydeon had always thought that their friendship was an innocent one. Korrd was the person that Gwydeon could always talk to about Gabrielle, and whenever he would have problems, Korrd was always there with a sympathetic ear. One day, Gwydeon went to Gabrielle's house looking for her. He should have been at the practice fields, but he wanted to see her. However, when he opened the door, he found Gabrielle curled up in Korrd's arms. They were both asleep, and it was all Gwydeon could do to keep from killing Korrd right then and there. Later the two men had it out, and Korrd left forever. Gwydeon never said a word to Gabrielle about the incident, and she never brought it up. After Korrd left though, it was as if nothing had ever happened, and Gabrielle was as loving as ever. The only problem was that a little voice in the back of his head would never let him forget what he had seen that day, and that part of him would never forgive Korrd.

Gwydeon pushed those thoughts of the past out of his mind as the passageway came to an abrupt end. There on the wall to his right was a small grate. Through the grate, he had a perfect view of the throne and most of the throne room. The grate itself was obscured by shadows, so there was no chance that anyone could detect Gwydeon's presence. On the golden throne sat Korrd Ranthall, the *Chosen One*, and to his left stood a very familiar woman. It was this woman that caused Gwydeon to open the grate and make himself known to everyone in the room. He had seen her before, but he had also seen her perish at the hands of the phase Caris. It was the streaks of red in her hair that ignited his memory. The woman standing there could have been the one controlling Korrd, and Gwydeon knew that the Lady Bryn he met could have been easily capable of more perfect manipulations than even Caris.

The Duel

Korrd didn't react at all when he heard the grate at the far end of the room drop to the floor. He had fully expected Arin to enter that way with his report on Logan's progress. The fullness of the reaction however came when he saw another man step into the light. In all the years that he had been running and hiding from himself, there had been one man who had stayed by his side. No matter what happened, he knew he could always count on Gwydeon Sandar to be there for him if Korrd ever needed help. Gwydeon had been the one who taught Korrd the art of swordplay, and that was the training that had kept him alive, far more than anything that Saurn ever taught him. Gwydeon was the first one that Korrd approached when he came back to Aradon wounded and a failure. Though he was supposed to be dead, Gwydeon still took to Korrd with all the kindness he would to a member of his own family. Gwydeon helped Korrd build a house on the far end of town, and then help to keep the secret of his existence when everyone started asking questions. Luckily, their combined efforts had been able to keep Logan in the dark for a long time. However, just like everything else in Korrd's life, something went horribly wrong. Early one spring, the spring when Korrd left Aradon for good, Gwydeon and his father traveled to a nearby town to do some blacksmithing for a friend. At the time, Gwydeon was passionately in love with a beautiful girl by the name of Gabrielle, and it was very apparent to everyone that the two of them were madly in love. Most said that it was only a matter of time before the two of them traded vows in the old church. Korrd knew that was exactly the case. Gwydeon and Gabrielle had both entered the upcoming sword tournament, and since Eldar had decided not to enter, Gwydeon was the favorite to win. Gwydeon's plan was to carry Gabrielle to the old church on the hill after the tournament and trade the ancient vows then and there. That night when Gwydeon was out of town, Gabrielle showed up at Korrd's house. This was not unusual at all. The three of them had spent many a night together talking and drinking, and whenever the two of them had quarreled, Korrd had acted as the sympathetic ear to both sides of the issue. However, this night was much different. Gabrielle had come for companionship, a light-hearted friend that she could spend the night with without fear or discomfort. That was how the night started.

Even as he stood there in those few seconds, watching Gwydeon emerge and walk slowly down the throne room, he ran through the scene in his mind. Gabrielle sat at the table in the center of the room laughing and joking as she always did, sipping at the mug of ale that Korrd had poured for her. Korrd was laughing too, and as he sat down on the chair, it slid out from under him and he went crashing to the floor. Being drunk had always thrown off his sense of balance. Gabrielle was hovering over him the next second, the smile and laughter gone from her lips. The look in her eyes concealed well what she was thinking, but in that next moment when her lips met his, her intentions were revealed. Korrd left Aradon that next morning and had never had to face Gwydeon again. When he received word that Gabrielle was dead, Korrd had so much wanted to go back and console his friend, but the risk was too great. Korrd closed off the scene in his mind, but not before Bryn looked up into his eyes and smiled that wicked smile that was remembered somewhere deep inside of him. She had read his thoughts, and now this whole situation had gone from bad to worse.

Bryn. She had come to Brea looking for the *Coromor*. It was as if she had known all along that Korrd and not Logan was the Dragon. There had been no pretense in her voice, and she never once made any overtures about controlling him. She had only said that she had some things to tell him, but that conversation never came about. Gwydeon was now the problem at hand, and soon enough Logan would come calling.

CHAPTER 21

"Korrd," Gwydeon said as he walked slowly down the long red carpet that led to the golden thrones, "it's been a long time my friend."

"Yes it has Gwydeon. I'm glad to see you're still alive. I didn't think that you would have escaped both Zarsi and Hawk, but you never were one to be dissuaded by being overmatched."

Gwydeon stopped short for a second. The truth was that he hadn't survived. If it wasn't for the fact that Pike and Talon were there to help, he would have died on the floor of Zarsi's throne room impaled by that shard of ice. That was a pain that he would always remember somewhere in the back of his mind, and his body would never stop feeling the burning in his chest.

"How did you...oh...Bryn must have filled you in on all of the plots and traps that we have slipped through. I must say that for a phase I actually find her meddling and manipulation almost helpful."

"Thank you Gwydeon," Bryn said shortly. "But as to the actions of Hawk and Zarsi I must claim ignorance. If there was anyone who would boast and complain about the botched plans of the phasia and their bastard children, it would be Saurn. He has always taken pride in succeeding where the others have failed. That's why he's here with Korrd. He is waiting for the real *Coromor* to kill the *Chosen One*."

"So it's true then?" Gwydeon asked softly.

"Yes Gwydeon," Korrd responded, "I am the true Lord Dragon of the prophecies. The *Coromor*."

Gwydeon simply stood there for a moment nodding his head. It all made sense, he didn't know why, but it all made sense.

"You're not surprised," Bryn said suddenly.

It was more of a statement than a question. She had been trying to read his mind ever since he entered her field of vision, but thus far she had been unable to glean anything from him. It was as if his mind was closed to her.

"No," Gwydeon answered coldly, "I'm not surprised. There has been something very wrong about all of this from the very beginning. I knew in my heart that Logan was too easily led by first Aryx, then Cedric, then Caris, then Emries. You and I both know that he has always been a strong and independent person Korrd, and it just isn't right to see him so easily manipulated. Besides, isn't the *Coromor* supposed to have this incredible pull to the side of the Light?"

"You're right Gwydeon," Korrd said pulling away from Bryn and walking down the dais toward his long-time friend. "You have always been very perceptive and that has always been one of the most impressive qualities about you."

Gwydeon stopped walking and looked right up into Korrd's face as he approached. Korrd stopped about arm's length from Gwydeon and put his hand on Gwydeon's shoulder.

"It's been too long old friend."

"Yes, Korrd, it has. I've been waiting a long time to see you."

Korrd smiled and was not in any position to see Gwydeon's fist speed toward him until it slammed full force into the side of his face. Korrd toppled to the ground and stared up into the face of his 'friend'. Gwydeon's sword was out of the scabbard in a second, and before Korrd could do anything, the tip of the blade was pressing against his throat.

"Now Korrd, it's time to settle up some old bets. You are in no position to do anything, even with your powers. The only thing you can do is kill me where I stand, and the chances are still good that I'll run you through."

Without letting his eyes leave the dangerous fallen opponent, Gwydeon cocked one eye in the direction of the other person in the throne room.

"Bryn," Gwydeon said with venom, "you can't do anything to me either, so don't try."

"This is foolish, Gwydeon," Korrd said trying to stay as still as possible. "You can't kill me. I'm the one that the prophecies have put the mantle of the *Coromor* upon. If I die, the battle is over for good. Don't seal the fate of the world because of one night's indiscretion."

"She was going to be my wife, Korrd," Gwydeon growled in anger. "Killing her was an accident, but I'll be damned if I'm not going to kill you on purpose."

Gwydeon raised the blade of his sword slightly and then...

* * * * * * * * * * * *

The storm clouds were just beginning to move in as Logan's group started out of the inn. Gwydeon's group had left only a moment or two earlier, and Logan hoped that they would be successful. Despite the apparent animosity in Brea for the People of the Dragon, there was little doubt in Logan's mind that he would make it to the throne room and confront Korrd; the only doubt was what would happen once the two brothers were finally face to face. The images of the Castle of Terror still floated through Logan's mind, and the fact that he had already failed once in resolving the situation with Korrd weighed heavily. Korrd was more valuable alive than dead, but if he put the fate of the quest at risk, then Logan would have no choice but to end his life. Logan knew from Basille that seven was the 'magic number' needed to defeat Shau-ling. For as long as the quest has been progressing, the number available to Logan had only sat at four. Now though the number was teetering precariously close to seven. Arin and Jerrard were not sworn to Logan, but he felt in his heart that they would follow the *Coromor* even if Korrd did not. That would bring the number to six, and from everything Logan had heard from Gideon and Jerrard, it was possible that Basille would come to the aid of the forces of the Light soon enough. That was the magic number either way. With or without Korrd, the battle against the Shadow would soon be over.

Jerrard led the way through the winding paths toward the royal palace that loomed in the increasing darkness. The pre-dawn sky should have been illuminated by the early morning moon, the dwindling light of the stars, and the red and orange hues of the impending sunrise, but that morning all of those wonders were shut out by the dark line of clouds that moved steadily in above. So far Logan had seen no movement, and travel seemed much too easy. Even the mysterious Gwillim in his red armor and this private security force could have been enough to take out an entire squad of the supposedly elite Light Keepers. As they walked, Fion and Pike flanked Logan, and Talon brought up the rear. Suddenly there was a flash of motion out of the corner of Logan's eye. He barely had enough time to see the steel of the sword glint in the dim light before Fion had run the Light Keeper though. The young man was very quick with the blade, and Logan was thankful that he had such good teachers. Before they could make an escape they were completely surrounded by members of the Light Keepers.

Jerrard was the first to strike. In the back of Logan's mind, he could feel Jerrard touch the string of power that was his to command as the son of a phase. By his own admission, Jerrard had no idea what he was doing, but he tried anyway. From his raised right hand, a beam of white fire danced out into the void between he and the nearest attacker. The soldier was quick enough to get his blade up in time, but upon contact with the bar of light, the sword vanished in a giant explosion that sent the soldier and two of his companions sprawling to the ground. It was apparent by the look on Jerrard's face that he was surprised at what he had done, but he was quick to recover and draw his sword. The unarmed soldier was unable to recover before Jerrard ran him through. The two other men however were quicker. As Jerrard withdrew his blade from the dying form, one of the men rounded on him and slashed with his sword. Jerrard was quick enough to dodge the blow and retaliate, sending the soldier crashing to the ground with a lateral slash to the knee. The other soldier took advantage of Jerrard's distraction by circling around him and striking at Jerrard's exposed back. Before Logan could intervene, a flash of steel struck the soldier in the throat and he was on the ground before his scream ripped from his chest. Jerrard's head snapped quickly around in time to see Fion recover his sword and return to the fray. Whatever his opinion of the man who was supposed to be Logan's son, Jerrard had to owe the man his life.

Jerrard was not the only one that Fion was able to assist. Many members of the Light Keepers fell to the combined onslaught of Pike and Talon. Any normal person would have only seen men falling to the ground clutching themselves in pain for no apparent reason. Logan knew however that Pike and Talon's elemental based attacks were enough to bring even the most powerful of men to the ground. Talon used his power over the wind to smother the on-rushing men while Pike drew the water out of their pores and caused their hearts to explode under the increased stress. However, there were too many of them to take out all at once. So, as men dropped to the ground, Fion danced through the broken ranks finishing those who Pike and Talon missed. Jerrard was also heavily engaged with enemy soldiers, and Logan helped to take the pressure off by igniting a soldier's heart or just running them through. After twenty or so minutes of continued assault, no more soldiers came. The five of men looked at each other confused, but Jerrard was the first one to notice the man clad in red armor approaching.

He looked no more than eighteen or nineteen years old by the smooth skin devoid of wrinkles and sparse whiskers on his chin. The problem was the fact that he walked with a power around him that Logan could not even begin to put into words. In his left hand he held a sword and as the golden etching glinted in the light, the symbol of the Dragon became apparent. This symbol was replicated in white on the breast plate of his armor. The armor and the symbol were the exact inverse of the banner that Lord Cedric had honored Logan with in Marcwell. Logan could only see these mockeries as Korrd's sick and twisted ways of confusing his mind. The worst blow was yet to come though. As the man came closer, his features took on a familiar cast. Maybe it was the way that his chin was sloped, or the way that his nose narrowed. The man called Gwillim had so many features that matched those of Gwydeon that it was difficult at a distance to tell them apart. However, as he closed the distance more, the features that sparked Logan's memories of Gwydeon changed. If Logan didn't know any better, he would have said that Gwillim and Fion could have held a family resemblance. Perhaps it was just an exhausted mind wandering in the face of the upcoming battle with Korrd and the fact that Elwyne was not there to temper Logan's imagination side. However, he could not help but compare Gwillim in his mind to both Gwydeon and Fion trying to figure out where he truly fit. Gwillim got to about three feet from Logan before Fion moved toward him to intervene. It was obvious that Gwillim sensed Fion's distrust, so he stopped well short and fell to one knee.

"Lord Logan," Gwillim said strongly and proudly, "I am glad to see that you are safe. We caught wind of this assault only an hour or so before dawn. Had we had any more advance warning, we might have been able to spirit you out of the inn without anyone seeing. However, it seems that we have done well enough with little warning."

"I appreciate your concern Sir Gwillim," Logan responded, extending him the courtesy that should be bestowed on him if it hadn't been already, "and I am glad that you and your force will be able to deliver us to my brother without any more interruptions."

"Yes Lord Logan," Gwillim said nodding and standing again. "Before I take you into the presence of my Lord Korrd, I have to ask your intentions for him."

"What right do you have to question the will of the Dragon," Fion raged. "Whatever his wish should be fulfilled as quickly as it was spoken."

Gwillim regarded Fion for a moment and then looked past him at Logan. It was clear what Gwillim was asking, but what wasn't clear was if the answer that was inside of Logan's heart was the answer that Gwillim wanted to hear. From the very time he had learned of his brother's existence, Logan had regarded Korrd as the enemy. One of the phasia was using Korrd to exterminate everyone and everything that stood in their path, and now he and Logan were about to collide. There was no telling how far Saurn had brainwashed Korrd into believing that he was the true *Coromor*, and as those thoughts of the Castle of Terror ran through Logan's mind again as he stood there and shivered. Korrd in that phantom place had told Logan that he was the Dragon and that Logan was the pretender. The test had cost the life of Talos, and Logan was going to make sure that no one else died because of his impatience.

"You're asking me if I'm going to kill him."

Gwillim nodded silently.

"If he attacks," Logan answered after a moment, "then I will have no choice but to defend myself. However, if I see any member of the phasia at his side, then I will have no choice but to strike him dead where he stands."

Gwillim nodded again and then whispered something to Jerrard. He looked back and Logan and then to Fion and closed his eyes. Something was wrong, but Logan could not put his finger on exactly what it was. Finally, Jerrard opened his eyes and shook his head.

"You should know," Gwillim started, "the phase Saurn is still here inside of Brea. Jerrard has informed me that you have split your party in an effort to save Gideon. That was a very wise maneuver, but it also may have tipped our hand. Logan, I would like to take you to Korrd's presence now, but I promise you that if you strike at my lord without cause, then my sword will be the first to pierce your heart, and there will be nothing that your powers or your powerful friends will be able to do to keep you from dying at my hand. Do we understand one another?"

Before Logan had a chance to answer, Fion rounded on Gwillim with his sword drawn.

"You dare to threaten the Dragon? I don't know who or what you think you are Gwillim, but I want you to back up your threats with your sword here and now!"

Gwillim had his sword up the next second ready to defend himself. His posture was one that Logan had seen Gwydeon use hundreds of times, and it was one that Logan remembered his father teaching in one of the first dueling lessons Logan ever had. Logan's father had always said that swordplay was to help you stay alive, and should only be used to take a life if there was no other option. The position that Gwillim was in was the first defensive position taught to any warrior student in Aradon. Fion was the one that surprised Logan though. He was temperamental, quick with unneeded words, and too quick to judge and make his judgments important. Before Fion had a chance to strike, Logan reached out and held his blade. Before Logan knew what was happening, Fion jerked his blade away from Logan's grasp slicing the tender flesh of his palm. Logan leaped away from Fion with blood pouring from the gaping wound. The next few happenings all coincided. Jerrard and Gwillim closed on Fion, disarmed him without too much trouble, and then forced him to the ground. Pike and Talon were at Logan's side in those same seconds, ax and sword drawn and *Debuisas* glowing their respective colors. The wound in Logan's palm was healed before he even had time to think about it, and then he motioned for Pike and Talon to put their weapons away.

"Release Fion gentlemen," Logan said without hesitation, "he meant no harm, it was only an accident. Return his sword to him and help him to his feet. When you are ready you may lead us to the throne room of Brea."

Gwillim and Jerrard both looked at Logan for a long second. Neither of them trusted Fion, but he had been a continued salvation during the battle with the Light Keepers, so there was no way Logan could deny the fact that Fion could continue to be useful. Not only that, his mission to save the next generation was one that Logan had no choice but to take heed of. Some mistake was made in the meeting with Korrd, and it would cost the lives of the majority of the human race. Fion may have been an angry young man who had no control over his passions and his rages, but from what he had told Logan of his life growing up, Logan had to give Fion more latitude than he would have any other member of the party. Jerrard and Gwillim both sheathed their swords, and Gwillim dropped Fion's sword to the ground beside him. Fion grabbed his sword after a moment and then rose and waited. Logan could feel Fion's anger building, and the tension in the other members of the force was growing by the second. Finally, Gwillim and Jerrard started toward the royal palace of Brea. The confrontation between Korrd and Logan was drawing closer and closer, but as the time grew shorter Logan's mind continue to swirl with doubt as to what he was supposed to do, as well as the true goal of the test in the Castle of Terror.

* * * * * * * * * * * *

...the door to the throne room opened and an old man sauntered into the room holding a long staff with a purple serpent coiled around the upper half. His hood was pulled over his face, but the way that he walked and the freeness that he entered the presence of the Dragon reaffirmed Gwydeon's belief that the man was a phase, most likely Saurn.

"Very good my young friend Sandar," the old man said in a strong and powerful voice. "I'm surprised that you got close enough to threaten the life of my little puppet."

"What do you want here Saurn?" Gwydeon responded. "If I were you I'd be on my way back to Shau-ling's palace to tell him that he is wrong about the identity of the Dragon, not that it would help him now. I doubt that there are enough phasia left alive to be hunters."

Saurn laughed under that cowl and then walked past Gwydeon and the fallen Korrd toward the woman who still stood on the dais.

"To tell you the truth Gwydeon," he said with an evil laughter, "I could care less about Shau-ling and his pitiful errand boys. I have larger concerns."

Saurn turned his attention to Bryn.

"I must say Bryn, I knew that you were a traitor, but I never imagined the depth to which you would sink."

Bryn dismissed Saurn with a flip of her hand.

"I stand beside Korrd because he is the true *Coromor* and because he deserves to know why he has been pushed so hard and why he must kill Shau-ling."

Saurn laughed again and then turned back to Korrd.

"My little one," he said as he pulled back the hood of his cloak to reveal white hair and wild violet eyes, "you are about to hear why your life has become such an interest to all of the members of the phasia, especially myself and Bryn."

Bryn's face was filled with disgust.

"Why don't I start the story with the man named Gideon . . ."

* * * * * * * * * * * *

Midarin, Arin and Gideon could hear the conversation in the throne room before they actually saw anything. As they stood looking out of the grate in the shadow-covered wall, they heard the banter between Gwydeon, Korrd and Bryn. Then, as they were about to step out into the room, Gwydeon struck Korrd and pressed his sword against the older man's neck. It took both Gideon and Midarin to keep Arin from rushing into the room to help his lord. It was well that they did, because in that next second, the

Proclaimer, the mad phase Saurn, entered the room. His speech was taunting, but when he started to speak of the past and the origins of the Ranthall family and the man Gideon, Midarin could feel Gideon's tension. He had a dagger in each hand, and it would not have been difficult for him to strike Saurn from that distance. And yet, he hesitated. Sensing that Saurn's unspoken words had frozen her friend, Midarin nocked an arrow on her bowstring and drew it back. It would not be a difficult shot from there, and her shot would most likely catch the phase by enough surprise that he would not be able to use his powers to defend himself in time. Gideon caught the flash of movement out of the corner of his eye in time to snatch the arrow out of Midarin's grasp.

"What did you do that for?" Midarin whispered, "I could have taken him."

"Not yet," he whispered in response, his eyes never shifting from the scene that was unfolding before them. "Dis information has ta come out first. Once ye hear it, ye'll know why I told ye ta wait. Saurn is about ta do us a big favor."

* * * * * * * * * * * *

The palace of Brea was as large as Logan expected it to be. It had broad columns throughout all of the long hallways, and between each of the columns were works of art that were on proud display. Many of the artist's names were very unfamiliar, but now and again Logan saw paintings that were signed with the initials A.D. Upon seeing the initials, Logan could not help but think that perhaps the fourth member of the *Erieal*, Arin Domae, was this mysterious A.D., but that bit of trivia would have to wait until much later. Logan's mind kept wandering from the task at hand. Suddenly, Jerrard ducked behind one of the pillars and motioned for everyone else to do the same. After a moment, Logan saw what had caused Jerrard to make everyone hide instead of attacking. There was an old man in flowing violet robes carrying a staff who was walking in a very deliberate manner toward the throne room. It was obvious long before Jerrard whispered back that it was Saurn. Part of Logan wanted to attack the phase then and there, but there was something that stayed Logan's hand. Saurn was not there and walking so slowly through the palace for no reason. Everyone said that Saurn was crazy, but plans with the complexity that Saurn seemed to operate with could not be explained by sheer madness. How could he have kept up this charade the whole time of being the Proclaimer if he did not have all of his faculties in full working order? Pike and Talon motioned to Logan from the far wall of the hallway and pointed to their glowing *Debuisas*. Logan shook his head and looked back at Saurn. They all wanted to attack, but the way that Saurn was walking was even more puzzling than his motivations and his supposed madness. Why would a member of the phasia in a deserted palace walk to the throne room to visit a person who already knows who and what he is instead of using one of those portals that they had seen so many times? Maybe it was because there was someone else in the room that Saurn did not want to reveal himself to as of yet. Or maybe if he did use a portal, there was someone in the throne room who could have felt it coming the same way that Stone had in the cave. That person couldn't have been Korrd because Korrd already knew Saurn was there. Maybe there was another member of the phasia in the palace that Saurn did not want to alert to his presence until the very last moment.

As soon as Saurn had entered the throne room and shut the heavy wooden doors, the hidden group emerged from their hiding places and started toward the throne room. Even as they approached, they could hear the conversations that raged inside.

"I say we burst in and take Saurn and Korrd by surprise, father," Fion said after only a moment. "We will have the tactical advantage. Pike and Talon will be able to immobilize and possibly kill Saurn before he has a chance to retaliate."

"We could have done that in the hallway, Fion," Pike growled. "But Logan ordered us to wait. I want to know why. We had a phase right where we wanted him, and yet you hesitated. The Korrd thing is really screwing you up Logan, and I'll be damned if I'm going to let you risk our lives just because of Emries' stupid little game that he played with you up on Mount Tantis."

"And I'm not going to let your temper cost us again like it did on Mount Tantis," Logan replied. "It was your anger and your fast words that made us take this long road in the first place, Pike. I know you have this personal vendetta against the members of the phasia, and I'm sure that Eldar is looking at you from the Other Side and is proud, but there has got to be a reason that Saurn is walking here instead of just using portals."

"He doesn't want Korrd to know he's coming," Jerrard stated.

"No," Gwillim said. "I see what Logan is saying. Why would Saurn be so deliberate if this was only to keep Korrd from knowing that he was going to enter the throne room? Maybe there is someone else in there who Saurn would have more reason to try and fool."

"Or trap," Pike continued.

"Another member of the phasia?" Jerrard asked.

"That's what I was thinking," was Logan's response. "Talon, I want to hear what they are saying before we crash the party."

"You got it."

The powers of the Wind captured the conversation that continued inside and pulled it to their ears as if they stood no more than two feet from the speaker. The voices were familiar, but the words shocked Logan to the core.

CHAPTER 21

Chapter XXII

Secrets Nevermore

Saurn seemed too pleased with himself for his own good. He was obviously ready to taunt Bryn with the information he possessed, and it was as though he could no longer contain himself and was about to burst. The way that the arrogant creature spoke, it was obvious to Gwydeon that the knowledge he had was knowledge that he was not supposed to possess.

"Gideon Viruci is more of a charlatan than any of you could ever imagine. The stories that I have heard are far more outlandish than my posing as a loving disciple of the *Coromor*. He has passed himself off as a thief, an assassin, and the ally of a prince who died long before Gideon ever could have known him. Gideon has been through Alimidar, there is no doubt of that, but his story that he was the son of the man at arms to the royal family is an utter lie. However, I must commend him on his wonderful ability to keep all of you fooled for as long as he has. Then, when he did finally admit that he was lying, he covered it with more half-truths. He told you that he was the ward of Lord Basille Mystic the phase, and that Basille was the one who taught him how to use his powers. It is true that Basille took him under his meddling wing and taught him how to become an enemy to the Shadow, but this was for another purpose my meddling little simpletons. A purpose that Bryn and her sister Ellis have known for a long time. Isn't that right Bryn?"

Bryn's face was stone cold, and it was obvious that she was trying not to react at all. However, she could not hide the fire in her eyes. Gwydeon didn't know Bryn as well as the memories that Korrd and Logan possessed allowed them to know her, but one thing had become clear. Despite her attempted reserved appearance at times, Bryn was a creature of passions, all violent and terrible.

"Her lack of response beckons me to continue with the sorted tale of betrayal," Saurn prodded. "Long ago, the phasia were locked in an eternal battle with the forces of the Light under the direction of a man by the name of Aralias Imstra, the very man who gave the world the prophecies of the *Coromor*. However, what was never known to the pathetic mortals fighting a hopeless war was that there was another war that raged on inside of the phasia. This war was the War for Power. As if you had not noticed, we members of the phasia do not love each other like one of your pitiful human families, and in truth we despise each other more than should be possible. If there is anyone that we hate more than the *Coromor*, than it would probably be Shau-ling. So, this War for Power was our way of determining our path of ascension to his throne. At this time, there were only the ten of us: Jeroch, Warron, Grawn, Bryn, Ellis, Caris, Aldridge, Farax, Erdric, and myself. Jeroch, being the first born of the phasia was Shau-ling's favorite, and so he was the top of the pecking order, and he was the one that every one of us wanted to knock off the top of the ladder. However, some of the phasia were more ambitious than just aiming their sights at the first born. Grawn, Bryn, and Ellis decided to combine their powers and their considerable intellects to find a way to destroy Shau-ling and propel themselves into power. Well, they found the way."

Saurn paused again, his eyes passing from Korrd to Bryn. Out of the corner of his eye, Gwydeon saw the woman ball her fist, the long sharp nails digging so hard into the palm of her hand that a trickle of blood squeezed through white knuckles.

"The beginning of this world was where they had to look, and they physically had to take themselves to the place where the whole world started, the place where the sides of good and evil were drawn once and for all; the birthplace of both the *Coromor* and the evil that calls itself Shau-ling. That place is called the Blight. The Blight has no real physical characteristics to it, but for us phasia, anything we think can take shape in the currents of power there. These currents formed this world, and allow the forces of both the Light and the Shadow to draw upon their powers. The Blight does not lead you, does not surrender its secrets willingly; you have to be smart and strong enough to find what you are looking for. Grawn, Bryn, and Ellis learned of the true nature Shau-ling and Emries, and saw how the war between Light and Shadow started. From this they learned the true nature of the strings of power that live within us, the *Erieal*, the *Coromor*, and the *Chosen One*. The *Chosen One* was the key to everything. It was the only being powerful enough to give birth to the *Coromor*. But they could not find exactly who or what this *Chosen One* was. They searched everywhere to no avail. However, after a particularly cutting betrayal, their queries came under the notice of our master. Grawn, Bryn, and Ellis were banished from the Council of the Brotherhood of Phasia and sent out on their own. They were shut out from drawing on the sheer awesome power of the Blaze, but they still had the power to draw on the string of power that they had been blessed with from birth. Shau-ling then created three new phasia to take their place. These phasia became known as Zarsi, Taron, and Basille. This was the worst move that Shau-ling could have ever made."

Here Saurn's voice filled with a barely restrained hatred, and the corners of his mouth fell into a scowl.

"From the beginning of time, there had to be a balance between Light and Shadow. This balance was observed first in the creation of Shau-ling and the *Coromor*. Then, there was the creation of the beings known as the phasia, the Flame, and the damnable *Erieal*. The Flame was a being of pure power made out of the Blaze and living of the same life-force as Shau-ling. The two of them battled recently, and Shau-ling conquered him with a little help from the first-born and our winged assassin Nightwing. When Shau-ling cast out Grawn, Bryn, and Ellis then created three more phasia to take their place, the Creator had to do something to recreate balance between the two factions. This equalizing factor came in the personage of Aerith Seth, the first *Chosen One*."

For the briefest moment, Gwydeon thought he saw the corner of Bryn's mouth raise into a smirk, and the color begin to return to her balled fist.

Something didn't add up in Gwydeon's mind. Was the glimpse one of Bryn's pride, or had Saurn misstated something?

"Aerith Seth from his birth was marked as special by everyone who came in contact with him. Of the children who were born in the same year as he was, Aerith talked, walked, crawled did everything up to a year before every other child. His faculty for language was incredible, and by the age of six, he could speak the Old Tongue and the common tongue in the same fluid and exceptional manner. But the true measure of his power could not be unlocked until like the best steel he was tempered with fire. His parents were lost to vile murder, his life became haunted by the harshness of depending on the kindness of a cold world. He became a ward of the kingdom, an orphan who had to prove his worth by working in the mines of Quea. But unlike so many others, Aerith survived his trials, was stronger, better, and harder than those who were many times his age. That was when I rescued Aerith. Like you Korrd, I taught Aerith the ways of this world. The best teachers from around the world were brought in to teach him the arts. From the very beginning he was a master of history and art, and it was soon obvious to all that he was going to be a master of the physical arts as well. It seemed that he did not even need to work on his physique because his muscles were hard and perfect by nature. So-called holy men proclaimed him the champion of the gods, and after he began to take up the sword, he was prophesied by the same small-minded men to become a holy avenger. If those puny minded fools had only known how true their statements really were."

Korrd ruffled at the description. Had Saurn been trying to recreate his success with Aerith Seth in his tutelage of Korrd? Was Korrd a poorer student than Seth because Korrd was truly the *Coromor* and not the *Chosen One* or had Aerith Seth simply been that extraordinary?

"Much to my chagrin, Aerith became restless. He was not satisfied in the role of puppet that I had cast for him, so he chose to wander and to seek his fortunes elsewhere as a professional soldier. I tried to steer him in a direction that would place him firmly in the hands of the phasia, where he could do more for the Shadow. He fell in with one of the most powerful armies ever assembled, the Army of the Fox. This was Bryn's personal army. Once she laid her eyes on Aerith, she knew that he was the one of the prophecies. She knew this because it was she who wrote the prophecies and gave them to Aralias Imstra. So, she took Aerith Seth as her personal guard and lover. But Bryn's short-sightedness would eventually cost more than she was willing to pay. Bryn and Grawn had been lovers from their birth, and still consider themselves married in every lifetime, but Grawn was more jealous then than he is now, and perhaps with good reason. The greatest secret that was never told is this…"

Gwydeon's anticipation of the words was palpable, yet at the same time they filled him with such dread that he could not explain. There was tension in both Gwydeon and Korrd, but Bryn's irritation had eased completely. In fact she seemed almost amused.

"Bryn withheld a prophecy from Aralias Imstra, and the one she gave him is vaguer than any of the others. This prophecy was the one that said 'From a *Chosen* hero the *Coromor* will rise.' What this meant was that the *Chosen One* carried the seed that would give birth to the *Coromor* of the next generation. Bryn thought that by taking Aerith Seth to her bed that she would be the mother of the first *Coromor* of the prophecies, and that with her help that child would be able to dispose of Shau-ling once and for all. However, what Bryn didn't know was that Aerith Seth had another lover before Bryn and that this woman was also carrying a child. Bryn's child would not turn out to be the *Coromor* but he would have power. But he would not be born into the first *Coromor's* generation. Grawn, in a fit of jealousy killed Bryn and sent her to the other side with her unborn child still in her womb. When she was reborn in the next generation, she was reborn with the child still inside of her."

Saurn's smile widened, his white teeth looking almost like fangs in the rippling shadows.

"That child was born and named Gideon Viruci. He was shuffled off to one of Bryn's longtime associates Basille Mystic, and the rest is history. Isn't that right Gideon?"

Gideon had been hiding in the secret passage longer than he should have. He knew that the story was true, mostly because he had admitted it to Saurn under his merciless torture. However, from the rest of the story, it was obvious that Saurn had already put together the pieces of the puzzle and he only pulled the information out of Gideon to make him feel more like and traitor than he already did. The time for silence was over, and he stepped into the light followed quickly by Midarin and Arin. Gideon didn't move away from the grate, but kept his eyes locked on Bryn and Saurn. Arin moved to the side of Korrd who still sat on the floor, and Midarin went to Gwydeon who had long since sheathed his blade.

"Hello mother," Gideon said in his strong, proud, non-accented voice, "you don't know how much I wanted to say something to you when we came to Nevi, but you and I both know that I couldn't have brought this to the forefront then while we were still dealing with Caris."

Bryn smiled.

"I know Gideon, my son, but you know why I had to intervene with Caris. She was going to try and do that same thing that Ellis did in the last generation, and I was not going to let that manipulative little bitch control the fate of the third generation's *Coromor*. She's probably sadistic enough to kill herself so the birth will be delayed, and then in the time before the birth after all of the phasia have been reborn plunge the blade of her own dagger into the unborn hero and seal the fate of the world. However, if I would have only known that the girl Elwyne was pregnant sooner, I would have found an easier way to take care of the bitch Caris."

"Wait," Midarin said with confusion thick in her voice, "I thought that the *Chosen One* had to give birth to the *Coromor*. So how would Caris having Logan's child give birth to the *Coromor*?"

"Because my dear displaced princess," Saurn teased, "Logan is the *Chosen One*, and his brother Korrd is really the *Coromor*."

Suddenly the doors to the throne room burst open.

* * * * * * * * * * * *

Logan had heard all that he wanted to hear, and something inside of him just snapped. He could not believe what Saurn and Bryn had just said and Logan would be damned if he was just going to sit idly by and listen while they destroyed the perception of reality that he had fought so long and hard for. So, that release of fire on the door might have been overly dramatic, but at the time Logan had to release his fury on something, but though every part of him screamed for it, killing Saurn was out of the question for the moment. The phase still had too much to answer for.

"Ah, Logan," he said as Logan entered the throne room, "it's good to finally meet the man who has been living a lie all this time."

Logan's fists were wrapped with power that ached to be turned lose, but still Logan stood just inside the doors of the throne room, fuming.

"Shut up Saurn, I'm not letting you live so that I can listen to that wagging tongue of yours spit out insults that I have heard many times before. I want you to continue your story, and as long as you have something worthwhile to say, I will stay my hand. But once you've outlived your usefulness, I can't guarantee what will happen next."

If Saurn was impacted by the threat, he gave no outward sign. Instead he shifted his position so that both of the Ranthall brothers were in view.

"Very well."

Bryn knew what was coming next, and though she had kept the secret for so long, she ached that this was the way that it was going to be told. She ached even more for the man who deserved to hear Saurn's words, but would likely never know the truth.

"You see the other woman that was Aerith Seth's lover was a lady of quite high standing in Lord Basille Mystic's kingdom, and she was promised to the newly crowned Lord of Marcwell to cement a treaty between Scalla and Marcwell. Eight months after the union between Lord and Lady Binosear, the twins Cedric and Anabel were born. Because Aerith Seth was the father, the first born, Cedric, was given the gift of the power of the *Coromor*. It is still unknown whether or not Anabel is a carrier of the power. So, as the first generation of the prophecies began and ended, there was no mention of the *Chosen One*. It is still unknown how the Creator determined what person would be blessed with that power, but in the first generation it was granted to a man named Arin Ranthall."

Korrd flinched at the mention of his father's name, and though Logan found himself filled with pride, there was something more menacing in Saurn's words, and the dread that began to grip Logan's heart deepened.

"Arin was a very powerful young man, much like Aerith Seth was when he was young. Arin was born in Aradon, and he lived his simple life as a farmer and teacher of the sword. His ability had always been uncanny, but no one ever looked at it with any sort of question, mostly because Arin himself could never envision anything more than the simple life that he lived. On his twenty-first birthday, Arin met and fell in love with his future wife Victorian Rhuiden. Ellis was the first to discover who the *Chosen One* of the new generation was, so she went to Aradon and possessed the body of the woman Victoria. During this time, Arin and Victoria had a child, a boy named Korrd."

The two Ranthall brothers locked eyes. Had everything they thought they knew been a lie?

"Ellis could have killed the child or just left with it," Bryn continued, "but in the time that she was with Arin, she had fallen in love with him. So, it was truly an act of love that she had his child. After the child was born, and her act accomplished, she left Aradon with the information stored inside her for no one else to know. Victoria retained all of the memories of that time when she and Ellis were one, but truly, she was not Korrd's mother. Arin and Victoria decided to have another child, but because of the joining with Ellis, Victoria was permanently weakened. The birth of her second son, Logan, killed her. Logan was endowed with the powers of the *Chosen One* because of the residual powers left over from the joining of Ellis and Victoria. I found out about the birth of the two boys only because of Saurn. It was not until I encountered Logan that I knew who and what he really was."

Korrd felt empty. All of the rage that he had in his heart for his father and his brother simply melted away. In a matter of words, Korrd had been hollowed out. Everything that he thought he knew was nothing more than a fabrication. He had been used by the phasia in more ways that he could have ever imagined. He, his father, his brother, his mother; they had all been pawns in a game they would never be able to fully understand. But when Korrd looked into Logan's eyes, all he saw was rage.

"So now you have heard the whole sordid tale of the poor unfortunate Ranthall brothers," Saurn prodded again. "I had hoped that the two of you would have killed one another, but this is even better. It is far better to see you beaten and broken, wading into a hell without hope. I would like to see the two of you make it to the throne room so Shau-ling can crush what remains of your souls. In the next generation we phasia will rule. Remember Logan, it is the first born child that inherits the power. Shau-ling has your precious Elwyne, and if he kills her, there will be no more *Coromors*. The world will be ours. If you still wish to kill me, little *Chosen One*, then come and find me in Quea, where your line truly began."

At that, a portal appeared below Saurn's feet, and he disappeared. Anger raged inside of Logan, and the scream that erupted from his chest the next moment echoed in the chamber, filled with power and fury. But even as Logan's eyes returned to those of his brother, Logan knew that there were more important matters that needed to be attended to. Then something clicked in Logan's mind.

Wait…the first born child…

The next moment Logan rounded on Fion with his hand firmly grasping the hilt of the Dragon Sword.

"My son," Logan said slowly in little more than a growl. "My son who was born from my wife-to-be, and had no powers what so ever. Tell me another one Fion. I am the *Chosen One*, and Elwyne's child will be the third *Coromor* of the prophecies. You are nothing but an impostor."

Before Logan could react, Fion raised his sword and slashed wildly. A sword crossed the distance between supposed father and son and diverted the attack. Logan saw the red armor out of the corner of his eye and briefly thanked the Creator that Gwillim was behind Logan when they walked into the throne room. Fion backed away from Gwillim, then thrust his blade quickly at the man. Gwillim parried Fion's sword right into the ground and then kicked one of his feet out from under him. Fion crashed to the ground, and then Gwillim ran him through. Instead of blood oozing from the wound, a thin black smoke seemed to rise from the cut. The smoke began to roll out in a thicker and thicker fog as the seconds past, and the body of Fion seemed to deflate like some kind of a punctured balloon. By the time a minute or two passed, there was nothing left of the man that Logan had accepted as his son.

"A Remnant," Bryn said with disgust thick in her voice. "Jeroch's creation, culled from the souls of his victims. They are designed to infiltrate into the ranks of the enemy and to sew discord wherever they can. They specialize in turning people against one another."

Pike frowned.

"It was doing a damn good job."

Logan looked in Bryn's direction.

"How could it have known so much?"

"Remnants steal bits and pieces of memory every time they touch someone. It allows them to learn and make their infiltration more effective. They can prey on the fears of their enemies."

Logan nodded. A moment later, Gwydeon moved away from Korrd, and the older man slowly got to his feet. Logan moved over to where Korrd stood and waited for a moment. There was so much that he wanted to say to his brother, but none of the thoughts would coalesce into anything tangible that would have translated into words. Finally, there was only one remaining course of action. When Logan's hand fell to the hilt of the Dragon Sword, he saw Korrd tense.

"Well Korrd, brother, it's been a long time. This was given to me by a great, and he wanted me to continue the legacy that he started. Cedric had the right family, but he wanted the first born son, not his younger brother. I now present you with the Dragon Sword, and I hope that you'll also accept my sword as an offer to be your brother again. This time, for good."

Korrd just stood there looking at Logan for a moment. Then, he nodded. Logan slowly drew the sword and placed it in Korrd's extended hands. The older brother looked at the blade for a long moment before slipping it into his scabbard. A moment later, Korrd bent down and retrieved his sword from where it lay at his feet, and took a long hard look at the blade before looking up at Logan.

"Logan," he said holding his sword in his hands, "I've used this sword to cut down member of the phasia and their misguided followers. However, in my acts of darkness, I'm afraid that I've also cut down some innocent men and women who deserved to live. I would be honored if you would take possession of my sword and bring some honor back to it."

"I would Korrd, thank you."

Logan took the sword from his brother and sheathed it. Then, he did the one thing that Logan never expected, Korrd reached out and embraced him as his brother. Logan had not seen Korrd in many years, and the last times that they were together were tumultuous at best. However, Logan was glad to have Korrd back in his life, even if he feared it would only be for a short time. After Korrd released Logan and stepped back, Logan remembered the ring that had been in his pocket since Marcwell.

"The Elder wanted you to have this Korrd, he said that it acted like a *Debuisa* for the *Coromor*."

He looked at the ring for a minute and the pulled something out of his pocket. What it looked like was a large coin, but on the coin was etched the symbol of a striking viper.

"I've been holding this for a very long time, but ever since Emries told me what I was, I've never used it. This is the last tie that I have to the forces of the Shadow, and now that I accept the symbols of the *Coromor* from you, I will destroy this coin and my ties to the phasia."

With that, he broke the coin and cast it to the other side of the room. Then, he took the ring and placed it on his finger.

"Well, now isn't that just wonderful," Talon said sarcastically.

"Yeah," Pike continued, "one big happy Ranthall family."

"Minus my wife to be," Logan replied, killing the levity with the seriousness that filled his soul. "What do you say Korrd, let's go find Saurn and make him pay for what he's done to you, and then we'll take out Shau-ling and get Elwyne back."

Jerrard was the only one who had another plan.

"Perhaps it would not be wise to jump right into Quea. Saurn will no doubt be waiting on us, and I don't feel like walking into a trap. Quea is one of Scalla's closest neighbors, and I think that we could get some valuable information and assistance from my father."

"Jerrard's right," Gwydeon said. "We should go to Scalla and talk to Basille. After all he's gone through to deliver Jerrard and Gideon to us, I think we ought to consult him on Saurn and Quea."

"Any information we can gather is valuable. Saurn has been one step ahead for too long, and it would be nice to be able to have the advantage for once," Korrd said after only a moment. "Jerrard, would you like us to wait while you get Erika, or would you prefer to leave her here."

"I think she'll be safe here Korrd," he said lightly, "besides, I plan on living though this quest, and this way I'll have some incentive to live knowing that she's safe."

"Funny," Logan commented, "I thought I was the only one who thought that way."

"No," Gwydeon chimed in, "I think that way too, but if I tried to leave Midarin behind, she would probably kill me."

Midarin hit Gwydeon on the shoulder which brought laughter from both Pike and Talon. Arin and Jerrard joined in, but when Logan looked in the direction of Bryn and Gideon, neither seemed to be interested in sharing in the levity. Despite the dour mood, the chances of surviving the quest had just gone up significantly. Korrd opened a portal to Scalla, and as each member stepped through, Logan could not help but feel the tides of fortune turning.

* * * * * * * * * * * *

Scalla, or at least, what used to be Scalla. After Nightwing's attack after his failure to kill Basille, there wasn't much left of it. That was why Basille came back. He knew the destruction that would probably have occurred, but he never imagined the utter devastation that awaited him. The foundation that his royal palace had been built upon no longer existed, and most of the buildings that he himself had commissioned were just smoldering piles of rubble. He had helped bury many of his subjects on that day, and there were still more bodies unaccounted for. So much destruction, and all just because he had wanted to live to see his son one more time. Was it worth it? He kept asking that question over and over again. That thought plagued him as he walked back to the ruins of his palace. Suddenly, he heard a familiar voice behind him.

"I thought that you might come back here, Raven, it isn't like you to just turn tail and run away from your kingdom."

Basille turned and saw two people approaching him. One he knew as both an enemy and an ally in some battles, while the other man had always been his enemy. The first man was older than any other being on the face of the earth, the other was his newest protégé.

"My lord Shau-ling," Basille said stiffening, "it is unusual to see you out of your palace."

"That it is Raven," the reptilian-faced lord of Shadow responded, "but I did not think that you would respond to a summons, so I came to see you. I am very unhappy with you, Raven, but I must say that your deviousness is refreshing. You have survived this long by playing both sides against the middle, and I must commend you on keeping Cedric Binosear in line for me. Your ploy with Caris was flawless, and his rage and hatred for me has made him more useful than I could ever imagine. And the fact that you then approached him as a sympathetic ear and friend was the master stroke."

"Thank you my lord."

"However," he continued, "these newest developments are very frustrating. I have told you all that you are not allowed to have children unless you first ask for my blessing. You all should remember what happened the last time with Bryn. Her child is now that thief Gideon. And I understand that you were involved in keeping his existence hidden from me. And now I learn that Ellis is responsible for the Ranthall brothers. My phasia are truly more willful than I ever wanted them to be, and it is going to cost you all in the next lifetime. The brotherhood must be rebuilt, and for that, I will have to bring Grawn, Bryn, and Ellis back into the fold. There are only two members of the phasia that I know I can trust now, and they are the two newest additions, Rael and Trece. Nightwing here is loyal enough, however, I believe that his inner desires may make him too dangerous to depend upon for too much longer. That is why I am here to offer you a choice, Raven. It is the same choice that I will offer Saurn. Come back to my Council of your own free will by giving your life to Nightwing, and I will give you the power that I have always withheld, the power to have a family. If you refuse, then I will banish you here and now."

Basille thought long and hard for a moment and then created a blade of pure Blaze energy and held it up to his master.

"I make you a counter proposal, Halicon. I use your name to show you the true gravity of my conviction. You said yourself that you might want to dispose of our impetuous friend Aryx here, and I know he wants another shot at me, so I give you this option. Let Aryx and I fight it out. If he wins, the striking blow will banish me forever. If I win, you release me from the Council so that I may fight alongside the forces of the Light as I wish."

Anger boiled inside of Shau-ling at the impetuous and arrogant reply of his son. But part of him could not help but take pride in the fact that his youngest up until the birth of the twins had the courage to stand up to him. It was almost difficult to imagine killing Basille.

"Why should I not just strike you down now?"

"Because I disgraced your perfect assassin in a fair fight. I proved that he was inferior to even the lowest born of the phasia, and so it would be easy to imply that he would not be a match for the *Coromor* who is supposed to be your equal. Let him prove himself in a fair fight, and the reward me if I can thwart your perfect creation."

"I agree to your terms, Raven," Shau-ling said stepping back. "Let the battle begin."

Nightwing stepped forward in that next instant with a sword of Blaze energy of his own. This time he was not going to play around with Basille, and Basille knew it. The two locked their pulsing blades and edged into each other. The taller Nightwing had too much strength for the man called Raven, and Basille was pushed to the ground. Nightwing struck quickly, but Basille was able to roll out of the way of the downward arching sword. Basille swung at the feet of his larger opponent, but Nightwing's reactions proved faster. His wings were out in a fraction of a second, and the simplest push against the air propelled him above the strike. Basille got to his feet quickly and jumped at the hovering monster. The two blades of power met and cracked with fury. The spark of the joined blades sent both combatants to the ground. Basille rose again and waited. Nightwing was up a second later, and he hesitated. The black armor retracted beneath the human skin, and the man named Aryx once again stood before Basille.

"You were arrogant like this last time, Aryx, and I made you pay for it," Basille taunted. "You can't match my speed or my ability with the Blaze and you know it."

"But you can't match me with the sword, so have at it."

Aryx charged in that next moment and swung hard at Basille's head. Basille ducked the slash and returned one of his own. Aryx's speed was not something that he had ever been known for, but augmented with the power of the Blaze, he was something more than human. His new speed enabled him to block Basille's attack where it would have killed him only a week earlier. Basille withdrew his sword and waited. As he expected, Aryx thrust his blade at Basille's heart. Basille hesitated only a second before leaping into the air and continuing in a full flip over the top of his opponent. This time, Basille was not content to just dodge the attack. The last battle, that same move had enabled him to escape with his life. This time, it was going to be the maneuver that won him his freedom. The flip now contained a half twist and allowed Basille to bring his sword to bear and bring it slashing across Aryx's back as he landed. Aryx screamed in pain as the glowing green blade met with human flesh and then black armor. Basille poured all of the Blaze power that he dared into the sword and watched as it left a nearly identical rip in the armor as there was on the breast plate.

Basille withdrew the Blaze sword and stepped back to admire his handiwork.

"Now Aryx, I've given you one on your back to match the one on your front. You know, it almost looks like that silly striking bolt of lightning that you used to wear on the back of your cloak. However, since you skin is not exactly white, maybe we should call you pale lightning."

Aryx growled and turned as if he were going to attack, but Shau-ling held him back.

"That's enough Aryx. I still have need of you in my battle against the forces of the Light. Basille, you have proven that you are more powerful than any of my creations, and for that I will give you the reward that you seek. I am glad to see that at least one of my creations was as undefeatable as I intended all of them to be. I hope you enjoy your stay in oblivion."

With that Shau-ling raised his hands toward his former son and lashed out with the full and awesome power of the Blaze. However, this Blaze was not like any that the phasia could wield. Intermixed with the pulsing green waves of power were peaks of white and black. This onslaught of energy struck true into the center of Basille's chest and pushed him to the ground. His screams of pain were overridden by the crashing of the waves of power inside the torrent of Blaze energy that continually pounded him. A moment later all that remained of Basille was dust. His task done, Shau-ling turned to his winged servant and smiled.

"Now," he said quickly, "let us pay our respects to the Viper."

* * * * * * * * * * * *

The portal opened and Logan found that they had not gone direction to Scalla, but rather that the portal had opened on the edge of Brea where Stone waited. There were very few words spoken, and though Stone seemed to tense at the sight of Bryn, the fact that Logan was there kept the situation from become tenuous. Pike and Talon still seemed to be enjoying the lightness of Gwydeon and Midarin's attempt at humor, but once the portal was opened again and the group stepped through, all humor ended when they saw what remained of the city known as Scalla. Fires still roared in some places, and the smoldering ashes of the palace caught everyone surprise, most of all Jerrard.

"This has to be the work of the Shadowwalkers," Pike said after a moment. "After seeing the kind of destruction that they were able to unleash on Aradon, they could easily have leveled this town."

"No," Bryn retorted, "the blasts are too random to have been done by the Shadowwalkers. This was done by one person, Shau-ling's new little toy, Nightwing."

"Let me guess," Talon replied, "big guy, black armor, horns, tail, looks like a Shadowwalker having a bad day?"

"That would be him," Bryn replied.

"Wonderful," Talon muttered.

"I'm just glad Erika isn't here to see this, it would break her heart. I wonder what happened to my father." Jerrard asked quietly.

The group fanned out trying to find survivors of the assault as well as any clues that could be uncovered at to Basille's fate. Jerrard and Bryn were the first to find something, and everyone came running when they called.

"Shau-ling has been here," Bryn said with fear in her voice, "and it's only been a few minutes ago. The traces of power all around suggest that there was a battle between Basille and Nightwing, and then Basille's power patterns seem to fade. I'm afraid the possibilities are good that Shau-ling banished him."

Silence fell over the group. They had just lost one of the best allies that they could have had, and now things were starting to look as if Shau-ling setting everything up for the end game. He was no longer going to allow any of his servants to get in the way of the final battle. It was only a matter of time before Shau-ling came after Logan and Korrd with everything he had.

"Come on," Korrd said finally, "we've got an appointment to keep with Saurn."

Civil War

Saurn laughed to himself as he checked the progress of his plans at Quea. Never before had he imagined a better trap for the forces of the Light, and now the hook was baited. The Ranthall family had been easy enough to control; all it took was dangling the right amount of information in front of them. Korrd had been the first to fall under his veil of darkness. He was nothing more than a vengeful boy looking for a direction to vent his long-building aggressions. The unwitting boy fell too easily for all the right words, and it took little convincing in the Blight. Within a day of the first message from Saurn, Korrd had become a murderer, and that cycle would repeat itself over and over. But no one could have ever realized the true depth of Saurn's planning. Bryn, Ellis, and Grawn were foolish enough years ago to think that loyalty and love were enough to hold the *Chosen One* back from his desired path of destruction. For a time they had been right. Before long the words of that fool Aralias Imstra swayed Aerith. Seth had always been one who would lend his sword the fight against the greatest challenge. From the beginning he had such power and intensity inside of him, he was told that there was no way that an army could be defeated if his sword joined it in battle. There was wanderlust within him, a desire to always see and be more, driven by forces that he would not understand in his lifetime. Bryn thought she had hidden him from everyone else's eyes, and sated his desire for new experiences in her bed, but Saurn been waiting for the moment when Aerith would take a full step into the light of his greater destiny. He began shadowing Bryn. Saurn smiled to himself as he remembered the night that all of his spying had paid off.

It was a late night in the fall before the great war of the light began. Bryn's forces had been surprisingly successful against the other armies of the phasia in every single battle. On no field had her army lost the day, and it looked as if she was going to be able to challenge Jeroch for the right to head the Brotherhood of Phasia. Jeroch may have been first born, but his power was not absolute. There was a law that read 'if the leadership of the phasia is contested in an open forum, then the first born of the phasia must relinquish his control over the Council.' Bryn took this law very seriously, as did the other members of the Brotherhood. As long as Jeroch was in control, the Brotherhood would serve the wants of Shau-ling without question. If another member of the phasia were to gain control, life would be very different. Factions would form inside of the phasia. If any one of those factions could gain control of the *Chosen One*, then there could be a chance of defeating Shau-ling once and for all. Then there would be no prophecies to protect the forces of the Light from the Shadows. Everything would eventually fall under the phasia's collective boot, and anyone or anything that opposed them would die. Bryn was not too far away from winning enough battles to make her a conscious threat to the leadership of the Shadow. There had been a secret meeting of the Council, and Bryn and Grawn had not been summoned. To no one's surprise, Ellis declined her summons, not intending to break ranks with her closest allies. At that time there was much more animosity between the members of the phasia, and there were a few harsh words and scuffles in the Council chambers before Shau-ling arrived and made his presence felt. The Voice had always been something that all of the phasia feared. Out of all of the powers that the Blaze had granted over the generations and lifetimes, the power to use the Voice had never come to any member of the phasia, even in a limited capacity. It seemed that this power was reserved for only Shau-ling, at least until he endowed the abomination Nightwing with a partial talent for the Voice. Whenever Shau-ling spoke fully with the power of the Voice, every phase, no matter where they were, felt a slight pain. If all of the phasia were addressed, all of them were driven to their knees and the sheer agony would almost drive them into unconsciousness. But, no matter the pain involved, the message never had to be repeated. The Council meeting that day went on as predicted. Jeroch whined to Shau-ling that

Bryn was doing something that she shouldn't have, and that Grawn and Ellis were helping her. Aldridge and Erdric sided with Jeroch on that point, but as expected applauded her efforts to challenge Jeroch. No one was a fan of Jeroch's leadership and obvious favored status, but most of the phasia were too cowardly to bring these opinions to light in the presence of Shau-ling. So, Erdric and Aldridge played it safe by keeping the law in the back of everyone's minds by mentioning it in passing. Warron and Farax kept their thoughts silent, and it was not until Basille was born as a replacement for the banished Ellis that anyone knew Warron's mind but Warron. Saurn had listened intently, but he also had his own agenda that would have continued that night had it not been for Caris. She spoke without fear in front of Shau-ling, and to her credit, she had always chosen her words with enough tact and grace to escape punishment.

* * * * * * * * * * *

"My lord Shau-ling," Caris said strongly, but with appropriate deference. "There are many rumors floating around the Council and in the world, and these rumors are disheartening to me and to the other members of the phasia, especially Jeroch. It is rumored that Bryn, Grawn, and Ellis have been leaking information to the human force that has been battling against us over the past few months. The man in the lead of this force, Aralias Imstra has been quoting prophecies in the language of the Creator and of his servants. He is predicting the coming of a great warrior of the Light, and a set of prophecies that would seal the fate of not only the phasia, but the forces of the Shadow including you my lord."

Most of the phasia had known about Aralias Imstra for the better part of two years, but up until recently, his words had not been heeded or even taken seriously in most circles. However, in the last few months, all of that had changed. Most had remarked that Imstra's Army of the Light was large enough to do some serious damage to all of the kingdoms controlled by the phasia, and in those wars it was logical to think that he would be able to turn people to his side. Though not much of a warrior or general, what Imstra excelled at was proselytizing and gathering willing warriors to his banner. At this point, it was still unsafe to bring the Kalbraks and the Shadowwalkers into the world, except for those crippling night attacks in which there would be no survivors. It was still necessary to make the followers of the phasia believe they were human. However, once open warfare broke out, that would all change, and the full force of the Shadows would be brought to bear, regardless of the possible consequences.

"What rumors, my daughter?"

It was not the question that took back all the members of the phasia, it was more the way that their master had asked the question. In his voice was a mixture of curiosity and anger, but there was also this quality that made Saurn believe that Shau-ling already knew the rumors and had known them before they were even rumors. Sometimes Saurn wondered whether or not there were times that Shau-ling feigned ignorance just to throw the phasia off the trail. Caris took a few moments before she answered the question, and it was obvious that she wished she hadn't said anything.

"The man who is leading the forces of the Light arrayed against you, the man we all know as Aralias Imstra, has been making pointed comments about a being that serves only the Shadows, and he has been using your birth-time name as the name of this being."

Shau-ling tensed at this, but Caris continued.

"The fact that your name has been waived around as the name of evil is not the only disheartening fact my lord Shau-ling, what is truly interesting is the fact that he is publicly denouncing all of the members of the phasia, except for Grawn, Bryn, and Ellis. It is this factor that makes me believe that Grawn, Bryn, and Ellis have been leaking information to the forces of the Light. Ellis' blatant disobeying of your summons is almost proof positive. You must admit my lord that her absence is the final proof to my accusations."

"But there is other proof my lord," Saurn spoke up before anyone had a chance to comment. "As the other phasia no doubt know, Bryn's army has been very successful over the past few months. On no field has her army been defeated, and more than one or two of us have lost kingdoms to her. Of late I have found the reason for her success, and these revelations by Caris have allowed me to make the connections that I needed to be sure. As Bryn's success began, I learned that she had named a new general to her armies, a man by the name of Aerith Seth."

Saurn thought he noticed tension in Shau-ling's face at the man's name, but something else, something akin to sadness in his eyes. However, the emotion was so brief that Saurn wasn't sure it was there at all. Undaunted, Saurn pressed on.

"Aerith's battle strategy and ferocity would rival even the most diabolical member of the phasia my lord, and that is why we have lost every day to her. Once I learned of Seth, I began to do some checking into his past. However, his past is mired in mystery. The story that circulates however is that he was born to rather lowly circumstances in one little town that I had never heard of that lies inside of Bryn's kingdom. By the age of eight, he had bested every warrior in his village and had one the kingdom's sword fighting tournament. In addition to this, he could speak ten languages and all of their different dialects. The most impressive of these stories is the fact that one day while riding, his horse spooked, and he was thrown from the saddle. The fall he took would have killed any normal human, and probably any member of the phasia. In fact, when they found him lying there on the ground, he was dead. He was not visibly breathing, and his body was lying as an angle that was impossible and grotesque. However, the moment that a member of the search part touched him, he straightened himself up and got up. To everyone's surprise, there were no broken bones, no cuts or bruises, and it seemed as if he had never taken a fall at all. To compound this, no wound inflicted by any mortal weapon has ever been able to pierce his skin."

Jeroch laughed at this depiction, but with a sweep of Shau-ling's hand, the laughter ceased.

"It is a pity to see that my first-born is taking these matters so lightly. I'll make sure that you do not do it ever again. In answer to the rumors, I have heard all of these rumors, and I know of the man Aerith Seth that Saurn speaks of. Believe me when I say this Shadow, that he is every bit of Saurn says he is, and he is also more dangerous than you could ever imagine. However, do not believe any story about his origins, for they will all be facets of a greater truth. In time however, he will be dealt with swiftly and decisively. The part of this that concerns me the most is the treachery of Grawn, Bryn, and Ellis. Of late I have marked certain behaviors of theirs as abnormal and puzzling. Now that I know what they have been up to, it all adds up. Your brother and sisters have greatly offended me and have wronged all who sit at the Council. Death and banishment are not enough of a punishment for them. So, this is my decree. From this time on, they are no longer phasia, and they are no longer welcome at the Council. They will no longer be nurtured by the powers of the Blaze, and they will use their birthright to merely stay alive. However, this is not the end of my displeasure. From this point on, in each lifetime, they will be hunted and open targets. My protection ceases now. To make my displeasure with them complete, I will create three new phasia to take their place."

Shock radiated through the Council, but Shau-ling would not allow emotion to distract his servants from the business at hand.

"Now, to take care of this Aerith Seth before his legend grows out of Bryn's control. Saurn, take an army and face Bryn. You are not to win, but you are to cripple them. If you can, bring Aerith Seth to me, and then Jeroch will be able to deal with him personally."

That had made Saurn's blood boil. Everyone hated Jeroch, but this was blatant favoritism. Not only that, now there would be three new phasia to enter the game. Jeroch was no safer than before, but this was the first time that stupidity had earned an honor. It was obvious that had it been anyone else, there would have been punishment. However, Saurn's displeasure with Shau-ling's treatment of Jeroch could wait. There was still Grawn, Bryn, and Ellis to deal with. Killing them would have been too easy, and definitely not any fun. Saurn had always been one that wanted to play with his prey before going for the kill. It was always more fun to make them miserable or confuse them before letting them die. Death was always harder to take when you died in confusion. The funny thing was that the weapon most effective to confuse an opponent was the truth. Secrets were always Bryn's way of staying on top of the game, well, on that fateful night; it was those same secrets that sealed her fate.

* * * * * * * * * * * *

Ever since Aerith Seth had been welcomed into Bryn's army, Bryn had taken him into her bed. The reasons for this didn't come out until later, but the fact that he was in her bed was enough. Grawn had always been jealous, and if any member of his army ever made a comment about Bryn, he would have the man killed without question or explanation. Unfortunately for Grawn, Bryn had never been one that was content to stay in one man's bed, and her appetites seemed to be without measure. She had been under the sheets of thirty other men before Grawn was able to find out about the first, but that all changed when Aerith Seth arrived. Seth was the only man that could hold Bryn's fancy for more than a night. The rumor was that she was his lover, not the other way around. This was the way that Saurn could ensure that Aerith Seth would not be there when he attacked, so he could not be called a failure. It was a brilliant plan, and it could not have played out any better.

That night, as usual, Bryn left the royal palace of Barer and went to the house where Aerith Seth lived. Saurn then used a portal and put himself into the throne room. As usual, Grawn was paranoid about the presence of other members of the phasia entering his kingdom, so Grawn was there waiting with a sword of ice in hand waiting on Saurn. When Saurn stepped out, Grawn took a defensive position and waited. Saurn spoke after a moment.

"Brother," Saurn said pleasantly, "I know that we are all at war, but has it gotten to the point that a friend cannot pay a visit without being attacked."

"If I would have attacked Saurn, you would not be talking right now. And I do not recall us ever being friends."

Grawn was always one to come to the point about everything, especially when it came to warfare. Saurn knew that if Grawn had truly wanted, Saurn would have been dead. But Grawn had hesitated, something that he was not known for when it came to other members of the phasia, and he had allowed Saurn to get his foot in the door. The first and hardest part of the plan was now over, and the rest would be easy. Grawn's distraction with his wife's infidelity was clear, and it had given Saurn the only opening that he would ever need.

"Grawn, I have come to deliver a message from Master. He says that you, Bryn, and Ellis have been banished from the Council, and that you are never again to be members of the Brotherhood. Your treachery has finally been rewarded, and you are now on your own."

Grawn didn't react for a moment; he just stood there intently watching. Grawn then smiled and lowered his sword.

"Why did you come, Saurn? Master could have just as easily used the Voice to inform us of this. And if you were the chosen messenger, then why is it that you did not appear to all of us tomorrow in court. I know you Saurn, and I know that you would not have risked your life unless there was something for you to gain, or something for the rest of the phasia to lose. For you to be this direct, it must be very important, so it probably has something to do with Jeroch."

Grawn had always been very perceptive when it came to matters of court, and especially matters that concerned the Council. Everyone detested Jeroch, but it seemed at times that Saurn had the most hatred inside of him. Grawn always held that little piece of knowledge close to his heart when he dealt with Saurn, and that was why he got what he wanted most of the time. But while Saurn's hatred of Jeroch paled to the rage that burned inside of Grawn. Grawn was the second-born, always reminded that he was in Jeroch's shadow. He would always be trapped between his infallible brother and his whore wife. This time, that knowledge and rage would prove to work against him.

"Yes," Saurn replied, "it does have something to do with Jeroch, but it also has something to do with Bryn."

Grawn backed away and sat down.

"Do tell."

Saurn sat across from him and then began speaking.

"Master knows of your traitorous visits to the Blight, and he also knows, thanks to Caris, that you have been leaking information to Aralias Imstra and that he is close to putting enough of that information together to create a prophecy that would destroy Shau-ling. Master is also aware of the man called Aerith Seth, and his uncanny ability with battle and his fabled invulnerability to mortal weapons. Master wants this man Aerith Seth, and he is to be given to Jeroch to kill. However, I think it only fair that you would be the one to deal with Aerith considering what he has done to you and your kingdom."

"What has he done?" Grawn said sitting up.

"Why he has taken your queen to his bed and she is going to have his child."

"That simple statement was enough to drive Grawn crazy. He shot up out of his chair and screamed at the top of his lungs. At that moment three armed guards ran into the room, but they didn't even see their lord before they were struck down by the bolts of lightning that radiated off of his body. In those days, Grawn's fury took physical shape in the form of lightning, and anyone who came near him would be struck down. In a matter of moments, a portal formed, and Grawn stepped through. Saurn knew where he was going, so he created a portal of his own and appeared just outside Aerith Seth's house. Grawn ripped the door to the house off its hinges, and there, just inside the bedroom lay Bryn wrapped in Aerith Seth's arms. They both awoke suddenly, and Bryn mumbled something, but Grawn cut her off with a cry of fury and rage. Seth was up out of bed in that next moment, and he had his sword in hand. The next moment Ellis bounded into the room.

"What are you two fools doing? If you kill each other now, then our plans and our banishment will be for nothing."

Grawn stopped in his tracks and turned to Ellis.

"How did you know we had been banished from the Council?"

Ellis answered him with a question.

"You haven't tried to touch the Blaze yet, have you?"

Grawn shook his head. By this time, Bryn was out of bed, and she strode over to Grawn and slapped him across the face.

"Your stupid jealousy almost cost us the war, Grawn. Aerith is more valuable to us than just as my lover, or your general. You know we need him if we are going to go up against Shau-ling. Now what's this all about?"

"Are you carrying his child?"

Grawn needed to only ask that question. There didn't need to be an answer. Bryn's look and her body language told the truth far better than any words could have. Ellis was also taken by the news; it was obvious to Grawn that she had not known.

"What were you thinking Bryn?" Ellis said shocked. "We are at risk now, more than you know. This goes against everything that we thought we could do safely without being permanently banished. If Shau-ling ever found out what you have done . . ."

"I know, Ellis," she said finally. "And we all know what we have to do now. Shau-ling will no doubt send a force after us and after Aerith. We have to get the rest of the information to Aralias Imstra, and Aerith will be safe with him."

"Now wait just a damn minute," Aerith said finally. "I should have a say in this, and I'm not going to leave you if there is a battle brewing. How could I walk away now, like this? Besides, you can't win without my sword and planning in the battle. Your soldiers aren't even strong enough to train without me. I know that you phasia are strong, but you can't be strong enough to take out a whole army by yourselves, especially since you have been cut off from the Blaze. I'm staying."

"No, Aerith," Bryn replied, "you need to go. The greatest challenge is for you to take up the fight against the phasia. Remember, you must give your life fighting for the Light, and the best way to do that would be fighting for Aralias Imstra. And Grawn needs to finish me so that my child will not fall into Shau-ling's hands when his forces invade. Do you understand what I am telling you, Aerith?"

The grimace that came to Aerith's face betrayed something that Saurn had not expected. Love.

"Yes Bryn, I do," he said in a defeated voice.

"Good, now go."

And that was how Aerith Seth came to be in the service of Aralias Imstra, and that was the beginning of the prophecies of the *Coromor.* But that did not last long. Saurn's attack on Bryn's forces went well, and the kingdom fell to the forces of the Shau. Some years later, Saurn was sent to deal with the forces of the Hand of the Light and Aerith Seth, only this time, he was able to recover Aerith Seth for his master. But true to Shau-ling's word, Jeroch was allowed to finish him, starting the war for the Light in earnest.

* * * * * * * * * * * *

Thoughts of the past still swirled in Saurn's mind as he stepped out of the portal into the Blight.

"You're still dwelling on that after all these centuries, brother?" a familiar voice said in the thinning darkness. "I would have thought that you would have been over that by now."

Saurn turned his attention toward the voice. He had not expected to see Jeroch in the Blight, and this was not a good time for their battle. The Ranthall brothers were ready to fall for his trap, and Saurn could not afford to be late.

"So, Jeroch," Saurn said mentally preparing himself for battle, "are you here for our little duel, or are you just here to give me one of master's warnings."

"I am indeed here for our duel."

"Then by the law of the Council, I openly challenge your leadership of the Council, and you are obligated to defend your seat or lose it by default."

"I accept," Jeroch replied.

In that next instant the shape of the Blight changed. It was no longer a formless mass, but it took the shape of the Council chambers. Out of Jeroch's hands grew two long blades of green energy, and Saurn was quick to form a Blaze sword of his own. This was the only way that a battle for ascension could be fought. Blaze against Blaze, no other powers. Jeroch charged his younger brother and slashed wickedly at his head. Saurn leaped back from the blow, and with his free hand created a patch of Blaze fire beneath Jeroch's feet. Jeroch spun out of the way, but not before one of the high peaks of flame caught him under the arm and burned his left bicep badly. However, as if he were immune to the pain, Jeroch dove toward Saurn, and one of the swords of energy struck true to Saurn's side. The pain made Saurn double over, but as Jeroch came in for the kill, a ball of Blaze energy enveloped him. It was not made to inflict damage, merely to hold Jeroch at bay long enough for Saurn to recover all of his strength. The moment Saurn made it to his feet Jeroch had broken free of the bubble of energy and was charging Saurn again. From Saurn's outstretched fingers, daggers of Blaze fire erupted and flew rapidly toward their on-rushing target. The Shadow lived up to his name by ducking and weaving though the projectiles as if he were merely a shadow. Jeroch then enveloped himself in a cone of Blaze energy and hurled himself at Saurn. Saurn had enough presence of mind to leap out of the way, and as Jeroch touched back down on the ground, Saurn launched an attack that would have been deadly to any other member of the phasia. Saurn extended both of his hands and a beam of pure Blaze energy exploded toward Jeroch. His reactions fueled by the Blaze that filled him, Jeroch was able to turn and created a beam of his own. The two columns of energy collided, and the shock waves reverberated through the Blight. Both members of the phasia were knocked to the ground as wave after wave of energy buffeted them. Neither of them had very much strength or energy left, but Jeroch had far more than Saurn knew. Jeroch stood and walked slowly over to where Saurn was recovering. When Saurn looked up, he saw that Jeroch was coated in an aura of energy very much like Taron's, only Jeroch's aura was constructed completely from Blaze energy.

"This ends here, Saurn. Your challenge has been met, and you have been defeated. From this time on, your right of challenge has been revoked, and if you ever again challenge my leadership of the Council, you will be banished by my hand. Do you understand?"

Saurn nodded and then prepared himself for his death. He knew that he would not see the blow that would destroy him, but as the aura around Jeroch began to pulsate, he knew that there was no defense that he could erect that would save his life. The power expanded from Jeroch in a shell that engulfed everything around him until it met with Saurn and before he knew what was happening, the burning was upon him, and Saurn's life was over. When the shell of Blaze energy finally receded, Jeroch nearly collapsed from the sheer exhaustion this battle had caused. From behind him, Jeroch heard a short laughter and some applause. He turned around to see Aryx standing behind him.

"Master sent me to make sure that you were alright."

"Yes," Jeroch replied, "just tired."

"Well, I'll take you back to the palace. You need to rest and prepare to meet the forces of the Dragon. They're on their way."

Warped Reality

From the ruins of Scalla, the newly constituted People of the Dragon proceeded north to the little border town of Quea. As they made their way through the countryside of the kingdom, they saw the truly magnanimous nature of the man they had all known as the phase Basille. For so long Logan had been blinded by rage and hate for the evil that were the phasia, but then he saw the work that Basille had done on behalf of his people. For lifetimes he had fought at the side of Shau-ling, but he did so differently than the other phasia. Caris was a woman who seemed that she could manipulate her way to the top. She wasn't interested in who or what she ruled, all she cared about was a lifetime's satisfaction in a few months' time. The lords that she used could have been anywhere from weak, like the King of Illimar, to the strongest in the land, like Lord Cedric, but they were all used. It was her timetable that they bowed to, and they had no choice but to listen to her soft words, cling to her silken body, and shudder at her masterful touch. It was a fact that Logan could speak on from experience, and could almost still feel her hands upon his body and upon his very soul. She was not content with manipulation of the body and mind. That was why Lord Cedric still pined over her to this day. Logan had been shocked to hear the true story of Erika Belnosian as they made their way to Quea, but to tell the truth it had not surprised him. Cedric had a weakness in his heart for the girl, and Caris had found a way to exploit it. It is not surprising that she wanted to make him her husband, and their child would have been more powerful than any of the other children of the phasia that they had met. Granted that the party had only met two, but they were prime examples of what the proper training could do. Jerrard was schooled in the arts of politics by his father Basille through Erika, and the man Hawk that Pike and Gwydeon had encountered was obviously trained in the art of treachery and deceit by his father Jeroch. Under Caris' apt tutelage, the child would have been able to command its powers with such precision that it probably would have been able to take on a full member of the phasia and win. Friend and foe alike would have been prey to this teaching, and from Gideon's story, that was why Basille took matters into his own hand and killed Caris on that fated wedding day. Had he not done that, matters would have been much worse than any of them could have imagined.

Still, as Logan thought about it, he could not help but feel a little sorry for their patron Lord Cedric. He has been fooled and lied to at every turn, and the man he thought was his best friend was really his mortal enemy. Cedric had been wrong about Logan, but yet he was still able to lead Logan down the right path to find what it was that he needed to find. For so long Logan had been going around in circles trying to find the reason that he was fighting. His life had been so happy in Aradon, but he too found out that his life was a lie. Logan's father had lied to him about his brother being dead, and his friends had kept Korrd's existence hidden from Logan as well. Logan also found it hard to believe that Lord Cedric had a role in the erasure of Korrd's existence, but then again, as Logan had found lately on the quest, nothing could be taken at face value. Logan had learned that the hard way with Leane Torne, Gideon, Jasmen, Aryx, etc. But if he had to pick, he was the most wrong about Basille. Here was a man who was supposed to be evil's most loyal servant, and yet in each and every lifetime, he came back to Scalla to find how his subjects had gotten along without him. During the War for Power, Basille returned to find a thriving town undisturbed by the rest of the phasia, and he took it for his own. At that time, no one knew of the war or the sides that were fighting it; what they did know was that they had a caring lord who wanted to make sure that their kingdom was prosperous and protected. And so from then on, he went back again and again, lifetime after lifetime. What it must have been like to know that through every generation the same kind and gentle lord would sit on the throne to take care of their needs. From what Gideon had explained, Basille saw over half of the townspeople born and then he would preside over their funerals and weep for them. He knew all of their names, their children's names, even their parent's names. Everything to Basille was a personal matter, and there was not one of the townspeople that would hesitate to make their way to the palace to talk with their Lord about a problem. For an agent of evil, Basille served as a truly blessed miracle to the kingdom of Scalla. But now it was all over. Basille Mystic of Scalla would never return to his kingdom to sit on the throne, attend births or funerals, and he would never have to serve the scourge that was Shau-ling ever again. Perhaps he was better off wherever he was. Spending a lifetime or several atoning for something you could not control was no way to live, and Logan hoped that in the end Basille was able to find peace in his final resting place. The only sorrow that Logan took from Basille's passing was a truly callous and greedy one. Logan never had a more knowledgeable, helpful and powerful ally than Basille, even though at times he got frustrated by Basille's lack of commitment to the side of the Light. And Logan was truly sorry that his son would not have the phase as an ally when he began his fight against the forces of the Shadow.

However, Basille had given Logan the one thing that he would be forever in the phase's debt for, Basille gave Logan his brother back. In the city of the gods Logan learned humility at the cost of Talos' life, but he also learned the truth. It had been Korrd and not Logan who had been the man fated to fight against Shau-ling all along, and thankfully he survived. For that Logan almost had to thank Saurn as well. It's funny to think that the very man whom Emries had chosen to carry his mantle fancied himself a servant of Shau-ling for a time. It was even harder to believe that Korrd and Logan were not from the same mother. Korrd was the son of a phase, and Logan was just the son of a warrior.

It was nightfall by the time they reached the edge of Quea, and Korrd decided that everyone should camp for the night. From the time that Logan's group had joined forces with Korrd, he had taken control of the group, and Logan had just stepped aside, bowing more to his power than to the fact that he was Logan's older brother. That wasn't the only change in the group that Logan noticed either. Arin Domae, the fourth member of the *Erieal*, seemed to fit in well with the members of Logan's group. He had stayed mostly with Pike, Talon, and Gideon learning to use his powers, and once Logan had given Arin the *Debuisa* that Logan had been given by the Elder, his learning curve accelerated greatly. But Arin also spent a great amount of time with Gwydeon and Midarin. This was the point that escaped Logan. Arin Domae was the man that had caught Midarin in the arms of the guard of the man she was supposed to marry, and then he reported her for the treason that earned her banishment. Yet they talked and laughed pleasantly, keeping close to Stone who was also an anomaly in this whole scheme. Jerrard Mystic, the son of the man they had learned to call friend was mostly at Arin's side. The knowledge that he was the husband of the real Erika Belnosian threw most of the group into shock, but that was only a momentary distancing. Before long, Jerrard was welcomed into the laughter and camaraderie. Apparently, he had picked up enough from Pike, Talon, and Gideon to begin to use his powers a little more effectively. Bryn had also had a hand in his tutelage, but that was very sparse and awkward. Bryn stayed very close to Korrd, and was not seen out of his company very much during the trip. Occasionally, someone pointed out to Logan that she was staring in his direction, but when Logan looked, she wasn't. The one time that her gaze met his, Logan could feel a pull at his heart from the being that was inside of his. It was the same feeling that Logan had the first time that he saw Bryn after the episode with Caris. Logan knew that Aerith Seth, the first *Chosen One*, had truly been in love with Bryn, and that she longed to have him in her arms again as well. He was still alive, and he could exact some control over Logan, but Logan would never betray Elwyne for the feelings of a man who had been dead for almost two hundred years. Gwillim was also sticking very close to Korrd. Logan didn't know how he was supposed to react to Gwillim. Logan clearly had to respect Gwillim as a warrior, and from what he saw in Brea, there was no doubting the young man's prowess with a sword. But there was another connection that Logan felt deep inside. He didn't know how to explain it. Gwillim was friendly enough to everyone in the group, but Gwydeon seemed to be avoiding him.

As Logan was setting up his bed for the night, Gwillim came over and tapped him on the shoulder.

"Korrd wants to talk to you alone."

That wasn't a request, it was an order. Logan didn't like orders, he never did. For some reason, Logan swallowed his pride, which he never was able to do before, and followed Gwillim over to where Korrd and Bryn sat by their own little fire. Korrd motioned for Logan to sit down, and when he did Korrd started speaking in a voice that made Logan realize that Korrd had been agonizing over the decisions that had been made.

"Logan," he said in a pained voice, "I've been doing a lot of thinking, and I have to say that these were not easy decisions that I have made. Bryn has given me the location of Shau-ling's palace, and after we take care of Saurn, we will leave for the Island of Mist."

Logan nodded absently.

"Fine, but why don't we leave now? Saurn is just sitting here waiting for us. If we take out Shau-ling, then we take out Saurn and any of the other phasia that we missed. This personal score of yours is not important enough to risk the lives of generations to come."

Korrd frowned.

"That's why you're not coming with me."

"What?"

Logan was dumbfounded. Korrd had always been the kind of person that wanted to do things on his own, even if there was no way that he could accomplish it on his own. Once he saw that he was in over his head, then maybe he would ask for help, but usually he was too proud. Headstrong and proud ran in their family, but Logan had never seen it taken to such an extreme. But, then again, if anyone asked Elwyne or any of the others, they would probably say that Logan did the same thing. This was different though. If Korrd found out that he was over his head, it would be too late, and his broken dying body would be laying at Saurn's feet in no time flat.

"Korrd," Logan said calmly after a moment, "you can't do this. If you take on Saurn one on one, you'll probably lose. Now before you say anything I want you to listen to me. You are good with your powers, but Saurn has had lifetimes to master his. Yes, he taught you, but he didn't teach you everything, and I'm sure that anything he taught you he would be able to counter or block. If you die..."

"If I die," Korrd finished, "you'll take the members of the *Erieal* and Jerrard to the Island of Mist, defeat Shau-ling and rescue Elwyne. You have been heading down this course from the very beginning, and the only reason that you are doubting yourself now is because I'm here. Bryn has assured me that the *Chosen One* with his powers and the backing of the *Erieal* will be enough to defeat Shau-ling."

"Yes," Logan agreed, "enough to defeat him, but we will be one short of the number needed to end it for good. That's the part of this whole thing that really bothers me. Bryn is just trying to keep herself alive for one more generation by getting you out of the way and letting us take on Shau-ling without the seven necessary to make the prophecies come full circle."

Korrd shook his head.

"Bryn is against my plan, Logan, and she is hoping that you convince me that it is in my best interests to either leave well enough alone, or take everyone against Saurn. She saw what Shau-ling did to Basille, and she is afraid that he will do the same thing to her. But, there is another piece to my thoughts that I have yet to air. According to Bryn, Stone is a danger to our group because anything a Bonded creature knows, Shau-ling knows. We have to kill him, Logan."

That was completely unexpected. Before they left Brea, Korrd was all for the idea of converting more members of Shau-ling's army into their ranks, and now at the word of Bryn, he was changing his mind and ordering Logan to kill a very valuable member of the group.

"Not only that," he continued after a moment, "but Bryn also has to die."

That struck Logan right in the heart. Even though he had no tie to Bryn, that part of Logan that was Aerith Seth was screaming. Logan couldn't stand by and watch as the woman that Logan...Aerith...they... Logan didn't know who he was anymore, or what he was feeling. That voice had been in Logan's head for so long that he couldn't tell it apart from his own. Regardless of who he was, Logan couldn't just let Bryn die in cold blood just because it might save them from some trouble later on. Too many people had died already, and Logan was going to do everything in his power to keep it from happening anymore.

"Korrd," Logan said shaking my head, "let's try and be rational about this. Shau-ling already knows we're coming, and if he can see through Stone's eyes, then the damage is already done. If he doesn't know about our parentage yet, I'm sure he will before too long, and by that time it will be too late for him to do anything about it. Stone can't hurt us as long as I have the power to hold the Blaze. With Bryn here and alive I can assure that. Besides, with Bryn here, I don't have to. As a member of the phasia, she is respected and feared by those creatures, so Stone will follow us without question. Not only that, but once we get to Shau-ling's palace, we're going to need her to lead us through. Trust me brother, the good of them being here far outweighs the bad."

Korrd sat there quiet for a moment and then silently nodded. He knew that Logan was right, even if he didn't like it. Maybe there was hope for the newly constituted group yet. He was the natural leader, but with both Ranthall brothers in the mix, maybe there was a chance that neither of them would be blinded by the situation. After he didn't speak for a moment Logan started to get up, but Korrd put his hand out and grasped his brother's shoulder.

"Thank you for being alive Logan, and thank you for helping me to see what I was so blind to for all those years."

Korrd paused for a long moment before continuing.

"I blamed you for our mother's death, and I blamed father too. I never got to apologize to him for what I did, but maybe in some way I can apologize to you. There is no hope for me at the end of this quest. Our friend Emries has assured me that I will pay for my evil deeds with my life. There is only one favor that I ask of you Logan, and it might not seem like much now, but you will understand in the future. When you have your child, make sure he knows that the powers he has will change him, there is nothing he can do about that. No matter what, don't let him follow anything but his own heart. Too many times the both of us have been misled by people who said they had our best interests at heart. Most of all

Logan, please tell him that he had an uncle, and despite what he did, he was still a good man at heart. Tell him that I wished I could have been there to see him born, or to fight beside him in the wars to come, but I couldn't because I was weak..."

His voice trailed off, and Logan saw the armor begin to crack, but that only lasted for a moment. The cold hard exterior returned, and he was again in control of the emotions that raged inside of him. He was never married, at least so far as anyone knew, and he would have no children if what Emries said was true. Logan knew what Korrd meant by his words, and Logan couldn't help but feel a blow to his heart. Korrd had gone through his life full of hate and anguish, and there would be no one to pass on his legacy to. There would be no one left to remember the man who gave his life to save the world. To everyone, Logan was the Dragon, and that proclamation came from the lips of the Lord Lion. No one would know that Korrd was actually the *Coromor*, and that Logan was just a role player like everyone else in the party. Korrd was the one who should have received the glory, but there was no real glory in dying for a cause. Your beliefs and the things that drove you are lost with you. They did not choose the path that they walked during the whole of the quest, it chose them. Neither of them asked to be heroes, and they never asked to fight against the forces of evil to save the world.

All Logan ever wanted was to live a peaceful life in Aradon with Elwyne, have a child or two, grow old, and die peacefully in his sleep. Logan's father taught him that war was neither glamorous nor terrible. It was a fact. As long as there were sides that could be taken, there was going to be war. The trick to war was learning which ones needed to be fought, and which ones shouldn't. This was a war that couldn't be ignored. However, when Logan was in Rama, he saw that little prideful war and knew that it was wrong. That's why Logan stopped that war and still fought in greater one. There was no pride in war, no glory, no power, no solution, no winner, no loser, just losses. People die in war, there is no escaping that fact, and to let one person die for something that could be solved with compromise is a truly evil thing. So few people were willing to find a compromise between good and evil, feeling that evil needed to be destroyed no matter the form it took. The only thing is, sometimes it's hard to tell which side of the line you're on. You think what you're doing is right, and your enemy is the evil one, but they say the same thing about you. You are the evil to them. There is no solution as long as we are all still small-minded enough to let what we see and what we think interfere with what is the truth. Wars for land, power, money, influence, hatred, revenge, and those fought just to be fought all share one harsh reality, at the end of the day there in the trenches lie the bodies of broken men. These men were husbands, fathers, lovers, friends, and sons. But it doesn't end there. If it did war wouldn't be that terrible. Women and children wouldn't cry when their husband or father goes off to the wars, and their lives wouldn't be destroyed when they get word that the man they loved would never come home ever again. And yet there is still more. If you've ever lost a friend, you know the hurt and anguish that passes through your heart when you learn that you will never see that person again. With every person that Logan saw die, he wondered who would mourn them, and who will stand over them and curse the fact that they were ever born? Was that the line between good and evil that they all faced? Was that what they had all become? Was there not a better choice than rugged dogmatic and blind dedication to an ideal as fraught with abstraction as good or evil?

"Well," he said after a moment, "I think you're right. Bryn and I will discuss what we should do about Saurn, and we'll go from there. If there is anything else that you think we should talk about, I'll be here. Oh, don't worry Logan, I think Elwyne will be alright when we get to Shau-ling's palace."

"I hope you're right, Korrd."

That was all Logan could manage. There were still too many feelings that were whirling through his brain, and Logan didn't have the time or the sanity to think about it all. Then there was still the unanswered questions about Bryn. Logan hated to bring his thoughts back to her, but there was no way that Logan could avoid it. There was a part of him that wanted her so badly that he could not stand it, and there was the other part of him that wanted her dead. Inwardly Logan wondered which part would win out in the end.

* * * * * * * * * * * *

Gwydeon sat alone by the side of a small brook that ran near where the party had camped for the night. Thoughts ran through his mind that defied everything that he had stood for over the last few months. For so long he had wished for the opportunity to find vengeance, but now he was faced with the man who had betrayed him. There was no excusing Korrd for what he did, and Gwydeon knew that there was no way that he could ever forgive the man for such blatant treachery. There in Brea Gwydeon had Korrd right where he wanted him, on the ground and in no position to defend himself. It would only have taken a little thrust of the wrist and it would have been all over, vengeance achieved. But there was something greater that he had to be aware of. Emries had given them both a great gift, and on top of that, each of them had a responsibility to live up to. Korrd was the second *Coromor* of the prophecies, and he was fated to defeat Shauling. Even before Emries proclamation that said Gwydeon would become the Brother of Angels, Gwydeon had always been special. His prowess with a sword was no exception. For as long as Gwydeon could remember, he had always been the one who was looked on to be the strength of the group. There was never a time in which he was allowed to be weak or let his emotions control what he did. That was always Pike and Talon's domain. They were the emotional ones who let their fits of fury lead the group into wild and charged battles that usually needed a cool head to resolve. That cool head inevitably rested on Gwydeon's shoulders. He had been the architect of the plan that had gotten them almost through the battle with Hawk's forces outside of Sador. However, the one time that he had allowed his emotions to control his behavior, he had almost cost six generations their lives. Never again could he allow his rages to control him.

"That is a foolish wish my friend," a voice said from behind him.

Gwydeon knew the man before he saw him. Emries was the name that he used, but there would never be a way to know whether that was his name or not. He was the first *Coromor* and known to the rest of the world as the Creator.

"To be totally cold to your emotions in battle would get you killed as surely as surrendering to them. You have always been able to balance the two well. The way you responded to Korrd was the same way that any man would have if they were in your position."

Gwydeon sat there shaking his head. He did not know why Emries was there, but it usually meant that either something was wrong or he was trying to lead them down the right path. Gwydeon had one question that plagued his heart, and he wanted so much to have an answer to it, but he knew that Emries would never tell him.

"Ask me Gwydeon," Emries said after reading his thoughts again. "If I do not want to answer the question, then I will not. You are in no position that you would risk any wrath from me. I understand your frustration with the situation that you have been placed in, but this..."

"Is just another test," Gwydeon finished. "I am really getting sick and tired of you and the gods making us jump through hoops just to see if we are ready to die for you. You and the gods have a really sick sense of reality. You make us go through things for a reason you say, and you say that people have to die for a reason. Tell me why Korrd had to sleep with Gabrielle. Tell me why I was so angry with her that I wasn't sorry that I killed her, even if it was accidental. Tell me why I didn't kill Korrd when I had a chance. Tell me that the Gwillim that I met a few hours ago isn't my son, but that he is really Korrd's."

Emries' face changed for the first time. Usually he had the calmest demeanor; calmer than should be possible, but now came the look of surprise.

"Give me more credit than that Emries," Gwydeon said looking back at the water. "I knew who he was the second that I laid eyes on him. And no, it wasn't just the name that gave it away. The first time I looked at his eyes, I knew. He has Gabrielle's eyes Emries, and believe me, after seeing those eyes every night in my dreams you would think that I would know them pretty well by now. But the face is more like Logan and Korrd's than mine. Tell me the truth Emries. Tell me who Gwillim's father is."

Emries shook his head and sighed hard. This was not an eventuality that he had expected. No one should have been able to tell that Gwillim was not the son of Gwydeon Sandar, and that falsehood should have protected him.

"He is Korrd's son, Gwydeon, but this knowledge cannot go past this place."

Gwydeon winced at the news, but listened as Emries continued with his explanation.

"The next generation will not be a pretty one. I cannot say more than this: the forces of the Shadow know enough to damage the chances of the Light forever. It was time for me to put a slight twist on the prophecies, and Gwillim's parentage gave me the edge that I need. Unfortunately, it also gave Shau-ling the ability to spawn two new phasia. I was not lying when I said that your son would eclipse the power of the Dragon, for it is true. The child that is growing inside of Midarin Rice will inherit my power and the calling to fight evil. I know that Logan's child should be the recipient of that power, but that child has already been taken care of. Take care of her Gwydeon, she is the Light's only hope."

"I'll send her back to Brea."

"No," Emries protested, "Shau-ling already knows that your child will be the next of the prophecies. If he were to learn that you sent her away, he would send his assassins to finish her, and then my ploy for the next generation will be a failure. No, if she goes, then Gwillim must go with her to protect her legacy."

Gwydeon thought for a moment and then remembered the words that had been said only an hour earlier. He had been taken into a confidence unintentionally, but it was information that he could use.

"Emries," Gwydeon said calmly, "I have a plan..."

The Island of Mist

The night had seemed so promising at first, even as they made camp near the ruins of the royal palace of Scalla. How was Logan to know that the moment he closed his eyes to try to sleep, all hell would break loose? There had been no sign of the forces of the Shadow since they had set foot in Scalla, and it seemed that Saurn was too busy with his trap in Quea to come after them directly. So, when the group all finally decided to go to sleep for the night, Logan hoped that they all might actually get a good night sleep. He couldn't have been more wrong. Logan had just settled down on his blanket and laid his head on a rolled up cloak when he heard the argument start. The voices were familiar ones, but Logan didn't think that it would have started again so soon, at least not after the events in the throne room of Brea. By the time that Logan was up out of his makeshift bed, the fight between Gwydeon and Korrd had escalated. Gwydeon was shouting at Korrd about Gabrielle, and Korrd was shouting equally as loud about not regretting what he did. Suddenly Gwydeon shoved Korrd to the ground and drew his sword. Logan rushed over to Gwydeon's side and tried to restrain him. Pike and Talon were also up trying to form a buffer between the two raging men. Arin and Jerrard were hanging back, but Gwillim had his sword drawn and was helping Korrd back to his feet. The situation was rapidly destabilizing, and the promising start to the unified People of the Dragon was crumbling before Logan's eyes.

"What the hell are you doing Gwydeon," Logan yelled, "you can't do this, we need him alive."

By this time everyone else was up and moving toward the confrontation. Midarin's bow was ready and pointed at the center of Korrd's chest, and Stone stood beside her, massive fists balled and ready for a fight. To Logan's surprise, Gideon stood near his mother Bryn, whose hands seemed to be radiating waves of intense heat that made the air around them warp and distend. Logan could feel the tension in the group rise as the seconds passed and Gwydeon didn't lower his blade. This was not the time or the place for petty disputes to take place, and if there was going to be bloodshed, Logan prayed that it would not be fatal. He had seen the look in Gwydeon's eyes though. That look only came over Gwydeon when he was ready to kill, and from the way he had slipped into a practiced defensive position, this time was no exception. Arin took the opportunity to interject himself, leaping between Korrd and Gwydeon and drawing his own sword. Matters had just gotten worse.

"Gwydeon," Arin said strongly, "drop your sword or surrender your life. We can finish the quest without you, but we can't finish this without Korrd. Either sheath your sword or prepare to be run though."

Arin was right, they could complete the quest without Gwydeon, but without his blade in battle, the chances of more of them dying than living went up by degrees of ten. There was no real way to tell how valuable Gwydeon was to them. In the end, they were all just men and women, no matter what powers the Creator had seen fit to curse them with, but despite that, Gwydeon fought harder than any one man should have. He had stared down members of the phasia who could have smote him with the simplest move of their hand, but they underestimated just how powerful his fighting spirit was. There was no question that Gwydeon was special, even Emries had seemed to fawn over the simple man. Naturally, Midarin was the first to step up to Gwydeon's defense.

"If you lay so much as a finger on him, Arin Domae, I'll kill you. You owe me for a lot, and I'll gladly take every bit of it out of you in blood if you don't step back and let Gwydeon and Korrd settle this."

"Only if he steps back and drops his sword," Arin responded.

"Stop this this instant," Bryn thundered. "You are all acting like children. Put down your swords and go back to sleep. We are so close, let us not let these petty disputes interfere with our mission. In the morning we go after Saurn, and we all need our strength."

"Shut up you lying heartless bitch," Midarin shot back.

The next few moments played out in slow motion, and there was nothing that anyone could do to stop it. In all of Logan's memories knew what Bryn's rage felt like and knew how she could keep control of an army not only with seduction but with sharp cruelty. Grawn had always been the intimidator, but when it came to lightning fast tempers and quick rages, Bryn had him beat by a mile or more. The memories from Aerith Seth were sketchy at best, but one scene played out in Logan's mind as he saw the catastrophe of the present unfold before his eyes. Bryn was touring her armies with Aerith one morning, and she heard two of her soldiers discussing her in very derogatory terms. One of them called her a bitch under his breath, and before Aerith or the soldiers knew what was happening, Bryn spun around and burned the soldier to ashes where he stood. That same scene played out in reality as it had in memory. Bryn's hands were up the next moment and the weave of fire and air leapt from her outstretched fingers and shot across the distance between her and Midarin. Gwydeon barely saw the attack before it slammed into Midarin's chest and her body crumpled to the ground, all the life taken out of her. Logan knew that Midarin was dead before she hit the ground, but he still couldn't believe that it happened. Gwydeon's resolve snapped and he cried out before dropping to his knees beside his fallen lover. But the carnage did not end there.

Stone had always seemed to be very fond of Midarin, and that had been true from the very moment that he joined the forces of the Light. However Logan never thought that such favoritism would ever carry it to such an act. The memories from Aerith Seth were able to help put this next act in perspective, as well as Logan's own experiences with Stone. Shau-ling had put a limitation on all of his beasts, and Stone had said as much himself. Most of the time, the creatures of the Shadow were able to function on their own, and when given missions by Shau-ling, they were left alone to deal with things their way. Well, the phasia also had the power to control the beasts of the Shadow because the phasia were able to hold the Blaze in a physical form. When Logan had captured the Blaze in the Dragon Sword, Stone was unable to attack Logan and was compelled to follow his orders. From that time on Logan had been able to pull Stone away from the Shadow into the Light. However Logan didn't think that they had pulled Stone far enough for it to attack a member of the phasia. But that was exactly what happened that next moment. Stone was not swift of foot but it was quick enough to react to Midarin's death before anyone could process what was actually occurring. Stone moved slowly past Midarin's fallen body and Gwydeon's grieving form, and as it passed by a stunned Arin Domae, Stone slammed its fist into Arin's chest sending him sprawling to the ground. It was not a strike designed to kill, but it was an effective and painful strategy to remove an obstacle. Stone was focused on its target, and it was not about to let anything stand in its way. Bryn was not through by any stretch of the imagination, and she sent volley after volley of green flame racing into the oncoming stone creature. However, Stone seemed to be unaffected by the use of the Blaze, and it continued undaunted. Bryn's final scream echoed through ·the forest with the sound of her bones snapping under the sheer force of Stone's grip. Time sped up in the next moment as Bryn's broken body slid from Stone's open hand and it turned back to face the fallen Midarin. However, the battle was not over there.

Stone had now become a threat to all who followed Korrd's lead, and it would only be a matter of time before one of them tried to take revenge for Bryn. Even though she was a member of the phasia, she still had the potential to be a powerful ally and guide. Logan wanted to take out Stone himself, but that was only because part of Aerith Seth was screaming in the back of his mind. Then as Logan thought about it more, he knew that Stone had just become a liability. From its actions with Bryn, it was apparent that Stone could snap at any time, and these bouts of indiscretion were fatal. It could just as easily have been Logan or Korrd sliding from Stone's grip as it was Bryn. Apparently, Gwillim was thinking the same thing. Gwillim leapt at Stone in the next moment, but from Logan's dealings with Stone's kind in the past, Logan knew that Gwillim would stand little chance of surviving a frontal assault against something that size. Stone grabbed for Gwillim. Apparently, Bryn's attacks had not been fruitless after all and had slowed Stone's reactions and its speed because Gwillim was able to dodge the attack and land a slash to Stone's chest.

Gwillim dodged three or four more blows, and landed a few slashes of his own. The sword slashes always left a gash in the stone skin of the beast, but it did not seemed to be doing any real damage. The next attack by Gwillim proved to be a costly one. He attacked wildly at Stone's chest, but one of his legs was unable to get out of the way of Stone's grabbing hand. Gwillim's death was a quick yet painful one. Gwillim had been trying to dive out of the way of Stone's hands, but when Stone caught his leg, it pulled hard and whipped Gwillim through the air. Stone then slammed Gwillim to the ground, shattering his skull upon impact with the ground. Stone just stood there.

Something was different about the way Stone moved. All of its movements were slowed and it was as if all of its will had been stolen. By this time Korrd was back to his feet and with the Dragon Sword drawn he approached the towering stone form. Logan could see that Korrd was not going to chance an assault as Gwillim had, and he was ready to kill Stone with his powers. Pike, Talon, and the others had also backed off, but there was a palpable change in the wind and the temperature. Logan knew from experience what the Dragon Sword could do when filled with power, but now that Korrd was in possession of both the ring from the Elder and the Dragon Sword, there was no telling how much energy he could draw on and focus at one time. Logan could see him reach for the strings of power and felt the energy draw from the four members of the *Erieal* and collect in the blade of the Dragon Sword. Stone did not react to Korrd's approach, and when Korrd thrust the tip of the Dragon Sword hard into the center of the massive creature's chest, the power flooded into its body, and Stone toppled over and shattered on impact with the ground. The conflict had ended more tragically than Logan could have imagined it would have.

* * * * * * * * * * * * *

The Island of Mist pulsated with the energy of its master and his life-force that powered it. The Blaze existed within everything that grew on the island, and it had perverted most of the plants and animals on the island turning them into beasts that would devour human flesh without a thought. The lake in the center of the island was blood red in color, and it also pulsed with a life of its own. Rael sat on the edge of the lake and watched as the creatures of the lake devoured one another and added to the richness of the color of the lake. He had been sent there to wait for the arrival of the forces of the Light, but he sat in boredom, wondering if they would ever arrive. Inwardly he desired a greater test for his abilities. He saw that the war for this generation was already lost, and it was only a matter of time before the forces of the Light would land on the Island of Mist, fight their way to the throne room, and defeat his master. Granted he had only been born of late, but that was not his fault. Had he been born earlier in this lifetime, he and his sister might have been able to make a difference in the war. But they were last born now, and they were two of the remaining five phasia. It was obvious that Jeroch would be sent to the Hall of Terrors in case Rael and Trece both failed, which they inevitably would. Rael knew that he had not been sent to stop the forces of the Light all by himself. If Shau-ling had wanted them stopped, he would have sent all three of the remaining loyal phasia to meet them in a winner take all battle. Rael inwardly wondered if Shau-ling were really trying to win the battle with the Light at all. Maybe Rael had been born into the wrong force. That was the thought that occupied his mind as the day turned to night.

Trece stood in the now empty Pen and waited. She felt her brother Rael's thoughts in the back of her mind and took comfort knowing that she was not the only one who had doubts. Jeroch had told her that the phasia were the most powerful force in the world, and when they dedicated their energies to something they could not fail. It was arrogance that got you killed, and that was why the other members of the phasia had died and failed. But not all of the phasia had died because of arrogance, and not all of them had lost their lives to the forces of the Light. There was one member of the phasia that died with honor. There was a member of the phasia that died knowing what he wanted. Basille was this phase. Shau-ling and Jeroch had tried to keep his death and the things he did in this generation a secret, but when Shau-ling banished him, all of the phasia felt the string burn and felt the flash in their mind. It was a pain that radiated through the Blaze, and all creatures of the Blaze could feel the sting and smell the charred flesh of their former brother. Basille had served the forces of Light and Shadow at the same time. He kept his kingdom and he followed Shau-ling's orders, but he sent his son and gave his time and advice to both Korrd and Logan Ranthall. Trece and Rael both knew in their hearts and in their minds that the side of the Shadow was corrupt and warped with arrogance and greed, but at the present time they were trapped. They had been born because of a rift between the Shadow and Light that created an imbalance. But that was what Shau-ling had told them. What if that were not so? What if there was no imbalance, and they were born with the ability to choose who they fought for, just like Basille did? Trece knew that she was grasping at straws, but when she felt Rael's heart jump at the idea, she knew that hope was not lost. Now was not the time for change, but the time would come, and in that time, Rael and Trece would be free.

In the Hall of Terror, the newly designed Flame and Jeroch stood speaking briefly. This would be where the final stand against the forces of the Light would take place, and Jeroch knew in his heart that if he failed, his master would not be able to defend himself, even without the surprise that Shau-ling had in store for the Ranthall brothers. Suddenly, Jeroch heard the roar of laughter come from his master, and Jeroch responded by entering the throne room. There sat his master, Shau-ling, on the throne laughing as loud as he could. Nightwing stood to his left, the armor retracted showing the still stomach churning form of Aryx Terian.

"What is it, Master?"

Shau-ling looked up and smiled with his reptilian eyes and mouth. It was a truly unusual sight to see Shau-ling smile, and Jeroch knew that something had happened that would change the course of history.

"Ah, Shadow. The battle is won. The little girl Elwyne has given me the secret of the next generation's *Coromor* and without having to act, the next generation is lost."

Jeroch looked at Aryx and then back at his master. When the subject of the *Coromor* came up, it was obvious that Jeroch only knew what he was told. He was never as perceptive as Grawn, Bryn, or Ellis, but he knew that if the *Coromor* were not born into the next generation, the prophecies were broken.

"What is this secret, my lord Shau-ling?" Jeroch asked.

"Emries made a grave mistake by forcing me to protect the life of Elwyne Tamerlane. He knew that once I found out that Logan Ranthall was the *Chosen One* that I would kill her. Because of this action, he has sealed the fate of the next generation."

"Master," Jeroch said approaching the throne, "forgive me for not understanding, but how, if we are not permitted to kill Elwyne Tamerlane, is the fate of the next generation sealed? If she were to be rescued and the forces of the Light were able to vanquish you in this lifetime, the third *Coromor* of the prophecies will be born and the cycle will start all over again."

Shau-ling laughed all the harder.

"I'll forgive your insolence this time, Jeroch. The forces of the Light will not defeat me in this generation, but if you fail, and the *Coromor* does make it this far, and defeats me, the prophecies will never be fulfilled, provided that you decrease the number of powered individuals below seven. Kill one of the *Erieal* and the prophecies end here."

"But how is that possible?" Jeroch questioned again.

Shau-ling sighed and then chuckled.

"Jeroch, your lack of vision amazes me. Upon learning the truth about the parentage of Logan and Korrd Ranthall, I realized something. The forces of the Light have been very obvious about their plans, and they have also been very obvious about who and what is important to them, almost to the point of making it laughable. Emries made me promise to protect Elwyne Tamerlane to make me think that she is carrying the next generation's *Coromor*. In truth however, she is not. She is not a factor anymore. When Ellis and Bryn figured out how the line was passed from *Chosen One* to *Coromor*, they used their gender as a weapon, and used their bodies as a vessel of destruction. Ellis completed her task but was too weak in the mind to carry out the task of destroying Korrd before he could become a thorn in my side. Then I thought, why would she want to kill the very creature that could destroy the vengeful father that tossed her away like she didn't exist? She didn't kill Korrd, because if he lived she could get revenge upon me. Bryn took her revenge by harboring Aerith Seth from me. In the next lifetime I will make good for wronging them by bringing the three of them back into the Council."

Jeroch took a step back and started to speak, but when Shau-ling raised a hand, he waited for his master to finish.

"This is not open for discussion Jeroch, but that is not where the story ends. Emries outsmarted himself and unknowingly walked right into my clutches. Because of Bryn and Ellis' discovery, Emries was forced to exercise his right as the first *Coromor* to pass his mantle to someone else besides the child of the *Chosen One*. This is where he failed. It was obvious to me though the reports from the other phasia, and through my operatives Stone and Fion, that Gwydeon Sandar would be the most logical choice. His child was prophesied by Emries himself to be greater than the Dragon. This was the secret that I was able to pry out of Elwyne Tamerlane. So, I decided to target Gwydeon Sandar as well as his lover Midarin Rice and their unborn child. The man called Gwillim that was Gwydeon's child, the child that Emries brought back to life from the city of the gods, is no longer a threat. Stone was strong enough to finish him too. The most wonderful development though is the fact that half of our job has been done for us by human arrogance and stupidity. Bryn has paid me back again by killing Midarin Rice and her unborn child, and then my Stone took care of Bryn so that she will be unable to lead them through the palace. All we must do now is make sure that Gwydeon Sandar does not leave this palace alive, and the next generation's fate will be sealed as well as the fates of all generations to come."

Shau-ling's evil laugh reverberated throughout the palace as Jeroch stood and smiled, waiting for the arrival of a true challenge.

* * * * * * * * * * * *

Logan thought the fact that three of their allies died was tragic and contemptible, but when Gwydeon started laughing, Logan's mind felt as though it were going to snap from the contradiction and confusion. Pike and Talon stared as though they thought Gwydeon had gone mad. Korrd sat down on the ground and looked at Gwydeon as if he lost his mind. Logan could not resist the urge to feel the same way. Perhaps the loss of Midarin had pushed Gwydeon past the brink. When Emries appeared the next moment with a wide smile painted on his face, Logan realized that they had all been fooled. Logan stood and approached Emries, but he waived everyone away.

"I know what you're thinking Logan, and I wouldn't act on it. It would not look very favorably upon you if you were to strike me."

Logan wanted to hit him anyway.

"Relax Logan," Gwydeon said calmly, "if you're going to hit anyone, it should be me. Believe it or not, this was all my idea, I just needed Emries' help to make it happen."

Logan nodded and tried to figure out exactly why this had all happened. Pike buried his ax in the ground and sat down on the ground, impatience and irritation hanging on him like a cloak. The rest of the group looked to thoroughly shocked and confused to react at all. Fortunately Emries' explanation followed quickly after Gwydeon's admission.

"I may be the first *Coromor* and I may reside among the gods," Emries started, "but that does not make me infallible. I am still subject to passions and frailties. The gods do not want to admit it, but they sometimes make mistakes too. However, the point you should take from all this is that if I can make mistakes, Shau-ling can to. You see years ago, Grawn, Bryn, and Ellis were banished from the Council, and they were left to go on their own and do what they pleased. This was because they had learned of the creation of a being called the *Chosen One*, later discovered to be a man named Aerith Seth who possessed extraordinary abilities. Bryn, and Ellis, because of their knowledge and frankly their arrogance, took him in and used him in their armies. Bryn also took him as her lover in the hopes of forcing a child that would be the next *Coromor*. But Aerith Seth already had a child, the man who would become Cedric Binosear, and Aerith Seth's death at Shau-ling's had would start the prophecies and allow me to bestow my mantle on a human. However, it did not end there. As you all know, Ellis is the mother of Korrd, and he is the *Coromor*. The problem that this causes is that the phasia are able to end the prophecies if Caris, Bryn, or Ellis are able to seduce the *Chosen One*. Logan, Caris nearly got to you, but luckily for you, Elwyne was already pregnant."

"Yes," Logan said with distress thick in his voice. "But Shau-ling has Elwyne."

"Don't worry Logan," Emries continued. "I have extended my protection to Elwyne Tamerlane, and Shau-ling knows it. He would not dare risk the vengeance of the gods if he were to kill her. When your forces win the battle, she will be safe. But I'm sorry to say that it does not matter now. Your child will not be the next *Coromor* of the prophecies, that much is certain, and as I prophesied before, it will be the child of Gwydeon Sandar that will strike the fatal blow in the next generation."

"But Midarin and Gwillim are dead," Gideon said shortly.

"Are they?"

With that Emries raised his hands and a bright light enveloped the bodies of Midarin, Gwillim, and Bryn. Within a moment the light receded and the three of them were standing. They looked around for a moment, but when Bryn's eyes fell on Emries she recoiled in horror.

"Worry not Shadow-spawn, I will not harm you. You will serve your purpose in this lifetime by leading my allies into the heart of Shau-ling's palace, and then in the next lifetime you will return to the Council of the Brotherhood of Phasia. It would behoove you to think of what will happen from this point forward as a terrible dream that you know you will wake up from. My protection will extend to the end of this lifetime, and will prevent other members of the phasia from being able to see you or act upon you. However, once you reach the door to Shau-ling's throne room, you will go to the Other Side and await your rebirth. You will not act without my permission, and you will reveal no information that has not already been preordained. Do you understand?"

"Yes."

Bryn crossed her arms at her chest, and Logan could see the familiar look of disgust in her features. She did not like the position that she had been relegated to, and it showed.

"Now, for the problem of the next generation," Emries continued. "Now that I have passed my mantle to Gwydeon's child, some truths must be known to you all. Gwillim Crill is the son of Gabrielle Crill, Gwydeon's former lover and the former friend to so many of you. However, Gwillim is not Gabrielle's child. Gabrielle always believed that it was, and it was her devotion that made me keep her in the city of the gods and to give her the gift of rebirth. So, she lived, as did Gwillim, but she was reborn in a time before her death, and that is why Gwillim is roughly the same age as Gwydeon. It helped to keep the mystery alive. As I said, Gwillim is not Gwydeon's child; he is actually the son of Korrd Ranthall."

Gwillim looked at Korrd for a moment, and Korrd returned the gaze. Logan knew the story of Korrd saving Gwillim from fire outside of Brea, but now that story took on a whole different meaning. Korrd always said that there was something that happened between him and the man that he saved, and that there was some kind of connection that he felt. He said that he couldn't explain what it was that he was feeling, but he knew that he wasn't imagining it. Well, now Korrd knew what the connection was. Logan could tell that Korrd was shocked, but he was trying to control his feelings and his reactions. The only reason that Logan knew was the fact that he could feel Korrd's emotions in the corner of his mind floating along the void where their powers lived. Logan was sure that the fact they were brothers had something to do with it as well, but when it came to their powers, there was never any way to be absolutely sure.

"However," Emries continued after a moment, "Gwillim's true parentage is only important in the narrowest scope of things. Shau-ling knows that if Gwillim was Gwydeon's son, he would inherit my mantle. Since this is the case, Shau-ling would have stopped at nothing to destroy first Gwillim, and then Midarin."

"So," Gwydeon continued seemingly unfazed by the revelations, "by faking their deaths we have accomplished two things. We have kept the mystery of Gwillim's parentage alive for the forces of the Shadow, and we have kept the true heir to Emries' power hidden away from Shau-ling. By the time he finds out, it will be too late for him to do anything about it."

Emries' smile widened.

"This knowledge of Gwillim and Midarin's death will cause Shau-ling to become over-confident, and will leave him ripe for the picking. Now he will not concentrate on the total destruction of your forces, but rather will settle for picking off one or two of you to prevent seven powered individuals from entering his throne room. I would like to see you all succeed, but in a way you already have."

With that Emries disappeared. As was always the way with his visits, there was this shroud of doubt and of hope that lingered. They all knew now what had to be done, but as always, whispers of secrets and schemes skittered into the darkness when any light was cast in their direction. It was obvious that there was more that Emries was hiding from them, and Logan wondered if they would ever know the real truth of it all.

"So, what do we do now?" Midarin asked.

"Now you and Gwillim return to Brea," Gwydeon replied softly. "He'll get you there safely. We can't let Shau-ling know that the two of you are still alive until it is too late for him to do anything about it. I know you don't like it, but..."

"I understand," Midarin replied, cutting off his attempts at defending his decision.

With that she kissed him and turned toward Gwillim who was standing near Korrd trying to find the words for what he wanted to say.

"Father, I..."

"No Gwillim," Korrd said shaking his head, "I'm not your father. I may have been the one responsible for giving you life, but I was never there for you while you were growing up. Your mother was an incredible woman, and I could never take anything away from the job she did raising you."

Gwillim's look changed from one of confusion to one of disappointment. Inside his heart had to be breaking.

"Though I won't allow you to call me father," Korrd continued in the next moment, "I would be glad to call you my son, and your stubbornness has proven you to be a Ranthall, if not in name but in action."

A smile came across his face then and the two men embraced. Logan could not help but think that they were a truly interesting family, the

Ranthalls, but when it came down to protecting their own, there was no family more devoted.

"Well," Logan said after the awkward moments of silence, "we should get on our way to the Island of Mist."

"Agreed," Korrd responded. "Bryn, will you be able to get us into the palace without too many problems?"

"It's difficult to say," she responded. "Shau-ling has probably increased the defenses on the island, but I should be able to get us there in one piece."

"Good," Logan replied. "I wouldn't want to keep Shau-ling waiting."

CHAPTER 22

Chapter XXIII

The Palace

Fear is the kind of motivation that you cannot help but follow, especially when the fear is driving you in the right direction. Logan had been afraid before during the quest, and he had been worried a lot, but never anything like what he felt as he got a first glimpse of the Island of Mist. For the most part, the fear that Logan had been feeling recently had been because of Elwyne. Having her taken away from him by Taron, and not knowing from one day to the next whether or not she was alive was starting to eat away at him from the inside. Insecurity was not something that Logan could fight and still be at his best, and that's exactly what would be demanded of him in the battles to come; his best. The last night when they camped in Scalla, or rather the remains of Scalla, Logan could not sleep. The nervousness of the situation had finally gotten to him, and it was all Logan could do to keep from getting sick. They had been asking for this, their chance to take on Shau-ling directly, and now they had it. Logan's father had always said be careful what you wish for, and Logan was truly beginning to understand why.

We shouldn't have been able to get this far, was the thought that kept echoing in Logan's mind over and over again. *We were just people, and young people at that, and the fate of the world was hung around our necks like a noose. One wrong step, and we end up falling over the edge and strangling ourselves with our own stupidity. The trouble was that we kept making the mistakes that should have gotten us killed, but each and every time we walked away. We should have been done for when the Tarnae had us in the forest outside of Illimar. The only reason that we lived was the fact that the Tarnae was playing with us. Then when we were blown off course and ended up in Sador, the Snags should have destroyed us and those that the Snags didn't get should have been wiped out by the Jeresei. The fact that Pike discovered his powers was the only thing that saved us, and without them, we would have been dead. Our powers have saved us too many times, and I can only guess how many times that Emries has saved us by his little clues and his careful manipulations.*

Why us? Why did we have to be the ones to take on the forces of evil for the rest of the world? Here I was, the son of a former warrior, raised to be a farmer, and I'm chosen to help save the world from Shau-ling? Why? There is something that is missing here. There has to be some greater reason that my brother and I were forced to fight. Could it be because our mother was the phase Ellis? Is this some kind of cosmic justice? I can't sit here and actually try to convince myself that I am here just because of my mother and father. But then my father was the Chosen One *of the first generation. Should I even ask why that is? I guess I'm just frustrated and trying to keep my mind off of the fact that the whole thing is coming to an end for us. In a matter of hours we will be face to face with the very thing that could well destroy all of us and the world as we know it. Scared? Yeah, I'm scared, but anyone would be too if they were in my position.*

From the small port in Scalla, Jerrard and Gideon were able to find a small ship that was still in one piece and large enough to carry the party across the sea to the Island of Mist. Bryn had explained that there was no way to use a portal to get the Island because of the protections that Shau-ling had erected to defend his palace. So, the only way to get to the island was the old-fashioned way. No one in the port was willing to crew the ship, but Jerrard and Gideon were confident that they would be able to ensure we got there safely with Pike and Talon's help. The trip would take several hours, and as the sun began to rise over the horizon, the small ship lurched out of port, and Logan stood on deck looking out into the distance waiting to get his first glimpse of their destination.

The Island of Mist loomed larger as the People of the Dragon approached. The seas were incredibly rough, and they were buffeted around so much that Logan thought that the waves were going to rip the boat apart. Off in the distance was a huge shroud of mist that hung like a low cloud over the island that housed Shau-ling's palace. They were not given much time to look at the island as Korrd called everyone below deck for a meeting in which Bryn would tell them what they were supposed to expect upon reaching the island. Logan could tell everyone what to expect without thinking about it too much. Whatever phasia were still alive would be throwing everything they had at them, Jeresei by the thousands would be trying to rip their throats out, enough Shadowwalkers to black out the sky would be breathing down streams of fire, moving mountains of Stone would try to crush them, and Tarnae would trap them in warped worlds long enough to devour them. Sounded pretty simple in Logan's mind, and he though everyone else in the group had a similar view of what would happen. So why the briefing? The reason was that Bryn was trying to be important, and Korrd was flexing his muscles as the newly appointed leader. But those were petty thoughts. The part of Logan that was Aerith Seth knew that Bryn had valuable information about the Throne Room and the Hall of Terrors, places only a few mortals had seen and fewer still had survived. Aryx and Cedric's council had been lost to them, and Bryn was the only source of information left; that and the broken and fragmented memories that Logan and Korrd could sometimes call upon. Logan was still on deck when the meeting started, and it took Korrd a minute or two to send someone after him. When Pike came up, Logan waited until Pike said something before Logan turned around.

"You know that Korrd wanted us all downstairs didn't you Logan?"

"Yeah Pike," Logan replied after a moment, still staring at the Island of Mist as it grew in the foreground, "I know. I was just thinking about Elwyne and the tasks ahead."

He didn't say anything for a moment and then walked over to the rail and leaned forward with his arms folded on the wooden rail. It took him a few more moments before he spoke, and Logan could tell he had a lot on his mind by the way that he was breathing and just sort of looking at the water.

"What do you think our chances are in there?" he said exhaling slowly.

"Better than anyone else in the world. Even better now that Korrd, Jerrard, and Arin are with us. We may actually survive the fight now."

Pike kicked at the rail absently, nervousness needing to find some outlet.

"I hate to seem like a pessimist Logan, but I don't think we're going to make it. There is too much wrong with the group now, and I know that we all don't trust one another. Jerrard and Arin are new to the group, and while their powers may be a help to you and Korrd, they won't be able to defend themselves against the Jeresei, let alone the Shadowwalkers. Korrd is too involved with Bryn to be thinking straight. Gwydeon's got a fixation on death, Talon's worried about me, and I'm just dying to kill something and get this whole thing over with. Then there's you. You've been screwed up since we lost Elwyne, and it's a wonder that you're still alive."

"You're saying that I'm a problem?" Logan said turning to probably his best friend in the entire world. "And what about you? Ever since Eldar died you've been running off and risking your life if there was the slightest chance that you could kill a member of the phasia or one of their little servants. At best you were reckless, and at worst you were stupid. Taron's dead, and still you haven't let up. If you go charging off when we hit the Island, you're dead. I know you're good with that ax and your powers, but surrounded by the worst that Shau-ling has to offer and on his own island, you won't last five minutes. The only way that we're going to get this done is together, so you have to put this vendetta aside."

Pike glared at Logan for a moment.

"You first. Just remember, you can't save Elwyne if you're dead."

Then he turned and started back toward the stairs. Logan just watched him walk away for a moment and then began to follow. In a matter of moments they were in the crew hold with everyone else. Gideon had fixed the rudder so that it would not deviate from their course, and Talon had surrounded the ship with a bubble of gentle wind that would keep them moving. Korrd only looked up for a moment before he started talking.

"Now that everyone is here, I'm going to give the floor to Bryn, and she is going to tell us what we should expect when we break the barrier of mist that shrouds the island."

Bryn stood from where she was sitting and looked over the group for a moment. Logan could feel the part of him that used to be Aerith Seth jump as her eyes met his. When Logan saw the smile come to her face, he knew that his reaction had been a more physical one than he had intended. It was hard not to react to a woman of her beauty, but when part of him that he can't control was also in love with the woman, it made it that much more difficult. Finally Bryn cleared her throat and began to speak. Her voice was calm and even, but Logan could detect the hint of fear just at the edges.

"The Island of Mist is a danger and a creature all of its own. Whenever Shau-ling chooses the place for his palace, he bonds with the land and bends it to his will. The trees, mountains, lakes, and even the grass has become imbued with the powers of the Blaze and will strike at his command. The island itself is ringed with a huge mountain range that completely encircles the island. There is a safe path through the mountain, but it will be heavily guarded by Jeresei and Shadowwalkers. Once we negotiate the path, we will have to make a stand at Blood Lake. There will most likely be a phase leading that army, and it will take the strength of all of you to make it through. After that I will be able to lead you into the palace. We will emerge in a place that we refer to as the Pen. This is where all of the beasts of the palace wait for their orders. It is mine to know that the Pen has been cleared, and so what awaits us will be an army hand-picked to try and defeat us. There is little doubt that this army will be led by a phase as well. Once we make it through that it will be time to negotiate the Hall of Terrors. However, I will give you information on that when you have survived the other battles."

"How many of the phasia are left?" Talon asked after a moment.

"Aldridge, Taron, Basille, Erdric, Farax, and Caris are dead by our hands," Korrd replied. "Zarsi died at the hands of Saurn."

"Warron, Grawn, and Ellis were exterminated by Nightwing," Bryn replied.

"Saurn is sitting in Quea waiting on us, and Bryn is on our side," Logan added.

"That leaves Rael, Trece, Jeroch, Nightwing, and the Flame," Bryn finished. "Jeroch and Nightwing will obviously not be deployed until we reach the throne room, and the Flame is not able to leave the Hall of

Terrors. So, that means that Rael and Trece will be leading the armies that we will face once we reach the Island of Mist. I don't know anything about them other than the fact that they exist, so I will not be much help."

"We've faced them," Pike replied, "and we didn't do too well. Of course they had help from Nightwing, but hopefully they'll be separated and without the help of that Shadowwalker from hell we should stand a pretty good chance of beating each of them one on one."

"Well," Korrd said as he stood, "we should all get some sleep. I'll wake the rest of you before we penetrate the mist. Good night."

With that he and Bryn left the hold and went up on deck. Everyone milled around for a few minutes before they found bunks and tried to sleep. Logan was too nervous and scared to sleep. It wasn't that he didn't want to sleep, but he just couldn't. However, he knew he had to try. That's the weird thing about being tired. Sometimes you don't know that you are. As soon as Logan's head hit the small thin pillow, sleep took him. Logan didn't hear or feel anything until Korrd shook him a few hours later when they were ready to cross through the mist.

"It's time," was all he said and then he went about waking the rest of the party.

Logan shook himself awake after a moment and then began to help rouse the rest of the sleeping members of the group. What sleep Logan had gotten hadn't been restful, and then and there he realized that he hadn't had a restful night's sleep since he lost Elwyne. Then came the caution from the back of his mind.

You haven't lost her yet Logan, she is still alive, and when you kill Shau-ling, you'll get her back. Don't lose hope.

But that was exactly what was happening. She was in the palace, had been for some time now, and every minute was one more minute that Shau-ling could have killed her.

Those thoughts still ran through his head when Logan finally made it to the top deck. Just at that moment, the bow of the ship was beginning to penetrate the mist. In a matter of moments, they were all enveloped by it.

As soon as the mist touched Logan's flesh, a cold chill ran through him like death had wrapped itself around his body and was feeding off of his fear. The shivering and horrible feelings didn't stop until they were clear of the mist. Korrd stood fast at the bow of the ship staring off into the mountains that now faced them. The island started with a small string of a beach and then the mountains stared out of nowhere, rising almost completely vertical out of the ground and continuing into the mist above. Off to the east, there appeared to be a fissure in the wall of rock, but it looked barely big enough to slip a piece of paper, let alone a human body through. But sure enough, as they all disembarked, Bryn and Korrd began to lead the group to the fissure.

Logan's opinion of the passage didn't change much when he finally saw it up close. The crack was perhaps large enough to squeeze through, but the rock was course and jagged enough to flay your skin off as you wedged yourself through.

"We're goin' through dere?" Gideon said coldly. It wasn't really a question, and the tone of his voice was one of disgust and disappointment. "Really Bryn, dere has ta be another way. I could always use me power ta open da t'ing up, but dat would probably let da big guy know we're here."

"Right as usual Gideon," she replied. "Besides, if you used your powers on the fissure, it would most likely decide to close on the first person through just out of spite. But in answer, yes, this is the only way through the mountain range. The peaks are too high and too perilous to climb over, and we would be sitting ducks for the Shadowwalkers once we make it into the mist. We would never see them until it was too late. Now the army of Shau-ling probably is sitting on the other side of this hole, but we'll deal with that when we get there. Right now I say we go through one at a time, each one signaling the next to go through."

"Agreed," Korrd said without waiting for anyone else's comments. "Who's going in first?"

Without any hesitation, Pike stepped forward and drew his ax.

"I'm going first."

Korrd was about to step aside and let him when Gwydeon grabbed him by the shoulder and pulled him away from the hole.

"Not this time, old buddy. The last thing we need is for one of you boys with the powers getting your heads chopped off by some over ambitious Jeresei. Let the professional mortals handle this stuff."

For a moment Logan thought that Pike was going to argue with him, but he stepped away from the hole and motioned for Gwydeon to go ahead. As much as they all hated to admit it, Gwydeon was right. They had the seven that it would take to destroy Shau-ling, and if one of them failed to make it to the throne room, then the battle would only be put off for another generation, and their chances for succeeding at all would be lessened. All Logan knew was that at that moment they had a chance to end it once and for all, and if they had to lose Gwydeon to do it, so be it. Though the thought turned Logan's stomach, he could not get passed the fact that one life for thousands was a trade that could not be passed up.

Gwydeon regarded the fissure for a moment and then wedged himself in. Everyone watched as he inched along the passage. The way that the fissure was situated was that Gwydeon had to stand up, keep his hands at his side and slide his body through the crack, adjusting to the formation of the rock with every step that he took. At one point Logan saw him wince as he pushed himself though a rather tight section of the rock. After three or four minutes of careful maneuvering, Gwydeon came out on the other side. As they watched him though the crack, he looked around and then motioned for the next member of the group to follow. One by one each member of the group slid through the crack. When Logan went through, he could feel the rock scraping at his skin, threatening to draw blood. Once he looked down and noticed a bloody smear on the wall that he was later able to identify by the huge tear on Pike's left arm. It was not a deep or painful wound, but it was one that would annoy and would also be a ripe target for a member of the Jeresei to strike for. A small wound could always be opened into a larger one.

The landscape on the other side of the fissure was not what Logan had expected at all. The grass on the ground was not green as it should have been. It was green, but it glow and burned with a fury and pulsed with a life of its own. As soon as Logan saw the glow intensify slightly, his memory sparked back to the battle with Aldridge and his use of the Blaze. The land was alive with that evil energy, and Logan could almost the power swelling around him. For a moment Logan stopped, took a breath, and opened his awareness to the land around him. In that split second Logan was pulverized by the amount of energy around him and fell to the ground, clutching his head in pain. Korrd and Bryn were at Logan's side in the next second, helping him to his feet.

"Careful Logan," Bryn said with that sweet voice, "if you reach out too much you are liable to inadvertently touch the Blaze and make yourself a slave to Shau-ling. Remember, you are within mere feet of the source of Shau-ling's power, and it would destroy you if you opened up to it fully. For your own sake, keep your attentions focused on the powers of your brother and the *Erieal*. That will keep you safe."

Logan nodded in ascent, and allowed them to help him back to his feet. For a few seconds Logan felt shaky, and when Korrd and Bryn let go of his arms, he nearly fell back to the ground. Korrd caught Logan and bore most of his weight. There was nothing that Logan could focus on, and his vision was blurred momentarily. It took a few attempts at blinking and refocusing, but finally his vision began to clear. Logan followed Bryn's advice and reached out to Korrd and the members of the *Erieal*. Pike, Talon, and Gideon's powers flowed into him quickly, and after a moment so did Arin's and Jerrard's. It took a few minutes before he began to feel any power from Korrd, but once he did, the feeling inside of Logan changed from desolation to elation. He felt that he was about to burst from the power inside, but Logan let it go again once he was sure that he had recovered. It was difficult to let the power go, but Logan knew that it wasn't needed yet.

Once they were ready, Bryn led the group toward what she had referred to as Blood Lake. The glade of grass ended abruptly in a twisted forest. The bark of the trees radiated with the same power as the grass, but this power seemed to be darker. Unlike with the grass, Logan didn't have to reach out to feel the power of the trees. It was like the trees had a will of their own and they were using the powers that they were imbued with to crush them with feelings of repression and doom. It was a physical feeling of hate that assaulted them as they walked down the path through the evil forest, and Logan kept waiting for the trees to reach out and attack.

However, the attack never came, and there had yet to be an attack made on them since setting foot on the Island of Mist. They walked through the forest for nearly an hour before a clearing became visible before them. More and more Logan was getting the feeling that they were being watched, but the source of the feeling was not evident. The trees themselves were oppressive, but they were not the source of the uneasy feeling. He was sure that there were Jeresei out in the forest somewhere, stalking them. He wasn't sure why he knew it was Jeresei, he just did. Then when the group made it out of the forest into the clearing, Logan saw a lake unlike any he had ever seen in his life.

The water in the lake was red, blood red, and it was a safe assumption that this was the Blood Lake that Bryn had spoken of. There beside the lake was a figure that Logan immediately recognized. It was the man who had called himself simply Rael when they had encountered the man and woman in that huge cave. As he did then, Rael now wore a totally black set of clothes and he held a long black sword in his right hand. Rael was not the most physically impressive of the phasia that they had met, but he had this fury in his eyes and in his posture that Logan had never seen in any other man or phase. His whole manner demanded fear and respect, and it was as if any moment he could strike any member of the party down, including Logan, and there would be nothing that any of them could do to stop it. He had yet to speak, but the threat was already there.

"Welcome, forces of the Light," Rael said slowly in a proud strong voice, "the High Lord of the Shadows wishes to congratulate you on making it to his Island, and also would like to express his sadness that you will not be able to see him in person. As my lord Shau-ling is a gracious and forgiving lord, he would like to make you an offer so that all of you would not have to forfeit your lives. Shau-ling would gladly let the rest of you live as his servants if you sacrifice the lives of Logan and Korrd Ranthall here and now."

"Why do you make this offer, Rael?" Korrd asked after a second. "Why don't you just loose your army on us? Surely Shau-ling would not send you out here alone to face us."

"Oh," Rael said hefting his sword and laying it on his shoulder, "my army is very close now, however they are holding for my order. Believe me, this offer from my master is a real one. You and your children will be protected in the age of Shadows to come. If you fight, you will surely lose, and your families will suffer greatly. If you sacrifice the Ranthall brothers now, you and your families will be spared a fate worse than death. This is your only chance to save yourselves."

The next second, Jeresei appeared all around then. There were thousands of them, all with claws and fangs bared, ready to rip the humans apart. Pike and Talon were already back to back with *Debuisa* glowing primal colors. Gideon was ready too, and Logan knew that it would only take one word or gesture to start the battle. However, the next twist was something that Logan would have never expected.

"Lord Rael," Gwydeon said stepping forward and drawing his sword. "I will make you a counter offer. I challenge you to personal combat with weapons only. If you are truly as confident of your skill as I think you to be, you will fight me without your powers."

"Why should I want to fight you at all when my Jeresei can just cut you down? I know of you Gwydeon Sandar, and I know of your skill with a sword. Fighting you would prove nothing."

"Oh, but it might," Gwydeon replied. "Here are the terms of the duel. If I win, your army will disengage and allow us passage into the palace. If you win, Logan and Korrd will sacrifice themselves. Remember Rael, I am to be the father of the third generation's *Coromor*, so if you kill me, even if my friends go against our agreement, you and your brothers and sisters have already won the war. The duel is of course to the death."

Rael looked Gwydeon over for several long moments, not quite sure what it was that he wanted to say in response. Logan could only imagine that Rael was trying to figure out whether or not he could take Gwydeon in one on one combat without powers. Though Logan did have confidence in Gwydeon's skill, it was never good to underestimate one of the phasia.

"I accept your terms, Sandar," Rael said after a moment, "my life, or the lives of the Ranthall brothers."

With that the black clad phase stepped forward and lowered his sword and his body into a combat stance. Gwydeon took only a moment to step forward and assume a similar stance. Gwydeon edged closer and closer to Rael until their swords touched. In the next second both of the combatants moved in unison, drawing back their blades and swinging fully at their opponent. The two swords met with a shower of sparks. Rael and Gwydeon both leaned into one another, fighting for some kind of leverage advantage, but the two were too equal in strength. They were nearly mirror images of one another in skill and power, and as they disengaged the leverage duel, they circled one another with swords lowered. Rael was the first to strike, as he leapt at Gwydeon with his sword raised high and it came down with a quick downward slash. Gwydeon parried the blow as he fell to one knee and raised his sword above his head. He then slashed at the phase's knees, but Rael was quick enough to jump away from his prey and avoid the strike. Gwydeon rose slowly to his feet, never taking his eyes off of Rael, and the two warriors began to circle one another again.

This time Gwydeon charged, marking Rael's right shoulder as the target of his diagonal slash. The lunge was foiled as Rael sidestepped and brought the blade of his sword down. The strike easily would have cleaved the head of a lesser opponent, but Gwydeon was better than most. As soon as he saw the strike would miss, he pulled his sword in and allowed his momentum to carry him into a roll that brought him under the path of Rael's sword. At the end of the roll, Gwydeon popped up to a knee and brought his sword up in time to stop Rael from hurrying into another strike. Rael stayed a safe distance from Gwydeon as he rose back to his feet. The two circled again, but this time a little faster. The respect was there, and the combatants were ready to fully test the skills of the other. Rael charged Gwydeon and their swords met time and time again as the two tried to find some inch of opening that they could exploit to draw first blood. Steel flashed and sparks flew as the two swords challenged one another for superiority. The blur of motion was almost too much to keep up with as Rael and Gwydeon danced around one another with deadly precision. The two were moving at incredible speeds, blocking slashes and thrusts that few other swordsmen could duplicate, let alone block. It was as if any moment one of the two would slip, and a strike would land that would prove to be fatal. In a battle like this, first blood was liable to be last blood, as the one who slipped would end up with a sword in the heart, or the loss of a head. It would only be a matter of time.

The combatants broke apart again. However, Gwydeon charged seconds later. Rael was ready. As the two combatants passed one another, both charging at full speed, time slowed to a crawl. Logan never saw either strike that landed, but when the two parted, a plume of blood burst from Gwydeon's side. Rael showed no sign of injury until he fell to his knees and then to his face, the blood pouring from a slash to the neck that all but severed his head from his shoulders. Gwydeon fell to his knees too, clutching the wound in his side. Pike and Talon hurried over to him, but as they tried to close the wound with their powers, it kept reopening. When Bryn looked at the wound she shook her head.

"That wound was inflicted by a weapon forged in the Blaze. A part of the Blaze exists in the wound and will prevent any type of healing until it is removed. However, if you touch the Blaze to remove it, you will become a slave to Shau-ling's will."

"Can't you remove the Blaze?" Logan asked.

Bryn shook her head.

"I am not to interfere. If I break the covenant set down by Emries that allows me to be here, we will all suffer. If you seal the wound with Fire, the bleeding will stop, but the Blaze will still eat at the man. Only the death of Shau-ling will heal the wound completely."

Jerrard stepped forward.

"What about me? I can touch the Blaze because I'm a child of a phase."

Bryn looked at Jerrard with a sympathetic smile.

"You have bravery Jerrard, but that is not enough. The process is painstaking and precise. If you were to make the slightest mistake not only could you kill Gwydeon, but you very likely could kill yourself. The risk is simply too great for someone of your lack of experience."

Jerrard frowned but finally nodded. The only course of action was clear. It only took a second, and Logan pooled his powers with Arin and Talon and sealed Gwydeon's wound as best they could. All of a sudden Logan remembered the army of Jeresei that had massed around us, but when he looked up, they were gone.

"Where did they go?" Logan asked out loud.

"When Rael fell, dey retreated," Gideon answered.

"Imagine that," Talon scoffed, "a phase keeping his word."

Bryn scowled at the comment and then turned toward a wall of rock that rose just past Blood Lake.

"This is the path into the palace," she said shortly, "follow closely."

Fortunately, the passage through the rock face was much more pleasant than the last one. Logan kept a close eye on Gwydeon, but he seemed to be doing all right. The passage was well-lit by torches that were mounted to the walls with black steel sculptures that looked to be in the shape of Jeresei heads. There was a constant downward grade to the path, and the glow of the torches seemed to get brighter the farther down the passage they traveled. It was obvious by the smoothness of the walls that this passage was not naturally occurring, but from Bryn's explanations of how Shau-ling effected the environment around him, Logan was not surprised. Within a few minutes of travel, the passage opened into a massive chamber that could have easily contained the entire city of Brea and still had room for Aradon and Illimar. In the ceiling was a large opening that was obviously an exit for those beasts that could fly. Again, Bryn's assessment of the situation was wrong, and there was not a force waiting for the forces of the Light in the Pen. Bryn looked around puzzled for a moment, and then turned to Korrd.

"I don't understand this Korrd, this place should be full. Shau-ling would be a fool not to set a trap here."

Korrd scratched his chin.

"Maybe he didn't expect us to be here so soon, or maybe he didn't expect us to get by Rael. Believe me Bryn, I'm not complaining. The less we have to fight, the less chance that we are going to lose someone vital to the plan."

Bryn nodded and led them around the edge of the chamber to a corridor that led out of the Pen. The corridor broke off in several directions, and Bryn led them carefully and quickly down a long series of twisting passages toward the place that she had called the Hall of Terrors. The further they walked, the more surreal and foreboding the atmosphere became and Logan began looking over his shoulder every few feet. Bryn was right, this was much too easy. They should never have gotten that far without any kind of resistance. Finally the passage widened into an oblong chamber with a large set of doors with intricate writing carved into them set into the far end of the chamber. Standing before the doors was the other half of the pair of new phasia, Trece. She was frowning, but did not appear surprised to see them.

"Welcome, scum. You were lucky to make it this far, and the death of my brother hits very hard. Realize that even if you defeat my force and I, you will never make it to the throne room. The horrors that await you in the Hall of Terror will claim you before you even know you are dead. However, I do not intend for you to make it through these doors. I have to avenge the death of my brother, and I will do so now."

Trece was in the air the next second, her sword raised high in the air. Her target was Korrd, and he rolled out of the way of the blow. She landed on the other side of him, out of the striking range of any of the weapons of the other members of the group. Talon turned his attention to her, and his powers flared, knocking her off her feet with a powerful gust of wind. That instant, the doors to the Hall of Terrors opened, and two dozen Jeresei charged into the chamber. As the People of the Dragon started to engage the army of the Shadow, twenty more sprinted in from the direction of the Pen. The trap had been sprung and the group were forced back into the center of the chamber with no clear line of retreat should the battle go badly. Korrd charged into the rank of the Jeresei coming from the Hall of Terrors with Arin and Jerrard at his side. Bryn moved to the edge of the chambers, hugging one of the walls, trying not to interfere. Gwydeon, Pike and Logan charged into the Jeresei that flanked the group, while Talon kept his attention on Trece. Logan heard the sounds of dying everywhere as swords and powers flared, meeting with the hard flesh of the red skinned beasts who were bent on their destruction. One by one the Jeresei fell, and Logan turned my head in time to see Talon and Trece locked in combat.

Her sword had cut him deeply across the chest, and he was parrying her flurry of attacks as best he could. The next instant, his hand shot out, and a gust of wind picked her up and slammed her violently into the wall. She staggered away, not knowing exactly where she was, and when she did, Talon ran her through. Just like their general, the Jeresei fell with surprising ease, leaving the group facing the now-open doors to the Hall of Terrors.

Hell's Doorstep

Trece was right. Even with her last breath, she was able to speak words of horror and despair. This so-called Hall of Terrors was quite aptly named. Logan only had a fragmented picture of the Hall in his mind, but whatever memories did exist could not prepare Logan for what waited behind the massive inscribed doors. There are many things in this life that people are in awe of. Logan had seen sunsets that had taken his breath away, and there have been waterfalls and fields of flowers that he had seen during their journey that have made Logan feel good to be alive. The Hall of Terrors was something else entirely. Those other things make you glad to be alive and glad that you can enjoy the beauty and splendor of nature. The Hall of Terrors made you wish you were dead. This is no exaggeration. As soon as the doors to the Hall were opened, a wave of dread and the smell of death wafted into the entryway. It was a feeling powerful enough to take all the fight out of a person, and had it not been for the fact that they were so near the end, Logan was sure that most of the party would have wanted to stop then and there. Logan felt as though a great weight had suddenly descended upon his shoulders, and he felt dozens of times heavier than he should have. It almost felt as though Logan wouldn't be able to lift his sword to fight. More than that, there was an oppressive heat that radiated from the Hall. Beads of sweat began to form on Logan's forehead immediately and as he took several breaths of the new warmer air, it was harder and harder to breathe. In fact, the longer Logan stood there, the more his head began to feel light and fuzzy, and for a few moments he wondered if he would be able to hold on to consciousness in a fight.

The Hall of Terrors was nothing more than that, a hall. There was a single stone walkway that stretched the entire length of the Hall to the doors of Shau-ling's throne room. The walkway itself looked wide enough for four people to stand shoulder to shoulder, but that was only a rough estimate, and from the look of the edges of the walkway, it was highly possible that some of segments along the way were not very stable. Extending off the main path every few feet were crossroads that led off into the darkness. These crossroads concerned Logan more than anything else. From the time that they had set foot on the cursed island, things had been jumping out from every direction, and danger had haunted their steps at every turn. Sometimes it seemed that there was nowhere for the creatures to come from, but they still poured out after them. In the Hall of Terrors however, it was rather obvious where the assaults would come from.

Whenever you're high up on a cliff or on a hanging bridge, the first thing they tell you is not to look down. And, naturally, the first thing you do is look down. In the Hall, Logan didn't need to be told not to look down, because after doing it he wished he hadn't. There was no "I told you so" needed. For those people who have been out to sea, you know the sensation when you first realize that you cannot see land anywhere around you. That suddenly makes you feel very isolated and for a time very insecure. In the Hall of Terrors Logan felt the same sensation overtake him when he looked down at the lake of fire that stretched down below their feet. The wall behind them that held the doors to the rest of the palace only extended about a foot below the level of the stone walkway, and below that was fire. The same held true for the wall on the other side of the walkway that held the doors to Shau-ling's throne room. The cross-paths extended to somewhere, but as Logan looked down at the fires below, he could get no perception of whether or not there were walls to their right or left. There had to be, at least if the palace bowed to any structural laws, but Logan had to remind himself that the place existed purely by the will of a mad evil god, so rules had very little sway. If it were only the isolation that the flames caused, the Hall of Terrors would only be the Hall of Annoyance, but the flame was definitely not there merely for decoration.

No, the roiling fires were certainly a deterrent for visitors. Gideon had taken a few steps down the path when a huge stream of fire erupted from below and brushed the walkway. Gideon dove back toward the entrance to the Hall and seemed to get away without a scratch, until they noticed the burn mark on the side of his shirt. The flame hadn't touched him, but the magnitude of the heat was able to singe his clothes merely from their close proximity. Hesitation filled every member of the party as sanity wrestled with what they were seeing. Another gout of flame burst up a few moments later, but was in a different place, and this time some of the liquid fire spilled out over the walkway making it impassible for a few moments.

"This is going to be fun," Pike mumbled under his breath.

"Let's try to stay optimistic here Pike," Korrd responded in a very strong voice. "We are only a few feet away from Shau-ling's throne room, and we still have the seven that we need to finish him forever. Just stay positive and we'll make it through here alive."

"Right," Pike said looking at one of the flame spurts as it leapt into the air and brushed heavily against the walkway, "positive."

Pike had said it well enough to express what everyone was feeling, and despite Korrd's dedication to the task, doubt was beginning to creep into everyone's heart. No one had been prepared for anything like what was stretched out before them, and Bryn had given no indication of what to expect. She had said that there were no words to describe the terrors and perils that were waiting for them in Shau-ling's palace, but if something like that could be understated, Logan was sure that she did. The longer they stood there, the more the sense of dread and despair tore at Logan's soul. It was like the Hall of Terrors was eating his heart and soul alive, making him not care about anyone or anything except getting the hell out of the Hall in one piece. From the looks on his friends' faces, Logan knew it was a shared sentiment.

"So Bryn," Jerrard said looking tentatively over the edge of the walkway, "what can you tell us now that we've seen this horrible place."

Bryn's expression had not changed since they had entered the palace. It was a look of anger and hatred mixed with despair and longing. She was a member of the phasia, and in a strange perverse way, this was her home that she was helping them destroy. Logan's memories of her came and went, and since they had entered the palace, Logan had gotten more and more from the former *Chosen One*. Aerith loathed this place more than Logan did, but Logan also got a sense of triumph in his anguish. The only time that he was ever brought to the Hall, it was to face his death at the hands of Shau-ling. Though he was going to die, which was what he was born for anyway, he went to his death with his head held high, and he did not let the dread of the Hall touch him. That was why the Hall was imbued with the characteristics it was. It was designed to destroy the hope of those who were going to meet with Shau-ling. It was a perfect way teach his creatures respect. By parading them though the Hall of Terrors, their wills were weakened, and it was easier for Shau-ling to bond them into service. Logan could not believe that it had taken him so long to figure it out. That was something else that he had to thank Aerith Seth for. Aerith had given Logan strength enough to give his life to the man that he would not have trusted a few days ago, and Aerith had given Logan the strength to make it through this ordeal. Apparently the conversation with his memories had drawn Logan farther away from reality than he had intended.

"Logan," Pike said as he looked back at Logan, "are you listening?"

Logan looked back at Pike and realized that he had taken a step or two away from the group and that they were all gathered around Bryn waiting for her words of wisdom and experience on the Hall. Logan walked calmly back over to where they were standing and locked his eyes on Bryn. Her eyes met his, and it made Logan shiver reflexively. Now that he was more in tune with the memories and feelings of Aerith Seth, she was having more of an impact on Logan's senses.

"As I was saying," she said looking back at Korrd, "this is the final leg of the journey, and it is probably the most perilous stretch. The fires below are not normal flame as you have probably all figured out by now. The flames are part of the Blaze. No one has ever been able to know fully whether or not they are the Blaze or not, but believe me they can drain the life from you if they touch you. The flame spurts have no definite timing, and no definite pattern. However, it is highly possible that the guardian of the Hall, a creature called the Flame, is able to control the spurts. The guardian will not make itself known until you cross the midway point of the Hall. That is why we are safe here. Shau-ling and the Flame choose not to monitor this inner door, and they wouldn't consider us a threat until we cross that barrier. Don't ask me why, I just chalk it up to Shau-ling's arrogance like everything else he does stupidly. The only other problem in the Hall are those crossroads. Each of those other paths leads to a cage where a unique creature lives. These creatures were experiments by the phasia back when we were given free run of the palace. There are twenty of these cages, two for each of the original phasia. You see, we were given the test to try and design better servants than the Kalbraks and the Jeresei. So, we each designed two creatures and presented them to Shau-ling. Every single one of the creatures failed to pass the tests that Shau-ling had devised, but he kept them all alive and kept them as pets. He calls them his creations now, as do we all, but the truth is that they were ours first."

"Can you tell us about any of the creatures Bryn?" Arin asked anxiously. "We need all the help we can get."

Bryn frowned.

"When we presented our creatures, we were not allowed to see what the other phasia came up with, so I can only tell you about the two that I created. The first one is a creature called the Vorton. The creature moves on four legs, and is very fast and agile. It has yellow and green lizard like skin, and it also has a long scorpion-like tail. This tail is one of its primary weapons. It first likes to pounce on its adversary, or catch its target with its jaws, and then sink the tip of its poisonous tail into the victim. Death happens rather quickly, but those last few seconds of life are filled with agony. My other creature was the Reak. The Reak is a wolf-like creature with scaled legs that paralyzes its opponents with a high pitched scream. After the opponent is paralyzed, it rips out the target's throat. Death is painful, and sometimes long and arduous."

"When you phasia do something you go all out don't you?" Talon asked.

"So what now?" Gwydeon asked in an attempt to gloss over Talon's comment.

Gwydeon had always been the one for getting down to business, but now his tone was sharper. He and Korrd both had a different take on the situation because they both knew that they weren't going to make it out of Shau-ling's palace alive. Korrd knew for sure, but Logan had begun to think that Gwydeon's fatalism was based more on fear than on anything else. But as Logan looked at the scar on Gwydeon's side, he knew that now Gwydeon had something to fuel that fear. In his mind Logan could see the scar, and he saw the touches of the Blaze in the wound that were eating away at the charred flesh that kept the wound from becoming a fatal one. If Arin and Logan had not used their powers to seal that wound, Gwydeon would have bled to death long before he made it to the Hall. As it was Gwydeon had already lost a lot of blood, and it was amazing that he still had enough strength to stand and fight.

"Well," Korrd said, "I think it's time that we introduced ourselves to the Flame and paid our respects to the creatures that live here in this beautiful place."

"My sentiments exactly," Pike said spinning his ax in his hands.

Bryn stayed at the threshold of the Hall of Terrors, looking at each of the members of the group. Finally she moved to Logan and stood eye to eye with him for several long moments. Finally she put her hand on his chest, leaned in, and then kissed him gently on the cheek.

"Another life, my love," she said softly.

A moment later, Bryn took a step across the threshold and disappeared. Emries had kept that much of his promise, and while Bryn had done her part, Logan wondered what retribution from both sides of the conflict waited for her in the next generation.

"Guess it's up to us," Logan said finally.

Korrd nodded, and put a hand briefly on Logan's shoulder before turning his attention back to the Hall of Terrors. In two staggered lines the People of the Dragon made their way down the Hall, and just before they reached the halfway point of the path, Korrd stopped. He turned around quickly and looked back at the group. Logan could see what he was doing, and Logan didn't like it one bit. Korrd's eyes moved from person to person sizing up abilities and deciding on a course of action.

"There are eight of us that can fight and there are going to be twenty-one of them. Right now I'm not worried about the Flame, but I am worried about those beasts coming from all around us. Logan, you and I will go take care of the Flame, and then we can help with the other creatures. We need Arin and Gideon at our backs so that we can draw on their powers. I'm not sure what kind of interference will be caused this close to the throne room, so I want to be assured that we can draw on at least two. Pike and Talon can hold their own in a fight, so I think that they can take a crossroad each. With Gwydeon and Jerrard together . . ."

"Korrd . . ." Gwydeon started.

" . . . . they can . . ."

"Korrd!"

Korrd stopped speaking and looked at Gwydeon.

"You know I'm the best swordsman here. I've seen Arin fight too, and I've been with Gideon long enough that he can hold his own. Pike, Talon, Gideon, and I can each hold two crossroads, and Arin and Jerrard can stay close to the two of you so that you can draw on their powers. Those two have the least use of their powers, so they will be mainly using their weapons in battle. Pike, Talon, and Gideon have more than enough experience and creativeness to take out four beasts by themselves, and with my steel..."

"What about your side?" Korrd asked point blank.

"I'll worry about my side, you worry about the Flame."

Korrd hesitated for a moment and the two men locked eyes. This was a battle of wills that Logan knew Korrd couldn't win. Even though Gwydeon was injured, but when hadn't he been during the quest, he was still a better swordsman than any of the other members of the group, and he was more than able to take on four of the Hall's terrors. Korrd knew it too.

"Come on Korrd," Gwydeon said after a moment, "you know I'm right about this."

Korrd nodded after a moment.

"Alright," he said calmly, "we'll use Gwydeon's plan. If any of you get into trouble fall back and fight back to back with someone else. It's bound to get ugly in here, so take whatever kind of kill that you can get. If you have to, kick the bastards into the fires below, just make sure they fall, you never know when one of them might be able to grab onto the walkway from below and come back to make your life miserable. Got it?"

There were nods all around.

"Good, let's go."

Korrd turned back around and took two steps forward. At the far end of the Hall, just in front of the doors to Shau-ling's throne room, two huge spurts of flame leapt up and created a barrier. Out of the barrier of flame Logan could see a form emerging. After a moment, the flame barrier receded, and the Flame stood defiantly before them.

"So, the forces of the Light have finally intruded in my charge," the Flame said in a demonic and vengeful voice. "I am glad that you have made it this far so that I might have the pleasure of finishing your petty attempt to save the world from the inevitable reign of the Shadows."

"I'll give you one chance Flame," Korrd said holding the Dragon Sword aloft, "open the doors to Shau-ling's throne room and stand aside."

The Flame's laughter resounded throughout the Hall.

"I think that was a no, Korrd," Pike commented.

"So be it."

The beam of energy exploded from the Dragon Sword the next instant and struck the Flame square in the chest. While that blow probably would have killed most of the members of Shau-ling's army, the Flame seemed to be unaffected by the attack. From somewhere in his body, an eruption of green flame shot down the length of the Hall. All of the members of the group were able to get down, but they now had a very good indication of what they were up against. This was not going to be easy, and if the creatures about to rush them were half as terrifying as Logan believed them to be, it could prove to be fatal for all of them.

"Now my pets," the Flame said in that same rolling laughter, "show these puny boys exactly why you have been kept here in the Hall of Terrors and why you have been chosen to hold the Master's door with me."

Logan heard the cages open and shrieks of laughter and joy echo through the Hall of Terrors. These monsters were different than any of the other ones that they had ever faced, that much was obvious. The Jeresei were vicious and arrogant, but they were too cold to be malevolent. The other creatures seemed not to have any personality at all, but from the cries of pleasure that resounded through the Hall, Logan could tell that these creatures did. They loved their job, they enjoyed killing, and they were ready to rip each and every one of the mortals that intruded in their home to shreds.

"Alright guys," Pike said readying his ax, "let's dance."

Sentinels and Sacrifices

Gwydeon readied himself for whatever was going to be the first of the creatures charging from their cages down to where the People of the Dragon stood waiting to face them. He stood poised on the walkway between the two crossroads closest to the door that led to the rest of the palace. It was almost as if he were on an island from the rest of the force, but still he waited. The threshold would offer him an advantage from the others who could have attacks coming at them from all sides, and since Gwydeon had only his sword and no abilities to draw from, it made sense for him to take the farthest position from the throne room. The Hall of Terrors was a tactical disadvantage for anyone who fought there, and the narrow path would make fighting in a group nearly impossible. If they had clumped up in the middle, any of the unique creatures with any form of attack that covered a mass area, like the one possessed by the Shadowwalkers could have wiped out the entire force with one blow. Splitting up was the best option, even if none of them liked to admit it.

From one of the crosses, Gwydeon saw something glinting in the firelight. As it came further down the path, its form became more and more apparent. It had the same size and shape of a man, but its skin was all silver, and it held a long silver sword in its hand that was nearly as long as the creature was tall. The striking feature that the creature possessed was the fact it had no face. The place where its face should have been was just a smooth piece of silver metal. The thing struck in the next moment.

Gwydeon brought his sword up in time to block the blow, but he had underestimated the power of the creature. The force of the blow drove him to the ground, and Gwydeon immediately wondered if he was completely overmatched. To make matters worse, his head landed near that of another of the creatures. From the glance that Gwydeon got of it, it was only about three feet tall with a large mouth, strong looking legs, and very large sharp teeth. It was the teeth that caught his attention the most as they came chomping down at him. However, the squat creature's attack carried its head into striking distance of the silver creature. The silver sword came crashing down on where Gwydeon was only moment earlier and severed the smaller beast's head from its body, sending green blood flowing across the walkway. Gwydeon pulled himself to his feet and came face to face with something very big and very hairy.

* * * * * * * * * * * *

Pike was ready for anything, at least he thought he was until he saw what first came down from one of the cages in his area of the Hall. He thought that he had seen the last of the nightmarish little creature when he left Sarmeel, but apparently as the black ball of hair and teeth came bounding down the path, he had been wrong. After a long bounce, the black Snag launched itself at Pike and slashed at him with its long lethal tail. Pike dodged the attack, but because of the speed of the creature, he was unable to return the attack. The black Snag moved too quickly for his slow ax, but it wasn't fast enough for his powers. As he spun toward where the Snag went, he extended his hand for an attack. Suddenly, he felt something leathery grasp his hand around the wrist, and Pike spun to see a human-like form behind him, and the tendril that grasped him around the wrist had extended from its chest. Pike had enough presence of mind to pull his ax up with his off hand and cut the tendril in two. The thing pulled the remaining portion of the tendril back into itself and lashed out again. Pike rolled away from the assault and stopped just short of the edge of the stone walkway. As he expected, the black Snag had turned for another assault, and as it hurtled toward him, Pike rolled again and the Snag flew over the edge of the walkway into the fiery depths below. However, this victory was short-lived as another leathery tendril shot toward Pike's face. It was nothing more than a reflex that allowed him to raise his hand and freeze the tendril mere inches before it hit his face. His ax spoke loudly as it connected with the black creature's torso and sent halves of the screaming creature falling to the ground. As Pike spun to face the next of his creatures, he didn't notice the two halves begin to slowly pull themselves back together.

* * * * * * * * * * * *

Talon looked over his shoulder only for a moment before turning to face the fleshy creature that pulled itself toward him. The body of the thing was very much like that of a normal human, except for the fact that it looked like it had no skin. It was as if the muscles of the creature grew and changed as it moved to compensate for what it was doing. Also as it moved, it secreted a red liquid that smoked as it came in contact with the ground. The smell of rotten eggs rolled off the muscular blob and Talon used every bit of his fortitude to keep from vomiting. It would have taken only a bit of his power to use the wind in the chamber to carry the smell away from his nose, but a trivial use of his power could mean he wouldn't have all he needed when it mattered the most. The blob had just come into full visual range when it raised one of its arms, and the arm seemed to extend toward Talon. Talon sidestepped the far-reaching appendage and struck at it with his sword. The sword struck true and cut deep into the muscle and sinew that held the arm together. Red liquid shot everywhere, and as Talon recovered his sword, he noticed that the blade had been scorched by the acid-like blood of the beast. The thing hesitated for a moment and then the arm shrank back to its normal size while the beast contemplated its next attack. Out of nowhere, a winged creature swooped down from above, and its bladed tail just missed Talon's shoulder by inches. Talon watched as the flying beast banked around for another pass and smiled. The creature's wings were like those of a butterfly, except they were transparent. The rest of the body was like that of a massive wasp that sported huge human arms where insect legs should have been. The tail of the beast was more like it had two legs that were fused together and whoever designed it had attached a dagger at the end of it. Talon waited until the creature had turned and then he hit it with a gale force wind that caused it to lose control of its wings and fall into the fiery depths below. Suddenly there was a huge crash, and Talon turned to see a ten foot green monster with blacksmith anvils for arms thundering down one of the cross-paths toward him. It was then that he felt the pain lance through his arm.

CHAPTER 23

＊ ＊ ＊ ＊ ＊ ＊ ＊ ＊ ＊ ＊ ＊ ＊

Arin and Jerrard were back to back waiting on their share of the monsters to come toward them. They figured that between the two of them they should be able to take on four a lot quicker than the others and then they could go help. The first two monster came rather quickly down the paths, and Jerrard ran to intercept the first, while Arin stood firm and waited for the second. The first thing to meet Jerrard's steel was humanoid in form, but that was all. The creature was about six and a half feet tall, but that was only because it was hunched over. Its face resembled that of a panther, and its black coat of hair was dull and lifeless. It used its cat-like paws to attack, and as it slashed at Jerrard, he saw the razor sharp claws as they passed close enough to tear at his short beard. Jerrard dodged the first slash, but met the second with his steel. The beast continued its assault and nearly forced Jerrard's sword out of his hand, as the creature's strength exceeded his own considerably. Jerrard held tight to the hilt of his sword and waited as the beast slashed at him again and again. When it recovered its paw from yet another strike, Jerrard drew on his powers and created a flash of bright light in the face of the larger creature. It staggered blindly for a moment, but a moment of distraction was all it took. Jerrard poised himself for the strike and attacked, piercing the creature through the brain with his blade. The creature fell to the wayside, and Jerrard turned to help his friend.

Arin waited only a second longer than Jerrard before coming face to face with his first foe. It was a creature about seven foot in height. Scales covered its entire body, but these were scales the size of shields. Large sword-like spines extended from its back down to the wide flat tail that dragged behind it. The creature lumbered forward and attacked, stepping to one side and swinging its tail at Arin. Arin jumped back to avoid the attack, but was unable to counter. The beast then lurched forward and slashed with its claws. Arin ducked underneath the extended hand of the monster and struck true with his sword to one of the shield-like scales on the thing's chest. The plate cracked and exposed the vulnerable skin below. Arin was able to dart out of the way again as the beast slashed with its other hand in an attempt to protect its newly formed weak spot. After several feints at the exposed spot, Arin finally darted in and buried his sword into the soft flesh. The creature roared in pain and then slumped to the ground. After recovering his sword, Arin turned to see if Jerrard needed any help.

"Arin," Jerrard shouted running back toward him, "watch out!"

* * * * * * * * * * * *

Before he knew what was happening, Gideon was surrounded by four very impressive and terrifying creatures. The first stood eight feet tall and brandished a large ax. Its head was very much like that of a bull, and the horns shone with bright sharp points. It looked very much like a Minotaur out of the old children's fables, but this one stank of death, and looked like it could make that smell a very terrible reality. The next creature was a human-sized skeleton, holding a sword in each hand. However, Gideon's powers instantly alerted him to the fact that the skeleton was not made out of bone, but rather out of one of the hardest metals Gideon had ever encountered in his life. In addition to having no vital organs to attack, the skeleton now posed and even larger threat. The next creature was made completely of ice. It had a very human shape and form, but the sharp spines of ice broke the monotony of smooth texture, and Gideon could see its breath crystallize the air around it. The other thing was horrible and intimidating. It was all mouth, and nothing more. The large opening that was rimmed with long sharp teeth slinked down its path slowly, leaving a trail of acid behind it that pitted the stone of the Hall. Gideon had two of his daggers drawn, and he had already taken hold of the string of Earth, but he waited for one of the creatures to make the first move. The Minotaur was the first to attack. Its ax came crashing down near Gideon, and rather than retreating from the blow, Gideon leapt toward the Minotaur with his daggers ready for fatal use. The first left his hand while he was still in the air, but it was hit by a beam of ice and frozen in mid-air. The second dagger contacted the chest of the Minotaur, but it was not enough damage to be considered a mortal wound. However, that was going to be taken care of for Gideon in another instant. The first beam of ice had missed, but as the second beam came, Gideon dropped to the ground and rolled through the legs of the massive bull-headed beast as the beam of ice struck the Minotaur square in the chest. Gideon popped up to his feet behind the Minotaur, channeled power into his fists and with one swift punch, the monster shattered. The skeleton's sword came crashing down from behind in the next instant, and Gideon missed being separated from his head by a slim margin. Before he came back to his feet once more, Gideon felt a sting on his shoulder and realized that he had rolled into the path of the large moving mouth. Without thinking about what he was doing, he channeled his power over the stone path that held the creature's weight. The rock lurched and rolled sending the creature plummeting into the fires below. As Gideon recovered his feet again, he waited for one of the other creatures to make a move.

* * * * * * * * * * * *

Korrd and Logan were face to face with the Flame. They knew that creature of pure Blaze flame was the final obstacle between the forces of the Light and Shau-ling's throne room. It was a truly menacing creature in that it stood taller than any of the creatures that they had ever seen before, including the Stone. The Flame seemed to exude the total power of the Blaze, and in doing so, one could feel the evil radiating from it like a fog. Korrd waited for a moment before he did anything, and as Logan expected, the Flame did not return the favor. As soon as the other creatures in the Hall had been turned loose, the Flame launched an attack of its own at Korrd. The beam of pure Blaze energy lanced across the distance between them, and struck at Korrd's feet. The Flame laughed again and launched another attack. The powers inside of Logan welled up in that next instant, and a beam of green energy shot from his outstretched fingers and intercepted the Flame's attack. The collision of energies sent a shockwave pulsing out in all directions, and nearly through Logan off his feet. The Flame recovered before Logan could, and a cone of Blaze energy erupted from inside of it and sped towards him. Korrd's outstretched hand released a bolt of energy that blocked the assault, and then Korrd turned his attention from defense to retaliation. From out of his pack, Korrd pulled the oddly shaped black crystalline structure that Logan had initially been sent to find by Lord Cedric. Logan had attempted to use it once, but with no success, and it had sat in Pike's pack ever since. Now it was in the hands of the man who could actually wield it to lethal result. Korrd pulled the living crystal free, and Logan watched as Korrd channeled his energies and the energies of the four *Erieal* into the Jeweled Dragon's Flame. The black crystal receded from the living flame, and Logan watched as the flame pulsed and cracked with renewed life. The Flame hesitated for a moment and then launched another attack, one that obviously should have been fatal had it struck true. Korrd held the living flame aloft and an explosion of pure white energy spewed forth and intercepted the assault of the Flame and pushed it back, finally engulfing the creature. After a moment the white light receded, and there was nothing left of the Flame. It was then that they heard Arin's anguished cry.

* * * * * * * * * * * *

Talon turned to see that the red fleshy beast had lashed out with its extending arm again, only this time the hand on the end had folded itself into a blade, and it had torn open the skin on his non-sword shoulder. The arm had not yet been recovered, so Talon slashed down with his sword and severed the creature's arm completely. The rest of the arm retreated back to its host, and the finally the fleshy blob charged Talon. Meanwhile, the huge green anvil-wielding monstrosity lumbered toward him with its arms banging the ground as it walked. After a moment of planning, Talon stabbed the remaining piece of the fleshy creatures arm with his sword. Talon could smell the acid burning at the blade of his sword, but that would have to be dealt with later. The lumbering green thing was close enough now, and Talon flung the piece of arm at the creature's eyes. The creature was unable to block the attack, and it wailed in pain as the acid from the fleshy creature's hand seared its eyes shut. Now unable to see, the green creature flailed around helplessly, its heavy arms crashing to the ground randomly. The fleshy creature was still charging, but as Talon sidestepped, he left his foot out. The creature tripped over Talon's outstretched foot and sprawled to the ground near the green creature. Within a moment, Talon heard the sound of the fleshy creature being crushed under the weight of an anvil-like arm. It only took a well-placed gust of wind to knock the large creature off the path and into the fires below. Talon turned to survey the scene, but found himself staring into the laughing face of a dog-like creature whose hooked bone arm was raised and ready to strike.

* * * * * * * * * * * *

Pike's gaze shifted to the next of his opponents, but he was not happy with what he saw. There in front of him was a creature that resembled a human, but its whole form was that of energy. Lightning-like energy crackled all over its body, and as Pike watched, a stream of lightning pulsed from its hands and sped past Pike's ear. Pike didn't dare use his powers against the energy beast, because there was a chance that water would only strengthen the creature's power. Suddenly, a familiar sound rang in Pike's ears. When he was fighting the creature that had the leathery tendrils, he remembered that every time that it retracted one, there was a unique sound. As another lightning bolt sailed over Pike's head, he heard the sound again, only this time it was ten times louder. He turned and saw that the creature had reconstituted itself. Pike's reintroduction to the beast was in the form of a tendril that struck him in the face and sent him reeling. Fortunately for Pike, the energy creature had not counted on any assistance, so its next attack was off the mark. Pike decided as he regained his senses that he was going to use the tendril creature to his advantage. Pike sprinted toward the energy creature and looked over his shoulder. As he expected, the tendril creature was following. The energy creature shot again, high and wide, and this was the time that Pike had been waiting for. Pike dove through the energy creature's legs and watched as tendril after tendril struck the energy creature. In a matter of seconds the energy creature was completely surrounded by tendrils, and with one pull, the creature engulfed its confederate. The explosion that finished them both happened away from Pike's sight, deep inside the tendril creature's stomach. As Pike rose back to his feet, he hefted his ax and looked around for his next adversary.

* * * * * * * * * * * *

Gwydeon looked up into the red eyes of the bear-like beast that bared down upon him. It had one of its claws raised, but Gwydeon never saw the slash fall. He dropped to the deck in the next second, and the silver creature buried its sword into the chest of the bear creature. The blow was not at all fatal, it just served to make the bear mad. The bear ripped the silver sword out of its chest and then picked up the silver creature and began to rip it apart piece by piece. Gwydeon took this opportunity to launch an attack on the larger opponent. His sword slash first struck at the knee of the larger opponent taking its leg out from under it. The next blow severed the other leg. By this time the bear creature had released the remains of the silver creature and was slashing wildly in Gwydeon's direction. Gwydeon ducked in and out until he was able to land two solid blows to the chest and pierce the heart. As the bear creature finally slumped to the ground, Gwydeon retrieved his sword and turned to look for his fourth monster. The flash of silver talons was the only thing he saw.

* * * * * * * * * * * *

The skeleton looked ready to make his play for Gideon's life, and as Gideon danced from side to side, he noticed that the ice creature was closing in on him too. It would only take a little to get them both in a single attack, but it would have to take split-second timing, and Gideon knew it. The ice creature shot again at close range, and Gideon was able to leap out of the way. The dagger was out of his hand in the next moment, and the ice creature was unable to dodge out of the way or block it. The ice creature was now enraged, and it started firing in all directions trying to hit Gideon. Gideon was able to dodge all of the attacks, but he moved toward the skeleton that lumbered toward him with each passing moment. Finally, Gideon was able to get the ice creature to fire at the skeleton. Gideon dodged out of the way and the skeleton was frozen in the stream of ice. Gideon rolled toward the ice creature, and using his powers he made his fist as hard as the stone that he rolled upon. When he came up, he slammed his fist into the creature's chest, and it shattered upon impact. When he saw Gwydeon fall, he ran toward his falling comrade, pushing the skeleton into the fires below as he ran by.

* * * * * * * * * * * *

Arin didn't hear the warning until it was much too late. The Vorton, Bryn's creation, leapt from the cross-path behind him and pinned him to the ground. Before Arin or Jerrard could do anything, the Vorton plunged its tail into Arin's thrashing body. The death was agonizing, but quick. However, before the Vorton could recover its tail, Jerrard plunged his sword into its head. There was no time for grief over Arin's death, because the last of their four monsters came running down one of the paths and leapt at Jerrard. The creature looked like a snake with four little legs that allowed it to run at incredible speeds. Jerrard dropped to his knees and hoped that the creature was not able to turn itself in midair. Even if the creature could have, it never got the chance. A beam of white energy shot from the hand of Korrd Ranthall and enveloped the beast. The only thing that landed on Jerrard were the beast's ashes.

CHAPTER 23

* * * * * * * * * * * *

Pike looked around and saw the final beast that awaited him. It was one that he recognized from Bryn's description as the Reak. Before Pike could move, the creature opened its mouth and let out an ear-piercing scream. The scream froze Pike in his tracks, but the Reak had not counted on the fact that Pike knew about the Reak's ability and had filled his ear canals with water in order to muffle the sound. Though he was no longer paralyzed, Pike remained rooted to the spot, waiting for his opponent to charge in for the kill. The Reak leapt at Pike, but not before he was able to raise his ax into a defensive position. The Reak couldn't do anything to defend itself and was soon lying in two pieces on the ground at Pike's feet. It was then that Pike saw Gwydeon fall.

* * * * * * * * * * * *

The creature with the bone hook arm looked down at Talon and smiled wickedly. Talon knew that the creature had him right where it wanted him, but it was waiting to strike. Suddenly the bone arm came down faster than Talon thought possible, and Talon was caught in the shoulder before he was able to roll away. The creature withdrew the hook and kicked Talon to the ground. As Talon lay there bleeding, the creature reached down with its other arm, an arm that ended with a red claw. The claw clutched Talon around the waist and started to lift him. Pain rocketed though Talon's body as the claw squeezed him and brought him up toward the creature's mouth. Though he heard bones cracking and blackness tugged at the edges of his vision, he pain was not enough for Talon to relinquish hold of his sword. It was a wild slash that caught the creature along the side of its face. The creature recoiled in pain, and Talon dropped to the ground. Talon tried to ignore the pain, but as he forced his way to his feet, he felt the surge of pain through his back and coughed violently, sending blood splattering to the ground. With the help of his sword, Talon was able to regain his balance, and then he slashed at the creature. The creature's bone hook lanced down in an attempt to block, but Talon drew all of the power he could manage, propelling his sword forward with the force equivalent to that of a hurricane. The force of Talon's blow was too much, and it shattered the bone. Red blood poured from the shattered appendage. Talon's next strike was enough to sever the beast's head from his shoulders. When Talon looked up after recovering his balance, he watched as a beast ripped at Gwydeon's side, and he fell to the ground.

* * * * * * * * * * * *

All they saw was a shaggy beast with silver claws come out of the shadows and rip at Gwydeon's already injured side. The wound was a quick and brutal, and Gwydeon went down to the ground in a heap clutching at the wound in his side that poured forth so much blood that it seemed to coat the ground of the Hall. The rest of the members of the party had finished dispatching the other beasts of the Hall, and they surrounded the beast that had wounded Gwydeon. It took only a few precise slashes before the beast itself crumpled to the ground dead. Logan knelt beside Gwydeon with Pike and Talon. The wound that Rael had inflicted had been reopened by the creature's attack, and Gwydeon had already lost a lot of blood. With Pike and Talon's help, they managed to mostly seal the wound, but there were still the threads of the Blaze in the wound from Rael's attack that they did not dare touch, as well as new threads that must have come from the claws of his attacker. To make matters worse it seemed that in the Hall of Terrors the Blaze was stronger and ate at Gwydeon's flesh with greater hunger. The wound was trying to reopen itself no matter their efforts, and it was only a matter of time before Gwydeon bled to death. Perhaps if Gwydeon could survive until they defeated Shau-ling, there would be a chance that he could be saved. It was then that Logan heard the laughter at the other end of the Hall.

Logan and Korrd looked up and saw that the doors to Shau-ling's throne room were open. Just inside the threshold of the doorway, stood the first born member of the phasia, the last line of defense between the People of the Dragon and Shau-ling. Jeroch wore only a pair of black pants and a tattered gray shirt that only covered his right shoulder. In his right hand he held a sword and he smiled as he walked into the Hall.

"So, this is the rabble that has come to challenge the mighty Shau-ling. What a pity that it must end here for all of you."

"Jeroch," Logan said rising to my feet, "it is good to see you. Get your steel ready, it is time for your death."

Logan started to move toward Jeroch, but found that he was unable to move. Logan could tell that the others were also trying to get at the cocky phase.

"Having a little trouble moving my little pigeons? Perhaps it is because of my powers in this generation. My special ability is a field that protects me from all powered individuals. Only a full member of the phasia is strong enough to break through it, and Jerrard is not a full member of the phasia. However, there is one among you that can come and fight me. Come Gwydeon Sandar. Show me why Emries chose you to be his mortal champion."

Gwydeon was sitting up in the next moment.

"Gwydeon don't," Pike said quickly, "we can figure out a way around this. If you move, the healing on your side will give way, and you'll bleed to death."

"I'm dead already Pike," Gwydeon said getting to his feet, "I have to do this."

Gwydeon rose to his feet and walked down the Hall with his sword ready for battle. Logan saw the cloth of his shirt clinging to the wound, but as the blood trickled down his side, the stain in the shirt grew in size. Jeroch took the sword off of his shoulder and brought it down in front of him, ready to fight. Without hesitation, Gwydeon launched himself at the phase, but Jeroch was able to bring up his sword in time to block the attack. Jeroch then pushed back and Gwydeon stumbled. Gwydeon may have been weakened by the loss of blood, but he was able to recover his feet.

"So, this is the powerful swordsman who will bring the next *Coromor* into the world? I am not impressed. When I am through with you I will destroy your allies, and there will not be a next generation to worry about."

"Come on then Jeroch," Gwydeon said obviously guarding his wounded side. "Show me how good you are."

Jeroch lunged at Gwydeon, but the blow was probing Gwydeon's defenses and nothing more, so it was easily parried and countered. On and on the two combatants circled each other, but with each step, Gwydeon winced a little more. He was trying to push the pain out of his mind, but Logan with his enhanced vision could see the threads of the Blaze starting to lurch through Gwydeon's body, no longer content to simply nibble at the edges of the wound. It would be a race to see which would kill Gwydeon first, Jeroch or the Blaze. Finally Jeroch lashed out again, catching Gwydeon's wounded side and another plume of blood erupted from the rapidly dying man. But Jeroch's quick success proved to be his undoing.

Jeroch started to get cocky in his attacks, and the slashes were wild and predictable. Gwydeon dodged two or three of the strikes to get Jeroch's timing and then he slashed at the phase catching his chest in a broad arching slash. Blood flowed from the wound and Jeroch leaped back stunned. That was a shock of reality to the phase, and he finally started to take his opponent more seriously. Again the combatants circled each other, but it was clear that the battle could not last much longer. If Gwydeon were not able to strike the final blow soon, he would drop to the ground because of loss of blood, and Jeroch would win. It was then that Gwydeon showed his true skill. Jeroch stepped in and slashed twice. Gwydeon parried both blows and landed another slash to Jeroch's chest. The target for the final strike was now perfectly marked. There was an X cut into Jeroch's chest, and as the phase came in for his final attack, Gwydeon stepped under the arching slash, pushing his tired and aching muscles to move as fast as they could and buried the point of his blade into the very center of Jeroch's chest. Both he and the phase dropped to the ground in the next moment, and Logan knew before they got to Gwydeon's side that he was dead. Much to Logan's surprise, his eyes were still open, and he motioned for Logan to come closer.

"My sword..."

His voice was strained, and Logan could practically feel his lifelong friend's life slowly slipping away. Logan moved to where Jeroch lay and removed the blade from the fallen phase. When he returned to Gwydeon's side, he raised his hand, and Logan placed the hilt of his sword into his open palm, then gently helped him prop the blade against his chest.

"Logan, my part of this quest is over, but I'm not finished. Emries said that I would dwell with the angels, but right now I'd trade it all to walk into that throne room with you and watch Shau-ling die. You were given the gift of power, and yet you stayed with your friends when you could have followed Lord Cedric's call without us. You didn't need me, but you brought me anyway. Thank you, my friend. You gave me the life I always dreamed about, and I don't fear death anymore."

He winced in pain, but then continued, his voice getting raspier as the seconds dragged on.

"I did what Emries wanted me to, and now my part in the story has to come to a close. The shadows didn't beat us, Logan, they never were stronger than we were."

Finally he lifted his hand away from the hilt of his sword and laid it on Logan's.

"You have to promise me something, Logan," he continued after a long pause. "When this is over, tell Midarin that I died on my feet, fighting, and that I love her. She isn't going to have me around to help raise our child. Tell her I'm sorry. But don't let her think that I won't be watching out for her. As long as she holds me in her heart, I'll always be with her. Promise me that, Logan, promise me."

"I promise, old friend," Logan replied, "I promise."

Pike was kneeling close, and when Gwydeon took his hand, Logan knew that he was nearly gone.

"I'll tell Eldar hello for you, Pike," he said weakly. "I know how you like to get the last word..."

His voice trailed off as he finally died. Their great and brave friend was gone, but he died the way that he lived; caring words, dry wit, and no sense of his own limits. Those qualities had endeared him in the hearts of everyone who had ever met Gwydeon Sandar. After a moment the remaining six members of the People of the Dragon stood, and without a word they entered the throne room of the master of the Shadows and prepared themselves to bring the second generation of the prophecies to a close.

The Shadow's Presence

Shau-ling's throne room stank with the smell of rotting flesh and the faint mixture of burning coals and stagnate water. The black dragon that was etched into the floor of the room pulsated with an eerie golden light that seemed to emanate from the very cracks in the floor. As the last of the People of the Dragon thundered through the door, the golden light oozed up from the floor and down from the ceiling, creating a pulsating barricade of light that held them in the presence of the master of evil and prevented any chance of escape. From the first moment that they had stepped into the palace, Logan had felt that the walls of the palace and every stone that made up the place were turned against them by Shau-ling and his minions. Moreover, the entire Island of Mist seemed to exude this same power and evil that wanted to halt their advance at every opportunity. Now this feeling in the pit of Logan's stomach intensified when his mind finally began to grasp the utter peril of their situation. For months they had been on the trail of the evil that had been known as Shau-ling, and now finally they were face to face with the terror that had gripped the hearts of the most powerful men in the world and had soured the courage of the bravest of soldiers. They now stood in the inner sanctum of the Lord of the Shadow that had attempted to rule the world for as long as it had existed. Shau-ling had seen the birth of the human race and had every intention of out-living them. Only Logan and Korrd were in a position strong enough to stop him from that. The two brothers, the *Coromor*, and the *Chosen One*.

Korrd had stopped dead in his tracks the instant he set foot on the black dragon in the floor. His eyes had been locked on the golden throne from the moment they entered the room, and his very attitude and posture spoke of hate and malice. Logan skidding to a stop beside him, and for the first time laid his eyes on the master of evil. However, even as Logan raised my eyes, he found that Korrd looked not at Shau-ling, but at the man who stood to his side. A man that they had all admired, no matter their positions at the time. A man both like a father and a brother. He had given them hope and guidance when they thought that their whole world would fall into the clutches of evil. The sword in his hand was familiar, but now glowed with an eerie green light that seemed to hang upon the blade like a sickness, mottling its once brilliant shine. Its golden hilt and etching spoke of the first of the prophecies, the Lion, but even the twin lions that made up the hilt seemed lifeless. Lord Cedric's eyes were cold and full of an angry, fragile fire that seemed to envelope him all the way to his soul. Logan's reaction mirrored that of his sibling. He could not believe the depth of the treachery that they were witness to, and he could do nothing but stare in a combination of rage and quiet confusion. Some of the other members of the group were not as quiet about the discovery. Pike's litany of curses was only out done by Talon's scream of rage. However, before their demonstrations could become rash acts, Korrd held up his hand and took three steps toward Shau-ling and the traitor.

"So," Korrd said softly after a moment, "this is how you've been one step ahead of us. How did you manage to convince Cedric to back you? Surely his depression could not have pushed him so far as to follow the likes of you."

"Not the introduction that I was hoping for Korrd," Shau-ling said after shifting on his throne, "but I suppose you have a right to be a bit confused by the Lion's defection from the light. Rather fitting isn't it that the circle begins and ends with him."

Shau-ling was rather enjoying his position of superiority and the effect his surprise was having upon his foes. His face was human in most of its features, but it also had many serpentine qualities. The eyes were bright yellow, much like Basille's, but they had a power and fire that Basille's did not. Shau-ling also did not have ears, and his mouth was filled with pointed, sharp teeth. Occasionally, a thin snake's tongue flicked out into the air for merely a second and then darted back into his mouth. Shau-ling's hands however were no more human than their shape. Where there should have been skin, there were only scales and a waxy looking residue that oozed from what would be comparable to human pours. His nails looked more like eagle's talons and were the same golden color as his eyes and the light that emanated from the floor. Shau-ling paused for a moment and looked over the remainder of the People of the Dragon. His army had cost them a great deal in the attempt to get to the throne room, and he knew it. Gwydeon died short of reaching the den of evil, and the loss of Arin had cost more than just another sword in the battle. Logan could feel the loss of power in his mind, and the more time that passed, the more the string of Fire died in the darkness. Shau-ling would live again in the next generation, and their chances on stopping him once and for all now were gone.

"But we are getting ahead of ourselves aren't we?" Shau-ling continued, his tone mocking, "There is still a battle to be fought and your lives to take. Tis a pity that I could not meet this Gwydeon Sandar that I have heard so much about. Emries was very careful about that boy, and I am glad that I have learned enough to end his life before his son could be born. Even if his life cost me Jeroch, the trade ultimately was worth the expenditure. Now, even if you do vanquish me, the third *Coromor* of the prophecies will never be born. Logan, I must thank you for taking in my little creation of stone. Thanks to him I was able not only to learn of Korrd and the mistake in Cedric's calculation that you were the *Coromor*, but I was also able to learn of Princess Rice's unborn child and that Gwillim boy that would have proven to be a large thorn in my side in the next generation. Your stupidity has condemned this world to my rule for the rest of eternity. Let me be the first to thank you."

Shau-ling laughed for a moment and then returned his gaze to Korrd. His look of triumph then faded into one of confusion. Korrd was smiling.

"Do you find the fact that you are beaten amusing Korrd, or perhaps has the strain of the situation finally driven you as mad as Saurn was at his end."

"No Halicon," Korrd said lightly, "I'm not mad, and you are yet to be victorious."

His voice now had a stronger quality that Logan had only remembered hearing in Emries' voice.

"Gwydeon's child is alive and well, and once we finish with you here, he will be glad to take his opportunity to avenge his father in the next generation."

Shau-ling's face now went from confusion to anger. Logan thought he saw that the color in the enemy's eyes changed from gold to red, and that was confirmed a moment later when the light in the room changed to a brilliant crimson.

"THAT IS IMPOSSIBLE," he screamed in a voice that seemed louder than all of the crashing thunder than had ever sounded, "I HAVE DESTROYED BOTH THE FATHER AND THE MOTHER, THE CHILD CANNOT LIVE."

"That child isn't dead," Korrd said calmly, "you thought you killed it early in its life, but you failed. Midarin is safe back in Brea, and there is no way you can touch her now. However, Gwillim is the one that will destroy you."

The look of confusion crept back onto the face of the master of evil, and he rose from the golden throne and advanced toward Korrd. Korrd took two steps forward himself and waited for Shau-ling to re-initiate the conversation. When Shau-ling stood there and stared, Korrd began speaking again.

"Don't you remember the prophecies that Aralias Imstra first spoke to you thanks to the research of your own children Grawn, Ellis, and Bryn? *A child that was never born shall come to hasten the end of the third reign of evil, and the tomorrows that have never been and shall always be shall turn their power against the master of evil. From the realm of angels shall he come, and to the realm of pain shall he venture to cure the world's ills. His blood will cleanse evil from the world, and his death shall help seal the coffin of evil.* You know the words better than I Shau-ling, and yet you ignore them and think that they are nothing more than words spoken by a blind fool before he met his own death. Wishful thinking by a stupid weak human trying to find a way to escape the evil that will eventually engulf the world? Arrogant misinterpretation of the words of your own children? Or is that why you discount the words. You don't think that they have any power because your children were not strong enough to survive without you. That is the only foolish arrogance that I see Shau-ling. Your stupidity has sealed your fate."

The rage was gone from Shau-ling's face and the victorious smile returned. He turned and walked back to the throne and sat down. After a moment, he spoke.

"We shall see. But perhaps I will not have to worry about Gwillim or any of the rest of the prophecies if I stop you here and now. Then perhaps I will hunt down and kill this third coming for my own amusement. His death will most likely be the first act of my new world domination. No, not my first act. My first act will be to dispose of all my sometimes willing accomplices."

He turned his gaze to Cedric and then laughed that defiant, pompous laugh that they had heard echoing though halls of the palace.

"So Cedric is no more than a pawn to throw our concentration off? I thought that perhaps he meant more to you than that. After all, he was the first and only man to ever beat you," Korrd prodded.

Rather than reacting with anger again, a bemused look came to Shau-ling's features.

"He is much more than that Korrd, he is a pawn that has a sword and can strike any of you with any time. Now that he has touched the powers of the Blaze, he is more than a match for any one of you now that the meddling Sandar has been eliminated. Not only that, but with his powers added to mine, you have no chance of destroying me. But let us not talk of the battle and your world's impending doom. Not all of the pieces have yet to be brought onto the board. Nightwing, I have need of you and our guest."

At Shau-ling's summons, a whirling blue portal appeared to his right. A moment later, the being they had learned was called Nightwing stepped out with a limp and motionless Elwyne in his clutches. From what Logan could tell, she was still alive, but the fact that most of her clothes were torn revealing long jagged scars made him worry. Anger swelled up inside of Logan, but he managed to keep it in check, even without Korrd putting a hand on his shoulder to reassure his brother. Logan knew that they could not afford to strike first, especially when it was obvious that was what Shau-ling was expecting them to do with all of the overt pokes and prods. As Nightwing lay Elwyne on the ground before his master, the blackness in Logan's mind that held the powers of the *Chosen One* began to overtake his vision as it had done so many times before. The whole scene that had been before him in his mortal sight faded to an echo cast in shadows and echoes of power. Cedric's body pulsed with a green fire that was peaked with strained white energy. The Elder's warnings about touching the Blaze had been true, but Lord Cedric had kept the fact that he was an unwilling servant of Shau-ling hidden from everyone. Then Logan remembered Lord Cedric telling Logan that he should try to draw on the power of the Blaze himself in an effort to learn the capabilities of the enemy. He had been trying to end the battle before it could even begin by turning the *Coromor* to the side of evil, but that was before the truth of Logan's true role in the war against the Shadow had been revealed. The fires around Cedric seemed to arch out and touch the thing called Nightwing. But the green fire around Nightwing seemed to be underlined by another power, a stronger one that held its connection deeper in Cedric than that of the Blaze. In Logan's mind he tried to push past the power of the Blaze and the strings of phasia energy that wrapped themselves around Nightwing's armor. Finally Logan found the way through the shield. There was a long jagged slash in the armor of Nightwing. They had all seen it when Nightwing dueled with Basille, but in the realm of power, that scar in the armor was like a window. Logan's power of vision lanced through the scar and found the ugly and bitter truth that lay beneath the armor. Logan saw Aryx wrapped in the fires of his *Erieal* energy imprisoned helplessly inside the armor. No matter what his body did, he was merely a spectator, a voiceless puppet in the service of Shau-ling. Horror filling his heart, Logan pulled himself out of the state of mind and started to say something to Korrd. Apparently, Shau-ling had read the look on Logan's face and had expected the discovery. He spoke first, muting any other words with stinging ones of his own.

"Ah," he said proudly, "I see that you have uncovered the truth dear Logan. Tis a pity that the rest of your group cannot see what your powers as the *Chosen One* have both blessed and cursed you with. But perhaps they can. Nightwing, show these good people the very thing that your friend Logan has discovered."

Nightwing looked up at his master and nodded. As it walked forward, Logan could see that the blade of its sword was still coated with the blood of the man they had known as Basille. He may have been a phase, and a servant of evil at birth, but he died a man and a friend of the cause of the human race. Nightwing dropped the sword and put both of its clawed hands at the scar in his armor that Basille had first inflicted and then widened. A howl of pain ripped from its throat as its strong arms began to pull apart the plates of armor that seemed to serve as its skin. The same pasty blue blood that had become easily recognizable as the viscera of other Shadowwalkers poured from the new wounds as pieces of the armor flaked off with each rip of the black claws. As the flow of blood dissipated, and the chunks of armor or skin fell away, tan human flesh came into full view. The human hands then removed the head of the beast known as Nightwing and revealed the face of the man once known around the world as White Lightning.

"Aryx..." Pike's words mingled with the other faint and confused reactions of the party. However, the shield of Blaze fire had not disappeared from around Aryx. Even though the armor was not in clear view, the Nightwing persona was still in full control, and the man they had known and once trusted would probably never surface again.

"Korrd," Logan whispered, "that's not..."

"I know Logan," he said squeezing the hilt of his sword tighter than ever, "but right now I'm more interested in finding out how we can turn this into our advantage than adding it to our already long list of disadvantages. If you have any suggestions little brother, now would be the time for you to take a shot."

Logan was surprised by how quickly Korrd was willing to defer to the younger man given the gravity of the situation. From the moment he joined the force, he had been the natural leader, and Logan felt that he was only called upon in times where he was the only option available. It wasn't as though Logan felt bitter or slighted, but going from the most important role to the second in line was a difficult transition. It may have been a selfish feeling, but in the grand scheme of things the role of the *Chosen One* was probably the better fit for Logan. He was not the leader that his brother was, nor was he as valuable with a blade or practiced with his powers. In fact, in the People of the Dragon, Logan often considered himself more a liability than a strength. It had been Pike and Gwydeon that had carried the most weight, and Logan had always taken solace in the fact that when the end came, he would be able to repay their blood and dedication in his role as the *Coromor*, but even that had been taken away. Still, Korrd was right. There was nothing that he could do about Aryx or Cedric short of initiating the final battle. His function was to kill Shau-ling and make sure that their generation would be safe. Because of Logan's abilities and the *Chosen One's* ties to the phasia and Shau-ling, he was able to see the strings of power that fed both Cedric and Aryx. They were now Logan's problem, and the responsibility that at times Logan wanted to run far away from sat firmly upon his shoulders.

"So Aryx," Logan said sheathing my sword, "have you enjoyed this little masquerade? I knew that you were evasive and uncooperative, but I never would have dreamed that you would become the servant of evil."

"He is not truly to blame, Logan," Shau-ling said as he walked down the dais toward Elwyne. "Aryx had no choice but to come to me when I called. You see, when Cedric touched my Blaze, my life-force, he became my servant. When I was reborn into the world, my connection to him was still very strong, and I began to slowly feed him pieces of my power and bits of my essence to affirm his allegiance to me. The so-called madness was my creation. The power that he possessed was mine, and he bent it to my will. But, there was an added bonus to my tinkering. Because I had enslaved the *Coromor*, the *Erieal* would also fall into line. Aryx was easy enough to turn. His allegiance to and hatred of Cedric made him the perfect target. So, through Cedric, I fed the powers of the first generation's *Erieal* and brought Aryx to my side as Nightwing."

"Why just Aryx?" Korrd asked before the question could form in Logan's mouth. "You could have had all of the first generation's *Erieal* to use against us. Their power matched with your own could be more powerful than all of your phasia put together, if they would ever stop fighting long enough to stand behind."

Shau-ling dismissed the question with the wave of a scaly hand.

"The other three *Erieal* were weak, and Aryx was the true prize of the lot. They do not possess the killing instinct that your *Erieal* do. Never would Mailock have used his powers to drain a man's life like Pike Rhuiden would. Arathorn Geoffry was worried too much about his sword to rely on the powers that my brother had bestowed on him. He would have rather died with a blade in hand than move the earth at his feet to save his life. Your Gideon Viruci is very adept at the use of his power, and thanks to Basille, my youngest and by far the most impressive phase, his powers have been honed to a deadly edge, much like his knives. And Diana, forgetting for a moment that she was a weak and frail woman, she could never use her powers as a man would. She does not have the killer instinct that is so well pronounced in Talon Aielin. His arrogance makes him powerful. Your companions would have made good phasia, were it not for that pitiful human instinct that you call mercy. My servants have no need of it, but you seem to feed on it and it makes you hold back when you should go in for the kill. Only Pike has shown flashes of true phasia ruthlessness. But not even all of your *Erieal* combined will rival that which I have created with Nightwing, and Aryx Terian with the Blaze burning in his blood is a truly terrifying creature."

Out of the corner of Logan's eye he saw Aryx frown and twitch slightly, but he filed the response in the back of his mind and prodded deeper.

"So the only reason was his strength?" Logan asked.

"Perhaps I should not have concerned myself so with you, Logan, it does not appear that you pay attention well enough to the truth that stands right before your eyes. No Logan, but strength and ruthlessness were very important pieces. Aryx had the power and the destructive instinct that I needed. Also, his prowess and speed with his sword made him invaluable. But I have you to thank for the most important part of my criteria Logan. After meeting you, Aryx began to doubt the fate of the second *Coromor* and the people he was supposed to protect. That doubt allowed me to pull on the strings of power inside him, and he came to my side in confusion and misery. He knew there was more than simply servitude and loyalty to an outmoded ideal handed down by a weak pretender masquerading as the great and powerful Creator. I ended the confusion and gave him the direction that he so desperately needed. The misery is of his own design and shall not even be ended by his death. Aryx has always been and shall always be my servant."

* * * * * * * * * * * *

The conversation between the forces of the Light and Shau-ling still droned on, but all Aryx could hear was that same sentence over and over again in his mind. It filled his heart with rage and began to turn the pieces of his mind to thoughts that had not been there in what seemed like lifetimes. 'Diana, she was a weak and frail woman.' The words bit at his mind. Perhaps it was only a slip of the tongue. Shau-ling meant to say is, not was. Aryx's heart cried in pain as the thought of his wife's body broken and bleeding ran through his mind. He had killed many people since he had become Nightwing, and he had seen many bodies lying in countless positions of death. Blood coating their bodies as their last breaths slipped from their lungs either in a scream of defiance or in a whimper of defeat. The cruelest twist was that he remembered all of them. Every face, every body. Their names in some cases, their words in others. As he thought about the possibility of his wife's death, the faces and bodies of his victims were now replaced with Diana's in his memories. In his mind, his wife died over and over again in every possible way. He could see her hair matted with blood from her shattered skull. He could feel the hot blood on his fingers from sword wounds to her chest. The sound of her screams and sobs of pain rang perfectly in his ears. Aryx, the real Aryx inside the shell of cold fire, began to shiver and grow restless.

* * * * * * * * * * * *

Korrd's fingers were still wrapped tight around the hilt of his sword, and Logan could tell that he was getting anxious. For the most part, the rest of the group had remained silent. There was so much that had happened in a short time, and there was no time to deal with it all yet. Basille, Arin, Gwydeon, Bryn, and Stone were all dead. Aryx and Cedric were traitors. But foremost was the fact that they were faced with the completion of the quest that had ruined their lives. Logan knew that Pike was ready to die for the cause, as were the rest. Jerrard was the first member of the party to speak openly to Shau-ling besides the Ranthall brothers.

"Shau-ling," he said stepping up to Korrd's side.

"Ah, my grandson. Jerrard Mystic. You were the piece of the puzzle that I couldn't place, even with the help of my Stone. When I learned that you were alive years ago, I dispatched my first-born to deal with you and your mother. Thanks to the Creator's own luck, you survived and were taken in by my companion here. Cedric was nice enough to make you one of his soldiers, and eventually you followed him to the foot of my palace where you fought and killed your own father by stabbing him in the back."

Jerrard's face went cold and pale. Clearly he remembered the incident, but Logan was sure that Jerrard had ever unraveled the truth about the identity of the phase he had defeated in the battle of Lakestone all those years ago. It was still hard to look at Jerrard and not think of him as a contemporary to the other members of the group. Though, the same could have been said of Gideon. The two men were anachronisms, caught out of time by flukes of their birth and the blood that flowed through their veins.

"So," Shau-ling said reading Jerrard's expression, "I see that your father never told you that you dealt the fatal blow in that lifetime. Ah, but that's not important is it? Your real importance in this whole game was that you were an unfettered link to my power. You can touch the Blaze without the pull to my service. You are much like Hawk, but you have a conscience which makes you completely ill-suited to be the son of a phase."

Jerrard smiled at the comparison. Logan had never personally had the displeasure of meeting the man called Hawk, but from the stories told by Pike and Talon, he was glad that Jerrard was nothing like Jeroch's son.

"Well," Jerrard said after a moment, "your phasia don't seem to be suited for the work you gave them now do they? After all, they're all dead, and here we are still standing. You even had to go out and recruit two of your own mortal enemies to combat us."

Shau-ling's eyes returned to the red that they had been when Korrd had taunted him, but before he could bellow a response, Jerrard continued with the verbal assault.

"And as for Hawk, he lasted maybe thirty seconds when faced with the People of the Dragon. Notice that I'm still alive. My father, he was strong. You taunt me with the fact that I delivered the final blow in his last lifetime. In answer, I would do it the same way if I had it to do all over again. Why you ask? He was about to kill Cedric when I put him down. Cedric was more important than my father, and had I known he was my father, I hated him so much at that point, I probably would have run him through for the personal gratification. Now, look what he became in this generation. He became a soldier for the Light. Granted he did it in his own way, but he helped to give us the edge. Thanks to his training of Gideon, his guidance of Korrd and Logan, and finally for pointing me in the direction of Arin Domae. He more than any other is responsible for your downfall, just like his brother and sisters Grawn, Bryn, and Ellis before him."

Shau-ling didn't react at all, he just sat there, the fires smoldering in his eyes. Logan heard some mumbling behind him that drew his attention to Pike, Talon and Gideon who were engaged in a quite animated but hushed conversation. They were planning something, and after a quick hand signal from Pike, Logan knew that he had to buy them some more time. It was too risky to try and speak through thoughts, considering Shau-ling could probably hear every words, so Logan gave Pike the 'what do you want me to do' look. His eyes shifted toward Cedric and then back to Logan. Pike smiled and returned to the conversation. However, just as Logan was about to restart the conversation with Shau-ling, he heard Korrd mumble, "enough of this," and reach for his sword. Using a little bit of his own power over the wind, almost little enough to escape notice, Logan nudged Korrd's hand back away from the hilt of his sword. He looked back at his younger brother and nodded in understanding.

"I'm confused Shau-ling," Logan said trying to disguise what had just occurred. "You knew all of this about us through Aryx and Stone. And you hold power over Aryx through Cedric. Why do you even need him here to fight us?"

Shau-ling relaxed back on the throne, his eyes shifting back to brilliant gold, so confident in his upcoming victory that he would tolerate a continued parlay.

"You could say that I have a weakness for poetic irony. He was the link to my first and only defeat by the power of steel. Emries was never able to defeat me, but Cedric did. His abilities endeared himself, no matter what side his allegiance fell upon. But in answer to your question, I was not the one that commanded Cedric be here for the final battle. Aryx was certain that his presence would be necessary, and so I allowed Nightwing to deliver my summons to the Lion. I was surprised to hear that Cedric also wanted to be here to face you and your brother. He is still hoping that I will allow him to die. I must say that when ultimately I am victorious, I may actually allow him to die. But even were you to be victorious in the coming conflict I shall have the comfort of knowing that you were forced to strike him down."

Again Logan saw the twitch of nervous energy from Aryx at the mention of his role in Cedric's appearance. There was something more to Aryx's conversion to the forces of the Shadow, and it was pushing to the surface the longer the taunts fired from each side.

"What reason would Cedric 'ave fer wantin' himself dead?" Gideon asked as he and Pike approached.

Talon also approached, but he stopped near Logan and the younger Ranthall saw that the metal of his *Debuisa* began to grow clearer.

"He's only become da biggest traitor in the history of da world. Emries must be cursing himself fer ever giving da mantle of *Coromor* ta ye."

"No Gideon," Pike said grasping his shoulder and pulling him back. "We all know that Cedric had his reasons for what he did. After what he's done, I'd want to be killed too."

Cedric sighed deeply and stepped away from Shau-ling. He descended the dais and stopped three of four feet in front of Pike. The Lion sword now came into a better light. The emeralds that served for the eyes of the Lions were now dim and covered with a black film. The state of the man had become the state of the sword. There was some strange power that flowed between the *Coromor* and the sword of his birth. Logan had never felt anything but raw power from the sword himself, but he was the *Chosen One*. Korrd had obviously felt the power of the blade from the moment that Logan had placed the sword in the true Dragon's hand. Cedric was still for a moment and then he spoke in a voice that seemed to be as weighted down as his soul.

"Pike," he said shaking his head, "you more than anyone should know the depths of darkness that my soul swims in. It feels as though there is a black veil that has descended upon my heart and my mind. You must have felt the same way when your Eldar died. The pain in my heart has come from the years of living with the memory of the only woman that I have ever loved or will ever love. The fact that her life was stolen away from me by my dearest friend Basille only scars my heart deeper. And before you say anything Pike, I know of the rumor that says my Erika was really the phase Caris. I will combat that ridiculous rumor with every breath in my body unless you have some proof to the contrary."

Pike smiled and nodded.

"I thought you would feel that way Cedric, and I'm almost sorry that you have to learn the truth now when your fate has already been sealed. You have been lied to all this time Cedric, and the proof I have will come from the mouth of Gideon Viruci, and a man that you trusted once in Jerrard Mystic."

"Dat's right Cedric. Think back to da day dat ye think ye fell in love with Erika. I can tell ye what day dat was Cedric. Dat was da day dat she was in dat riding accident."

"Oh yes," Cedric said, his whole attitude seeming to lift a degree. "She looked so frail when her horse rode back into the gates. She was barely clinging to the saddle, and I remember I had to carry her to her house. Arthur was so pleased that she was alive, he barely noticed the way that I was looking at her. For the next week, I checked on her every day, bringing her the best cuts from the palace flower garden."

"Dat's right Cedric," Gideon continued, "dat is da day of da biggest lie of all. Erika was out riding, and her mount was spooked by a man and a woman who just happened to be walking through dat field. Da man was yer best friend and my caretaker, Basille Mystic. Da woman was Caris, da only remaining daughter of the Council of phasia. Caris could touch anyone's soul and steal their form, memories, and voice. Da plan was dat Caris would take Erika's place ta get close ta ye. Basille was supposed to dispose of Erika, but he showed pity on the girl, and she was taken ta Basille's palace where she was told dat her parents were killed and dere was no reason for her ta ever go back ta Marcwell. Basille raised her as a daughter, and once he learned that Jerrard was alive he sent her to Illimar."

"Which is when I first met the woman I knew as Erika Belnosian," Jerrard said taking up the story. "I knew the name Belnosian from my time with the Lion's Mane, but I never thought that she was of any relation. In fact, I was so surprised that a woman so beautiful would have taken an interest in me that I don't remember ever asking her last name. In time, I just began to see my life and hers together forever, and I must say that she seemed to have the same thoughts in mind. We were married a month after meeting, and we lived in Illimar until the war that claimed the life of the woman we had known as Queen Saris. That woman turned out to be Caris, and her assassin would later be found out to be Korrd. When the Army of the Dragon took control, I was named the head of the standing army, which was made up of mostly peasants. I went to Illimar to escape the constant fighting, so I gave up the commission the next day. In the middle of the night a few days after the battle, two men snatched me from my bed, tied me up, blindfolded me, and threw me in the back of a wagon. The next voice I heard was Erika's. She was there with me, but from the way she held me and talked to me, I knew that somehow she had either sneaked aboard the wagon, or that she wasn't a prisoner. I later found out that the latter was true but the abduction was not a heinous act. That's how I met my father and learned the truth about Erika's origins. You were fooled into believing that ruthless hag Caris was really my sweet and loving Erika. I know that you loved her with all your heart, but your love was never returned. Caris was incapable of love, and she would laugh at the fact that you are still torn apart by her. It's not too late Cedric. Listen to reason."

For a moment Cedric stood perfectly still, as though the great turmoil that must have been raging in his heart and mind were being contained in a statue of cold stone. But then finally the corners of Cedric's mouth raised slightly and a maddened laughter shook the former *Coromor* from head to toe. It looked for a moment that he would laugh so hard that it would snap the bones in his frail figure, but finally the laughter subsided, and the eyes of a killer locked on Jerrard.

"I would were reason being spoken," he said gripping tightly the hilt of his sword. "I see no reason why we should prolong this pointless discussion any further do you? The dying starts now. And my blade will speak the truth!"

The Final Battle

Aryx stood near Elwyne and listened as the conversation with his former lord and master droned on. The words of love and caring tore at his heart, and he could not help but look at Elwyne as he thought of the life that he had once had. Those last few days when he was with Logan's force, he could see the kind of devotion that Logan and Elwyne felt for one another, and every time he did, he thought about Diana and counted the days before he could see her again. And now he would never be able to see her. Shau-ling had probably realized that the only reason Aryx wanted to deliver the message to Cedric in Marcwell was that he might have stolen some glances at his former bride. It seemed impossible, but he achieved his end. One day, after he had met with Cedric about the time and place that Cedric was supposed to go, Aryx had put on an old tattered cloak and made his way to the palaces holy temple which was built on the far side of the palace courtyard for privacy. The other reason it was built there was because Cedric wanted it as far away from him as possible. After his fight with Shau-ling, Cedric became increasingly intolerant of religion and would have renounced the gods altogether had it not been for Arathorn's cool-headed persuasion. Aryx had walked slowly across the courtyard, trying to fake a limp and not draw too much attention to himself. That day, Wednesday, was the public day at the palace. Peasants were allowed to come and voice their opinions or give their praise to Lord Cedric. While in the palace, they were also allowed to worship in the temple. It was still early and most of the peasants were still in the great hall making themselves heard. As Aryx entered the temple, he saw Diana kneeling in front of the altar. She was dressed in black, and her head was covered in a mourning shroud. Aryx could only stand for a moment watching her, and then he left with his heart aching for the life that had been stolen from him. He had lost once too, a loss that he still felt deep in his heart. It was a scar that could never heal, one that would haunt his steps. It wasn't until he touched the Blaze through Nightwing that the loss reawakened in his mind, and it made him ache for Diana all the more.

Now the conversation between Cedric and the force of the Light had begun to turn ugly. Gideon and Jerrard were speaking the truth, but Cedric had been so brainwashed by his years of sorrow and regret and the words of Shau-ling that he was incapable of hearing it. Now Cedric was becoming angry. Aryx could feel the surges of power run through his body as Cedric began to pull on the powers of the Blaze. As the Lion tightened the grip on his sword, the power began to flow into the blade until he Aryx could see a faint glow of green down the length of the sword. The battle would to begin at any moment, and Aryx had to decide if he were to follow his heart or follow his head. Were the years of living in the Light strong enough to make a difference, and was the chance of seeing Diana's face one more worth an eternity of pain?

* * * * * * * * * * * *

Logan had not expected the conversation to turn as ugly as rapidly as it had. Gideon's plan most certainly had been to aggravate Cedric to the point that he would initiate the battle and Shau-ling and Nightwing would be unprepared. Personally, that wasn't a strategy that Logan favored, especially considering they had no idea how far Cedric had traveled down the path into the bosom of the Shadow and what new powers that he had found. His grief and anger would make him powerful, ever so much powerful than their short confrontation in the frontier. There would be no limits this time, and Logan was sure that he would be unable to rob the former *Coromor* of his powers this time around. Cedric brought his Lion sword to bear, and as it slashed out into the air at Jerrard, Logan noticed the glimmer of green fire that surrounded the blade. Logan started to shout something in Jerrard's direction, but Talon pulled Logan quickly to the ground as a ball of fire sailed over their heads. When Logan looked up, he saw that Shau-ling was off his throne and using his powers to their fullest killing potential. As he shuffled back to his feet, Logan drew upon the energy in the room. The powers of the three *Erieal* and Jerrard filled him, and Logan unleashed and bolt of gray-green energy in the direction of Shau-ling. His hands flashed for a moment, and the beam was intercepted with one of his own. Korrd was three feet from Logan, ducking and weaving away from the bolts of lightning that flew from various places around the room. Talon started to move toward where Jerrard and Pike were dodging the blows of the Lion. Logan grabbed him by the shoulder and pulled him back.

"Talon," Logan said keeping one eye on Shau-ling and the other on Korrd. "You have to make sure that Elwyne is protected. Weave a shield of Wind around her and make sure that Shau-ling, Cedric or Nightwing don't get close enough to do her any harm."

"But that will take me out of the battle, Logan," Talon frowned. "I'll have to concentrate all of my strength on the shield with all of the stray energy flying around."

"Please Talon," Logan implored.

Time was growing short. Another beam of energy lanced over their heads, and Logan shook Talon's shoulder again.

"I'd do it myself but..."

"I know, Logan," he said moving toward the dais and Nightwing. "Don't worry, I'll take up her protection where Gideon can't. Nothing will happen to her, I stake my life on it."

He moved quickly toward where Nightwing stood motionless, still waiting to enter the battle, and created the shield that Logan had asked for. As Logan looked back toward Shau-ling, there was a brilliant flash of green light that he caught out of the corner of his eye, and an audible cry of pain that sounded like it came from Jerrard. Shau-ling's laughter confirmed Logan's fearful expectation.

"You see how easily your people can fall?" he said mocking their fallen friend.

Logan ran over to where Jerrard lay. There was a huge burn mark across the front of his tunic, and in Logan's mind, he could see the Blaze energy eating away at Jerrard on the inside. Cedric's sword had stored up enough energy that when it finally struck true, the full force of the Blaze energy was released into his victim. Logan knew that Jerrard was dying. The only way to save him was to physically pull the Blaze energy out of him. But, as they had faced with Gwydeon, in attempting to save his life, whoever touched the Blaze would become a slave to Shau-ling.

"Interesting quandary isn't it, Logan?" Shau-ling mocked as if he read the younger Ranthall's thoughts. "Do you save your friend's life and become like Aryx and Cedric, or do you let him die and forever live with the memory that you could have saved him? You humans would not have to worry about such things if you didn't have those terrible consciences. Decide quickly, for time grows short for all of you and your world."

Logan stood to face Shau-ling.

"Well then," he said sitting back onto his golden throne, "Cedric, finish this rabble."

Cedric smiled, and then raised his sword again. This time the powers of the Blaze began to mix with those that he had been granted as the *Coromor*. Korrd kept his eyes focused on Shau-ling, and Pike and Gideon were watching Cedric. Just as Logan was about to unleash another bolt of energy, Aryx, wrapped in his Nightwing armor, flew across the room and cut off the attack that was meant for Logan. The blow reflected off the dull black armor and struck a far wall. Shock held the room silent and still. Nightwing stood defiant as Cedric waited for some guidance on what he should do. Before any such guidance came, Nightwing pulled his still bloody sword to bear. He charged Cedric the next moment. Nightwing's blade was also charged with energy, and as the two blades met, the energy crackled and sparks flew. This was a battle that had waited a lifetime to occur. Logan and the others had heard of the challenge of Arathorn to Aryx, and the fact that Aryx had lost that battle. Cedric's swordsmanship though had never been that impressive. The two combatants circled each other and their blades met again and again. Cedric slashed wildly and missed, but Nightwing was not in a position to follow up and get a clean shot at the kill. However, Logan forgot for a moment that Nightwing was more than Aryx and more than a Shadowwalker. What would have been impossible for either alone was very possible for Nightwing. As Cedric reeled forward, off-balance from his latest wild slash, Nightwing's tail leapt out and tripped his former friend. Cedric fell forward and the impact sent his sword skidding out of his reach. Nightwing looked up at his former master who looked on not with shock but more a knowing disappointment, and then plunged his blade into Cedric's back. That instant, the bond between Cedric and Aryx shattered. The shield of Blaze energy began to weaken, and there was no telling how long his power would hold out before he was simply Aryx again.

"ENOUGH OF THIS," Shau-ling roared. "THIS WILL ALSO BE THE END OF THIS PITIFUL REBELLION AGAINST THE FORCES OF THE SHADOW. NOW, WITNESS THE TRUE POWER OF THE MASTER OF THE BLAZE!"

As Shau-ling spoke those words, the golden light in the room began to fade. The golden throne that glittered behind Shau-ling now sank away into the floor, and a huge column of green energy lanced through the floor and burned a hole through the top of the throne room. Shau-ling stood motionless for a moment and then stepped back into the channel of energy. As soon as he was completely immersed in the violent flow of green power, he floated a foot above the dais and closed his eyes, extending his hands out. The look on his face was very much like that of pure joy. As all of this was happening, the still upright members of the group all gathered around Korrd. Talon was the first to speak up.

"Is that what I think it is?"

"That's the very core of his power," Korrd answered in a voice that was not at all his. "He has opened himself up fully to the power of the Blaze."

Pike shook his head and started giving orders.

"Korrd's gone to a place that I don't intend on going just yet, so what we have to do is make sure that he gets his shot. Whatever is happening is going to be very bad when it all comes down, and I think that something needs to be done about it. If we hit him with all of our powers at once, with Logan and Korrd channeling as much as they can, we might have a chance to get out of this."

"As long as the Blaze is still feeding Shau-ling, there is no way that you have enough power to defeat him."

The voice had come from the singular man who stood away from the group. Aryx had let the armor retract, and he stood in the same clothes that Logan remembered last seeing him in, minus the cloak. Part of Logan was happy to have the real Aryx back with them, but the fact that he had once served the Shadow made it hard to be entirely trusting.

"So we have to figure out some way to stop Shau-ling from drawing on the Blaze. After he's out of the column of energy. I'll form a shield of wind to keep him out of the Blaze."

"That plan might work except for the fact that just being here in the throne room gives Shau-ling access to the full power of the Blaze," Aryx countered glumly.

The sound of Aryx's voice had a faint aura of morbidity to it that struck a discordant tone. It was as if he had already condemned them all to death.

"So we have to get him out of the throne room," Talon interjected.

Pike shook his head and looked back at me.

"That will never happen. Shau-ling knows that he has the advantage here, and we would have to kill him to get him out of this place."

"And that leads us back to the same question again," Logan replied. "There has to be some way of stopping Shau-ling from feeding on the Blaze. Aryx, you've been in here and you've seen the Blaze. You know what it's capable of, and I'm sure you have some idea of how to stop it."

Aryx looked up at the floating form of Shau-ling and then slowly nodded.

"I have an idea Logan, but it's a slim chance at best. You need to follow Pike's suggestion and use everything that you have to try and keep Shau-ling off balance. I'll do what I can. Talon will have to be responsible for creating a shield of wind. Logan, your powers are much too valuable and are needed in the real fight."

"What about Elwyne?" Logan said looking back at her still motionless body. "She's still well within the line of fire."

"Logan," Korrd said looking back and joining our conversation for the first time. "You have to choose what's more important, the life of the woman you love, or the lives of six generations of people. One life for millions is a fair trade."

"For you maybe," Logan shot back. "You have known from the beginning that you're going to die as a result of this battle, and you don't have enough human compassion left in you to care about anything. Talon can make sure that nothing touches her, and I'll keep Shau-ling from turning back to the Blaze."

"No!" Korrd barked grabbing my shoulder. "You heard Aryx. As much as I don't trust him, he's right. I need you for the first strike. Now that the powers of the Jeweled Dragon's Flame are lost to us, I can't let our powers be divided, and because there is a chance that Aryx's plan won't work. I need you now more than ever. Isn't this what Gwydeon sacrificed for? And Arin? And Eldar and Lane? How many others? Are your desires so much more important than theirs? Now you either . . ."

"Korrd," Pike said staring at the motionless body of Shau-ling that we had ignored for the past few seconds, "you're not going to believe this."

At Pike's insistence, the group looked back at the column of power, and watched in horror as the body of Shau-ling began to change. His eyes were open again, but the face had taken on far more reptilian features. As the moments passed, Shau-ling's skin transformed into black scales, and his eyes were beginning to glow into a deep red. That was when the rest of his body began to change.

Shau-ling's arms began to thicken, and the small green scales there began to grow and turn black. The middle two fingers on each hand began to grow together and then became one as the hand flexed back and took on the appearance of a great paw rather than a hand. The arms too looked much different. At one point, each elbow straightened and then bent the opposite way. Both arms now looked like legs with a giant paw on the end. The new paws still had the gleaming golden talons, but each one's size had been greatly increased. It looked to Logan that each one of the talons were as long as he was tall.

Shau-ling's legs underwent a similar change. His pants ripped and then were shredded as the breadth of the limbs increased exponentially. Black scales cascaded down each leg, and gleaming golden talons grew out of each toe. The middle two toes merged, and soon Shau-ling's legs were almost identical to the arms, except laden with more muscle to support the growing bulk. His torso expanded and the black scales seemed to erupt from the human-like pours that dotted his frame. As everything else on his body seemed to expand, his neck started to lengthen. With each addition to the length of the neck, black scales appeared to cover the human skin of the previous section. When the neck had finished lengthening and thickening, the head too began to grow. His jaw jutted forward and lengthened as his nose sank back into nonexistence and his head flattened. The top part of Shau-ling's mouth then began to lengthen and stopped when its length matched that of the jaw. Where a human's head seems to sit atop the neck at a square angle, Shau-ling's neck and head seemed to sit in a straight line. As the head and neck moved into their new configuration there was the sound of snapping bones and ripping flesh. The unnatural angle the face formed made Logan's stomach turn. The tail of the dragon was the next piece to be formed. That same sound of skin breaking accompanied the formation, and as the remaining People of the Dragon watched, a small snake-like projection came into view. It twisted and moved as if it were fighting to pull itself from the rest of the body. More and more pulled itself out as the seconds passed until it had grown to at least sixty feet in length. But the transformation's most spectacular portion had yet to be seen.

The dragon rolled onto its side, and two large slits appeared in the dragon's back. The scaly liquid substance that had formed on the legs and chest of Shau-ling now dripped from the open wounds, and then started to solidify the further they dripped away from the rest of the body. It was like the wings formed from the tips inward. Most of the wing was a lighter color, almost gray. Black veins arched across the seemingly thin skin and attached to the black tendon-like framework of the wing. The wings themselves looked like those of a bat, much like those of the original Shadowwalkers. When the transformation was complete, the dragon stepped out of the column of energy and glared down at the forces of the Light with its brilliant red eyes. It was the same dragon that Logan had seen during his dream-like confrontation with Shau-ling in Rama.

Korrd stepped forward and waited. The look on the dragon's face was familiar, and if Logan would have compared the look to a human expression, he would have had to say that the dragon smiled. Korrd seized all of the power he could and pointed his hands at Shau-ling. Logan could see a faint outline of energy surge around Korrd's fingers before the burst of energy erupted. A stream of power erupted from Korrd's extended hands and sped toward the head of the dragon. Shau-ling was quick to react, opening his huge jaws and sending a stream of Blaze energy leaping from his mouth where it met the blast midway between the combatants. The streams of white and green struck in a dazzling array of small explosions that lit the chamber in reds, blues, and yellows. But as the seconds passed, Korrd's attack was pushed back by the awesome and limitless power of the master of the Blaze. It was clear that the power of the *Coromor* was not enough to turn back the full power of the Blaze, and Korrd's stream of power was being beaten back faster and faster. Korrd hesitated only a moment before raising his other hand and releasing a stream of white force from the combined energies of the three *Erieal*, Aryx, and Jerrard. With that energy added to his power alone, a stalemate was achieved. Reflexively, Logan pulled the powers of the *Erieal* and the *Coromor* into himself and released a beam of energy of his own into the face of the dragon. Shau-ling reeled from the combined assault, and he staggered backward. The dragon lost its balance and flailed around for something to steady itself. In Logan's mind he saw Talon bring up a shield of wind to keep Shau-ling from retreating into the Blaze. The dragon however was too worried about not losing its balance to think about the damage done to it. While it flailed, one of its forearms struck the stone arch over the dais and knocked loose a large chunk. The newly created boulder fell downward and was headed straight toward Elwyne. Logan tried to exert his powers of the Wind and Earth to stop the piece of stone, but either his powers had no effect on the stone because of Shau-ling's control, or because the previous release had left Logan too weak. Talon was in no position to shift his powers because of the crucial role his shield of wind played. Pike had not seen archway crumble, and was using his powers to try and keep the dragon off balance by freezing different places on the dais. The ice never lasted long because of Shau-ling's control over the surroundings, but it seemed to be enough of a distraction to keep Shau-ling's focus shifted to more than just Korrd and Logan. Gideon was the only one left. Before Logan knew what was happening, Gideon was sprinting toward Elwyne. Apparently he had tried to use his powers and failed to change the trajectory of the falling stone. The whole scene seemed to play out in slow motion. Gideon was moving faster than it seemed possible to move, and he dove toward Elwyne, pushing her out of the falling arch's path. But his dive had not carried him past the point of impact. His legs and lower back were crushed under the heavy stone, and he cried out in pain. The pain pushed him into unconsciousness, but he was still barely hanging on to the last threads of life. The echo of the trauma radiated through the strings of power inside Logan's mind, and he could not help but nearly lose his grasp on the string of Earth. The power of Earth wavered for a moment, but was still there, but it was unclear how long that would last. He shouldn't have survived the impact at all, but the stubbornness of the former thief could not be denied, and Logan hoped that the man could hold on until the battle for the future of the world was over.

The dragon finally regained its balance, but was clearly shaken. The small window of hesitation due to Gideon's injury had given Shau-ling the time he needed to bring himself back to the battle. Korrd had not moved from where he stood, and when the dragon stared back down at him, Korrd lashed out again with his own powers. The dragon was ready for the assault this time and used a more focused burst of power that not only forced back Korrd's beam of energy, but also knocked the *Coromor* to the ground. Talon had been near Korrd when the strike hit, and he was thrown hard against one of the columns. When he didn't move right away, Logan began to worry. Then Logan felt the twinges of power inside him begin to groan and die. The string of Wind had been snapped as quickly as Talon's neck upon impact. The death of their friend had been quick and relatively painless, but its impacted upon the strength available to both Logan and Korrd would echo through the remainder of the battle. Korrd proved to be more resilient of the brothers and he was up on his feet lashing out again with his significantly diminished powers. Korrd knew that with Talon dead, the shield of wind that held Shau-ling out of the Blaze was gone. Shau-ling could retreat and revitalize himself at any moment. As soon as Shau-ling realized what had occurred, the forces of the Light would all be reduced to red smears on the floor of his throne room; trophies of his ultimate defeat of the People of the Dragon.

Logan started lashing out with his powers, and for the moment they seemed to have achieved only a stalemate where before their powers had been enough to shake the huge beast. It was then that Logan saw Aryx's plan start to take shape. Aryx, back in his Nightwing armor, circled above Shau-ling and unleashed an assault with what power he had left. The strings of Fire slammed into the dragon's back knocking him forward. Had it not been for the force of the combined powers of the Ranthall brothers, the dragon might have been sprawled over the floor of the throne room.

The dragon recovered slightly, enough to continue to force back Logan and Korrd's powers with his own. He could have retreated, but apparently his anger was not allowing him to think logically. Then Aryx did the one thing that would send his name into the annals of history as one of the most selfless heroes in the history of the world. He turned his attention away from the dragon and flew toward the column of Blaze energy as fast as he could. When his armor touched the Blaze, there was a sound like thunder that echoed through the throne room with deafening intensity. Aryx continued flying through the burning and the pain that echoed through the blackness in his mind. Aryx had the powers of the phasia inside of him, and the pain he was enduring was so intense that it sent shock-waves down the lines of power that were so powerful that Logan almost could not stand. Yet the former knight in the service of the Kingdom of Marcwell fought through it all and continued downward into the torrent of energy, until finally he entered the core.

The only explosions that Logan had ever seen in his life were those shown to them by magicians and through the tinkers and their 'fireworks'. Those things were usually beautiful sparkles of different colored lights that inspired amazement by the crowd. When Aryx struck the core of the Blaze, a different kind of explosion took place. Flames shot from the column of energy. The ground and the walls shook with the power of the explosion that happened deep beneath their feet. Parts of the floor began to rise and steam streamed from the openings. One giant crack appeared through the center of the dragon that was etched in the floor. After the initial shocks were finished, they watched as the transformation of Shau-ling's body reversed itself, and he lay on the dais in his near-human form. But this would not be the end for a being as powerful as the master of the Shadows. Shau-ling picked himself off the floor and knew immediately what had happened. His power may have been greatly diminished, but he was not about to admit defeat. He looked down at his palm, and instantly a sword of pure Blaze energy appeared. He had enough left for that one last act, and he was going to go down fighting.

"If I kill all of you, I win, and I rule the world for every generation to come. If you kill me, I'll be back in the next generation to fight Gwydeon's child. I win either way. But right now, it comes down to the pretender and I. Are you feeling up to it, Korrd, or will you defer this duty to your brother as well?"

"Whenever you're ready, Halicon. I've been waiting a long time for this."

"As have I."

Korrd took a few steps toward Shau-ling and then raised his sword. Just as Shau-ling could bend the Blaze into the form of a sword, Korrd had the power to bend the power of the *Coromor* and push it into the sword that had been made for just that purpose. The blade sang with power, and the two combatants regarded each other cautiously as they approached.

The swords struck and created sparks much like when Cedric and Aryx had fought. However, this battle would have more than just a momentary impact in the scheme of things. This was the battle that would decide the fate of six generations of life, and they could not afford to have it surrendered to the forces of evil. While Shau-ling was weak and off-balance, he was clearly a swordsman of formidable skill. They rounded each other, and then Korrd lunged forward. Shau-ling sidestepped the thrust and parried Korrd's sword to the ground. Before Korrd could recover, Shau-ling's fist struck the side of Korrd's face and sent him sprawling to the ground. But the older Ranthall brother was not to be defeated that easily. He scrambled to his feet and recovered his sword. From that point on the battle looked as if it could go on forever. Every single thrust and slash was parried, and neither man could land a single blow to his opponent. They rounded one another again and advanced toward each other at the same instant. Shau-ling's back was to Logan, and he saw the tip of the Dragon Sword emerge from Shau-ling's back. The power of the sword rushed into Shau-ling's body and he slumped against Korrd, the life stolen from him. But something was wrong.

Korrd had not moved since the fatal blow was struck, and Logan climbed to the top of the dais slowly, not knowing exactly what would happen in the next moments. Logan was about to congratulate Korrd on his victory, but when Shau-ling fell to the ground and his sword crashed beside him, Logan saw the hilt of the dagger that had been thrust through Korrd's heart. Logan ran up the dais to try and give him some assistance, but Korrd waived his off and fell to both knees. Emries' prophecies had come true and Korrd's life was forfeit for the greater good of the world. When Korrd finally fell, a light emerged from the wound in his chest. The light became bigger and bigger, until it filled the entire room. Then, it flashed once and disappeared, and the surviving People of the Dragon were left there in the throne room, alone.

CHAPTER 23

Epilogue

Victory

Victory.

Never did that word sound as hollow as it did when Logan spoke it there in the middle of the throne room. Korrd still lay there just in front of the dais, all of the life stolen from his body. Only two weeks prior, Logan had discovered that his brother was still alive. For most of that time though, hatred was the only emotion that filled Logan's heart, a feeling fully and completely reciprocated by Logan's older sibling. But when Logan and Korrd finally met again though, Logan learned that Korrd was the true hero of their story, and any animosity between them had been manufactured and misplaced. Logan had actually started to admire Korrd the more that they were together, his strength and his heroism pulling them through the darkness and loss to their ultimate goal. Shau-ling had been defeated, but now Korrd was gone. Never would the true reasons for his departure and faked death be aired. The only information that would exist about Korrd would be found with Logan's friends who had hidden him for years. But Korrd was not the foremost on Logan's mind.

There on the ground by the unmoving forms of Gideon and Talon was the motionless body of the woman Logan loved. As he knelt beside Elwyne, Logan began to worry that she was not alive. Her skin was cold to the touch, and her lips had a trace of blue in them. It looked as if she was suspended just at the edge of death. The only thoughts that ran through

Logan's mind was that she had to live, and that everything they had gone through would have been meaningless without her by his side. There was no way that he could live without her. Logan's heart felt as if it would leap out of his chest, and there were no rational thoughts left in his mind. Merely on impulse, Logan felt his arms reach out and pull her in close. He had never felt her body as limp as it was then, and fear gripped Logan's heart and mind so completely that he held her tighter than he had ever held her before. What happened in the next few seconds defied any rational explanation. If you've ever been in love, you know that there is a part of you that would gladly give up your life for that other person. If there was any way that you could stop that other person from feeling pain by taking it upon yourself, you gladly would. That is the way that Logan had always felt about Elwyne, and those promises that he had always made to her kept ringing in his mind.

'No matter where you are and no matter what you do,' Logan used to say to her, 'just know that I will do everything in my power to make sure that nothing ever harms you. If there is anything you ever need, any time, any place, anywhere, all you have to do is call and I will drop whatever I'm doing and I will come for you. You are more precious to me than anything in this world and I would do anything for you. I love you with all my heart.'

Those thoughts ran through Logan's mind over and over, getting louder and more insistent as each heartbeat passed, and then he started to get angry and frustrated. They had fought so long and hard together, only to be torn apart at the very end of the story. Logan had broken a lot of promises to Elwyne in the past, but that promise, the one that kept reverberating in his head was one that he thought he could keep until the day he died. In the end, Logan had failed her when she needed him the most. But in true Ranthall fashion, even in the face of death, part of Logan didn't want to admit defeat. The fighting spirit in him would not let her die. In that last moment, where it was either live or die, Logan pushed all of his strength and will and love and soul into that limp vessel that lay in his arms. If love can ever be a tangible thing, he let it flow through his arms and into Elwyne's body. When nothing happened, Logan felt as though his own body would give out, and his arms were numb. He pulled her body even tighter as the tears began to fall. Then the most wonderful thing happened. One of Elwyne's arms moved. She pushed herself away from Logan a little and then looked up at him with those beautiful eyes. When she smiled, more tears fell from Logan's eyes. She wiped them away lovingly and then started to look around the room. When her eyes fell on Korrd and Gideon, she looked back up at Logan with horror and sorrow in her eyes.

"It's over, Elwyne," Logan said as tenderly as he could. "Korrd did what he had to do, and Shau-ling killed Korrd. Emries was right, and it ended just like the prophecies said it would."

"And Gideon?"

"During the fight, he made the sacrifice of his own life so that you could survive. He said that he would protect you at the cost of his life, and he did. If there was ever anything bad that I ever said about the man, I take it all back."

"Talon too?"

All Logan could do was nod somberly.

Elwyne was frozen for a moment, sorrow and pain overcoming her, and after a moment all she could do was hug Logan tight, as though she was in the middle of an ocean of darkness and Logan was the only thing keeping her from going under. Once she stopped shaking Logan helped Elwyne to her feet and together they walked slowly to where Pike knelt by Jerrard. The burn mark on his chest was still there, but when Logan looked back into the fading blackness in his mind, the place where the powers of the *Chosen* One dwelled, Logan saw that the Blaze fires within the wound were gone. Jerrard began to stir a little, and with Pike's help he managed to make it to his feet.

"Well Jerrard," Pike said laying his hand on Jerrard's shoulder. "Now you have responsibility for two kingdoms. With your father dead, Scalla is yours, and thanks to your wife's connection to Marcwell, that's yours also. I think you'll make a fine king."

"No Pike," Jerrard said straining a bit, "my days of being a hero ended here. Erika and I will go to Scalla and live in the royal palace, but I think that Talamon will make a better king than I would. Besides, I have to rest up or Erika won't be able to have the three children that she wants."

They all laughed and then Jerrard turned the tables.

"Where will the rest of you go?"

"I'm going back to Taren," Pike said after a moment. "I know I shouldn't, but Eldar deserves a proper burial. After that, I don't know."

"And you Logan?" Jerrard asked.

"Elwyne and I are going back to Aradon to be married. I'd like you all to be there, but if you can't make it I'll understand. The adventure is over, and it's time to go home and get ready for my real son to arrive. I already had a taste of it with Fion, but now I'm ready for the real thing."

Elwyne hugged Logan tightly and smiled.

"You're right, Logan," she said guiding him toward the open door that led out of the throne room. "It's time to go home."

* * * * * * * * * * * *

Many years passed, some would consider them uneventful, but not Logan. He knew what was coming, and as the days became weeks that became years, Logan could not help but dwell on what was not said in that throne room after their seemingly hollow victory. It still haunted him, both in his waking moments and in his nightmare-filled nights. They had not really won the war on that fated day, nor did they even come close. Each time Logan looked back on the battle, he tried hard to figure out what they did wrong. They knew all along what it took to make everyone's lives safe from evil, but in the end they weren't able to get the job done. The best Logan and Korrd were able to do was buy the world some time. But the third generation was still saddled with a bloody future, and Shau-ling would soon return ready to start the war all over again. Logan could not help but hope that Gwydeon and Midarin's child would be able to succeed where Logan had failed. One day, Logan's son would stand strong beside the rest of the chosen warriors of the Light, and together they would change the face of the world forever.

Appendicies

Dramatis Personae

Cedric Binosear
The Lord Lion
First *Coromor* of the Prophecies
Lord of the Kingdom of Marcwell
Twin Brother of Anabel Binosear

Erika Belnosian
Daughter of Arthur Belnosian
Sister of Erdric Belnosian
Betrothed of Cedric Binosear
Wife of Jerrard Mystic

Aryx Terian
White Lightning
General in the Lion's Mane
Fire *Erieal* of the Prophecies
Knight of the Kingdom of Marcwell
Husband of Diana Geoffry Terian
Host of Nightwing

Logan Ranthall
The Lord Dragon
Second *Coromor* of the Prophecies
Son of Arin Ranthall and Victoria
Rhuiden
Brother of Korrd Ranthall
First Cousin of Pike Rhuiden
Relationship with Elwyne Tamerlane

Korrd Ranthall
Second *Chosen One* of the Prophecies
Son of Arin Ranthall and Victoria
Rhuiden
Brother of Logan Ranthall
First Cousin of Pike Rhuiden

David Tamerlane
Blacksmith's Apprentice
Son of the Mayor of Aradon
Brother of Elwyne Tamerlane

Pike Rhuiden
Water *Erieal* of the Prophecies
Former Blacksmith's Apprentice
Apprentice Carpenter
Son of Tam Rhuiden
Best Friend of Talon Aielin
First Cousin of Logan Ranthall
Elder Merin's Former Lover

Talon Aielin
Wind *Erieal* of the Prophecies
Apprentice Carpenter
Best Friend of Pike Rhuiden
Professional Carouser

Lane Toridon
Apprentice Magician
Orphan
Adopted by the Town of Aradon

Gwydeon Sandar
Apprentice Blacksmith
Sword Master
Son of Torris Sandar
Brother of Bella Sandar

Eldar Merin
Daughter of Noble Family of Trelon
Sword Master
Champion Duelist
Best Friend of Elwyne Tamerlane
Pike Rhuiden's Former Lover

Elwyne Tamerlane
Daughter of the Mayor of Aradon
Sister of David Tamerlane
Relationship with Logan Ranthall

Arin Ranthall
Member of the Lion's Mane
First *Chosen One* of the Prophecies
Husband of Victoria Rhuiden
Father of Logan Ranthall
Father of Korrd Ranthall

Victoria Rhuiden
Member of the Lion's Mane
Sister of Tam Rhuiden
Wife of Arin Ranthall
Mother of Logan Ranthall
Mother of Korrd Ranthall

Tam Rhuiden
Master Carpenter
Aradon City Council Member
Brother of Victoria Rhuiden
Father of Pike Rhuiden

Torris Sandar
Master Blacksmith
Aradon City Council Member
Father of Gwydeon Sandar
Father of Bella Sandar

Arathorn Geoffry
Leader of the Lion's Mane
Earth *Erieal* of the Prophecies
Brother of Diana Geoffry Terian

Mailock
Member of the Moridon Tribe
Water *Erieal* of the Prophecies

Diana Terian Geoffry
Member of the Lion's Mane
Wind *Erieal* of the Prophecies
Sister of Arathorn Geoffry
Wife of Aryx Terian

Gideon Viruci
Earth *Erieal* of the Prophecies
Professional Thief
Member of Alimidar Thief's Guild

Ren Manderis
Former Member of the Lion's Mane
Former Pirate
Dock Master of Illimar
Alias: Seelious Monk

Midarin Rice
Former Princess of the Kingdom of
Brea
Banished for High Treason
Master Archer

Zar Elouix
Lord of Rama

Captain Antrobus
General of the Army of Rama
Murdered by Korrd Ranthall

Alexander Mealon
Standard Bearer
Squire in the Army of Rama

Talos Berder
Member of the Moridon Tribe
Advisor to the Kingdom of Rana

Emries
The Creator and First *Coromor*

Anabel Binosear
Sister of Cedric Binosear
Queen of the Kingdom of Trelon
Mother of Cairyn Binosear
Mother of Allan Binosear
Alias: Camille Talaat
Murdered by Allan Binosear

Cairyn Binosear
Daughter of Anabel Binosear
Niece of Cedric Binosear
Queen of the Kingdom of Trelon

Allan Binosear
Son of Anabel Binosear
Nephew of Cedric Binosear
Crown Prince of Trelon
Second in Line of Succession
Alias of Aldridge Farran

Leane Torne
General in the Army of Rama
Former Member of the Army of Brea

Aerith Seth
General of the Hand of the Light
The *Chosen One*

Hawk Yetre
General of the Army of Sador
Son of Jeroch Yetre

Asperon Thorne
Guardian of the Jeweled Dragon's
Flame

Jasmen Hiedra
Traveling Minstrel
Part-Time Adventurer
Assassin in Service of Shau-ling

Jerrard Mystic
Soldier in the Army of Illimar
Former Member of the Lion's Mane
Son of Basille Mystic
Husband of Erika Belnosian

Christine Goldenlake
Former Member of the Lion's Mane
Master Archer
Murdered by Jeroch Yetre

Allahanna
Member of the Moridon Tribe
Former Member of the Lion's Mane
Sister of Corin
Murdered by Warron Ysamaran

Corin
Member of the Moridon Tribe
Former Member of the Lion's Mane
Sister of Allahanna
Murdered by Warron Ysamaran

Galanax Pryde
Master Blacksmith
Former Member of the Lion's Mane
Murdered by Basille Mystic

William Hathaway
Former Pirate
Former Member of the Lion's Mane
Murdered by Taron Steen

Khisanth Alghri
Member of the Moridon Tribe
Former Member of the Lion's Mane
Murdered by Basille Mystic

Shau-ling
Master of the Shadows
Father of the Phasia

Jeroch Yetre
The Lord Shadow
First Born of the Phasia
Father of Hawk Yetre

Warron Ysamaran
The Lord Boar
Member of the Brotherhood of Phasia

Basille Mystic
The Lord Raven
Lord of Scalla
Member of the Brotherhood of Phasia
Father of Jerrard Mystic

Farax Soar
The Lord Vulture
Member of the Brotherhood of Phasia

The Flame
Personal Guardian of Shau-ling
Keeper of the Hall of Terrors

Zarsi Aeron
The Lord Cobra
Lord of Sador
Member of the Brotherhood of Phasia

Aldridge Farran
The Lord Hawk
Member of the Brotherhood of Phasia

Saurn Macco
The Lord Viper
Member of the Brotherhood of Phasia

Caris Vale
The Lady Wolf
Queen of Illimar
Alias: Queen Saris
Member of the Brotherhood of Phasia

Erdric Yarrow
The Lord Scorpion
Member of the Brotherhood of Phasia

Taron Steen
The Lord Jackal
Member of the Brotherhood of Phasia

About the Author

Brian Kershner is a life-long dreamer, writer, and problem-solver. He grew up absorbing anything and everything he could get his hands on, and as a child of the Star Wars era he constantly wanted to see the worlds beyond the little Indiana town he grew up in. There was no adventure too far, and no problem too big.

Emboldened by parents who always supported his curiosity and his thoughtfulness, Brian found himself bounding from Space Camp to Laser Summer Camp to Athletic Training Camp to Piano Lessons to Football Practice to Basketball Practice to Choir Practice and back again. Despite all of the roaming and traveling, his family remained close-knit and supportive.

Though he flirted with the idea of becoming a doctor, Brian's attentions always fell back to the computer world. He got his first computer when he was six, and not long after found his way into a word processing program and began crafting his own fantastic worlds and even more fantastic characters.

As he has grown and changed and experienced life, so too have his characters. He continues to write, craft, and create; whether it is websites for his customers, or characters and worlds for his audience.